SEA OF SORROWS

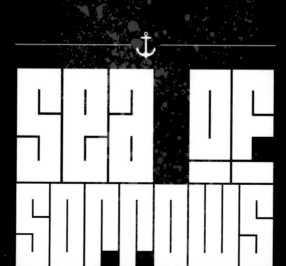

Cover Art by
Alex Cormack

Series Edits by
Bobby Curnow

Collection Edits by
Alonzo Simon
and Zac Boone

Collection Design by
Shawn Lee

Nachie Marsham, Publisher | Blake Kobashigawa, VP of Sales | Tara McCrillis, VP
Publishing Operations | John Barber, Editor-in-Chief | Mark Doyle, Editorial Director,
Originals | Erika Turner, Executive Editor | Scott Dunbier, Director, Special Projects
Mark Irwin, Editorial Director, Consumer Products Manager | Joe Hughes, Director, Talent
Relations | Anna Morrow, Sr. Marketing Director | Alexandra Hargett, Book & Mass
Market Sales Director | Keith Davidsen, Senior Manager, PR | Topher Alford, Sr. Digital
Marketing Manager | Shauna Monteforte, Sr. Director of Manufacturing Operations
Jamie Miller, Sr. Operations Manager | Nathan Widick, Sr. Art Director, Head of Design
Neil Uyetake, Sr. Art Director Design & Production | Shawn Lee, Art Director Design &
Production | Jack Rivera, Art Director, Marketing

Ted Adams and Robbie Robbins, IDW Founders

WRITER
RICH DOUEK

ARTIST
ALEX CORMACK

COLOR ASSISTANT
MARK MULLANEY

LETTERER
JUSTIN BIRCH

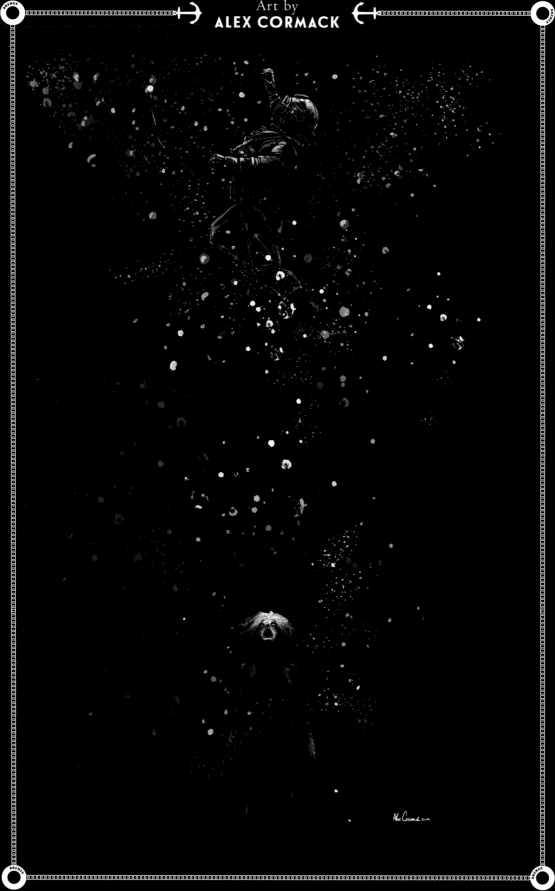

Art by
ALEX CORMACK

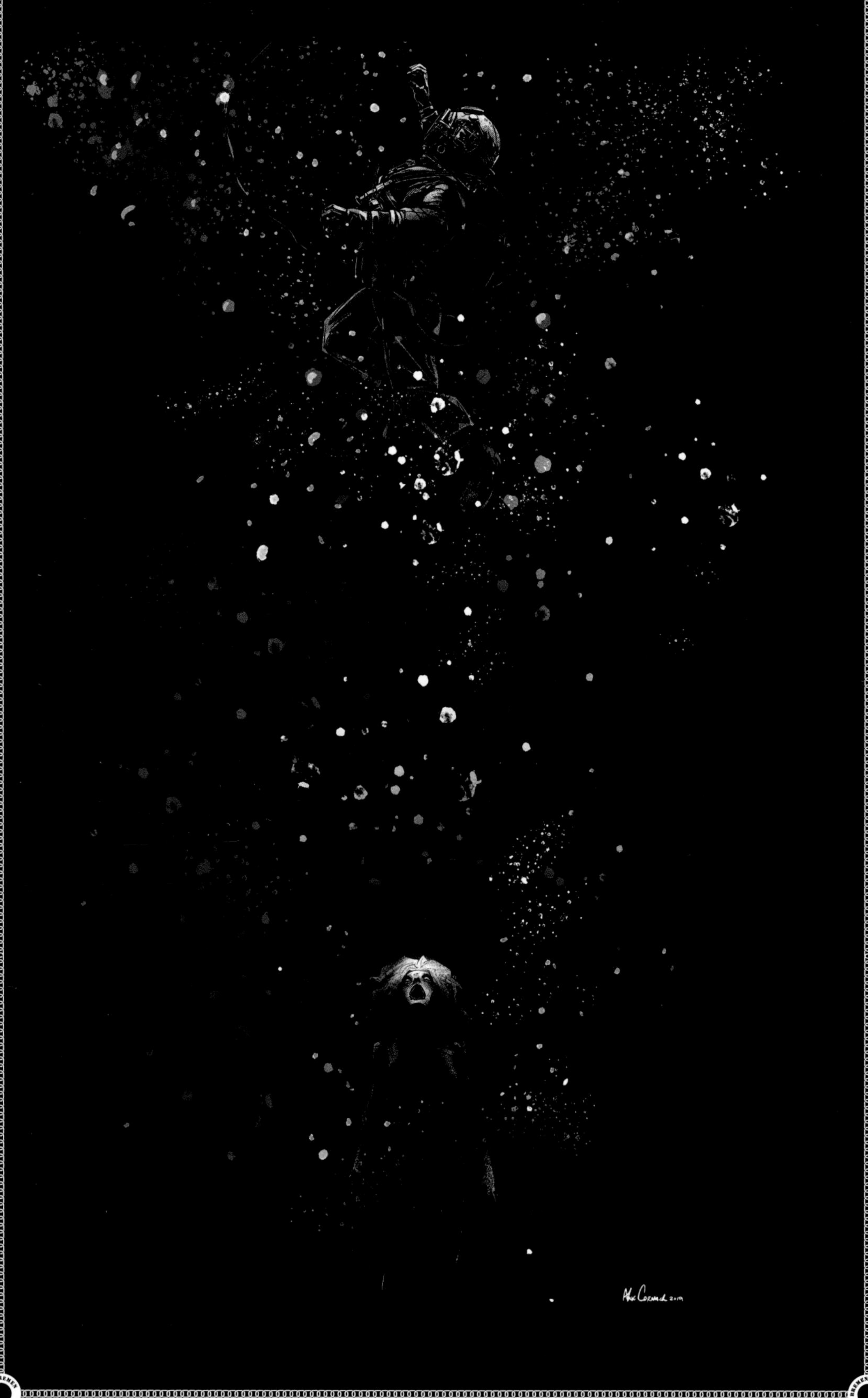

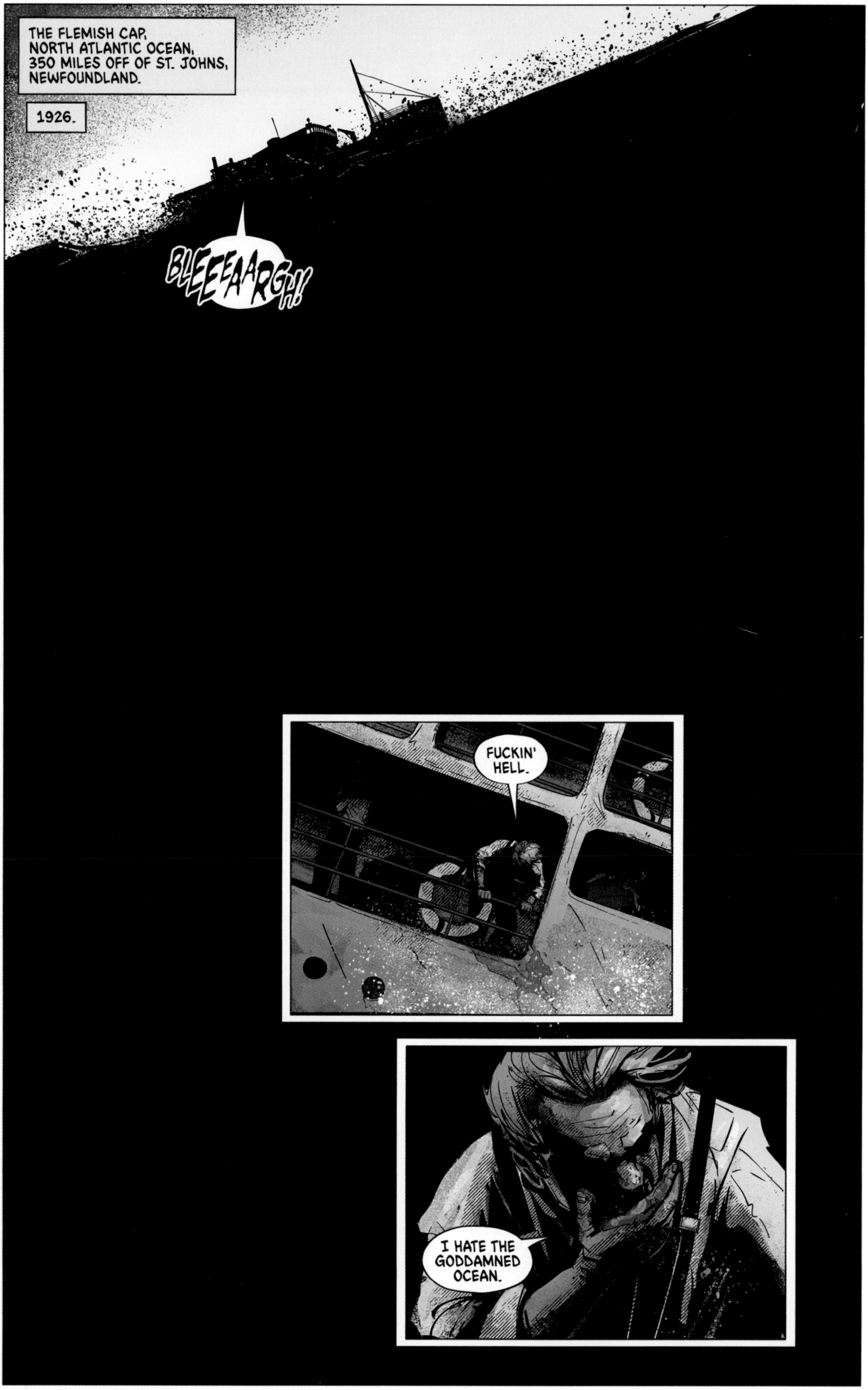

THE FLEMISH CAP, NORTH ATLANTIC OCEAN, 350 MILES OFF OF ST. JOHNS, NEWFOUNDLAND.
1926.
BLEEEAARGH!
FUCKIN' HELL.
I HATE THE GODDAMNED OCEAN.

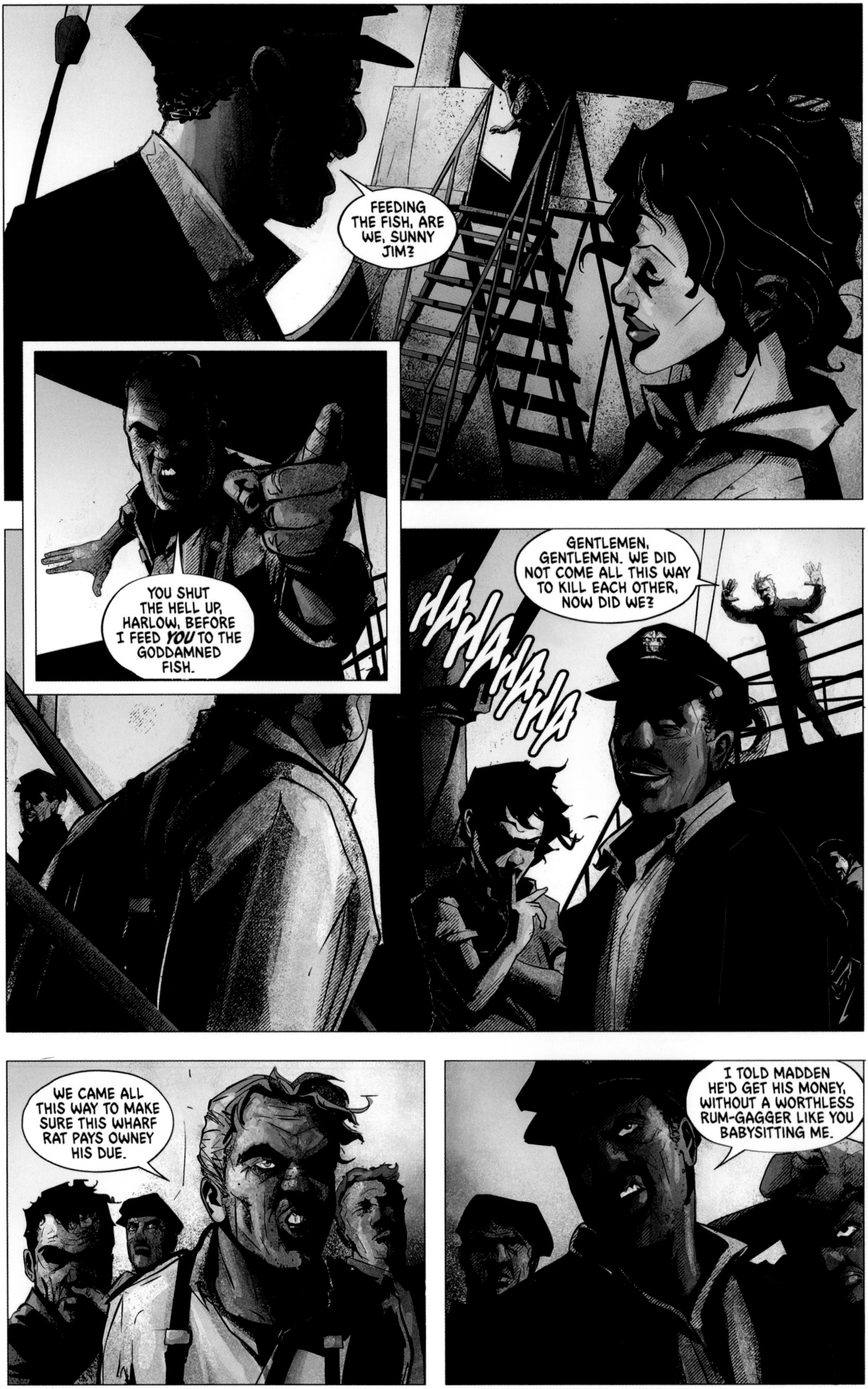

FEEDING THE FISH, ARE WE, SUNNY JIM?
YOU SHUT THE HELL UP, HARLOW, BEFORE I FEED *YOU* TO THE GODDAMNED FISH.
HAHAHAHAHAHA
GENTLEMEN, GENTLEMEN. WE DID NOT COME ALL THIS WAY TO KILL EACH OTHER, NOW DID WE?
WE CAME ALL THIS WAY TO MAKE SURE THIS WHARF RAT PAYS OWNEY HIS DUE.
I TOLD MADDEN HE'D GET HIS MONEY, WITHOUT A WORTHLESS RUM-GAGGER LIKE YOU BABYSITTING ME.

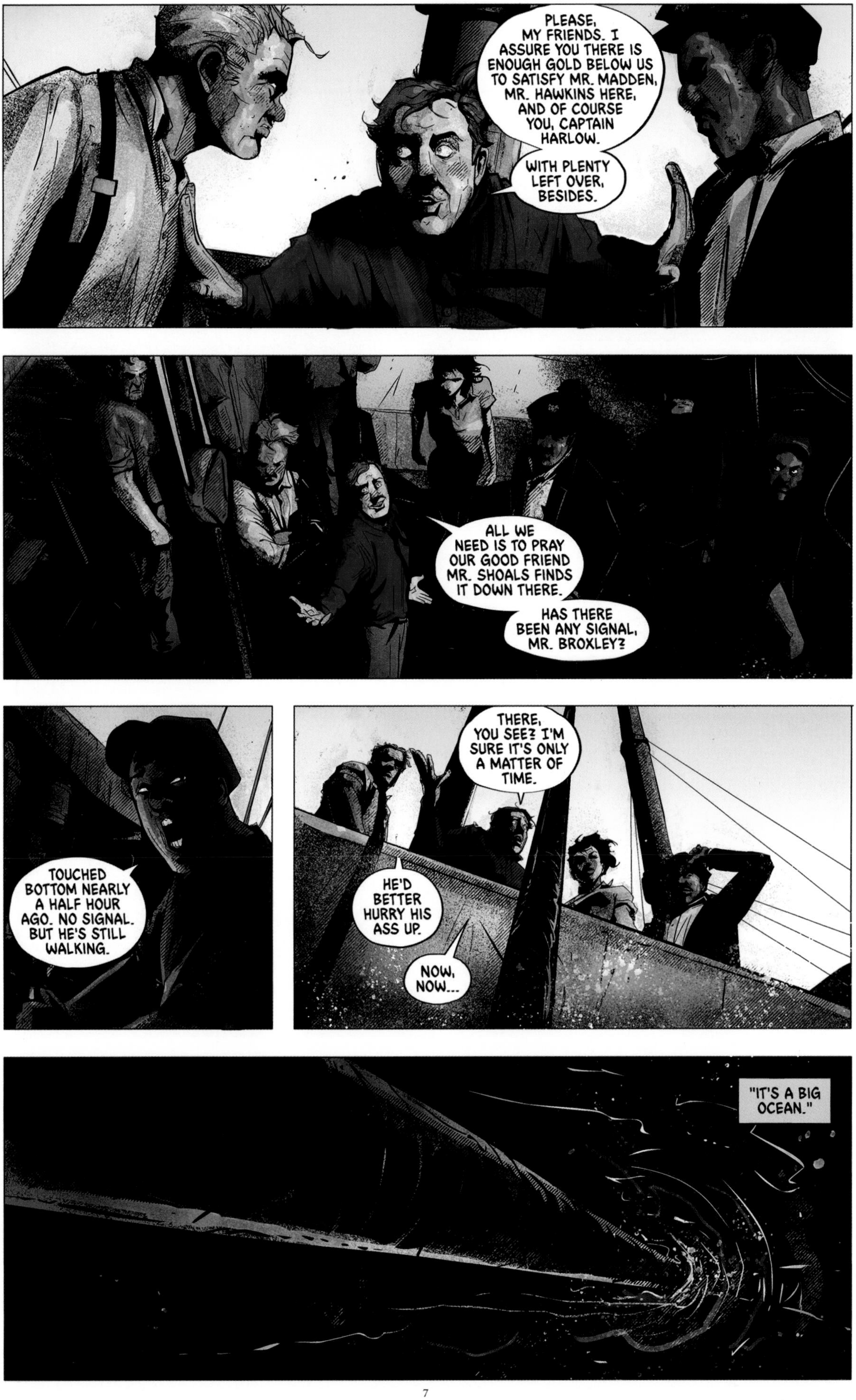
PLEASE, MY FRIENDS. I ASSURE YOU THERE IS ENOUGH GOLD BELOW US TO SATISFY MR. MADDEN, MR. HAWKINS HERE, AND OF COURSE YOU, CAPTAIN HARLOW.
WITH PLENTY LEFT OVER, BESIDES.
ALL WE NEED IS TO PRAY OUR GOOD FRIEND MR. SHOALS FINDS IT DOWN THERE.
HAS THERE BEEN ANY SIGNAL, MR. BROXLEY?
TOUCHED BOTTOM NEARLY A HALF HOUR AGO. NO SIGNAL. BUT HE'S STILL WALKING.
THERE, YOU SEE? I'M SURE IT'S ONLY A MATTER OF TIME.
HE'D BETTER HURRY HIS ASS UP.
NOW, NOW...
"IT'S A BIG OCEAN."

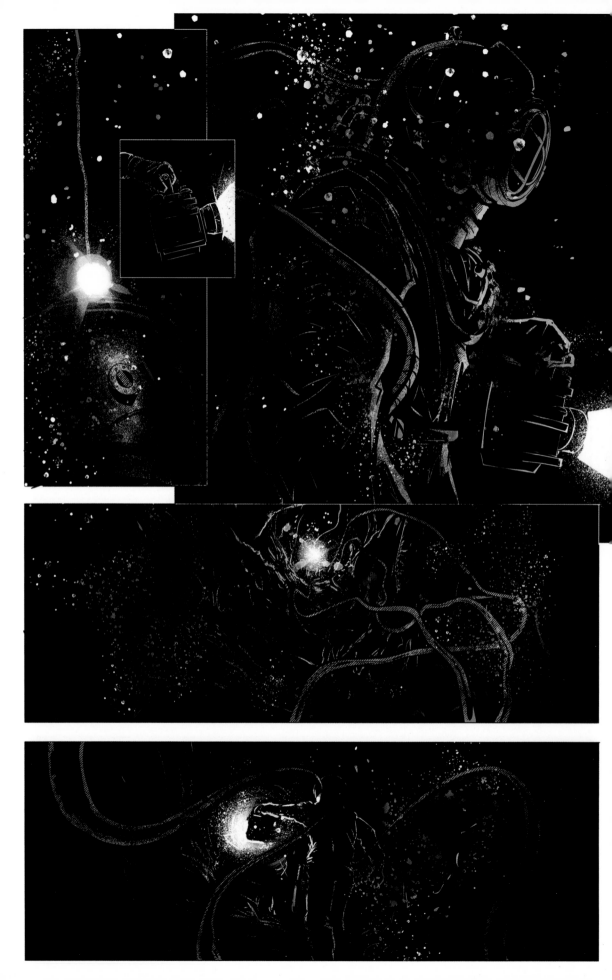

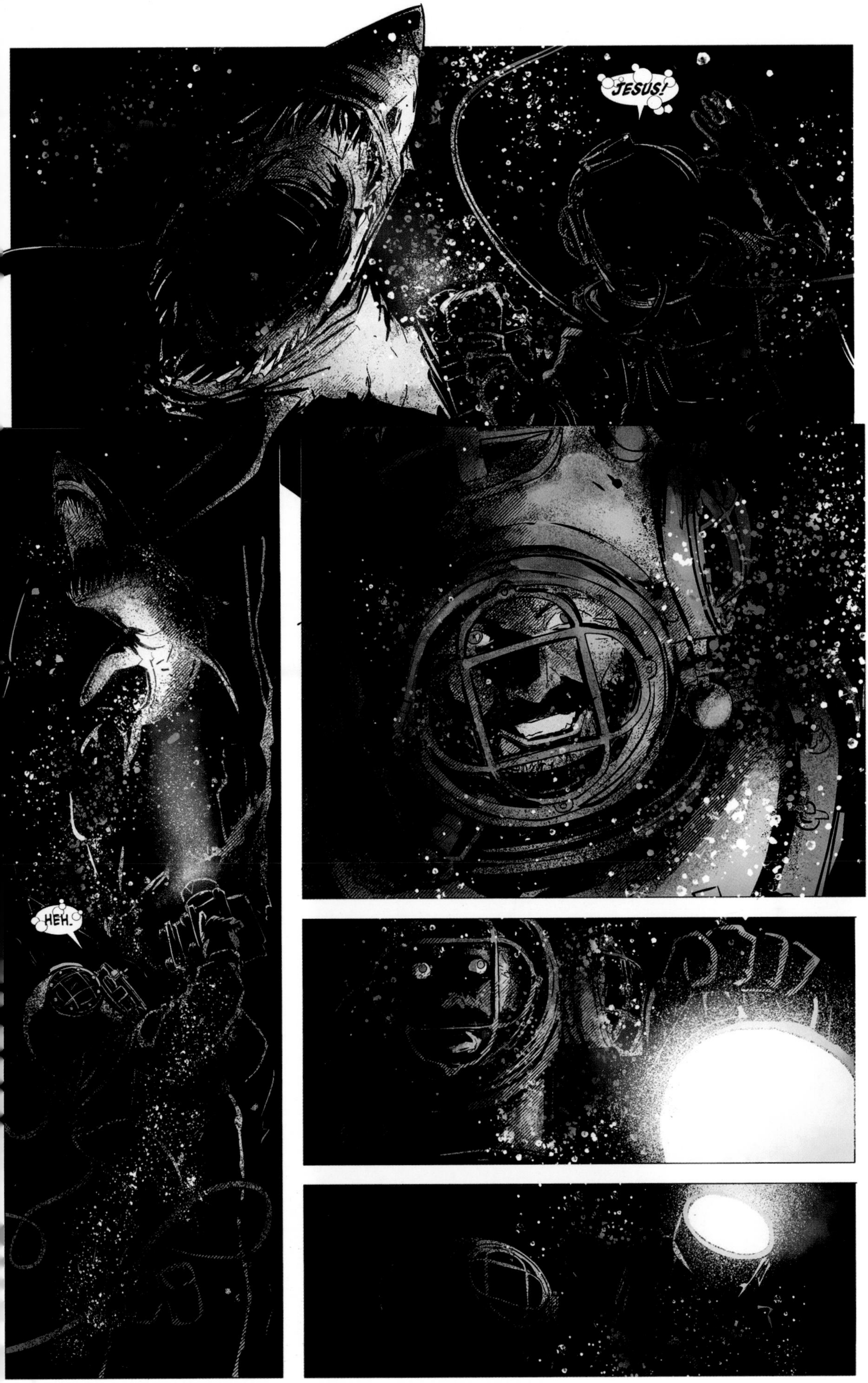
JESUS!
HEH.

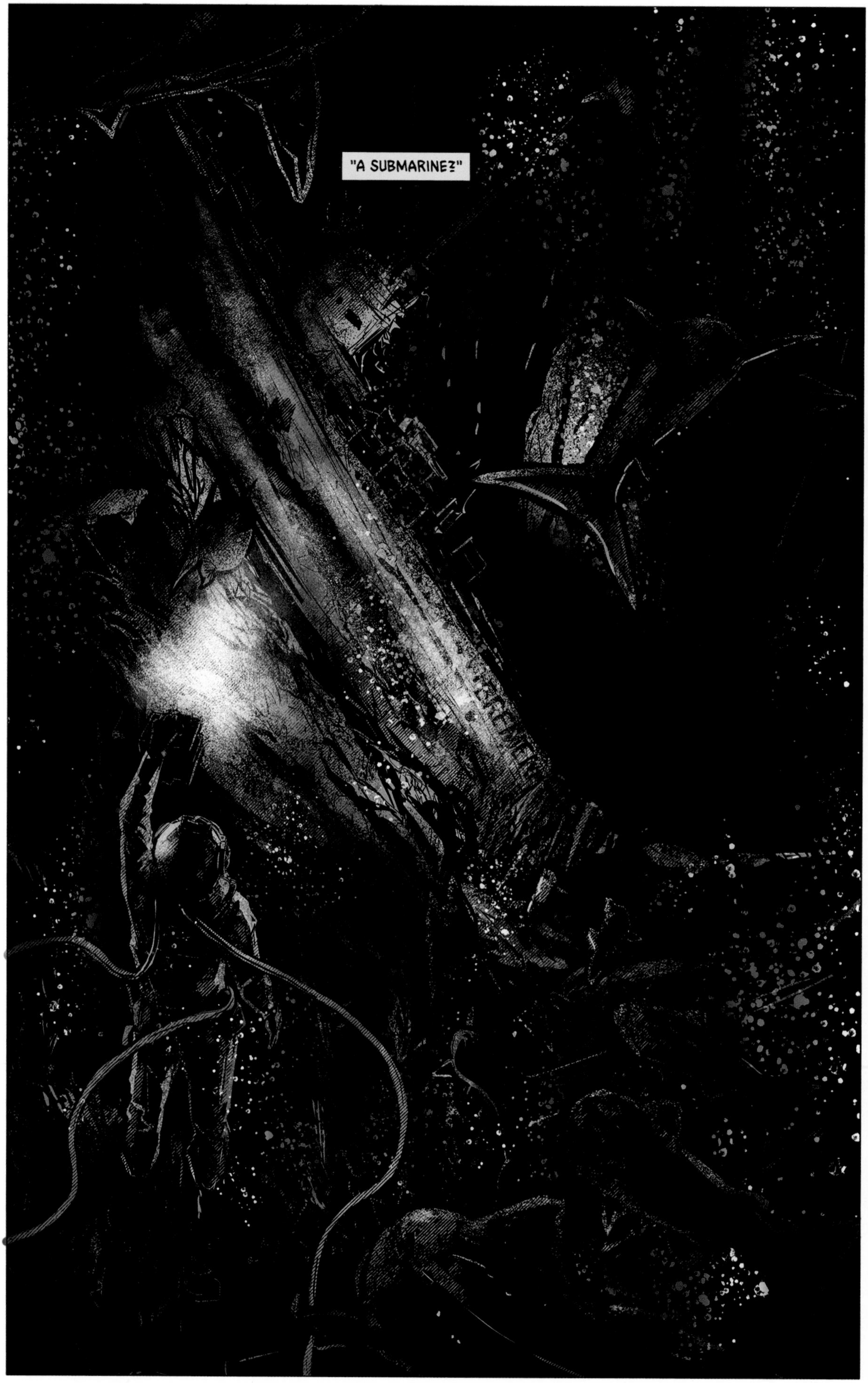
"A SUBMARINE?"

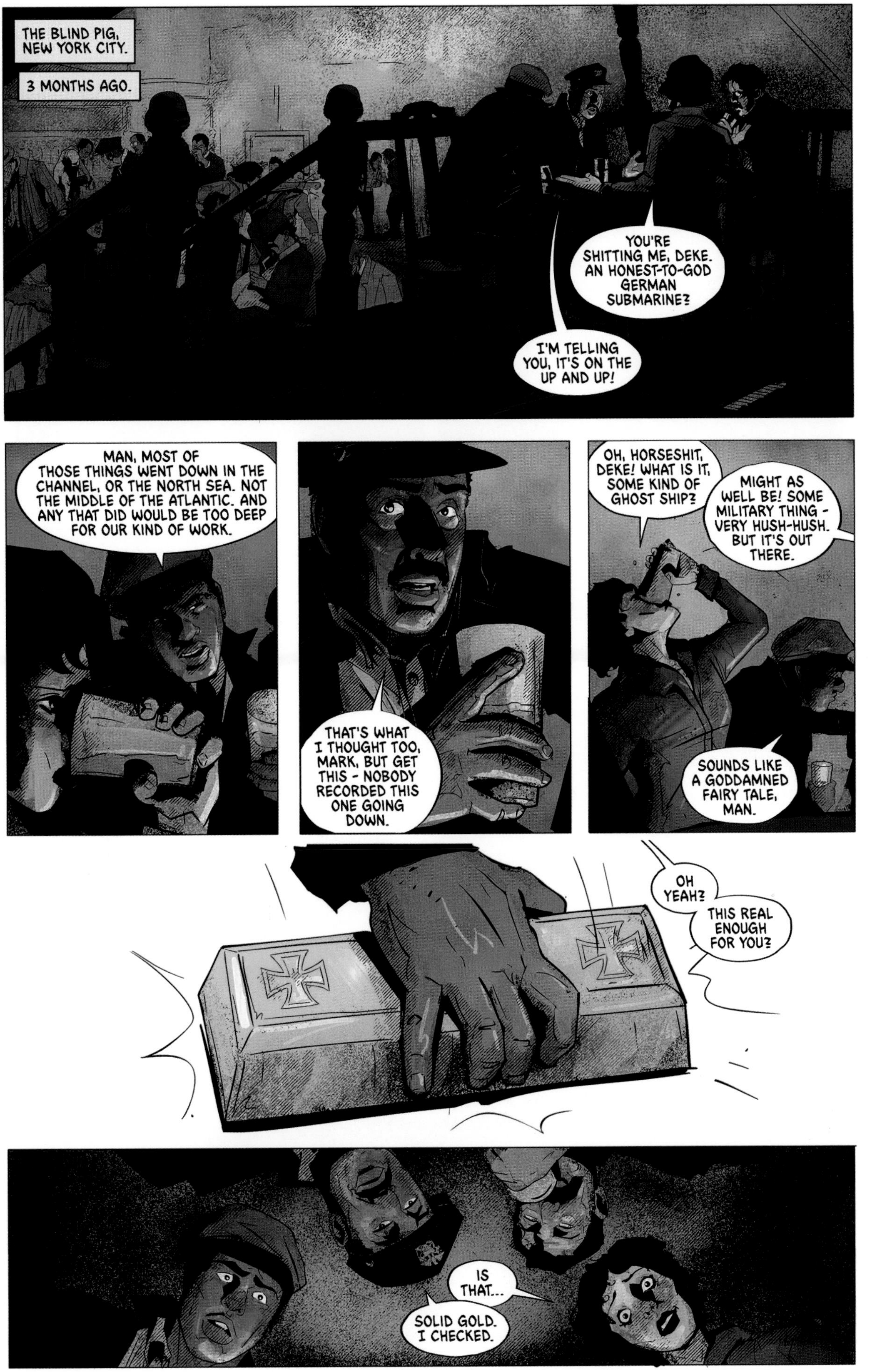
THE BLIND PIG, NEW YORK CITY.
3 MONTHS AGO.
YOU'RE SHITTING ME, DEKE. AN HONEST-TO-GOD GERMAN SUBMARINE?
I'M TELLING YOU, IT'S ON THE UP AND UP!
MAN, MOST OF THOSE THINGS WENT DOWN IN THE CHANNEL, OR THE NORTH SEA. NOT THE MIDDLE OF THE ATLANTIC. AND ANY THAT DID WOULD BE TOO DEEP FOR OUR KIND OF WORK.
THAT'S WHAT I THOUGHT TOO, MARK, BUT GET THIS - NOBODY RECORDED THIS ONE GOING DOWN.
OH, HORSESHIT, DEKE! WHAT IS IT, SOME KIND OF GHOST SHIP?
MIGHT AS WELL BE! SOME MILITARY THING - VERY HUSH-HUSH. BUT IT'S OUT THERE.
SOUNDS LIKE A GODDAMNED FAIRY TALE, MAN.
OH YEAH?
THIS REAL ENOUGH FOR YOU?
IS THAT...
SOLID GOLD. I CHECKED.

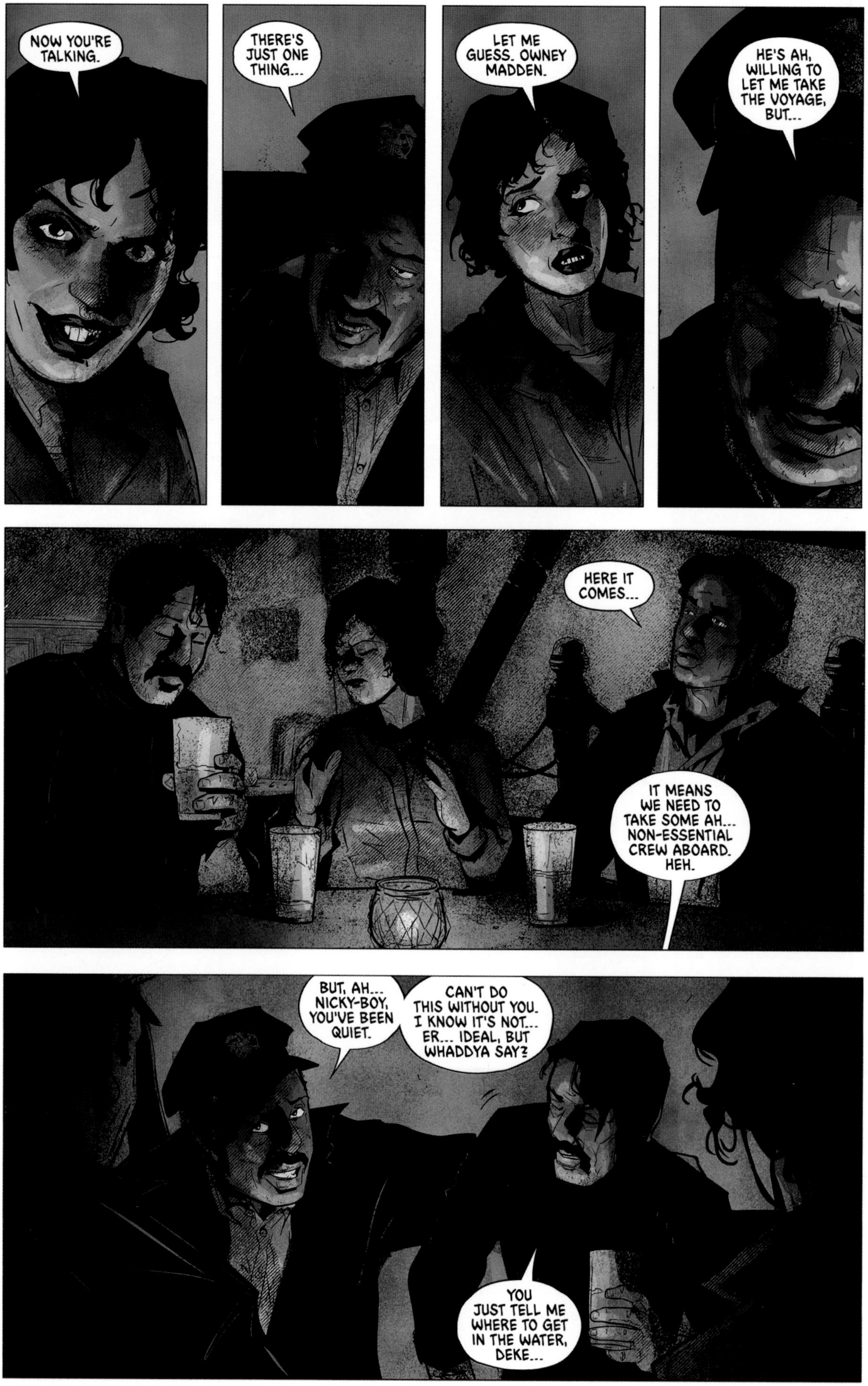
NOW YOU'RE TALKING.
THERE'S JUST ONE THING...
LET ME GUESS. OWNEY MADDEN.
HE'S AH, WILLING TO LET ME TAKE THE VOYAGE, BUT...
HERE IT COMES...
IT MEANS WE NEED TO TAKE SOME AH... NON-ESSENTIAL CREW ABOARD. HEH.
BUT, AH... NICKY-BOY, YOU'VE BEEN QUIET.
CAN'T DO THIS WITHOUT YOU. I KNOW IT'S NOT... ER... IDEAL, BUT WHADDYA SAY?
YOU JUST TELL ME WHERE TO GET IN THE WATER, DEKE...

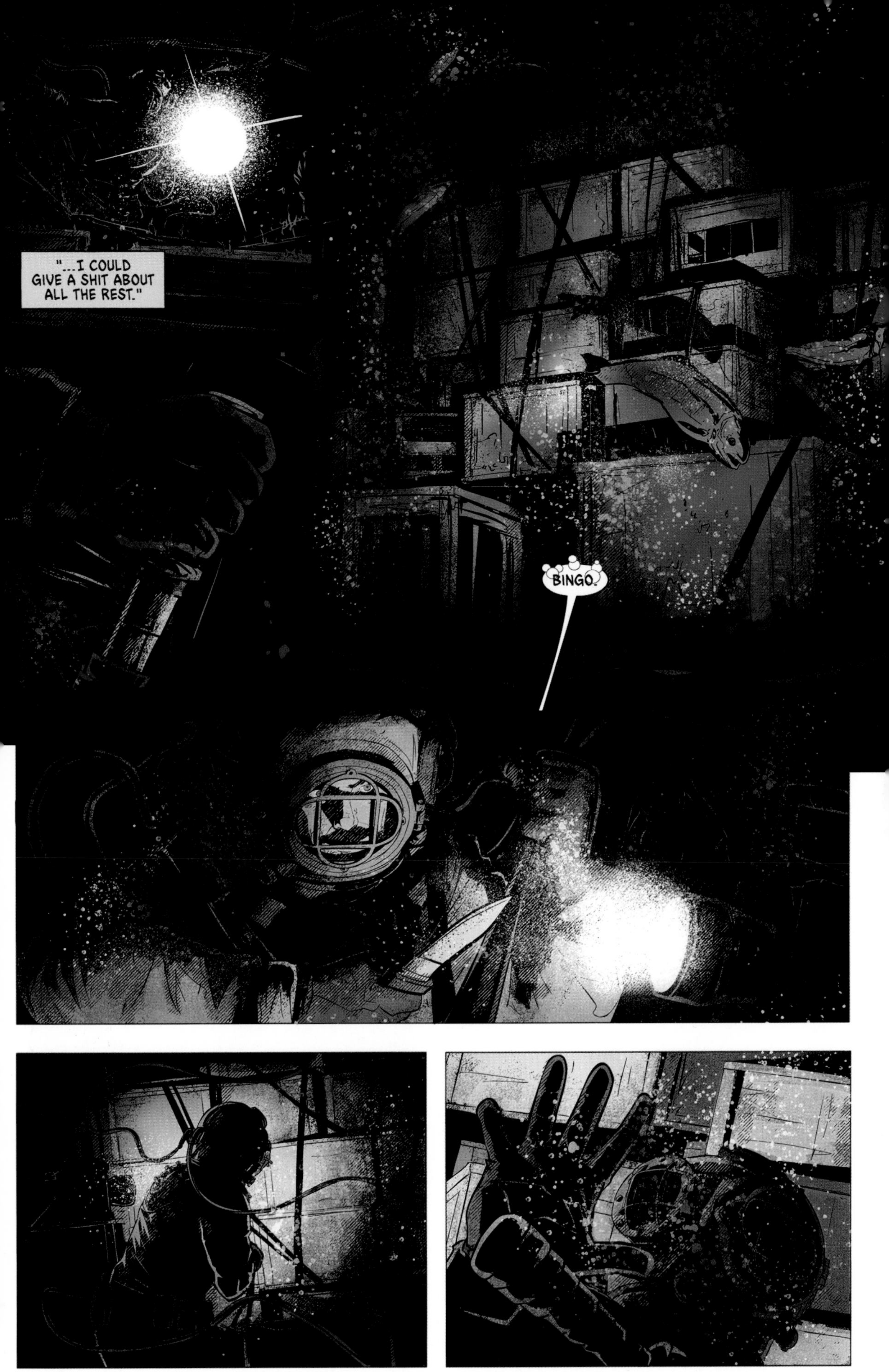
"...I COULD GIVE A SHIT ABOUT ALL THE REST."
BINGO.

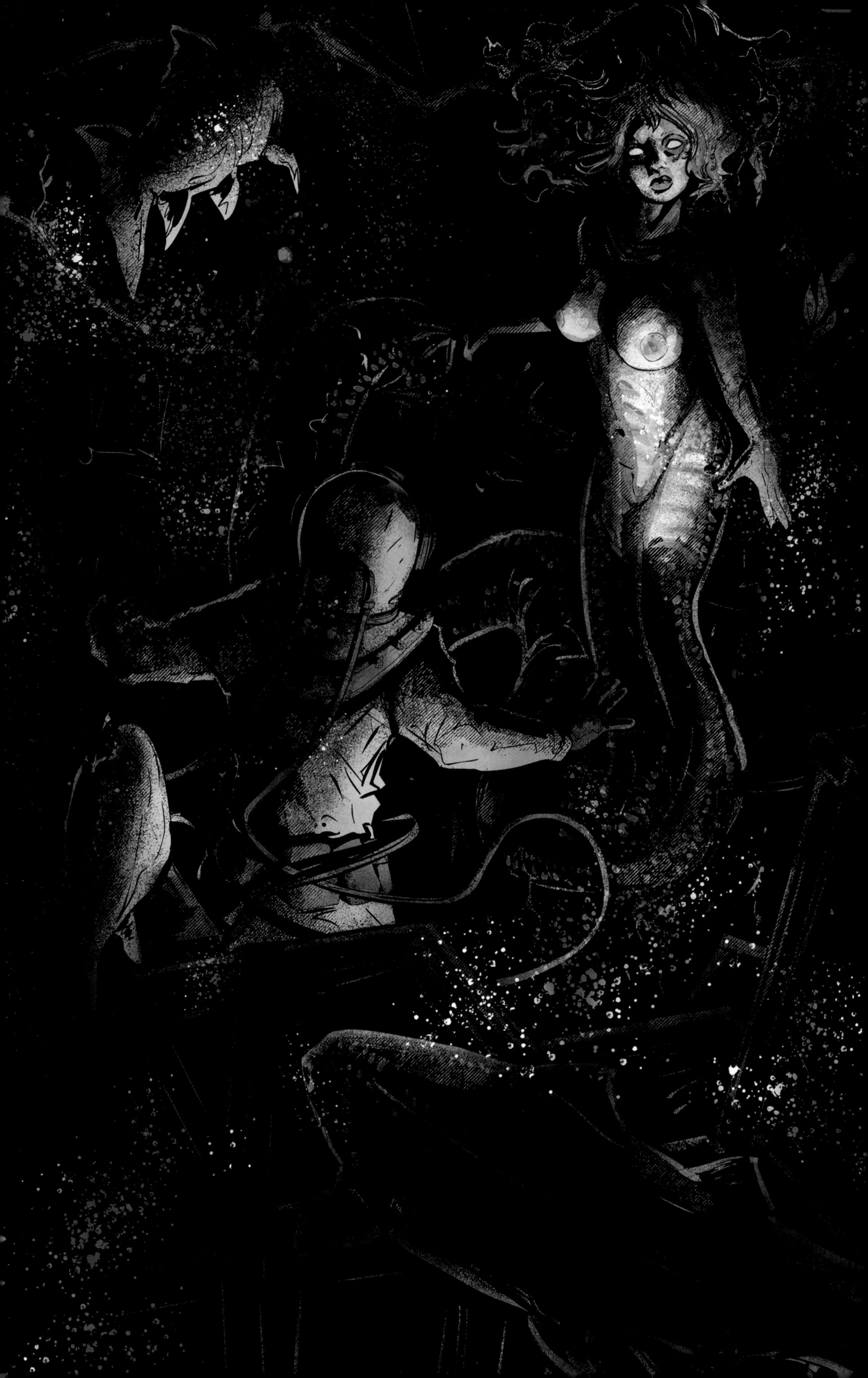

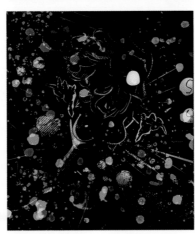

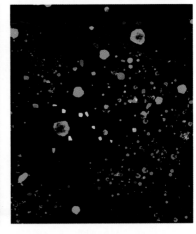

HUH. AIR'S FINE.

SEEING THINGS.

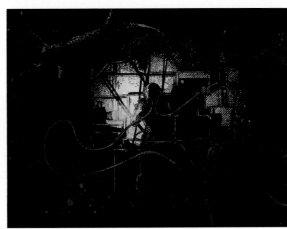

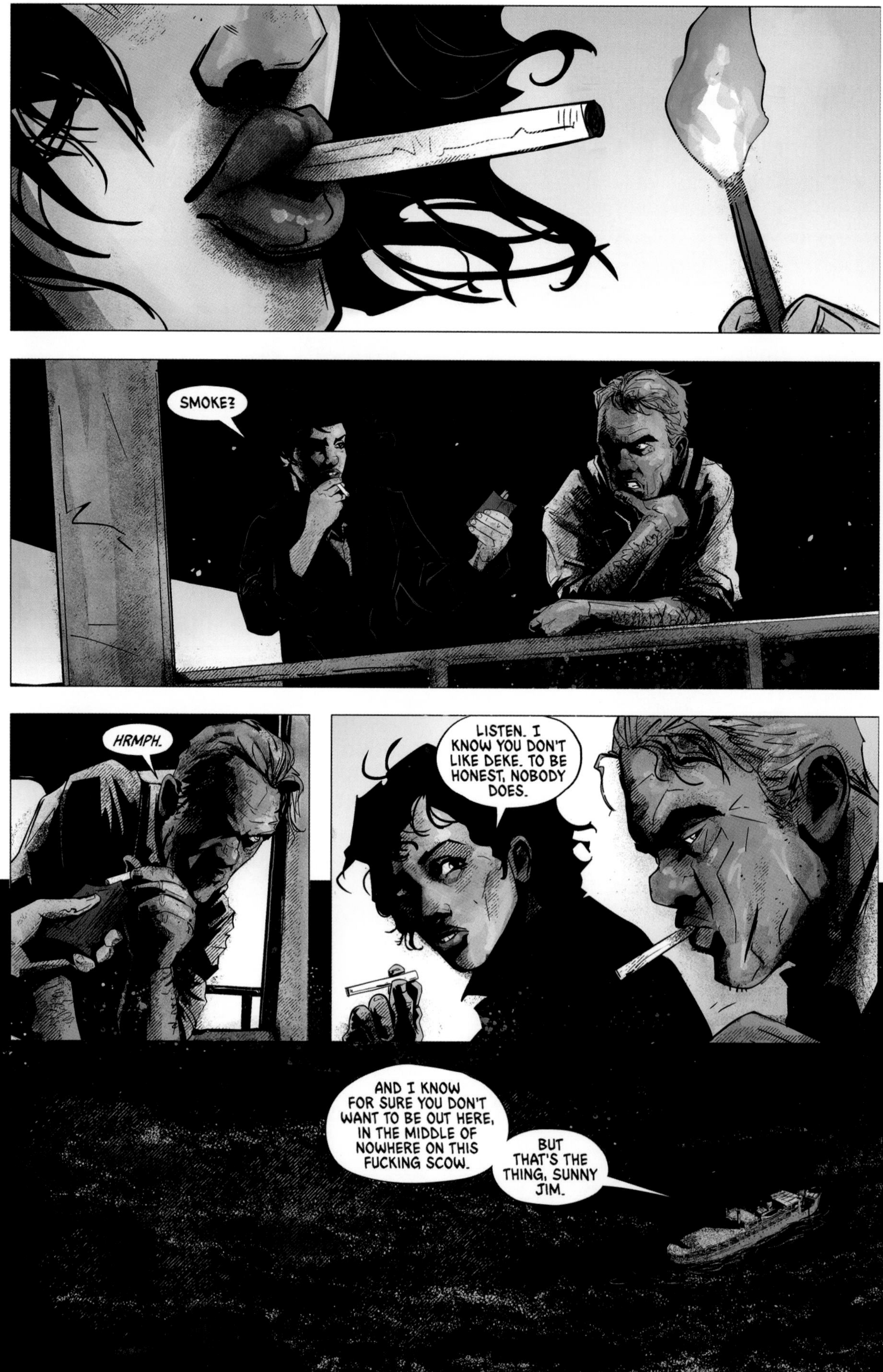
SMOKE?
HRMPH.
LISTEN. I KNOW YOU DON'T LIKE DEKE. TO BE HONEST, NOBODY DOES.
AND I KNOW FOR SURE YOU DON'T WANT TO BE OUT HERE, IN THE MIDDLE OF NOWHERE ON THIS FUCKING SCOW.
BUT THAT'S THE THING, SUNNY JIM.

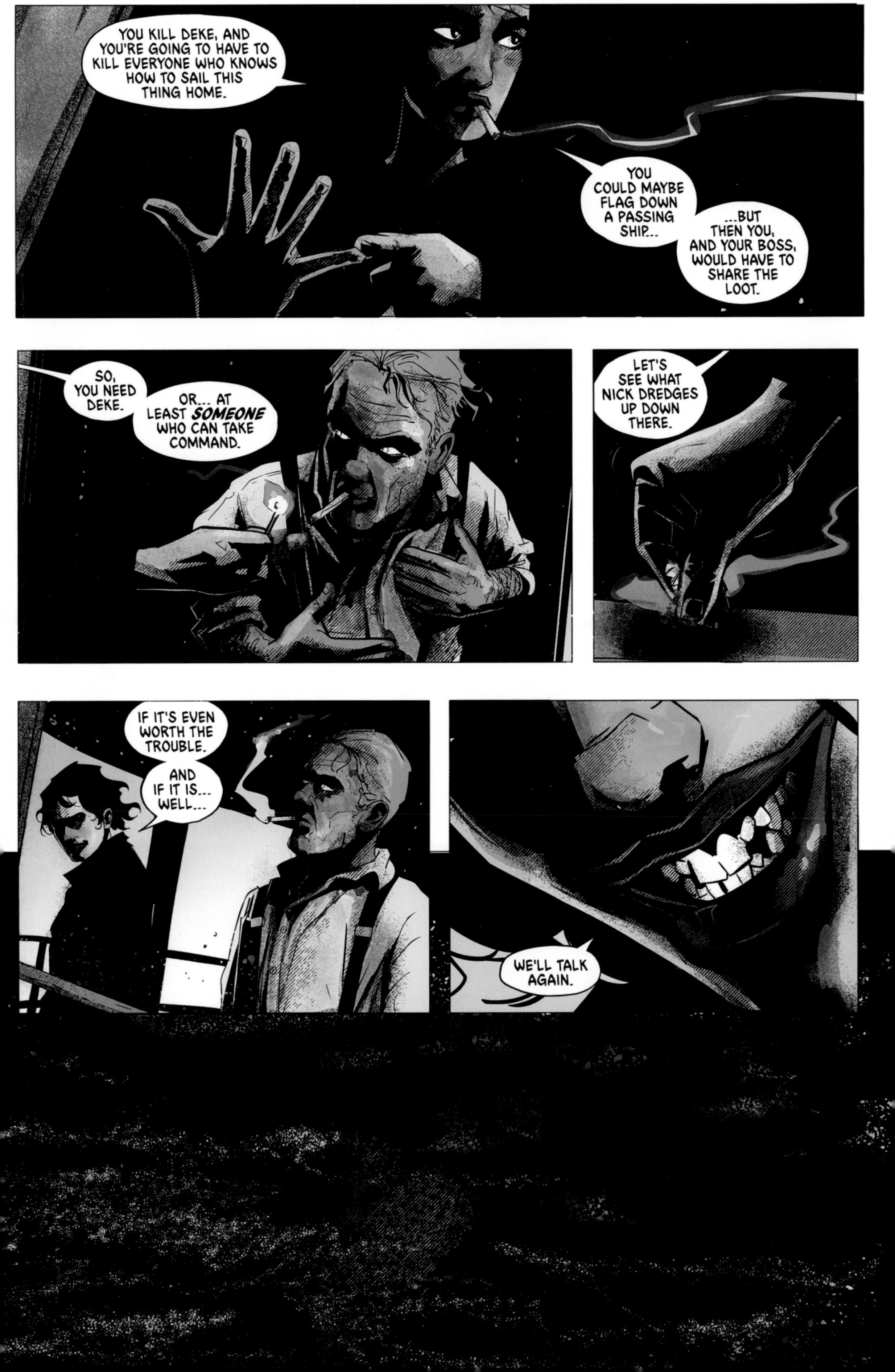
YOU KILL DEKE, AND YOU'RE GOING TO HAVE TO KILL EVERYONE WHO KNOWS HOW TO SAIL THIS THING HOME.
YOU COULD MAYBE FLAG DOWN A PASSING SHIP...
...BUT THEN YOU, AND YOUR BOSS, WOULD HAVE TO SHARE THE LOOT.
SO, YOU NEED DEKE.
OR... AT LEAST SOMEONE WHO CAN TAKE COMMAND.
LET'S SEE WHAT NICK DREDGES UP DOWN THERE.
IF IT'S EVEN WORTH THE TROUBLE.
AND IF IT IS... WELL...
WE'LL TALK AGAIN.

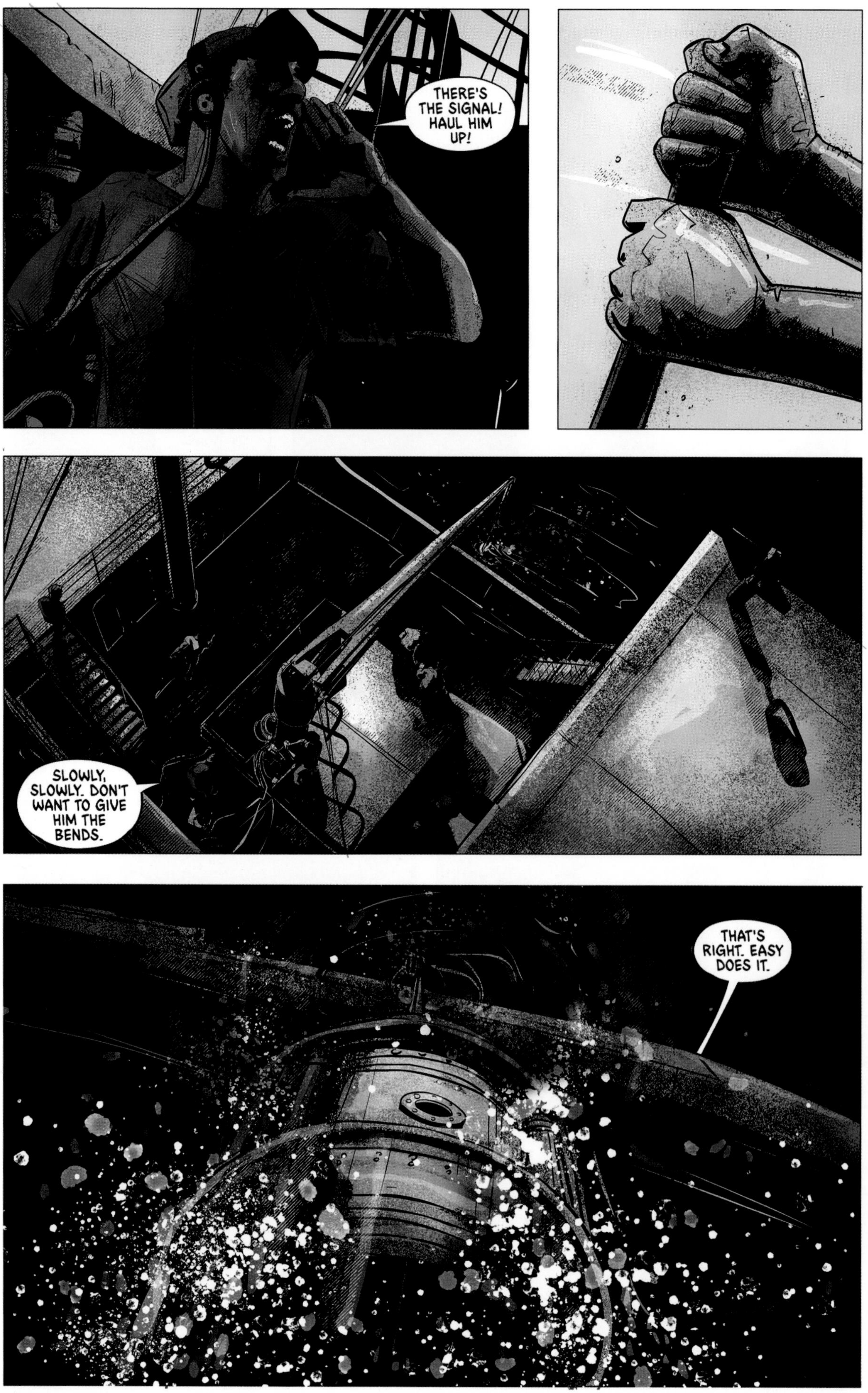
THERE'S THE SIGNAL! HAUL HIM UP!
SLOWLY, SLOWLY. DON'T WANT TO GIVE HIM THE BENDS.
THAT'S RIGHT. EASY DOES IT.

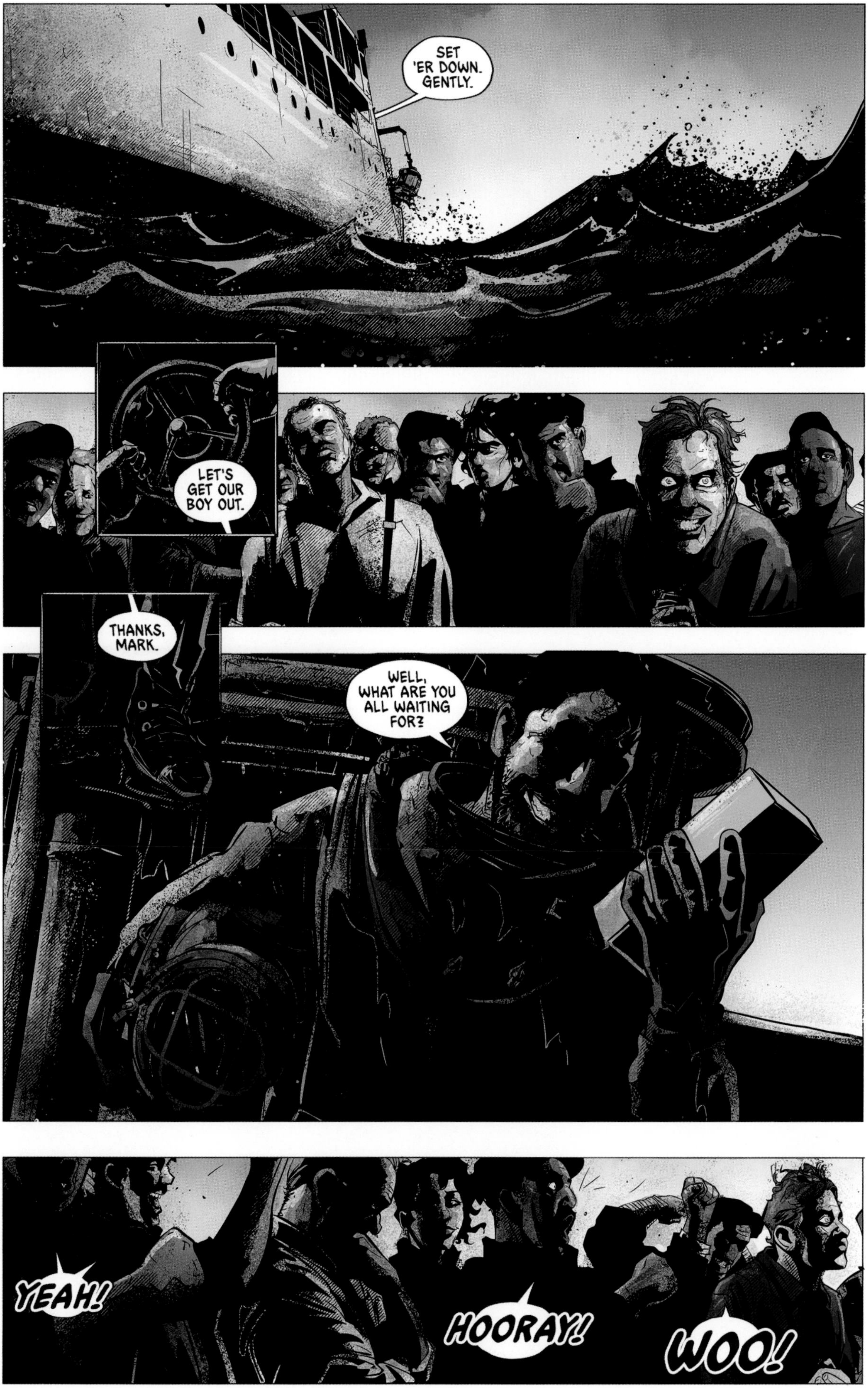
SET 'ER DOWN. GENTLY.
LET'S GET OUR BOY OUT.
THANKS, MARK.
WELL, WHAT ARE YOU ALL WAITING FOR?
YEAH!
HOORAY!
WOO!

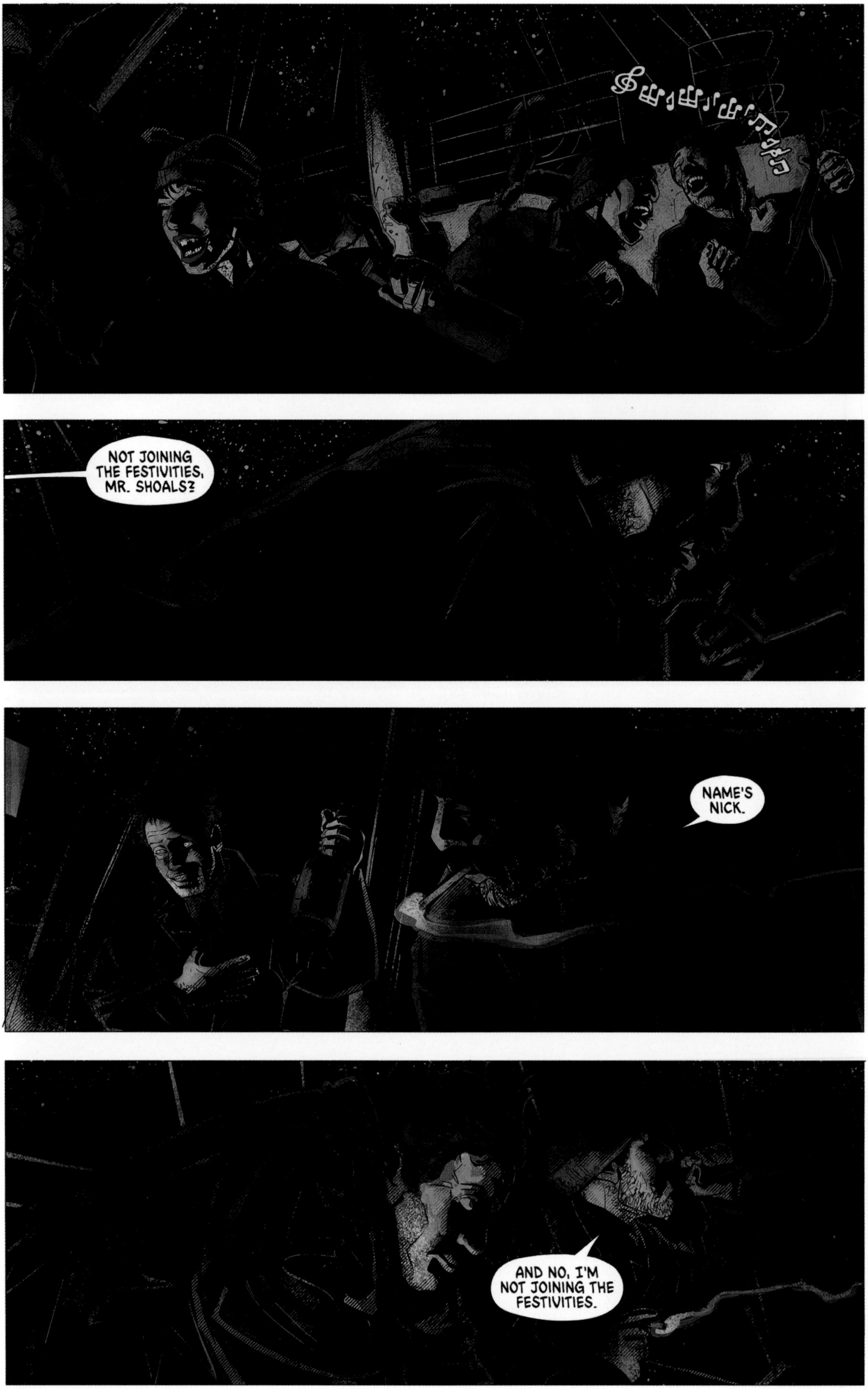
NOT JOINING THE FESTIVITIES, MR. SHOALS?
NAME'S NICK.
AND NO, I'M NOT JOINING THE FESTIVITIES.

I JUST WANT TO GET BACK DOWN THERE. AWAY FROM ALL THE NOISE.

IS IT PEACEFUL? DOWN THERE?

YEAH.

MORE PEACEFUL THAN A MAN LIKE ME HAS ANY RIGHT TO EXPERIENCE.

FWOOSH

COME NOW, NICK, YOU DON'T SEEM A BAD FELLOW.

SURELY YOU'RE NOT SOME KIND OF MONSTER.

A MONSTER? NO.

AT LEAST...

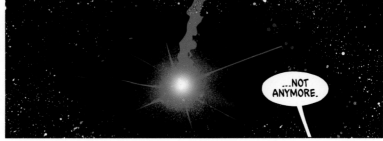

...NOT ANYMORE.

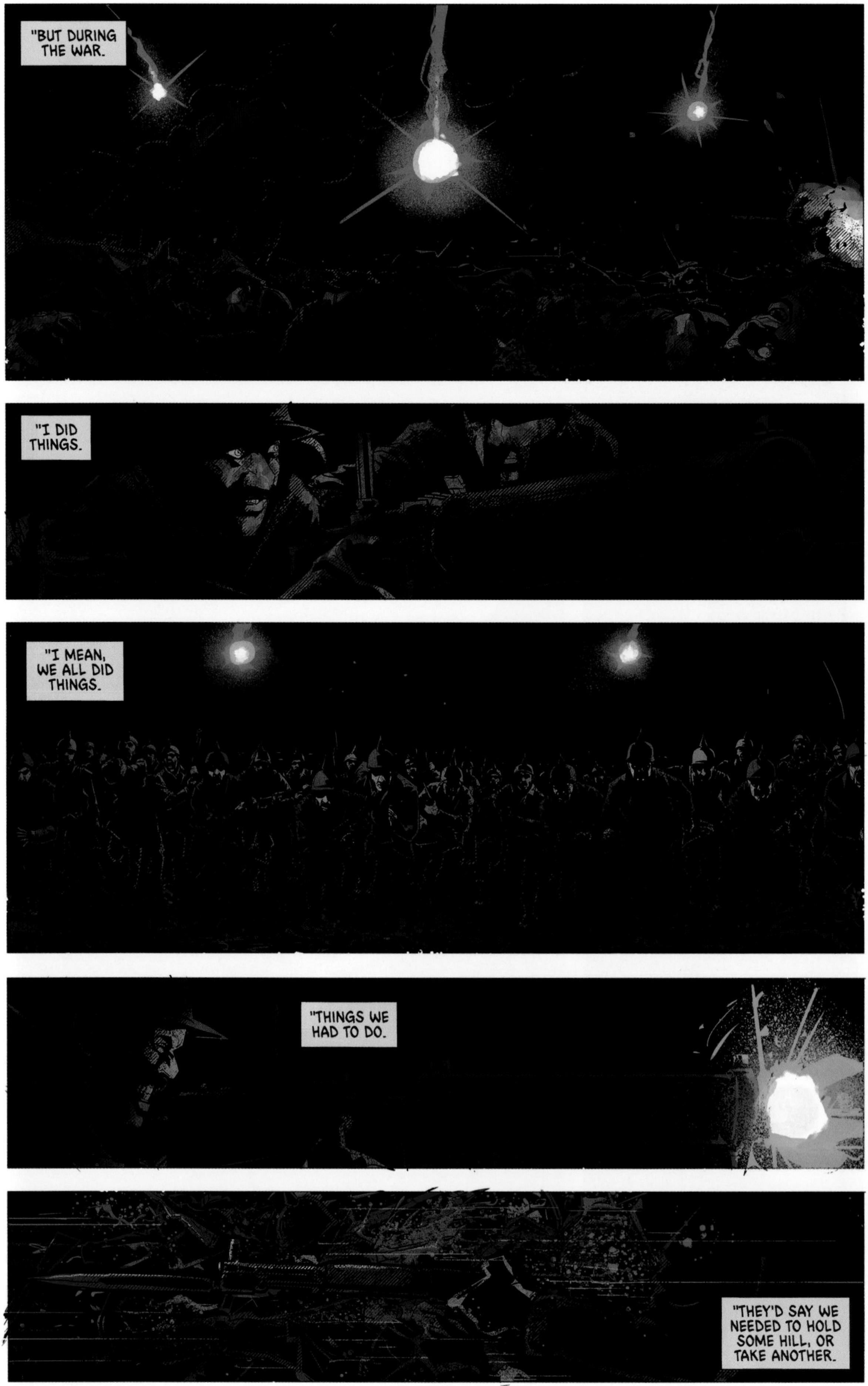
"BUT DURING THE WAR.
"I DID THINGS.
"I MEAN, WE ALL DID THINGS.
"THINGS WE HAD TO DO.
"THEY'D SAY WE NEEDED TO HOLD SOME HILL, OR TAKE ANOTHER.

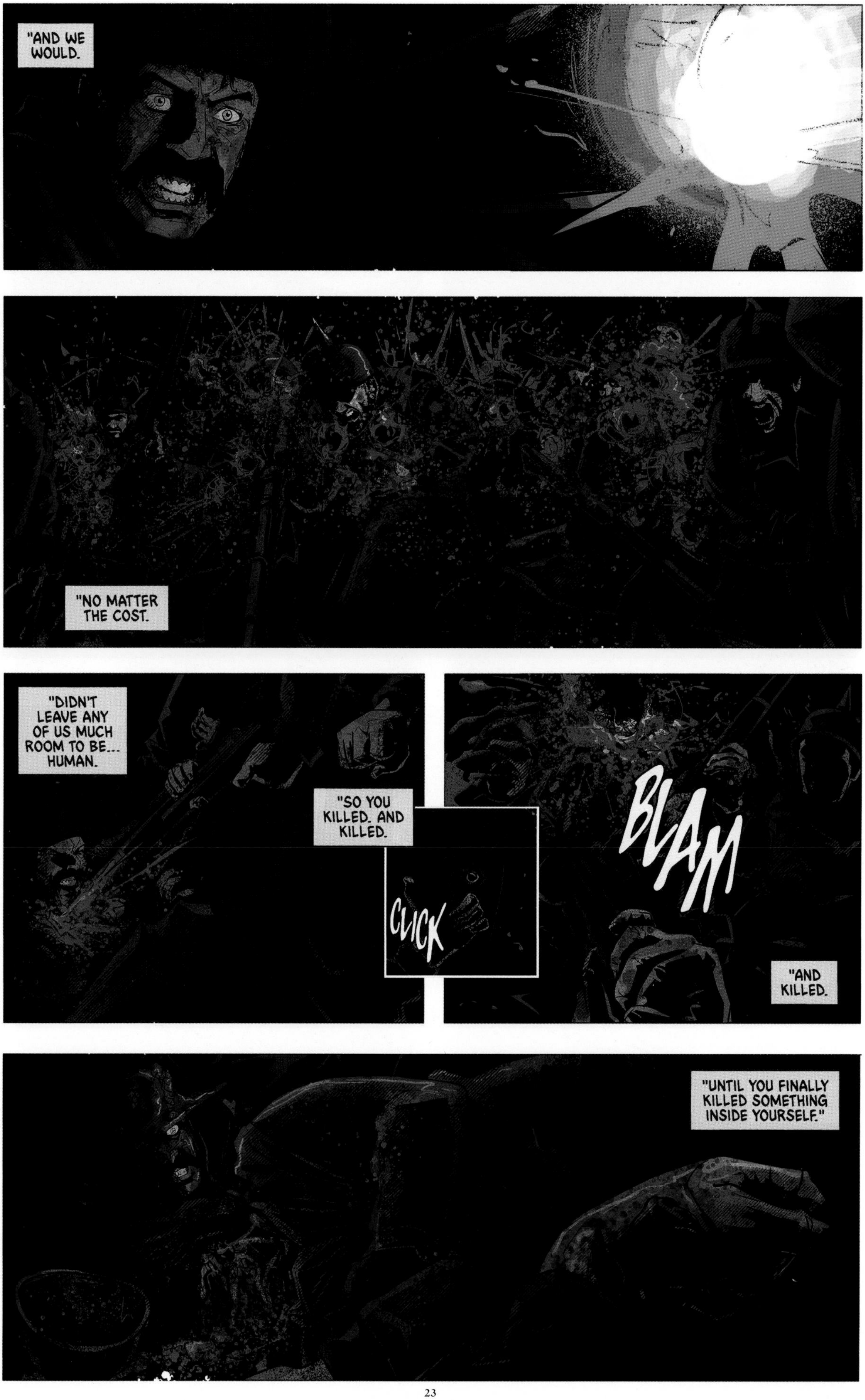
"AND WE WOULD.
"NO MATTER THE COST.
"DIDN'T LEAVE ANY OF US MUCH ROOM TO BE... HUMAN.
"SO YOU KILLED. AND KILLED.
CLICK
BLAM
"AND KILLED.
"UNTIL YOU FINALLY KILLED SOMETHING INSIDE YOURSELF."

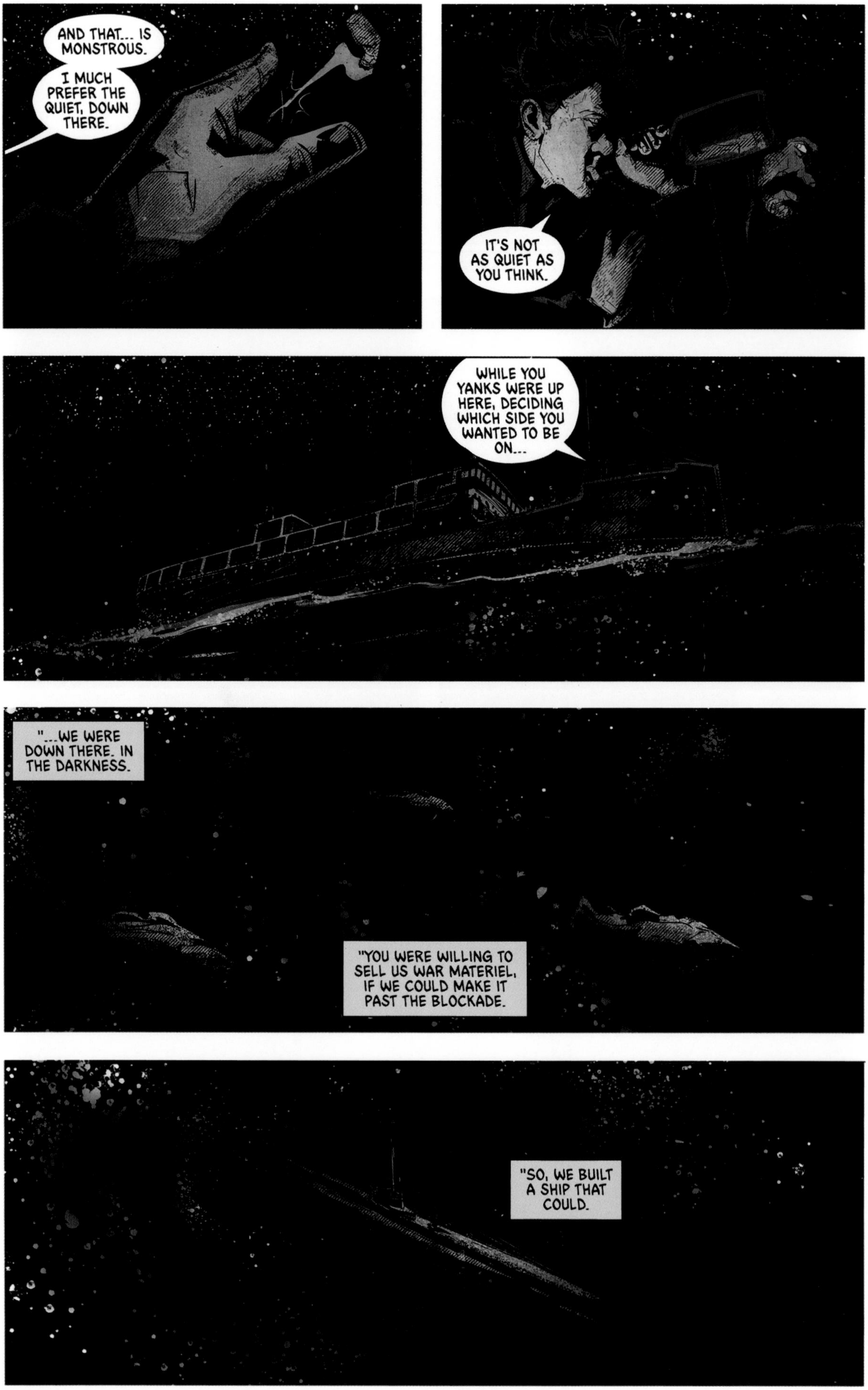
AND THAT... IS MONSTROUS.
I MUCH PREFER THE QUIET, DOWN THERE.
IT'S NOT AS QUIET AS YOU THINK.
WHILE YOU YANKS WERE UP HERE, DECIDING WHICH SIDE YOU WANTED TO BE ON...
"...WE WERE DOWN THERE. IN THE DARKNESS.
"YOU WERE WILLING TO SELL US WAR MATERIEL, IF WE COULD MAKE IT PAST THE BLOCKADE.
"SO, WE BUILT A SHIP THAT COULD.

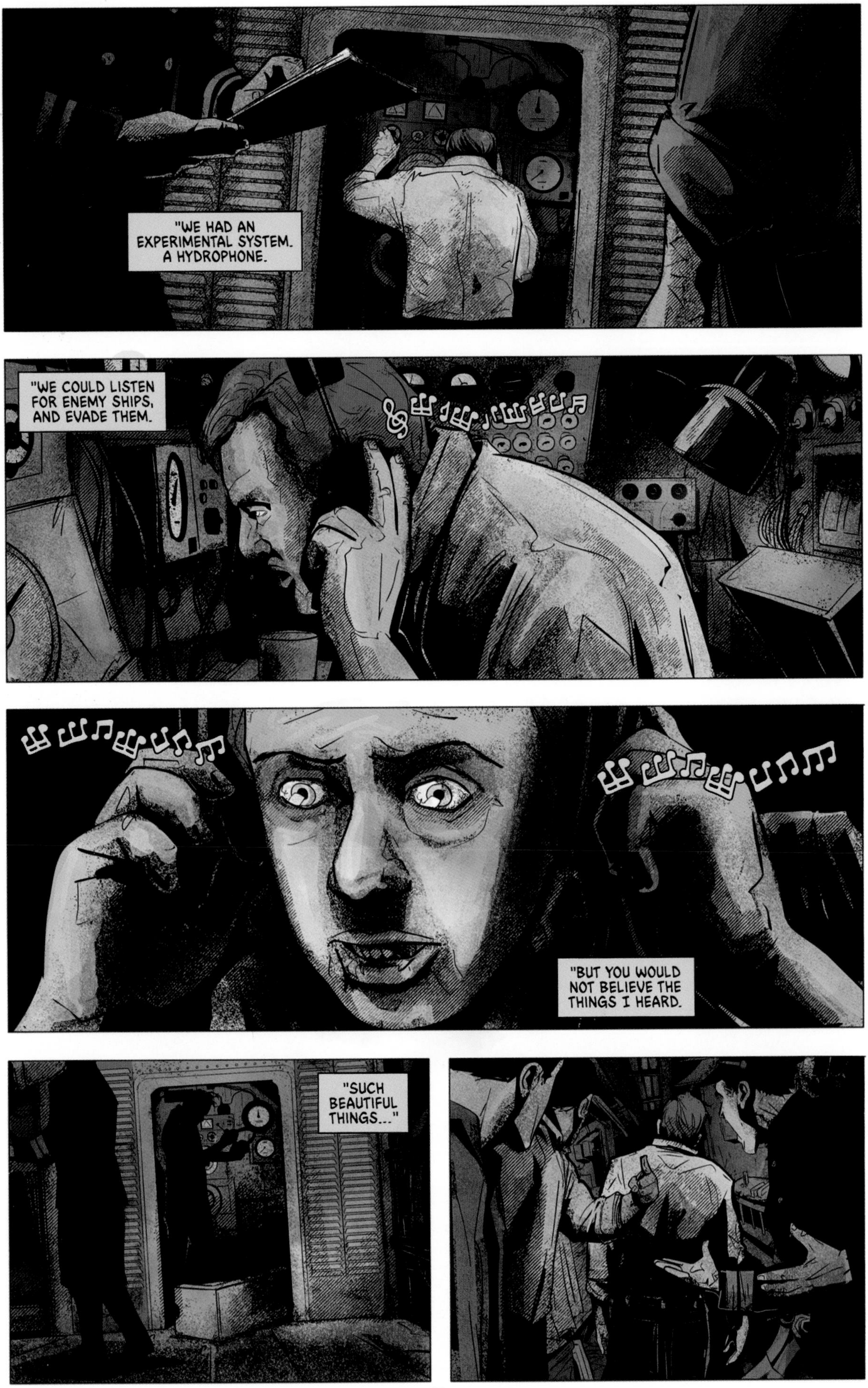
"WE HAD AN EXPERIMENTAL SYSTEM. A HYDROPHONE.
"WE COULD LISTEN FOR ENEMY SHIPS, AND EVADE THEM.
"BUT YOU WOULD NOT BELIEVE THE THINGS I HEARD.
"SUCH BEAUTIFUL THINGS..."

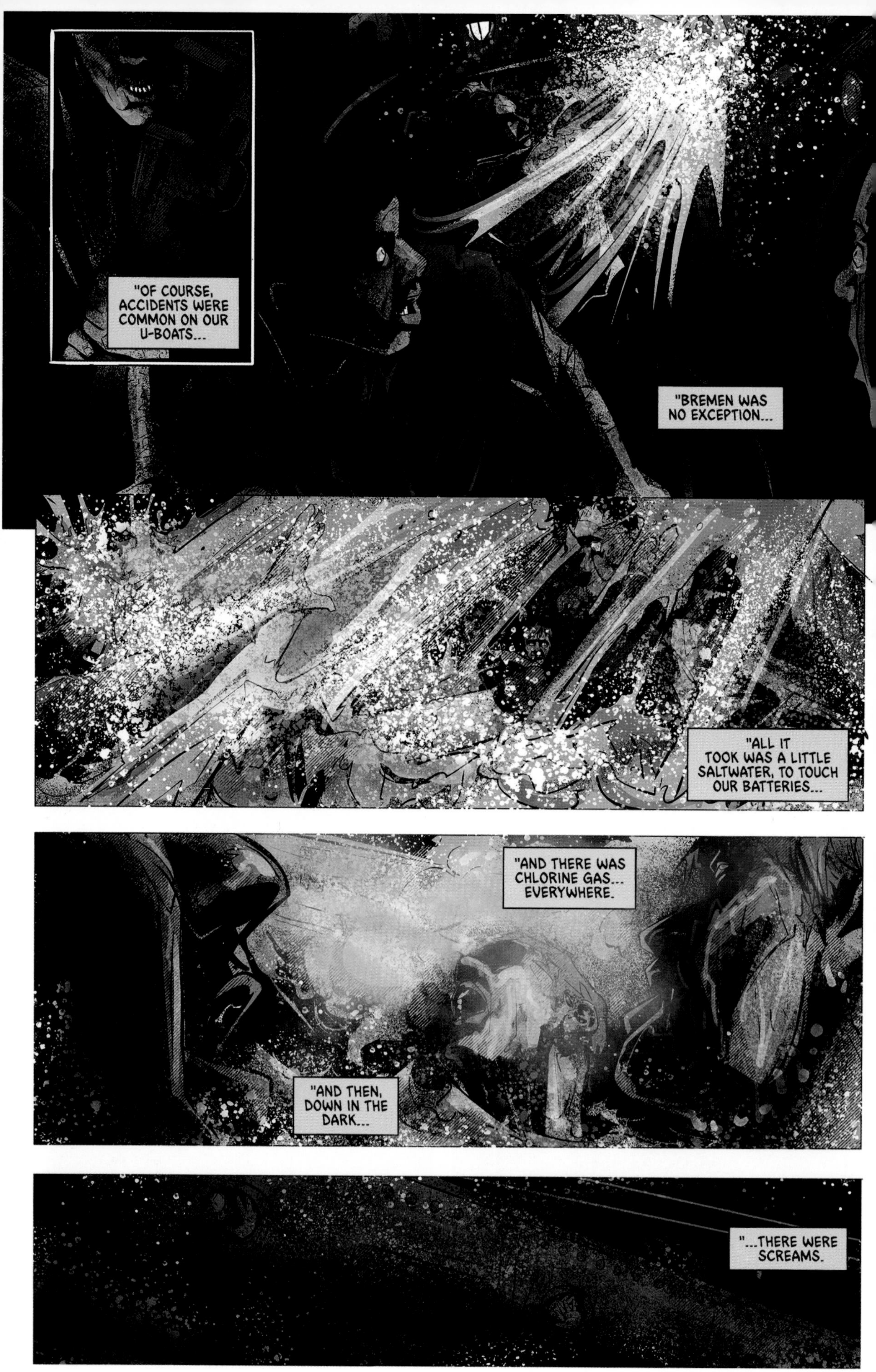
"OF COURSE, ACCIDENTS WERE COMMON ON OUR U-BOATS...
"BREMEN WAS NO EXCEPTION...
"ALL IT TOOK WAS A LITTLE SALTWATER, TO TOUCH OUR BATTERIES...
"AND THERE WAS CHLORINE GAS... EVERYWHERE.
"AND THEN, DOWN IN THE DARK...
"...THERE WERE SCREAMS.

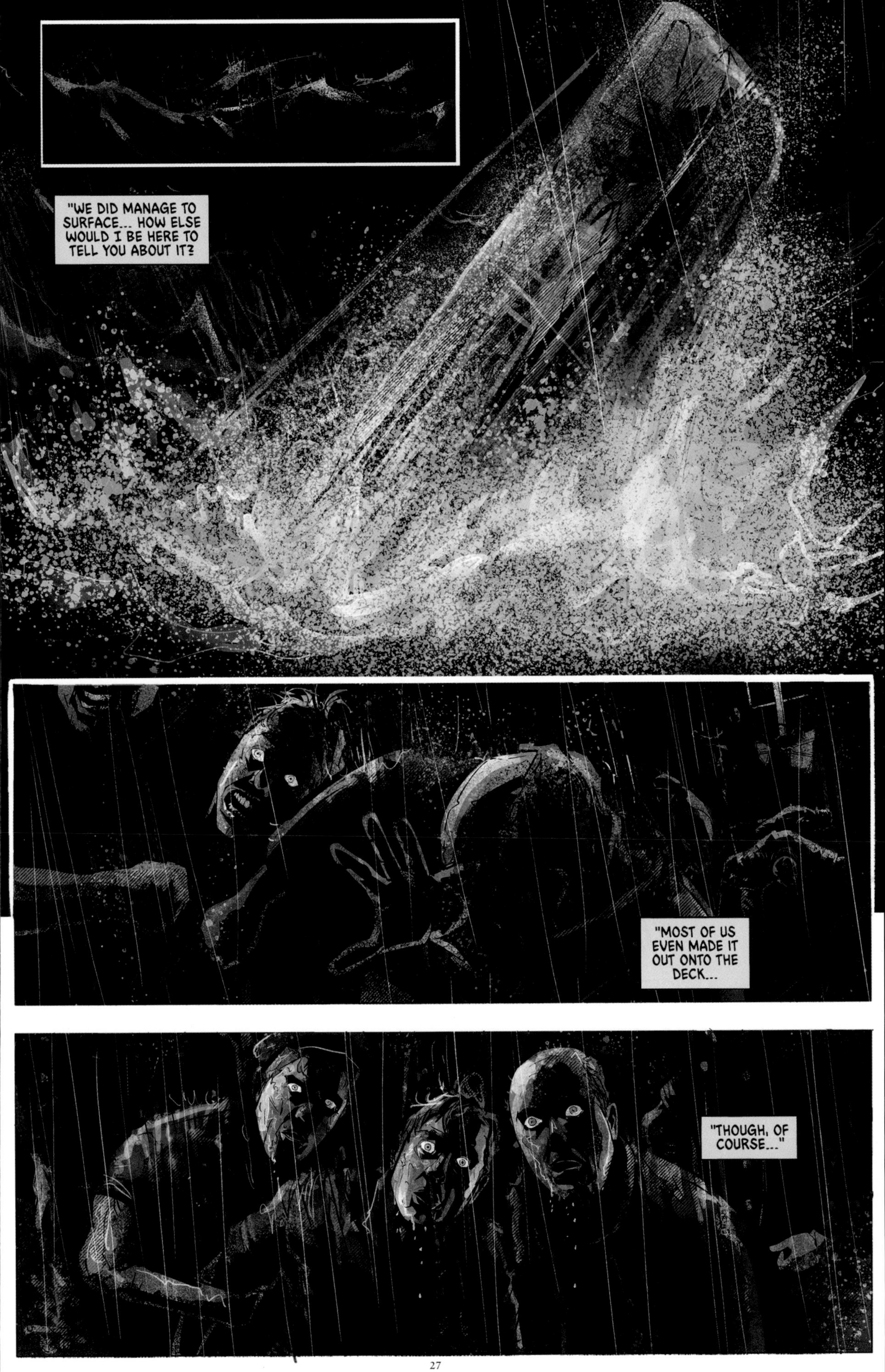
"WE DID MANAGE TO SURFACE... HOW ELSE WOULD I BE HERE TO TELL YOU ABOUT IT?
"MOST OF US EVEN MADE IT OUT ONTO THE DECK...
"THOUGH, OF COURSE..."

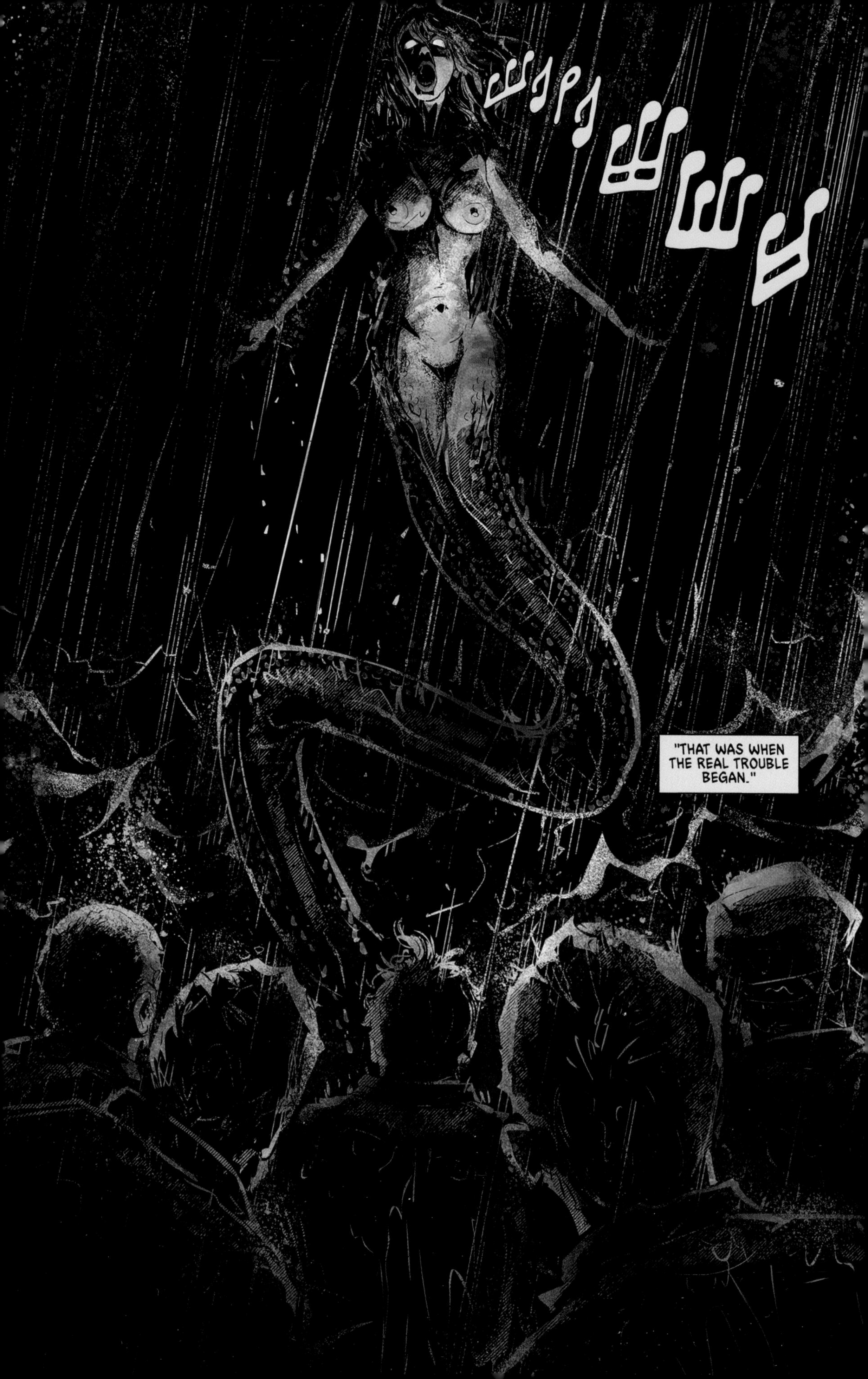
"THAT WAS WHEN THE REAL TROUBLE BEGAN."

Art by
KATIE SAWATSKY

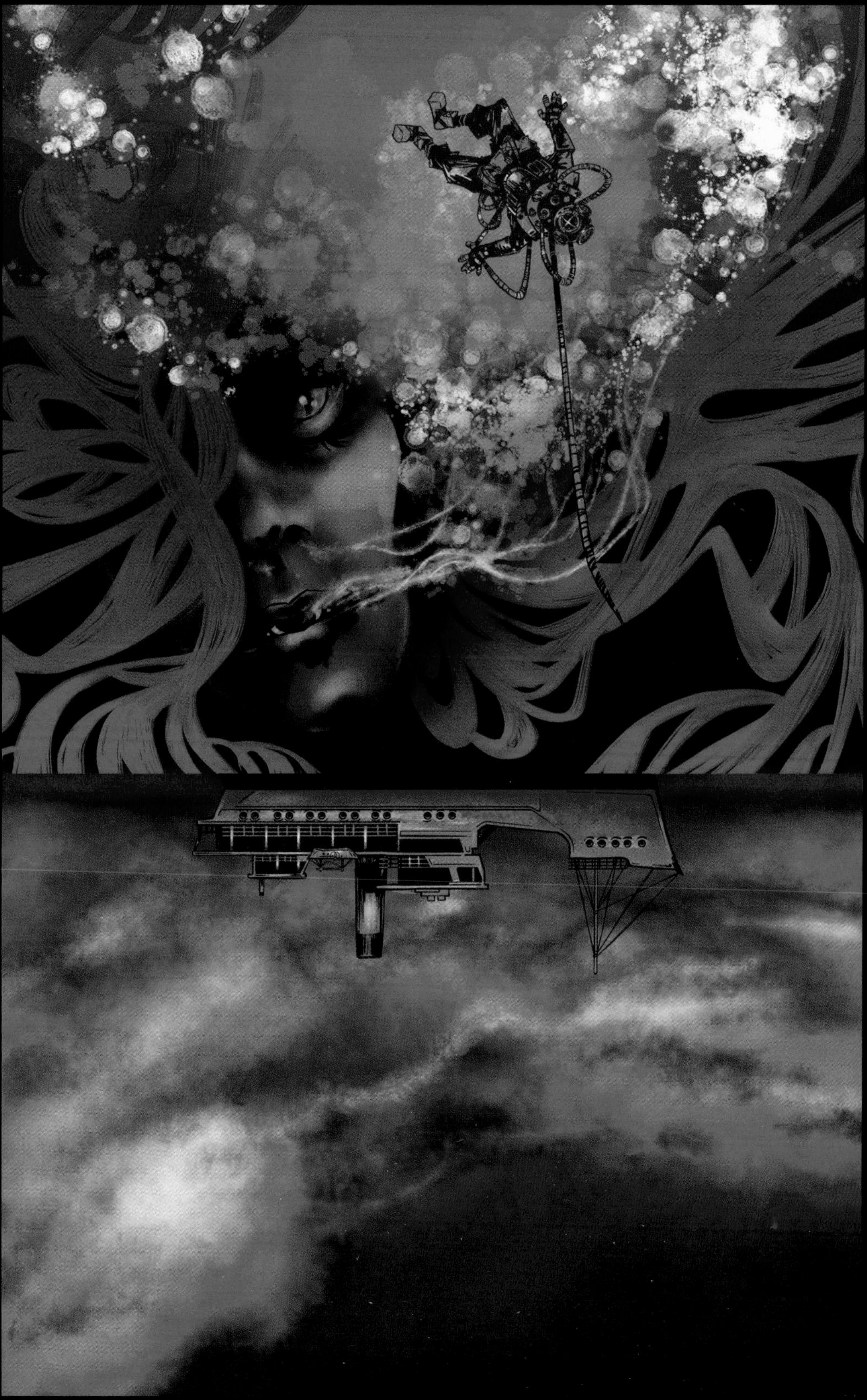

BREMEN
BREMEN
BREMEN
BREMEN

Art by
ALEX CORMACK

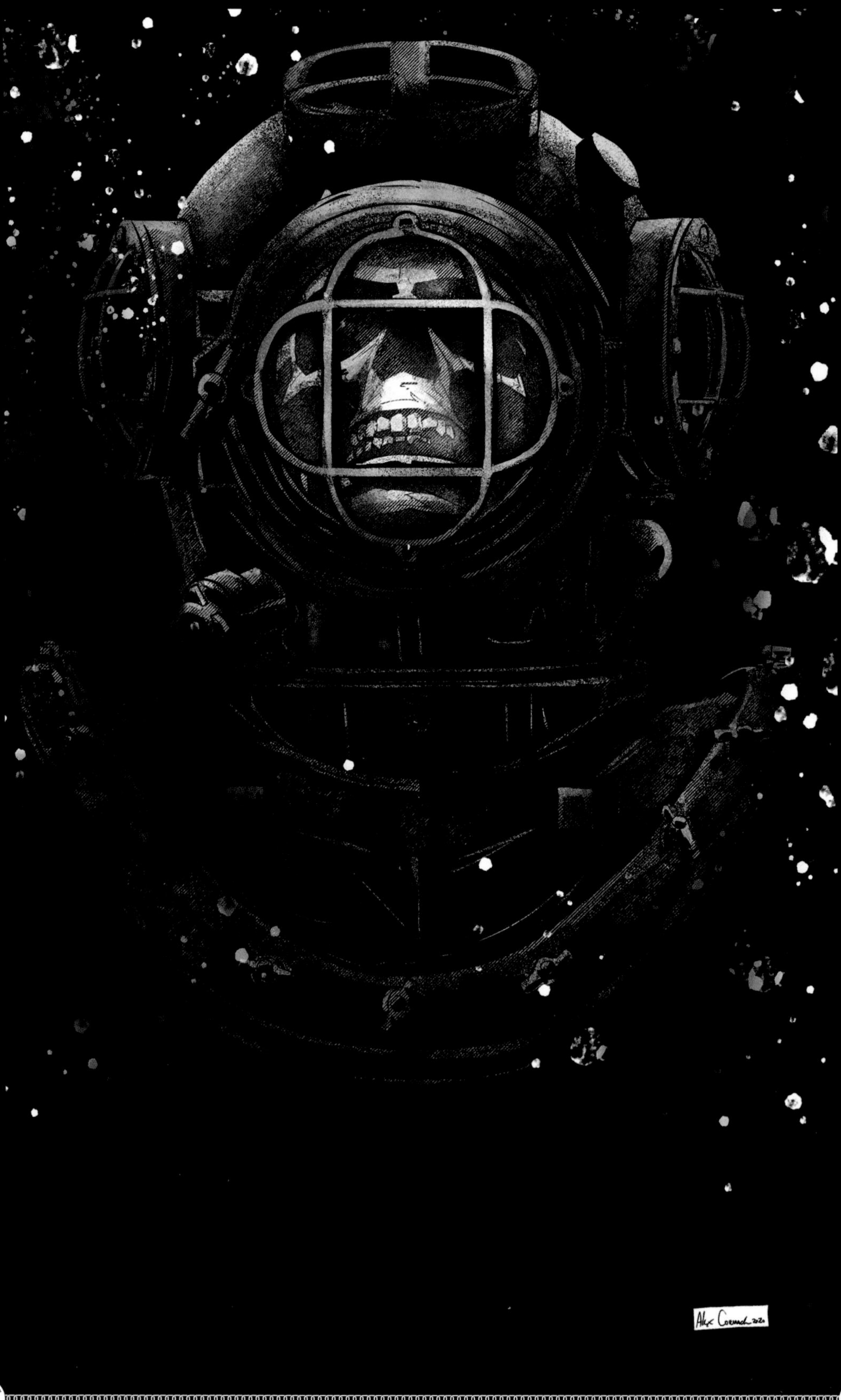
Alex Cormack 2020

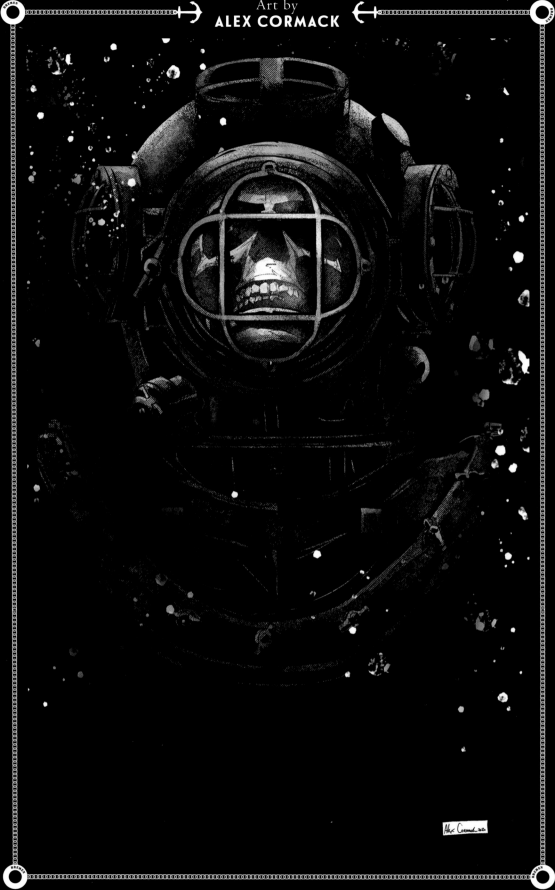

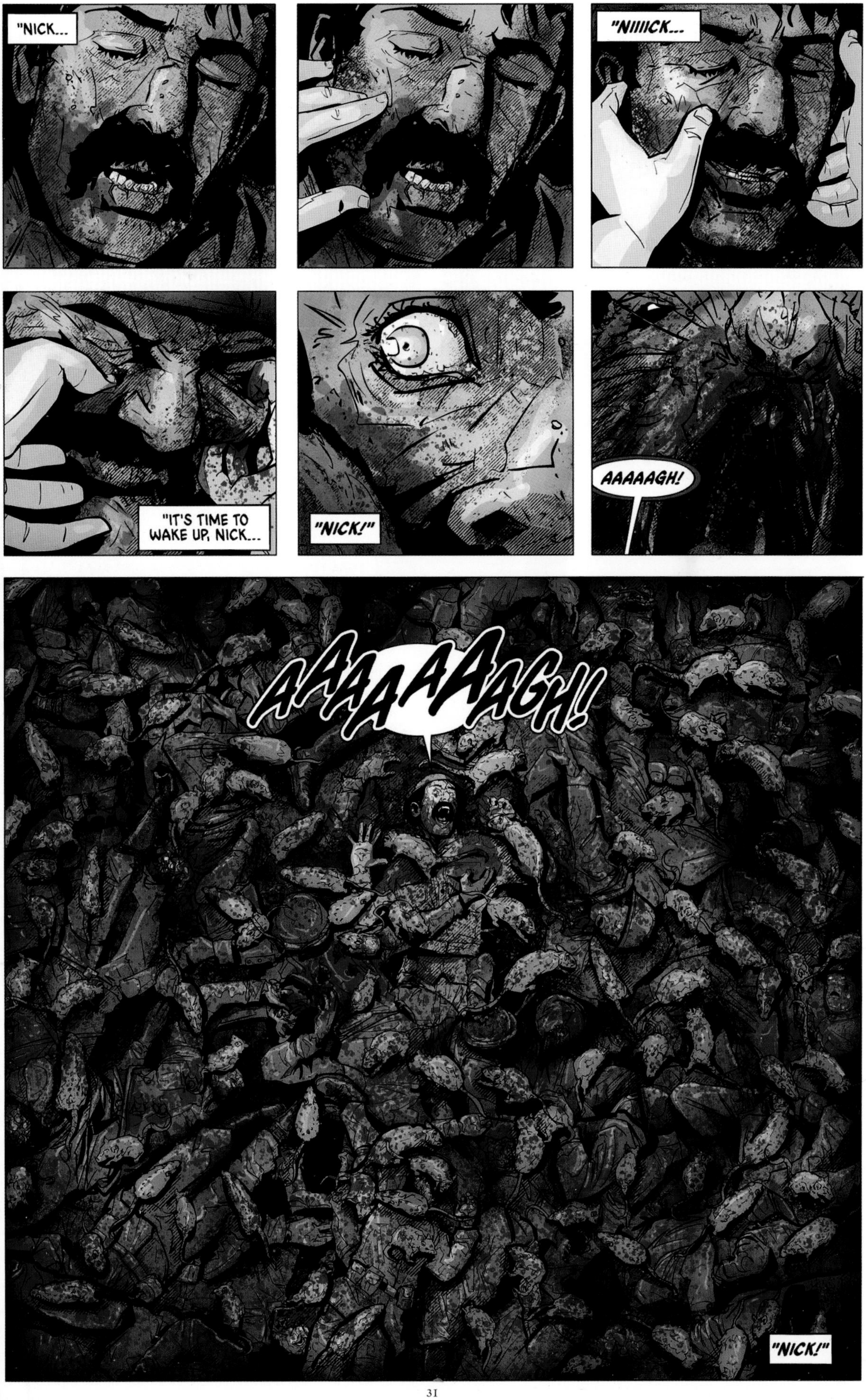
"NICK...
"NIIIICK...
"IT'S TIME TO WAKE UP, NICK...
"NICK!"
AAAAAGH!
AAAAAAAGH!
"NICK!"

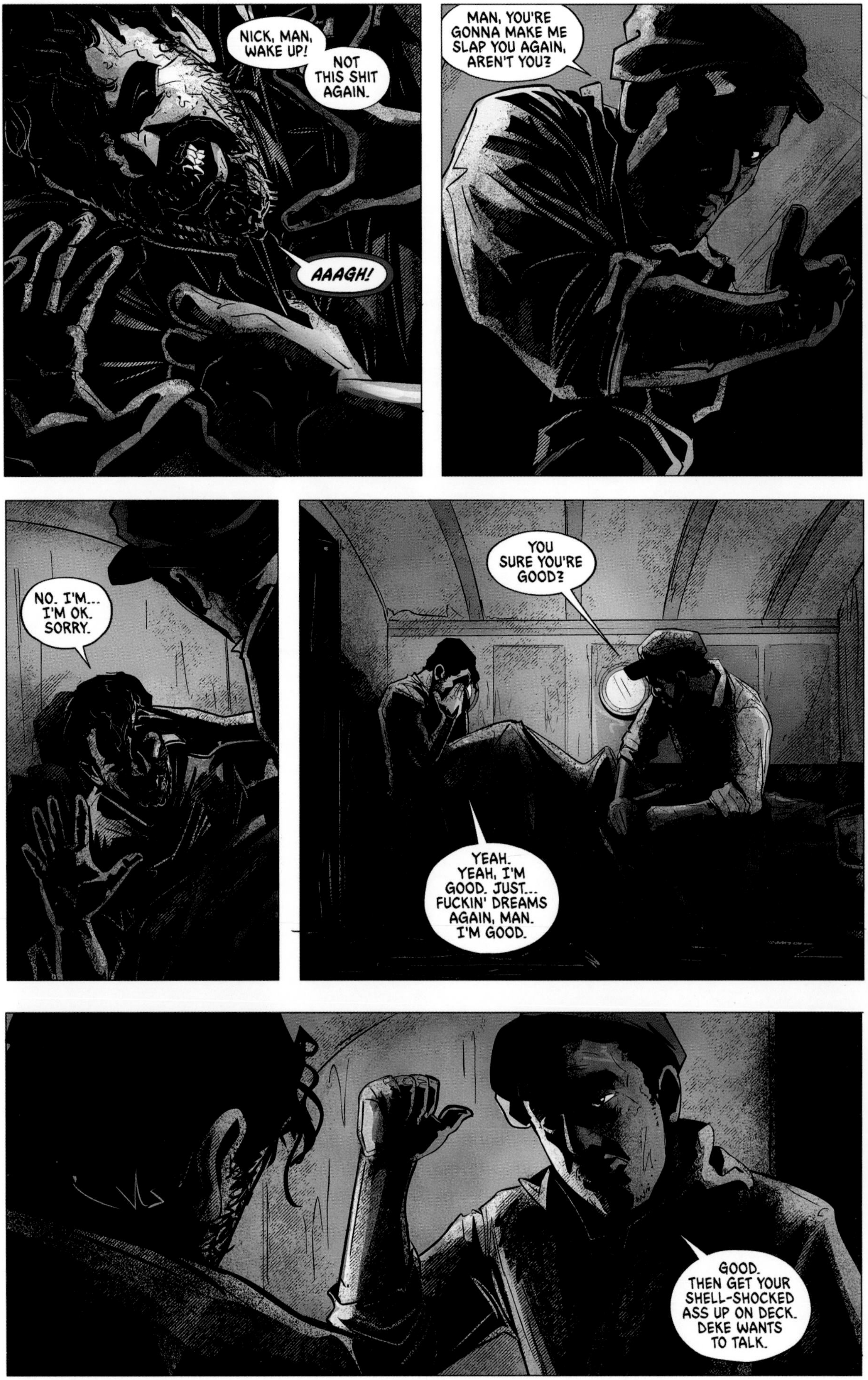
NICK, MAN, WAKE UP!
NOT THIS SHIT AGAIN.
AAAGH!
MAN, YOU'RE GONNA MAKE ME SLAP YOU AGAIN, AREN'T YOU?
NO. I'M... I'M OK. SORRY.
YOU SURE YOU'RE GOOD?
YEAH. YEAH, I'M GOOD. JUST... FUCKIN' DREAMS AGAIN, MAN. I'M GOOD.
GOOD. THEN GET YOUR SHELL-SHOCKED ASS UP ON DECK. DEKE WANTS TO TALK.

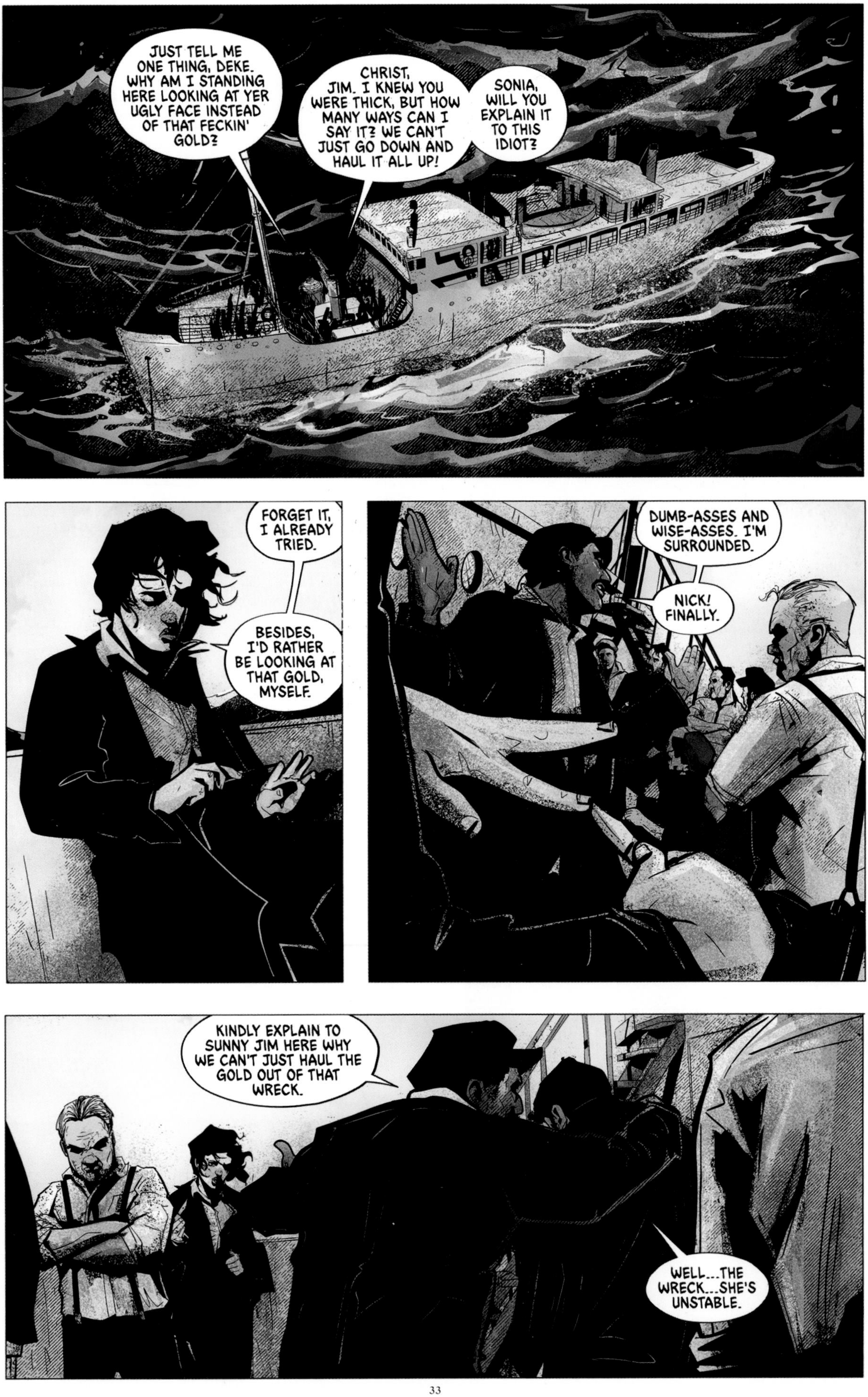
JUST TELL ME ONE THING, DEKE. WHY AM I STANDING HERE LOOKING AT YER UGLY FACE INSTEAD OF THAT FECKIN' GOLD?
CHRIST, JIM. I KNEW YOU WERE THICK, BUT HOW MANY WAYS CAN I SAY IT? WE CAN'T JUST GO DOWN AND HAUL IT ALL UP!
SONIA, WILL YOU EXPLAIN IT TO THIS IDIOT?
FORGET IT, I ALREADY TRIED.
BESIDES, I'D RATHER BE LOOKING AT THAT GOLD, MYSELF.
DUMB-ASSES AND WISE-ASSES. I'M SURROUNDED.
NICK! FINALLY.
KINDLY EXPLAIN TO SUNNY JIM HERE WHY WE CAN'T JUST HAUL THE GOLD OUT OF THAT WRECK.
WELL...THE WRECK...SHE'S UNSTABLE.

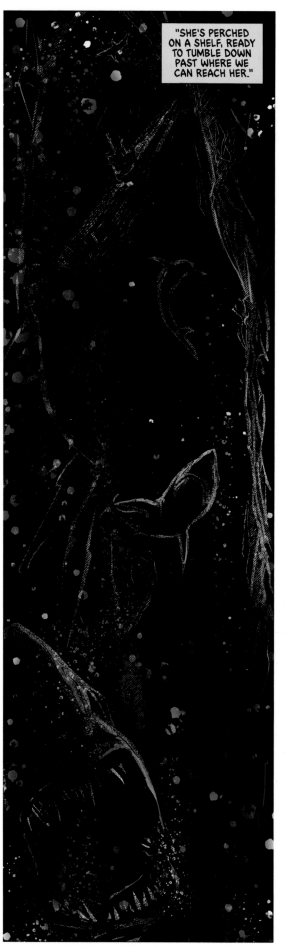

"SHE'S PERCHED ON A SHELF, READY TO TUMBLE DOWN PAST WHERE WE CAN REACH HER."

THE WEIGHT OF THE CARGO IS PROBABLY THE ONLY THING KEEPING HER THERE.

WE START TO REMOVE IT... COULD BE THE WHOLE BOAT GOES OVER.

SO YOU DIVE DOWN DEEPER!

NOBODY CAN DIVE *THAT* DEEP. PRESSURE WOULD CRACK MY HELMET LIKE AN EGG.

YOU WANT TO SHOOT US, GO AHEAD AND FUCKING SHOOT US, THEN.

WON'T CHANGE THE FACT THAT NOTHING IS GETTING HAULED UP UNTIL THAT WRECK IS STABILIZED.

GET ON WITH IT, THEN!

"NOW REMEMBER, WE'RE JUST SURVEYING.

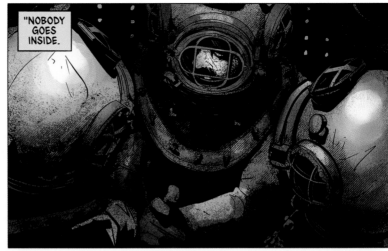

"NOBODY GOES INSIDE.

"NOBODY MOVES SO MUCH AS A ROCK.

"IN FACT...

...NOBODY TOUCHES A GODDAMNED THING WITHOUT MY SAY SO."

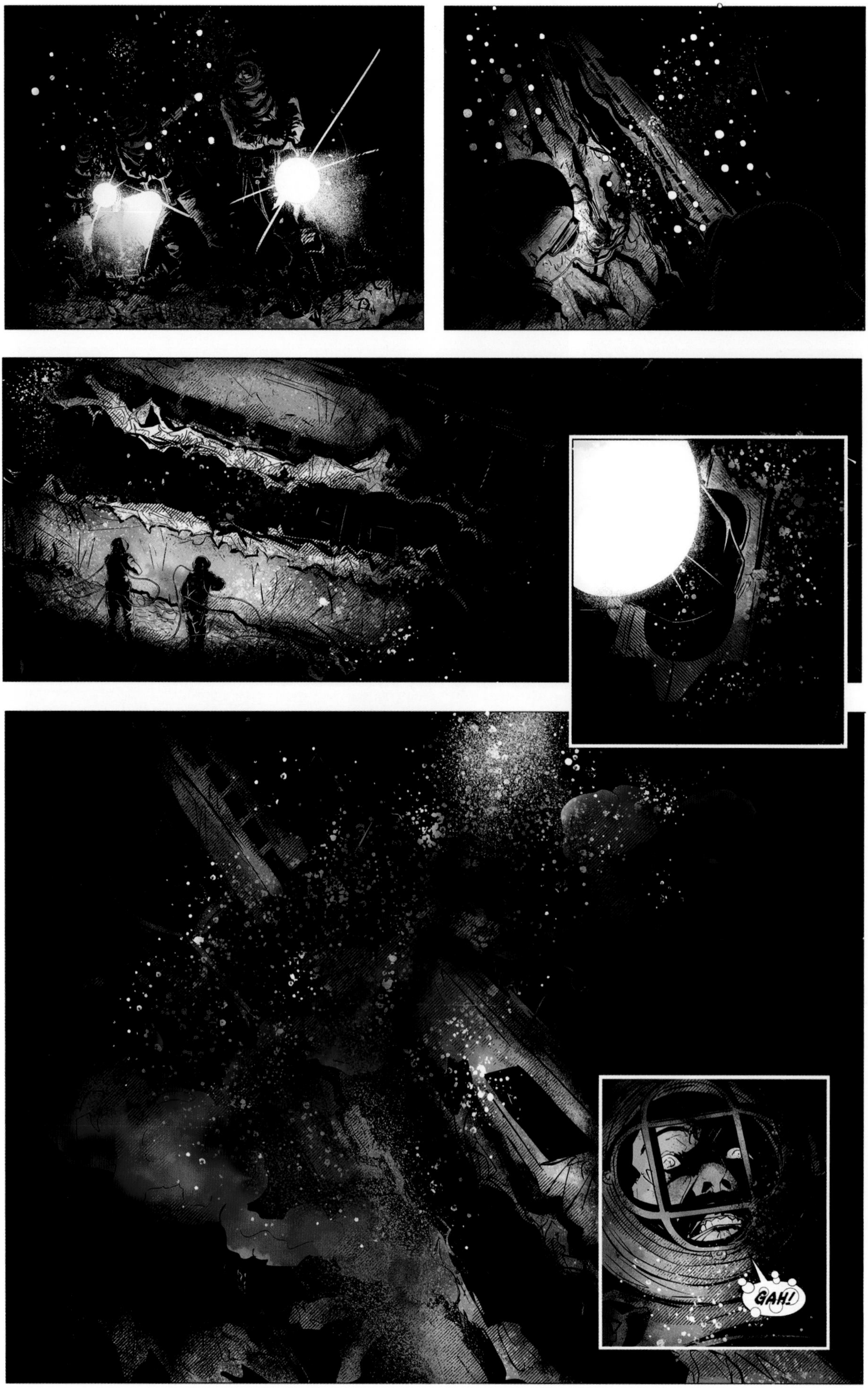
GAH!

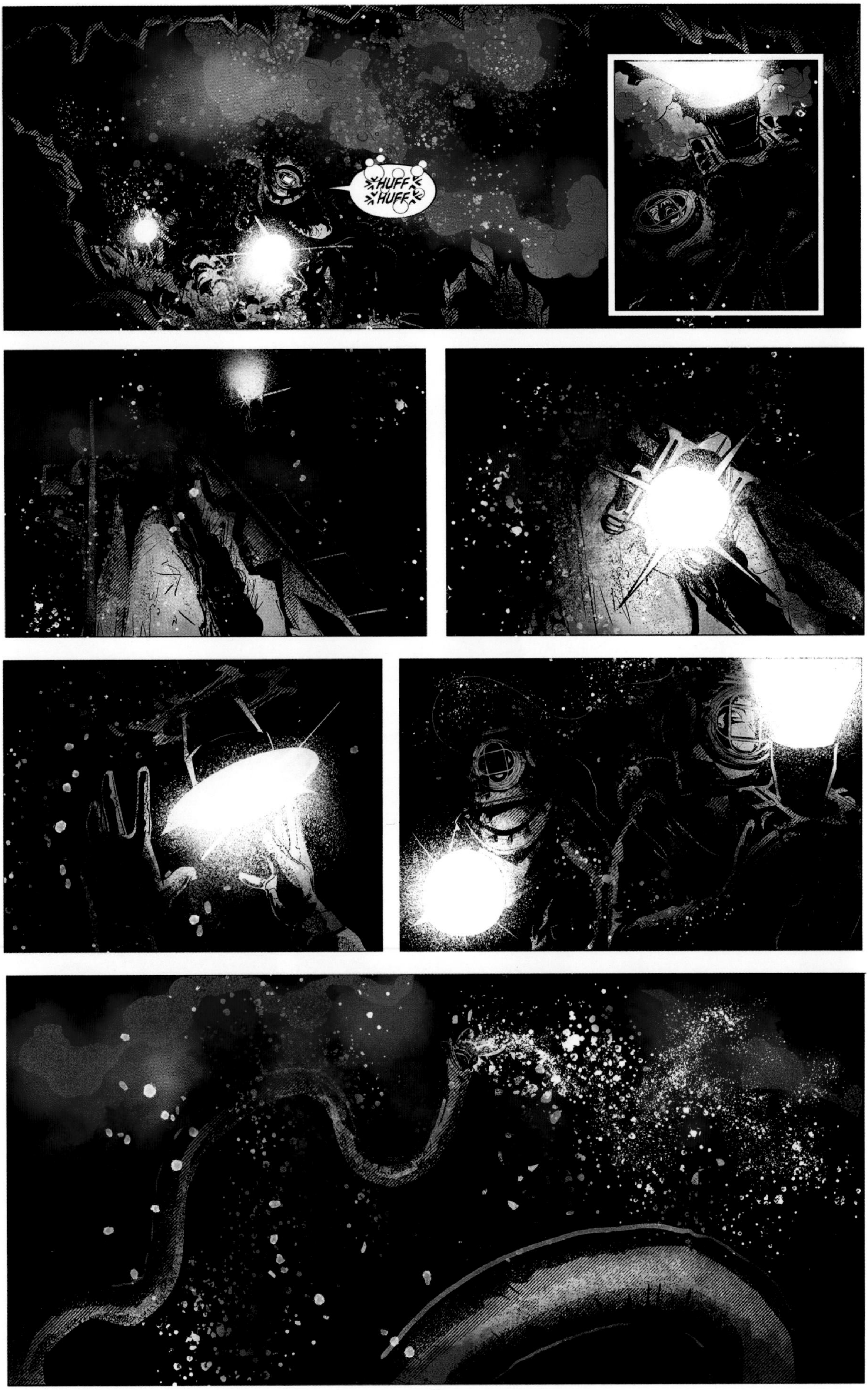
HUFF
HUFF

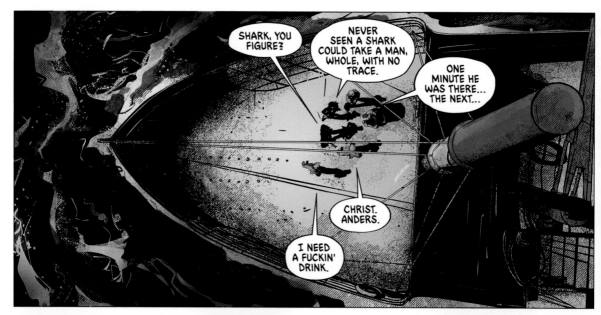

SHARK, YOU FIGURE?

NEVER SEEN A SHARK COULD TAKE A MAN, WHOLE, WITH NO TRACE.

ONE MINUTE HE WAS THERE... THE NEXT...

CHRIST. ANDERS.

I NEED A FUCKIN' DRINK.

I'M AFRAID IT'S ALL TOO POSSIBLE, MY FRIENDS.

AS I WAS TELLING MR. SHOALS LAST NIGHT...

YOU SAID SHE SURFACED...

LONG ENOUGH FOR US TO GET ON DECK. BUT IT WAS ABUNDANTLY CLEAR SHE WAS GOING RIGHT BACK DOWN. SO WE TOOK TO THE WATER...

AND IN THE WATER...

SHARKS. WE GET IT.

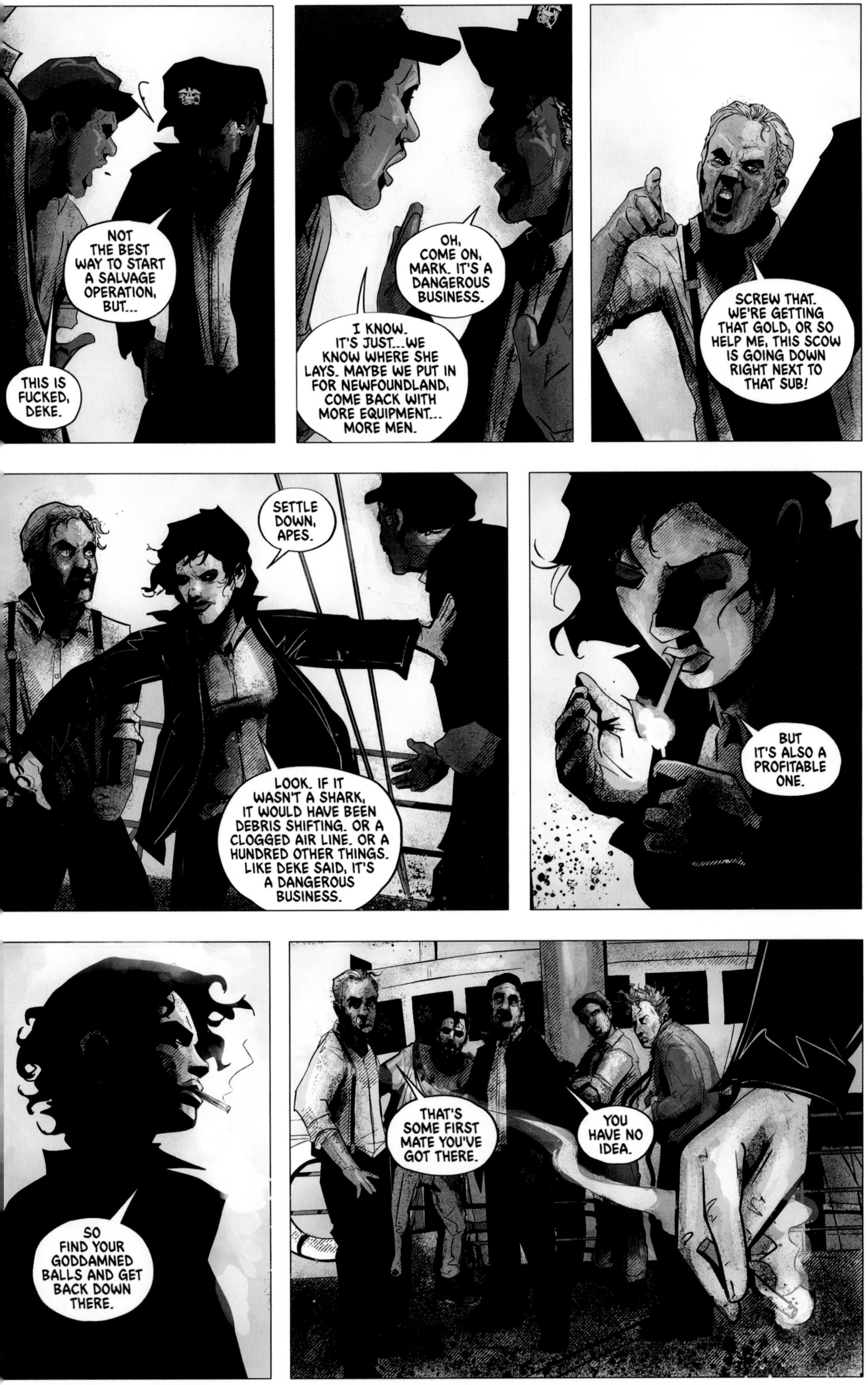
NOT THE BEST WAY TO START A SALVAGE OPERATION, BUT...
THIS IS FUCKED, DEKE.
OH, COME ON, MARK. IT'S A DANGEROUS BUSINESS.
I KNOW. IT'S JUST...WE KNOW WHERE SHE LAYS. MAYBE WE PUT IN FOR NEWFOUNDLAND, COME BACK WITH MORE EQUIPMENT... MORE MEN.
SCREW THAT. WE'RE GETTING THAT GOLD, OR SO HELP ME, THIS SCOW IS GOING DOWN RIGHT NEXT TO THAT SUB!
SETTLE DOWN, APES.
LOOK. IF IT WASN'T A SHARK, IT WOULD HAVE BEEN DEBRIS SHIFTING. OR A CLOGGED AIR LINE. OR A HUNDRED OTHER THINGS. LIKE DEKE SAID, IT'S A DANGEROUS BUSINESS.
BUT IT'S ALSO A PROFITABLE ONE.
SO FIND YOUR GODDAMNED BALLS AND GET BACK DOWN THERE.
THAT'S SOME FIRST MATE YOU'VE GOT THERE.
YOU HAVE NO IDEA.

LISTEN, GUYS, YOU DON'T HAVE TO DO THIS. TELL THEM ALL TO GO SCREW.

SHIT, I'LL TELL THEM MYSELF.

LOOK, ANDERS WAS A GOOD MAN. BUT...

BUT WHAT?

WE JUST...WE JUST WANT THE GOLD, MARK.

OH, COME OFF IT, CARL.

NICK, MAN, THINK ABOUT WHAT YOU'RE RISKING!

WE'RE RISKING IT ANYWAY, MARK. DOWN THERE. UP HERE. DOESN'T MATTER.

SO WHAT, YOU *WANT* TO DIE, OR SOMETHING?

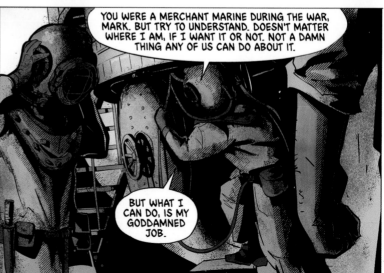

YOU WERE A MERCHANT MARINE DURING THE WAR, MARK. BUT TRY TO UNDERSTAND. DOESN'T MATTER WHERE I AM, IF I WANT IT OR NOT. NOT A DAMN THING ANY OF US CAN DO ABOUT IT.

BUT WHAT I CAN DO, IS MY GODDAMNED JOB.

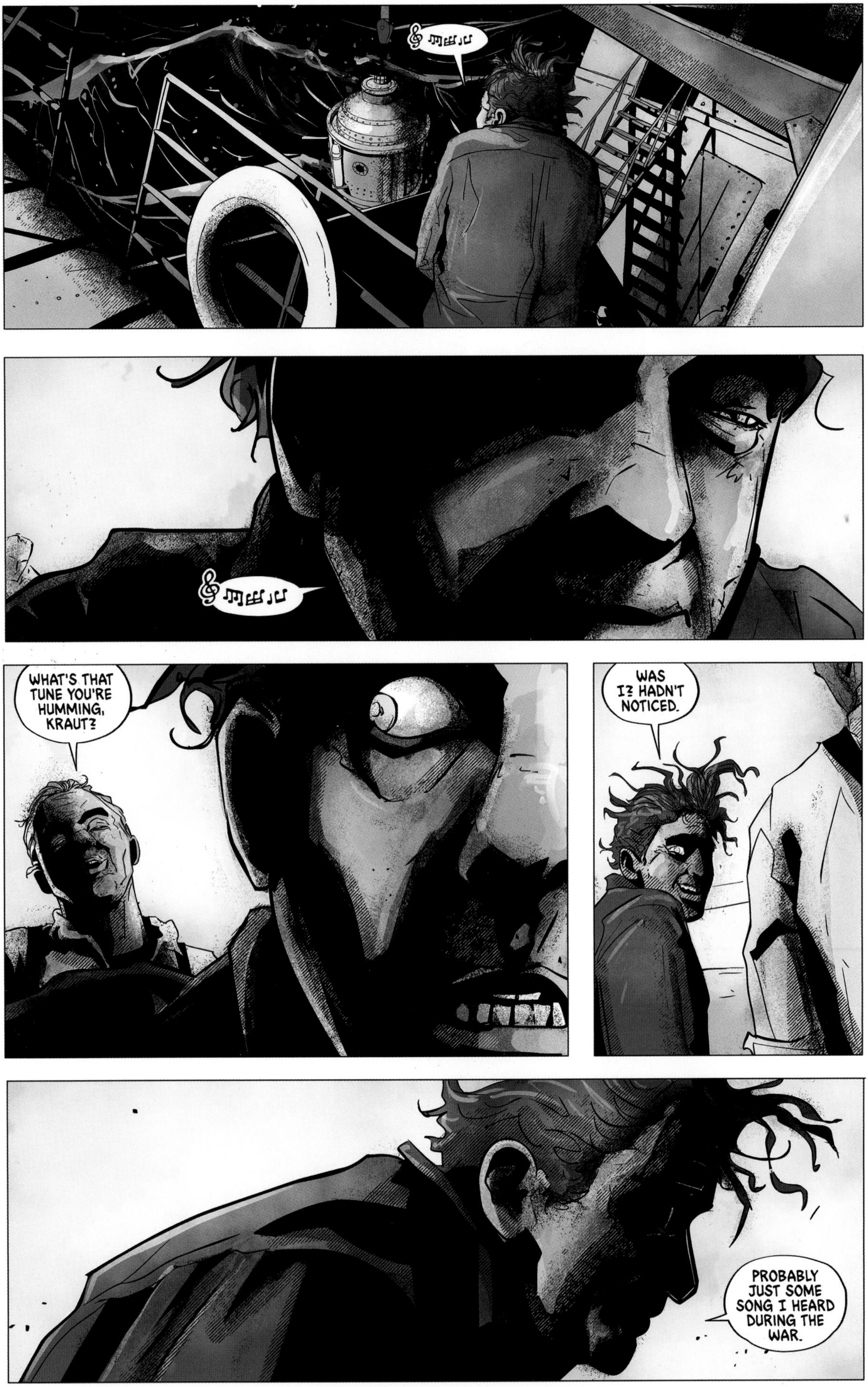
WHAT'S THAT TUNE YOU'RE HUMMING, KRAUT?
WAS I? HADN'T NOTICED.
PROBABLY JUST SOME SONG I HEARD DURING THE WAR.

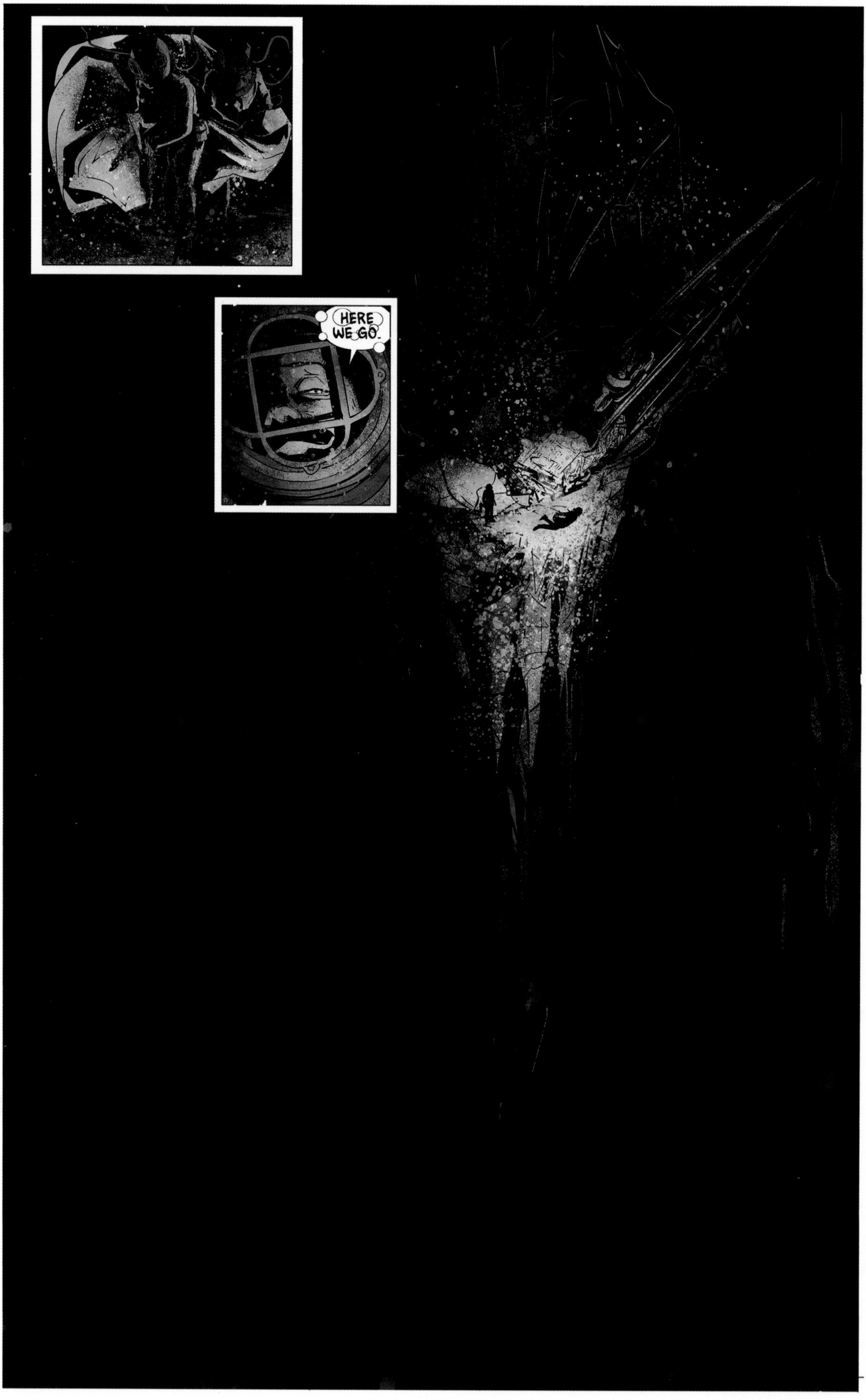
HERE WE GO.

STEADY...

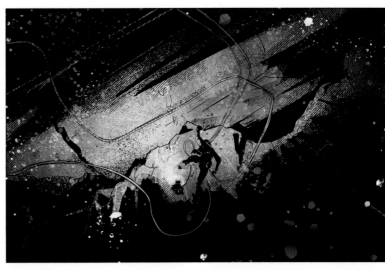

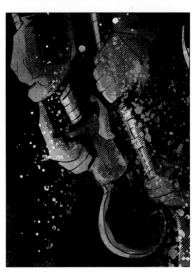

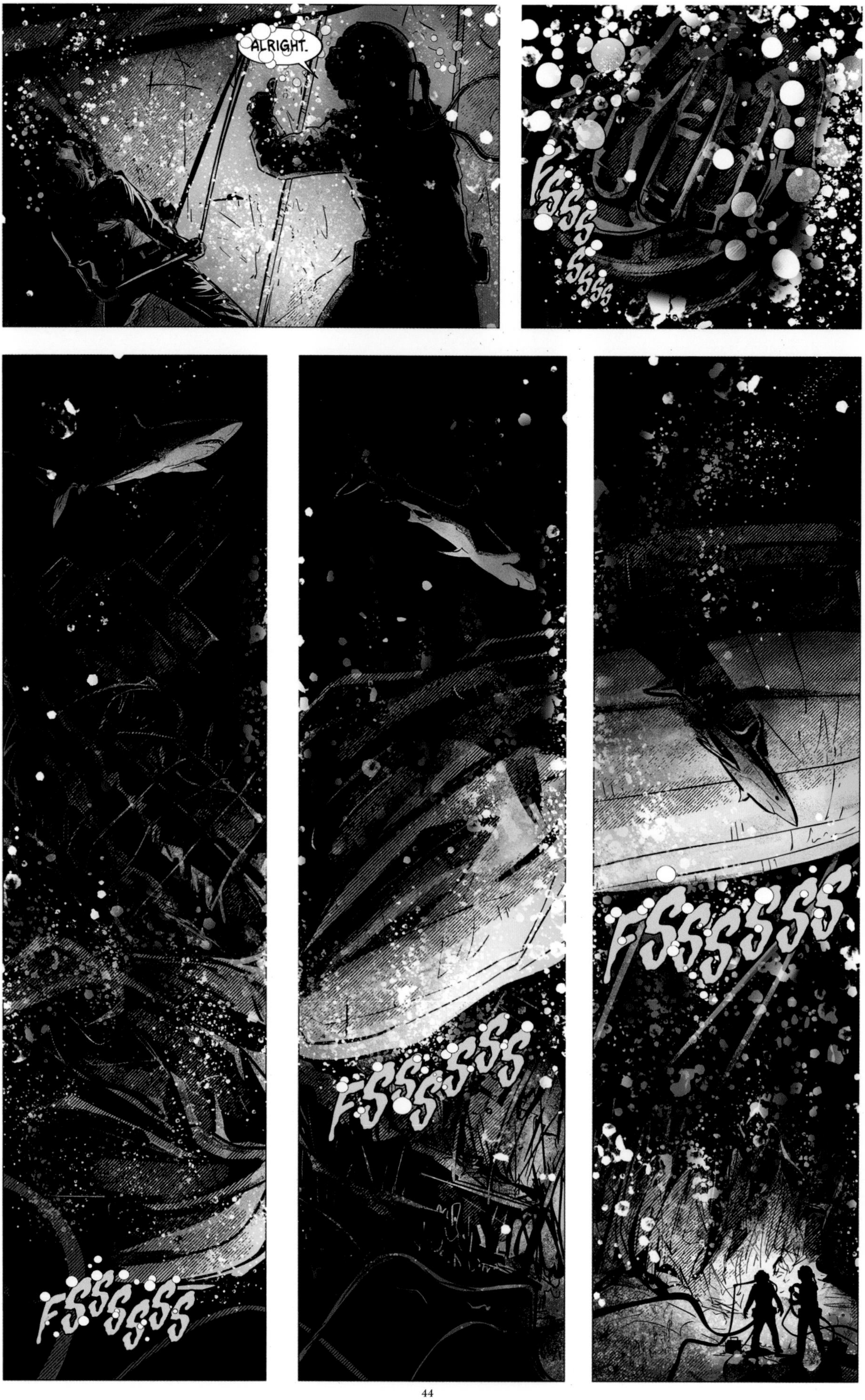
ALRIGHT.
FSSSSSS
FSSSSSS
FSSSSSSS
FSSSSSSS

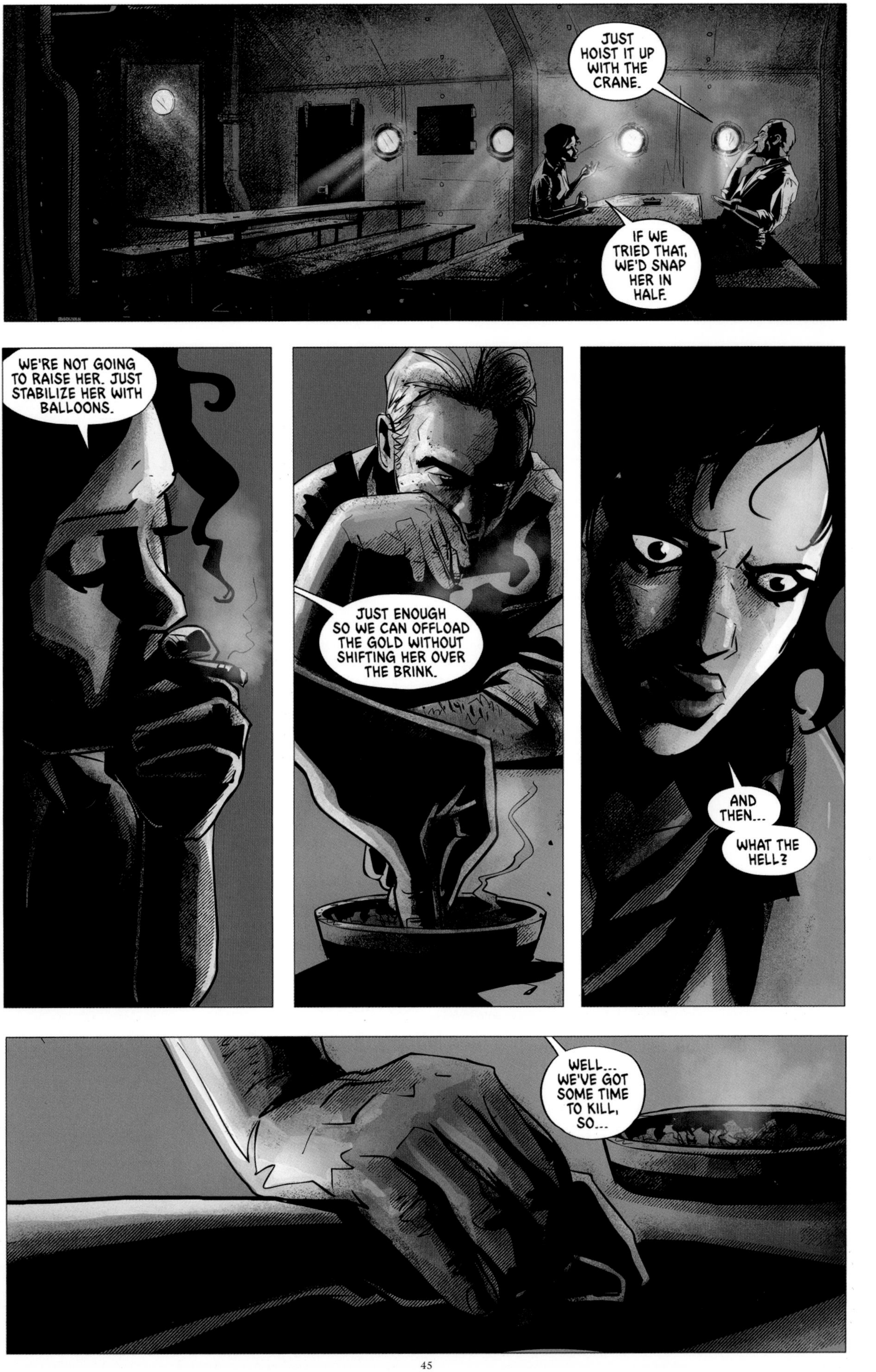
JUST HOIST IT UP WITH THE CRANE.
IF WE TRIED THAT, WE'D SNAP HER IN HALF.
WE'RE NOT GOING TO RAISE HER. JUST STABILIZE HER WITH BALLOONS.
JUST ENOUGH SO WE CAN OFFLOAD THE GOLD WITHOUT SHIFTING HER OVER THE BRINK.
AND THEN...
WHAT THE HELL?
WELL... WE'VE GOT SOME TIME TO KILL, SO...

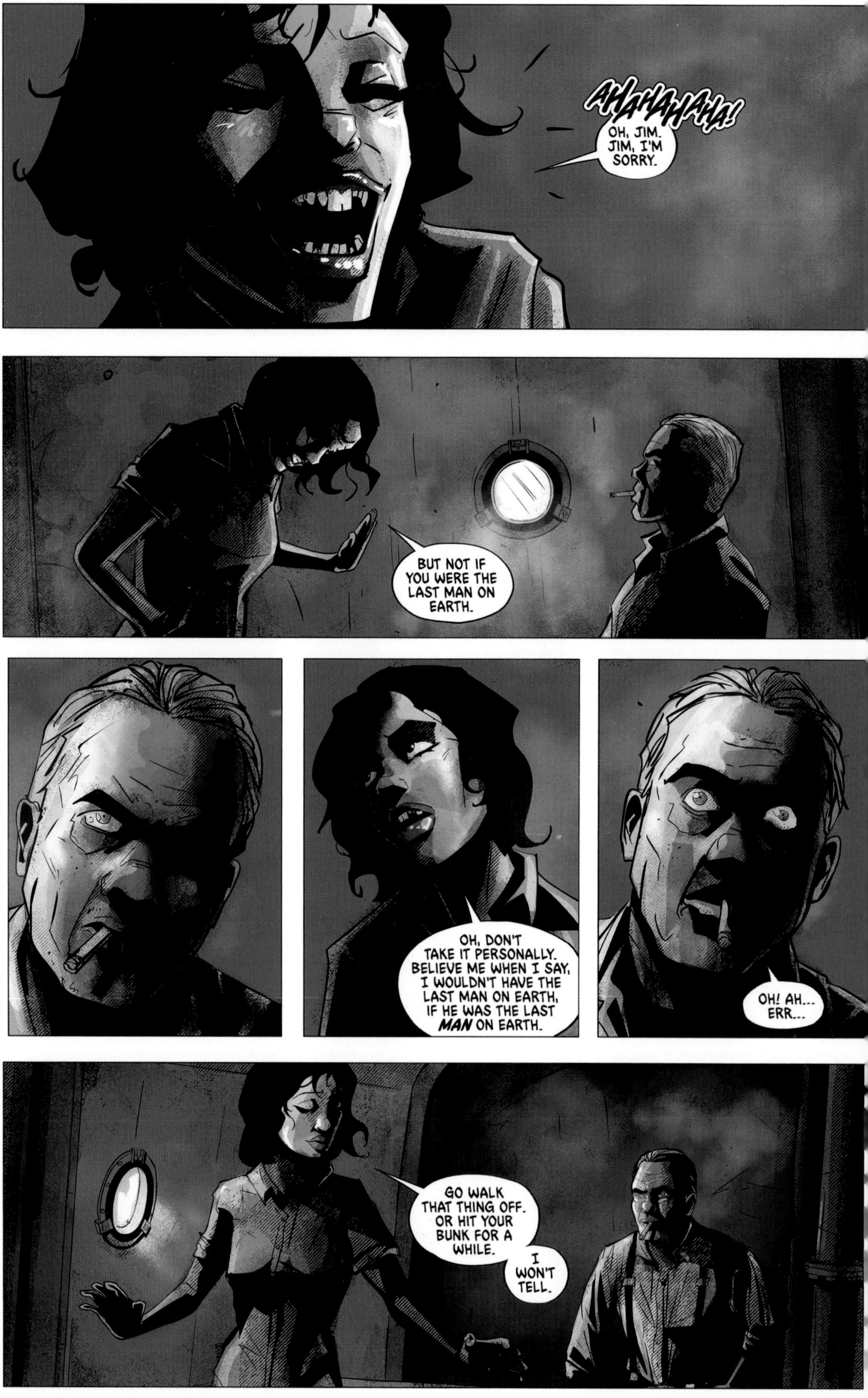
AHAHAHAHAHA!
OH, JIM. JIM, I'M SORRY.
BUT NOT IF YOU WERE THE LAST MAN ON EARTH.
OH, DON'T TAKE IT PERSONALLY. BELIEVE ME WHEN I SAY, I WOULDN'T HAVE THE LAST MAN ON EARTH, IF HE WAS THE LAST *MAN* ON EARTH.
OH! AH... ERR...
GO WALK THAT THING OFF. OR HIT YOUR BUNK FOR A WHILE.
I WON'T TELL.

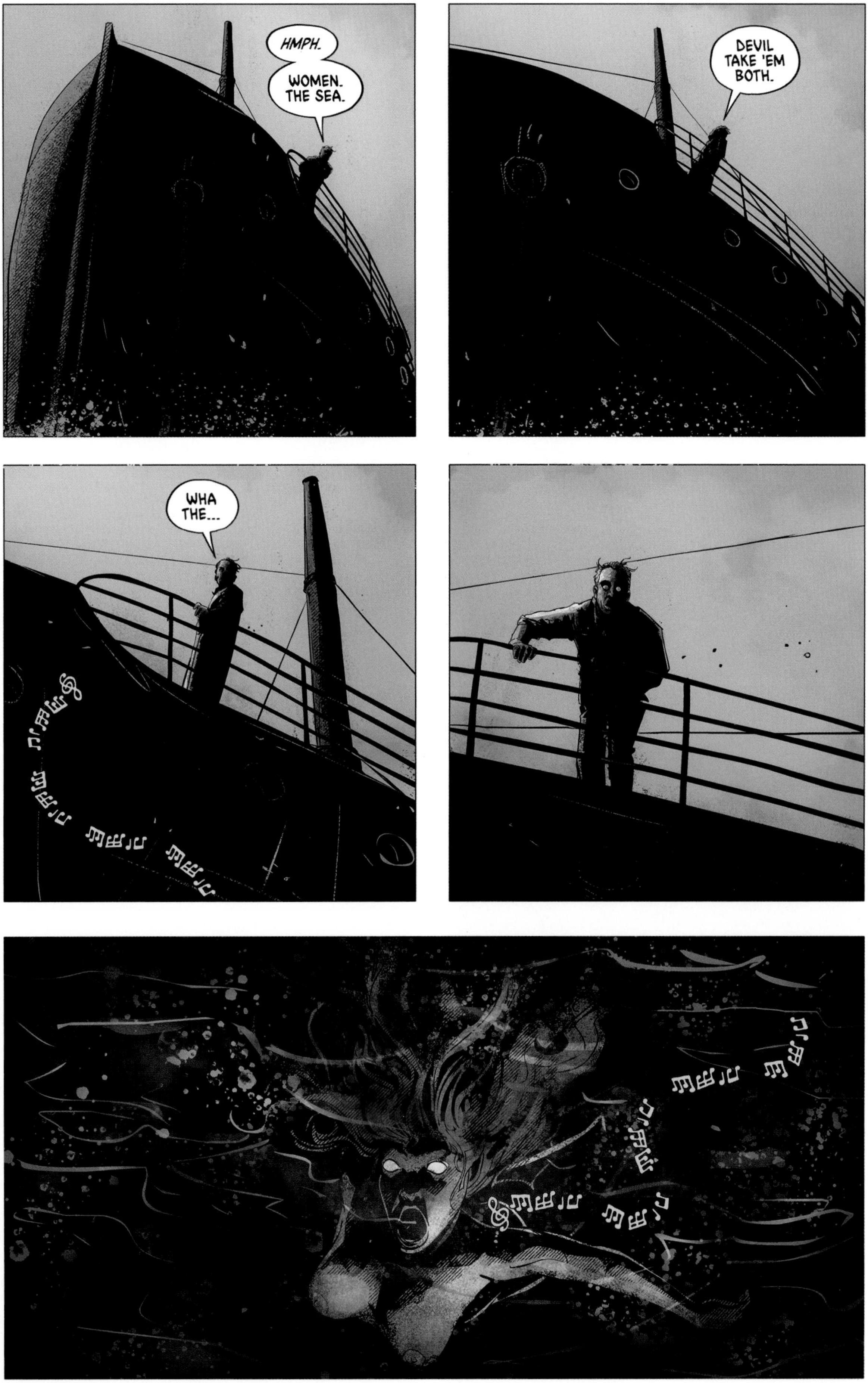
HMPH.
WOMEN. THE SEA.
DEVIL TAKE 'EM BOTH.
WHA THE...

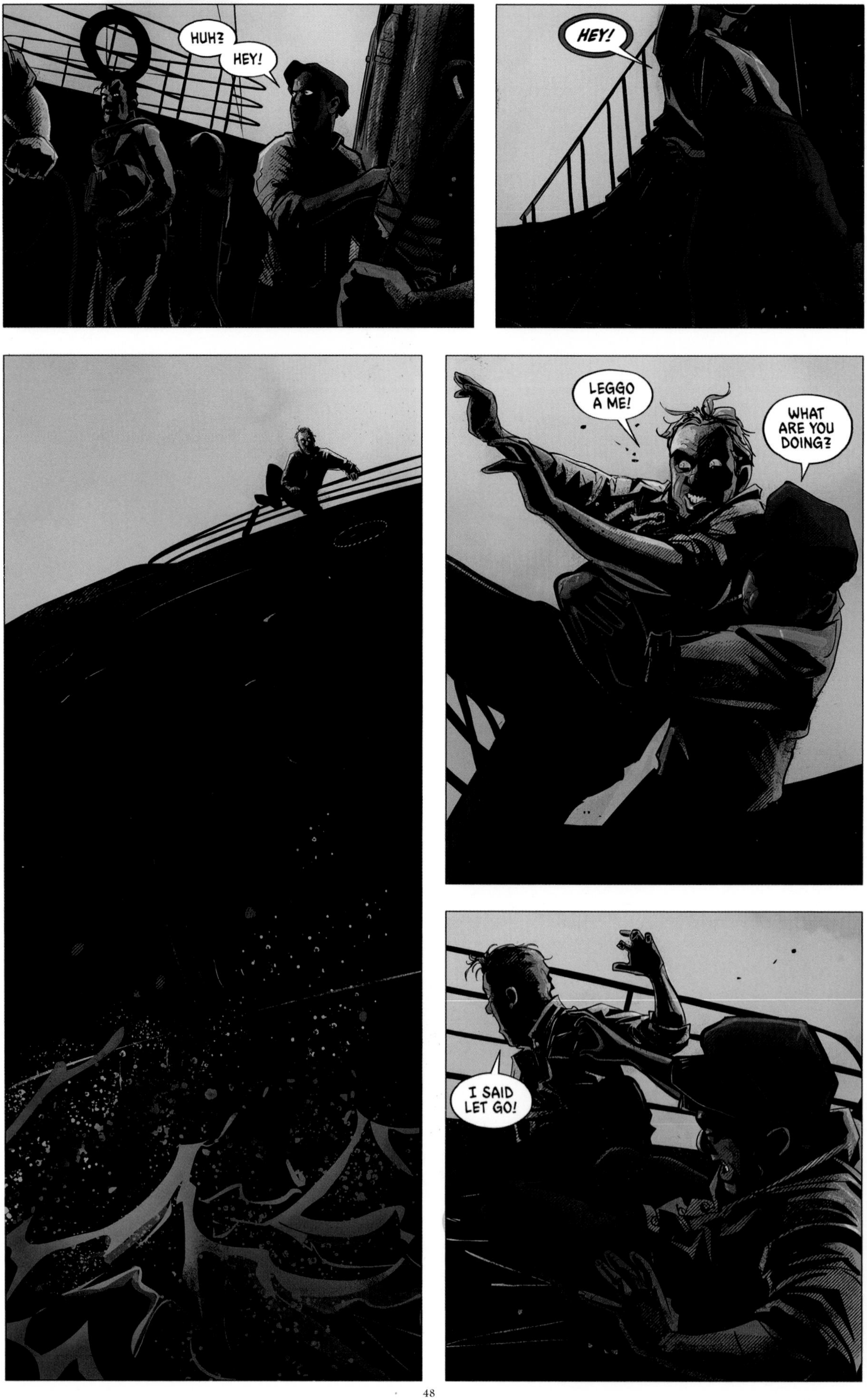
HUH?
HEY!
HEY!
LEGGO A ME!
WHAT ARE YOU DOING?
I SAID LET GO!

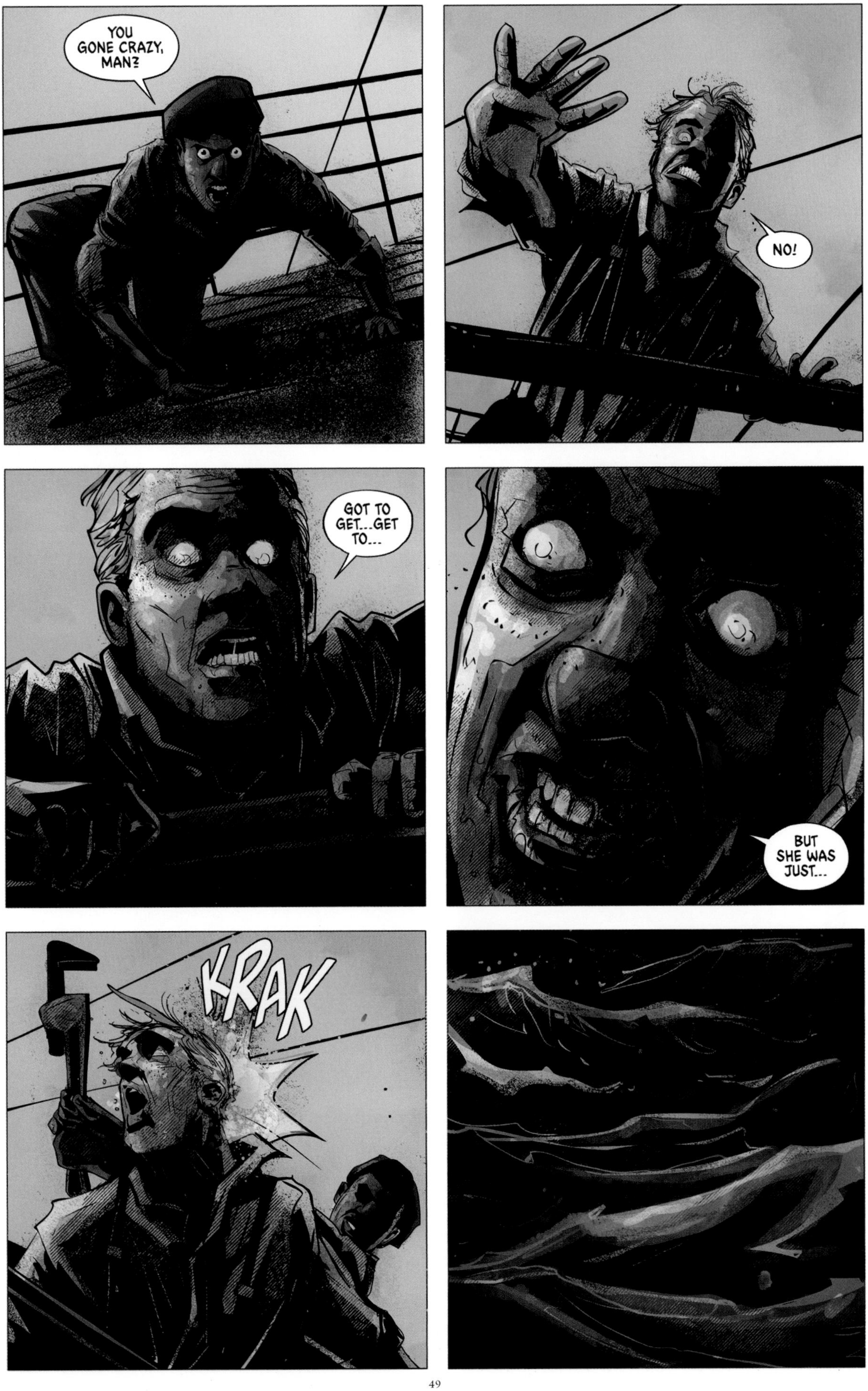
YOU GONE CRAZY, MAN?
NO!
GOT TO GET...GET TO...
BUT SHE WAS JUST...
KRAK

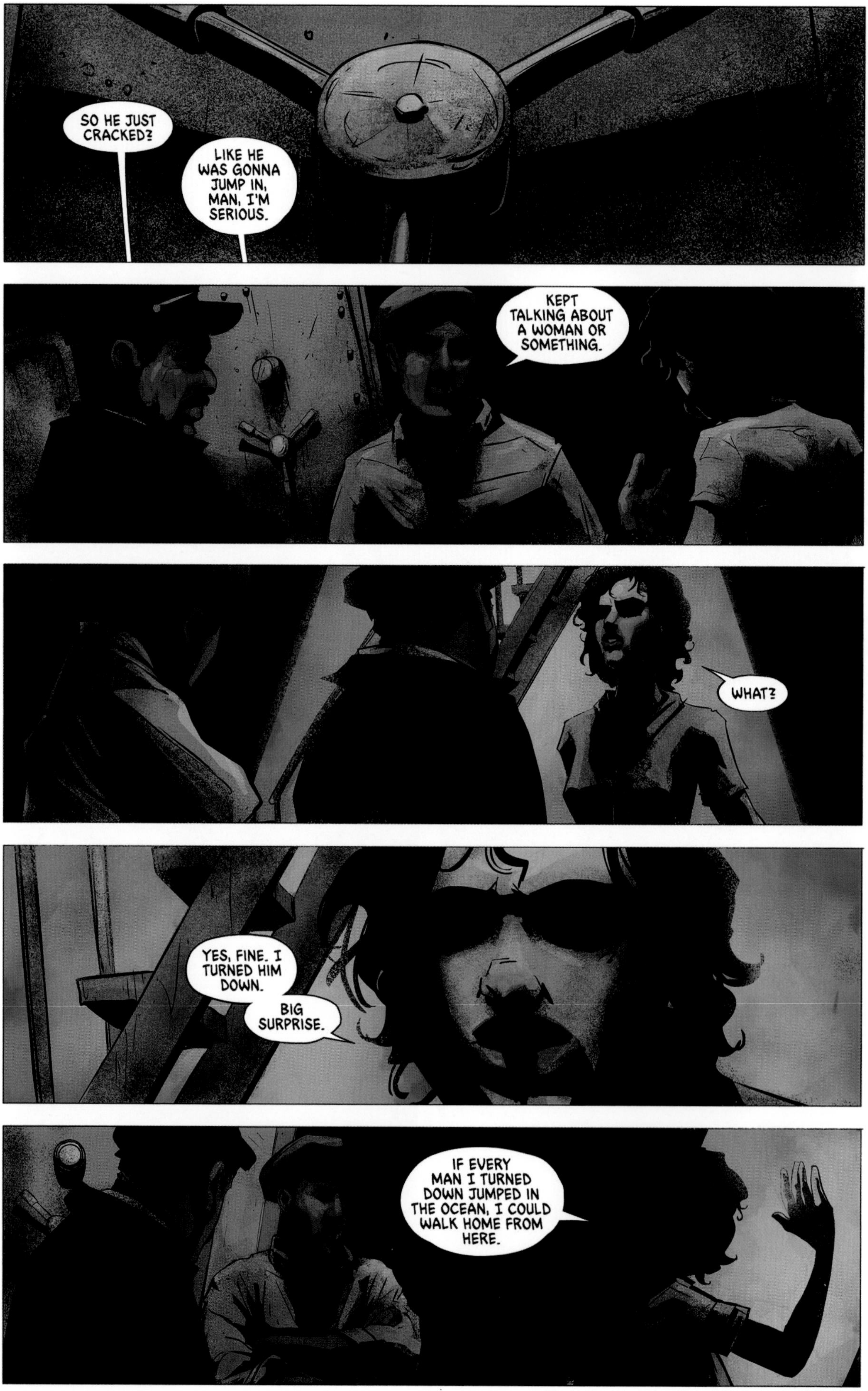
SO HE JUST CRACKED?
LIKE HE WAS GONNA JUMP IN, MAN, I'M SERIOUS.
KEPT TALKING ABOUT A WOMAN OR SOMETHING.
WHAT?
YES, FINE. I TURNED HIM DOWN.
BIG SURPRISE.
IF EVERY MAN I TURNED DOWN JUMPED IN THE OCEAN, I COULD WALK HOME FROM HERE.

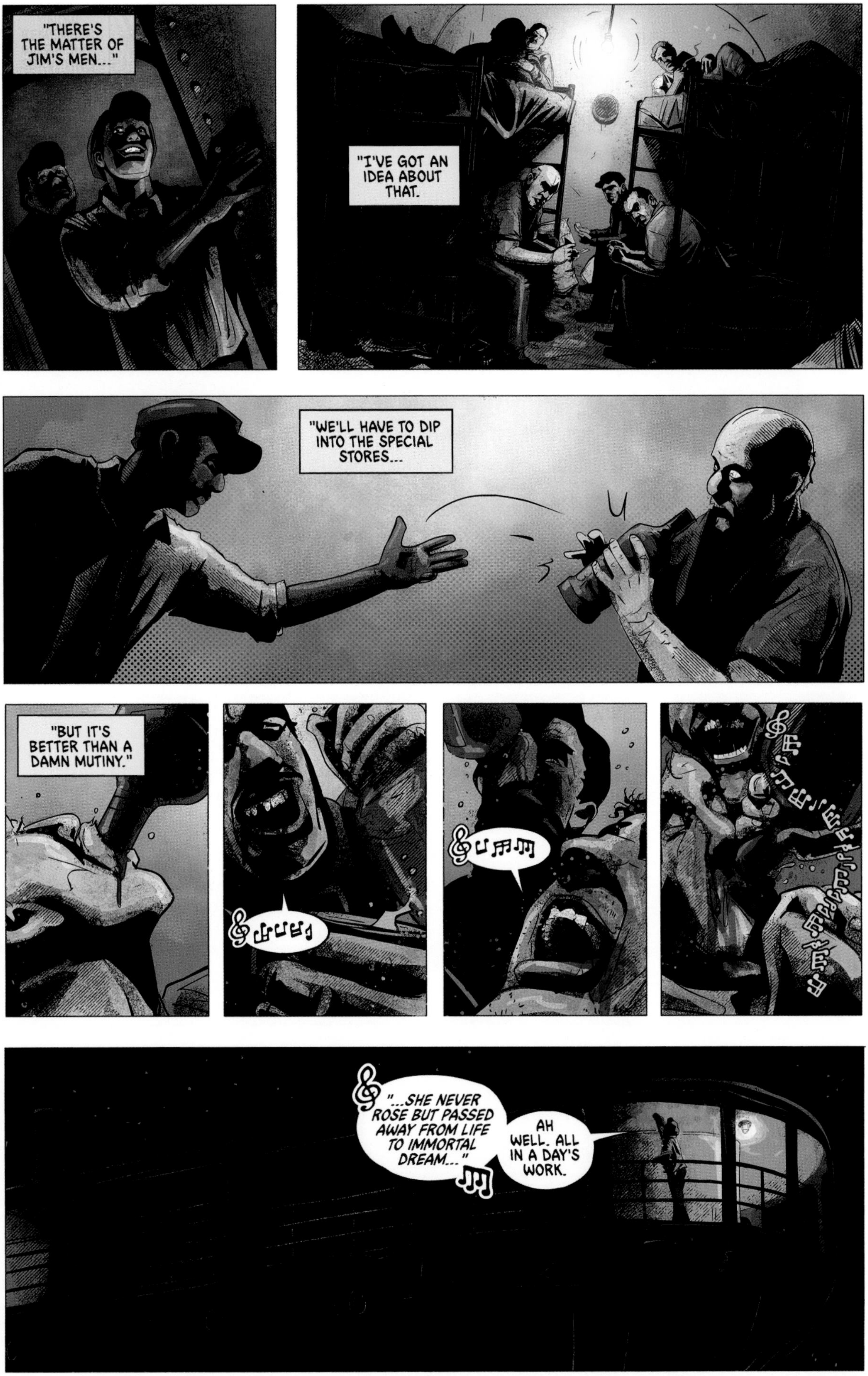
"THERE'S THE MATTER OF JIM'S MEN..."
"I'VE GOT AN IDEA ABOUT THAT.
"WE'LL HAVE TO DIP INTO THE SPECIAL STORES...
"BUT IT'S BETTER THAN A DAMN MUTINY."
"...SHE NEVER ROSE BUT PASSED AWAY FROM LIFE TO IMMORTAL DREAM..."
AH WELL. ALL IN A DAY'S WORK.

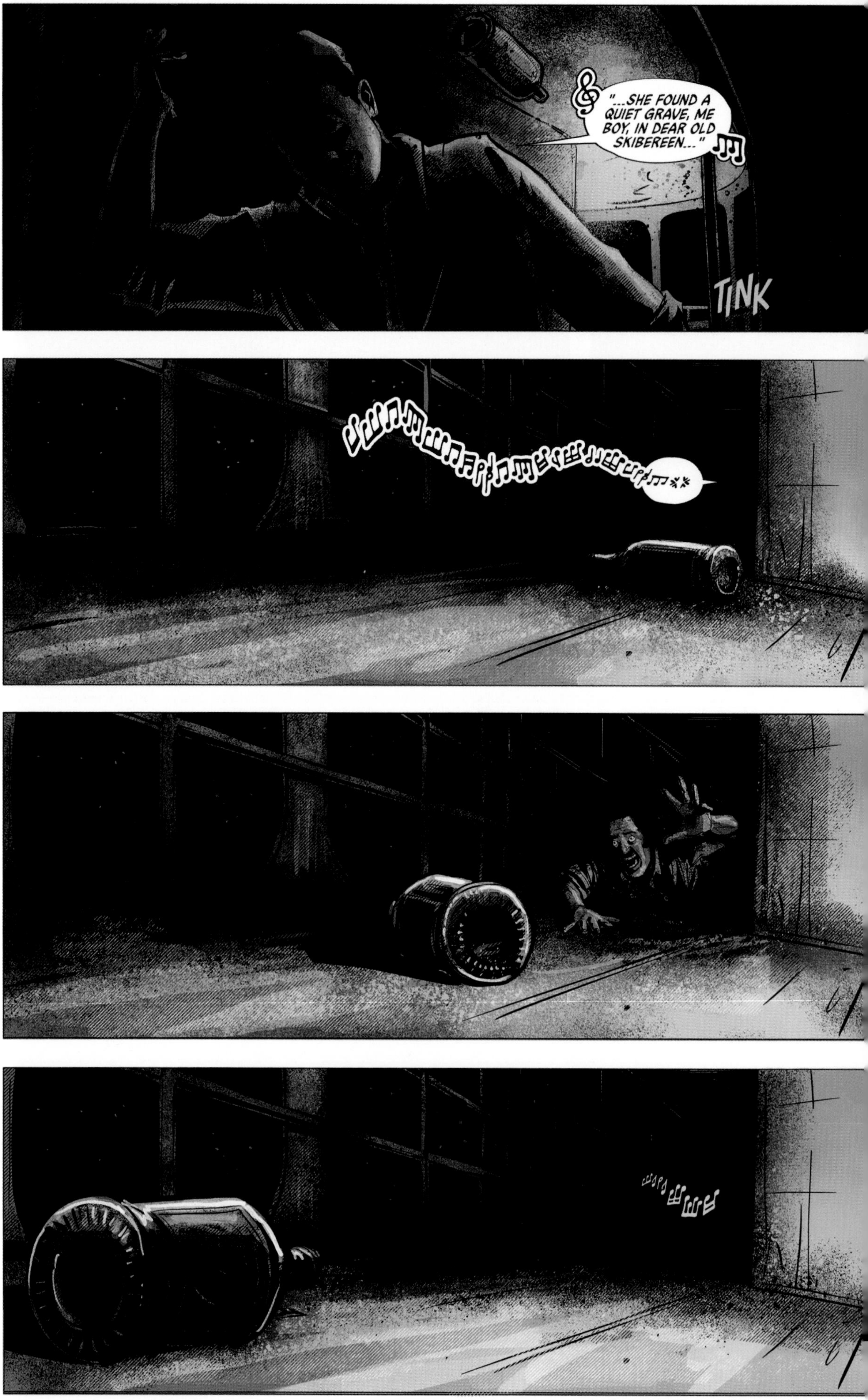
"...SHE FOUND A QUIET GRAVE, ME BOY, IN DEAR OLD SKIBEREEN..."
TINK

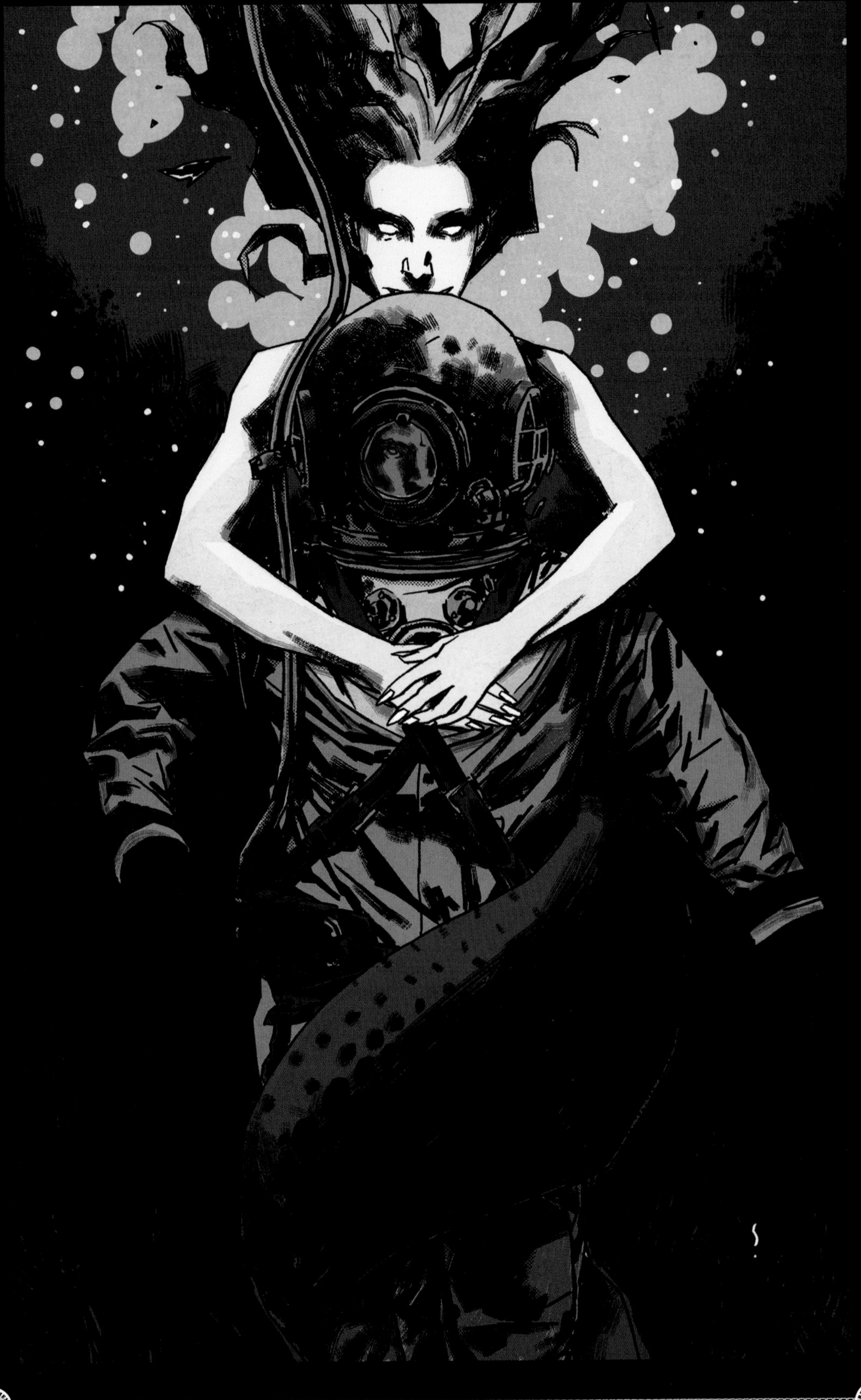

ALEX CORMACK

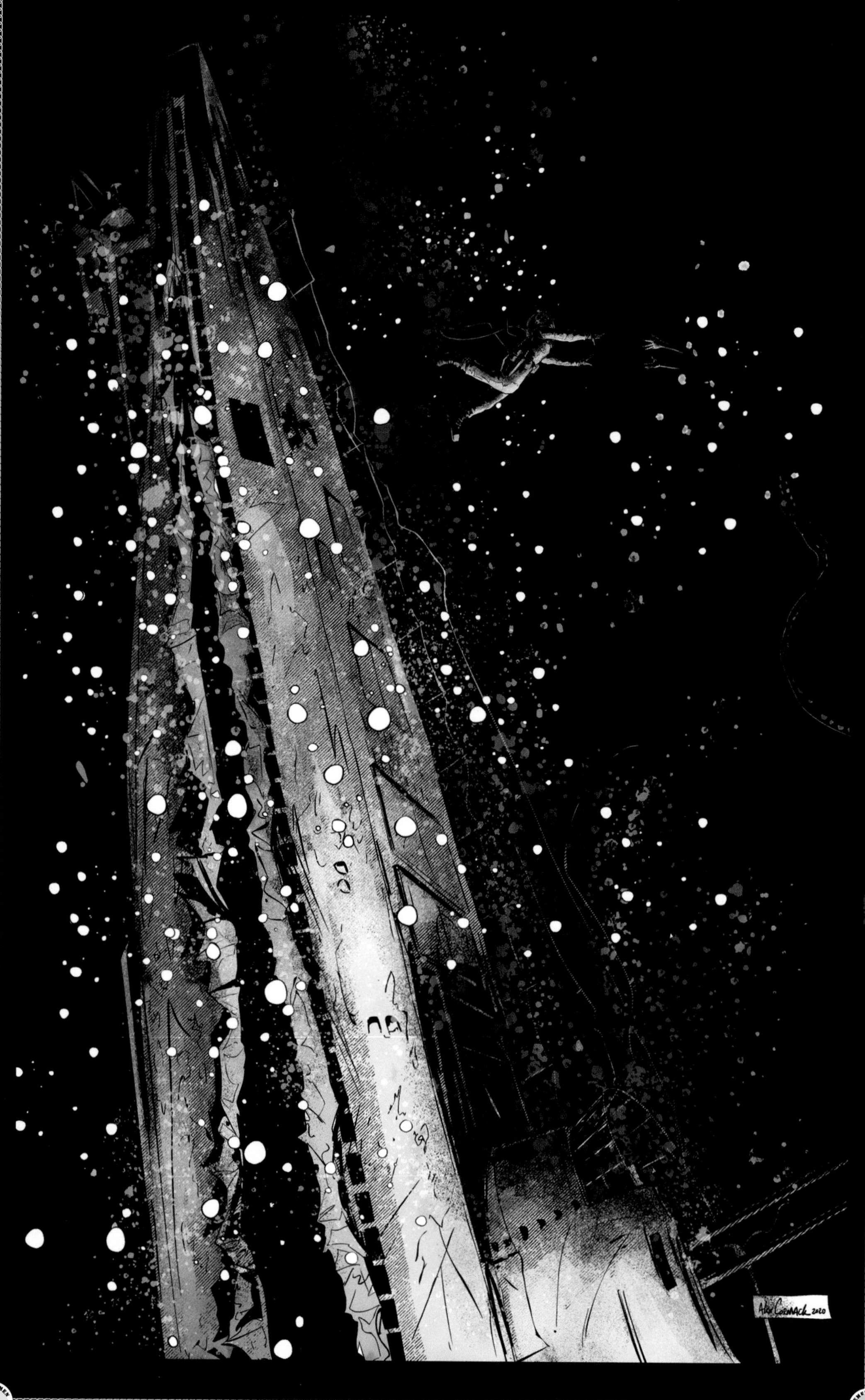
Alex Cormack 2020

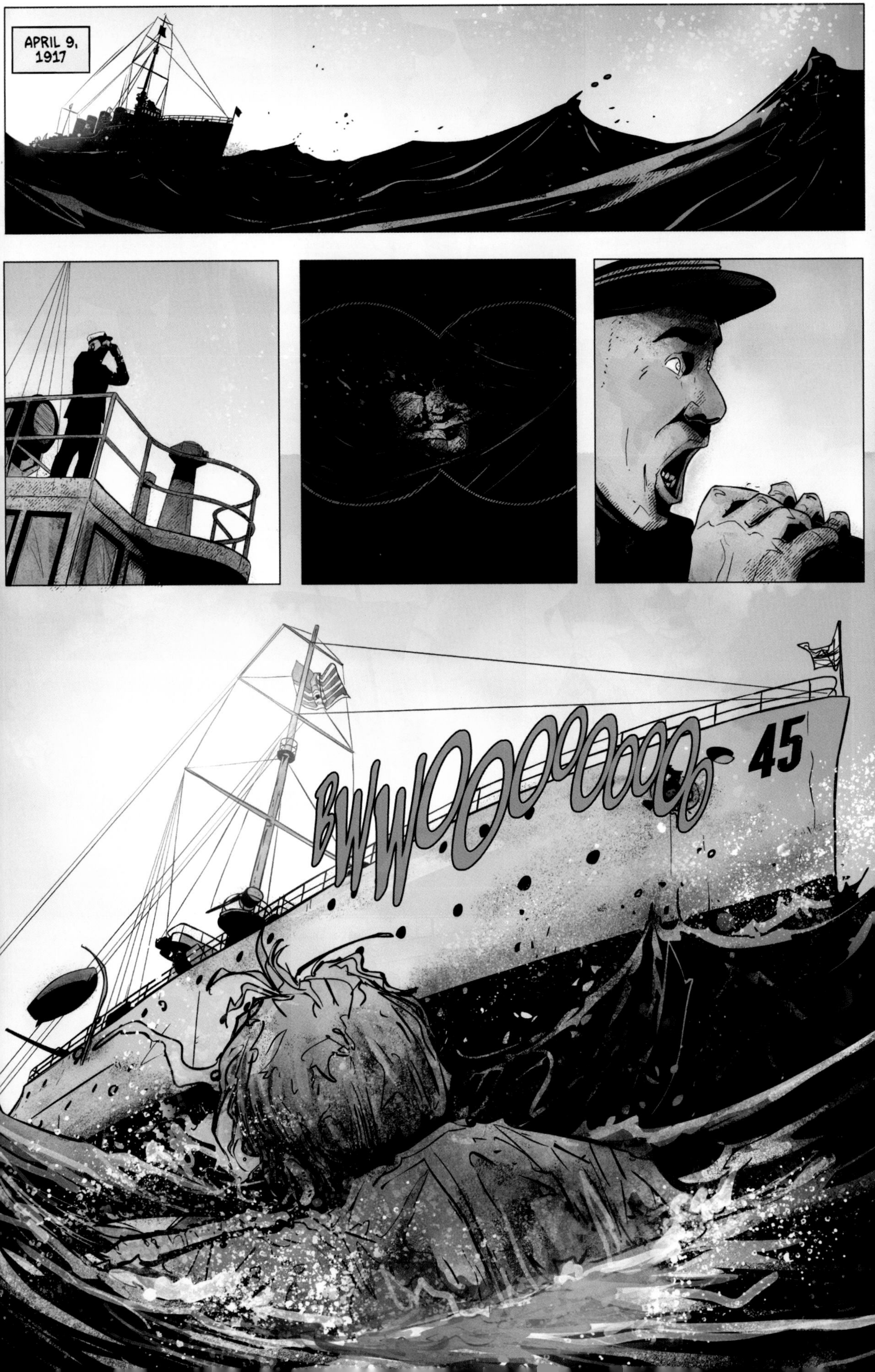
APRIL 9, 1917
45
BWWOOOOOOOOO

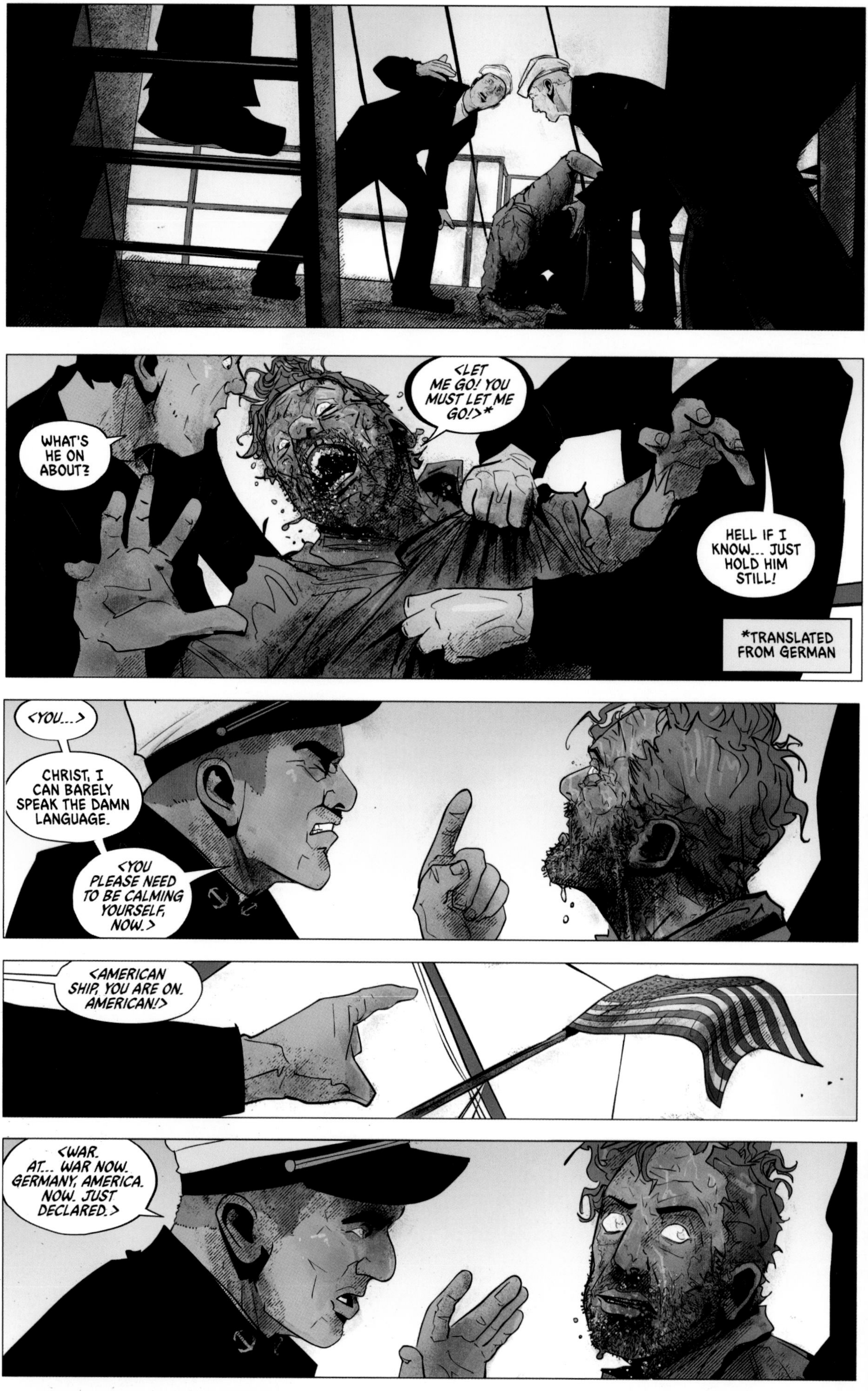
<LET ME GO! YOU MUST LET ME GO!>*
WHAT'S HE ON ABOUT?
HELL IF I KNOW... JUST HOLD HIM STILL!
*TRANSLATED FROM GERMAN
<YOU...>
CHRIST, I CAN BARELY SPEAK THE DAMN LANGUAGE.
<YOU PLEASE NEED TO BE CALMING YOURSELF, NOW.>
<AMERICAN SHIP, YOU ARE ON. AMERICAN!>
<WAR. AT... WAR NOW. GERMANY, AMERICA. NOW. JUST DECLARED.>

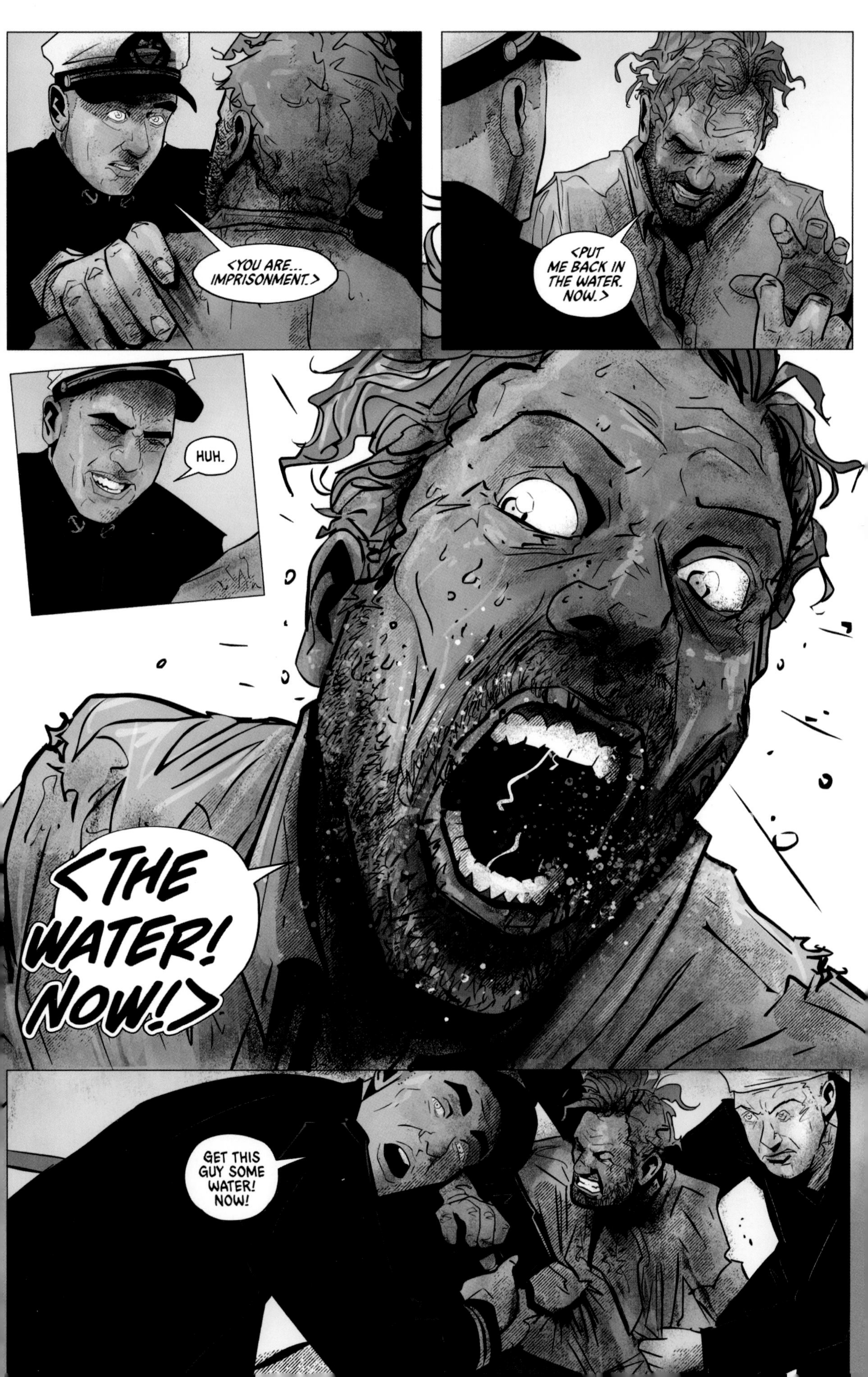
<YOU ARE... IMPRISONMENT.>
<PUT ME BACK IN THE WATER. NOW.>
HUH.
<THE WATER! NOW!>
GET THIS GUY SOME WATER! NOW!

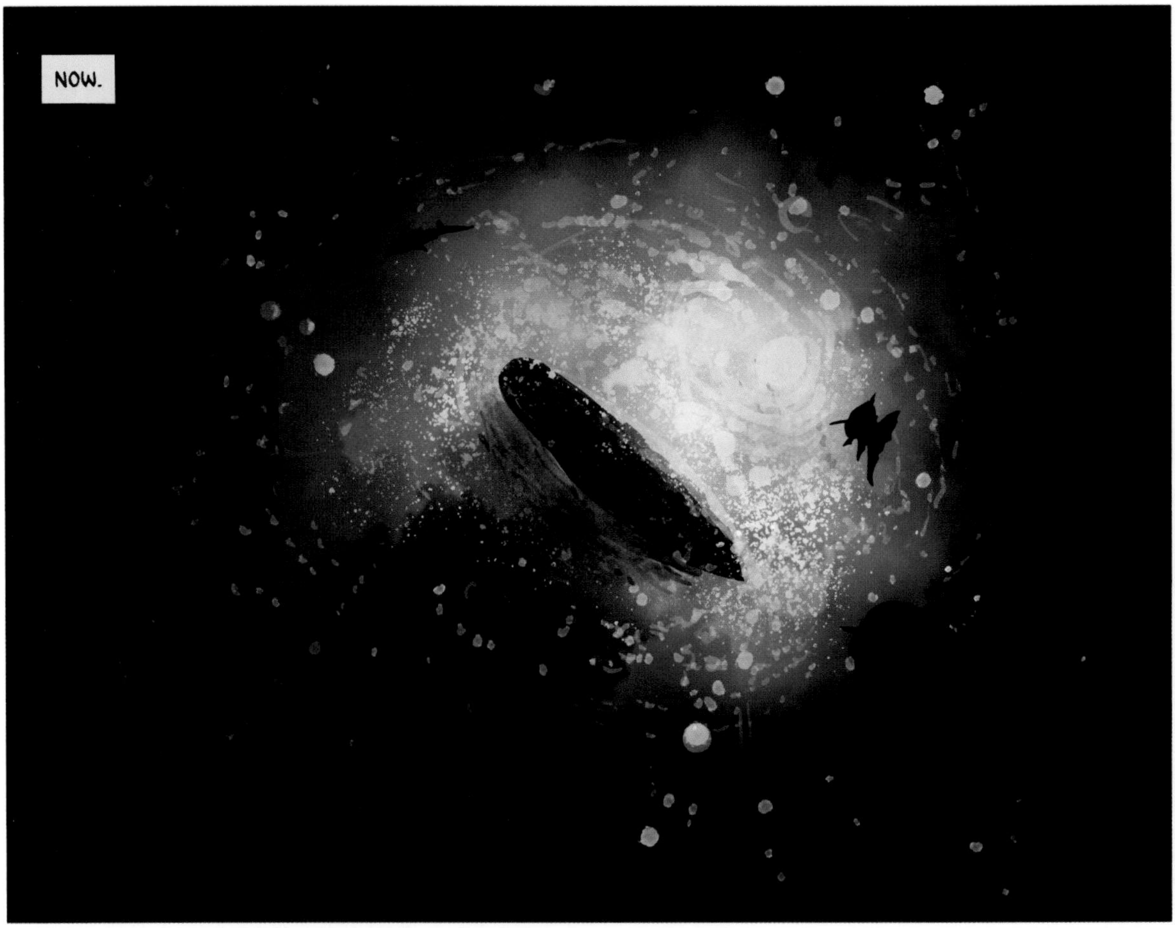
NOW.

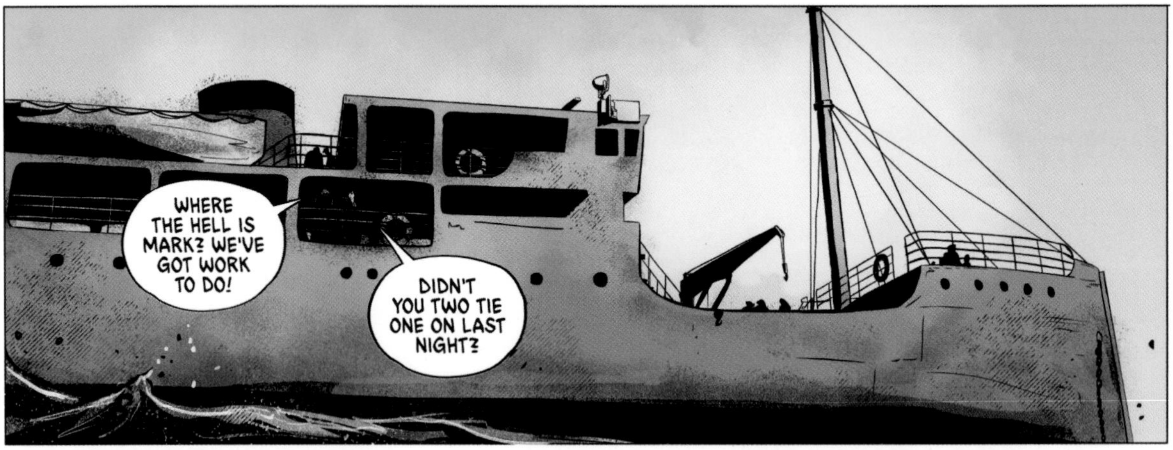
WHERE THE HELL IS MARK? WE'VE GOT WORK TO DO!
DIDN'T YOU TWO TIE ONE ON LAST NIGHT?

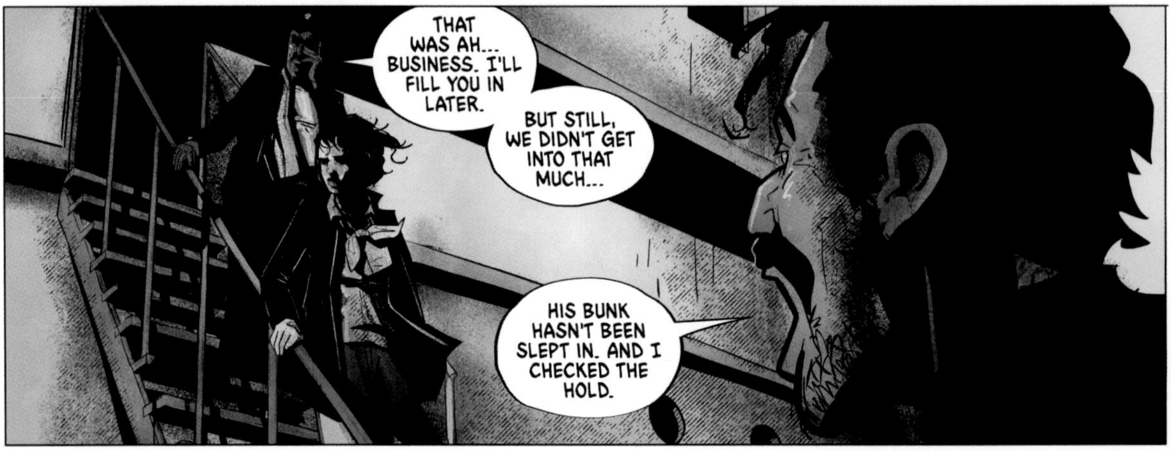
THAT WAS AH... BUSINESS. I'LL FILL YOU IN LATER.
BUT STILL, WE DIDN'T GET INTO THAT MUCH...
HIS BUNK HASN'T BEEN SLEPT IN. AND I CHECKED THE HOLD.

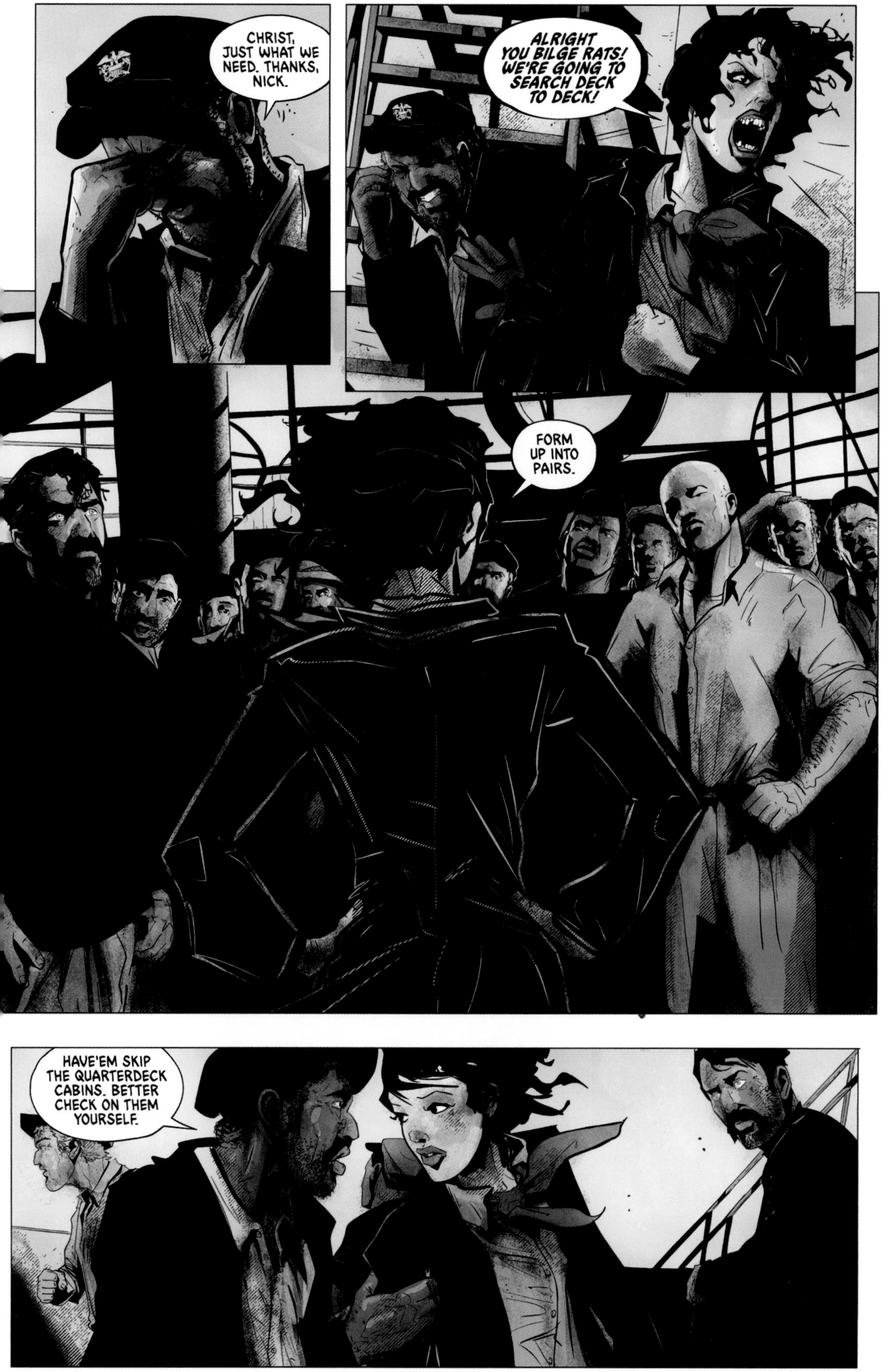
CHRIST, JUST WHAT WE NEED. THANKS, NICK.
ALRIGHT YOU BILGE RATS! WE'RE GOING TO SEARCH DECK TO DECK!
FORM UP INTO PAIRS.
HAVE'EM SKIP THE QUARTERDECK CABINS. BETTER CHECK ON THEM YOURSELF.

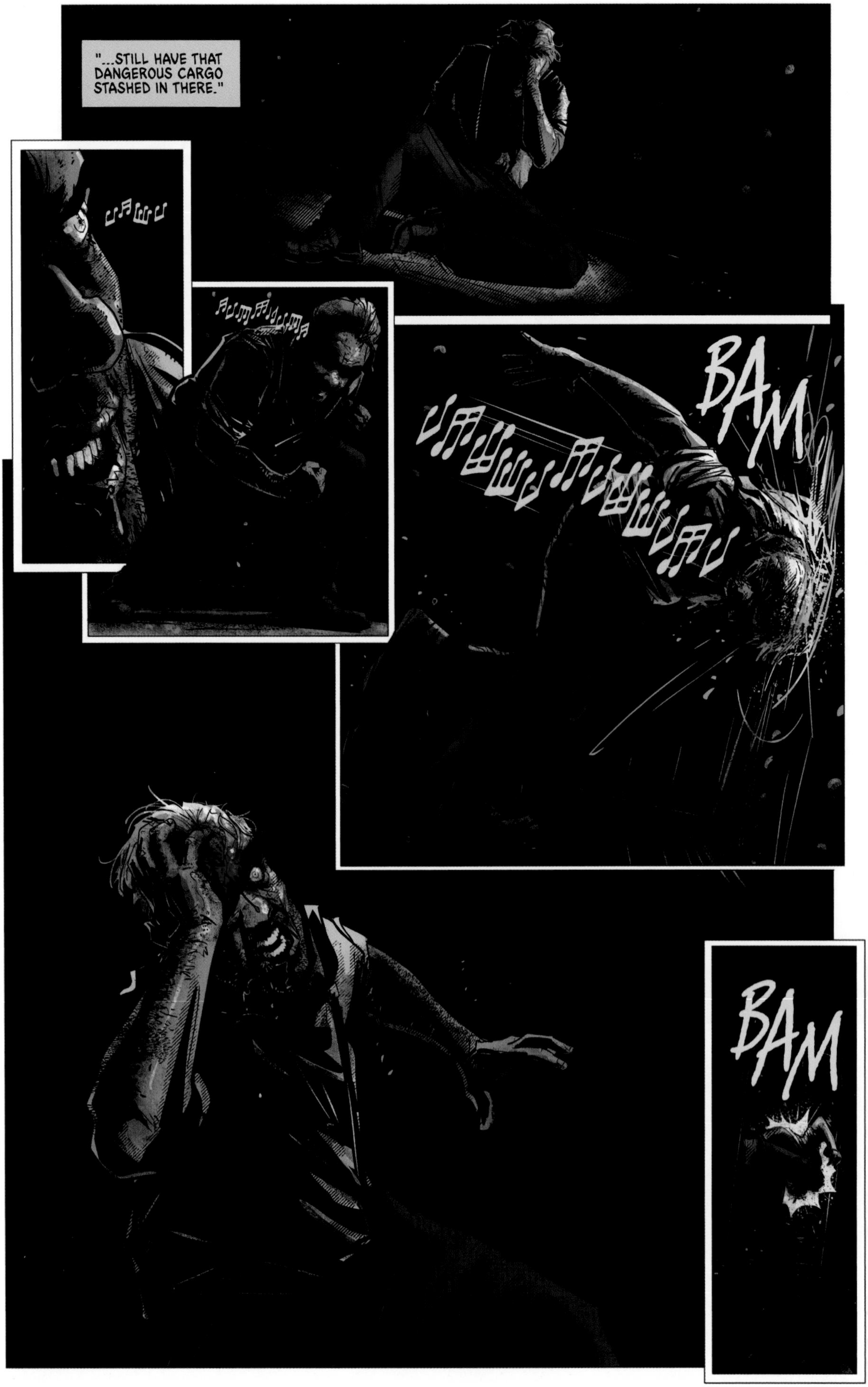
"...STILL HAVE THAT DANGEROUS CARGO STASHED IN THERE."
BAM
BAM

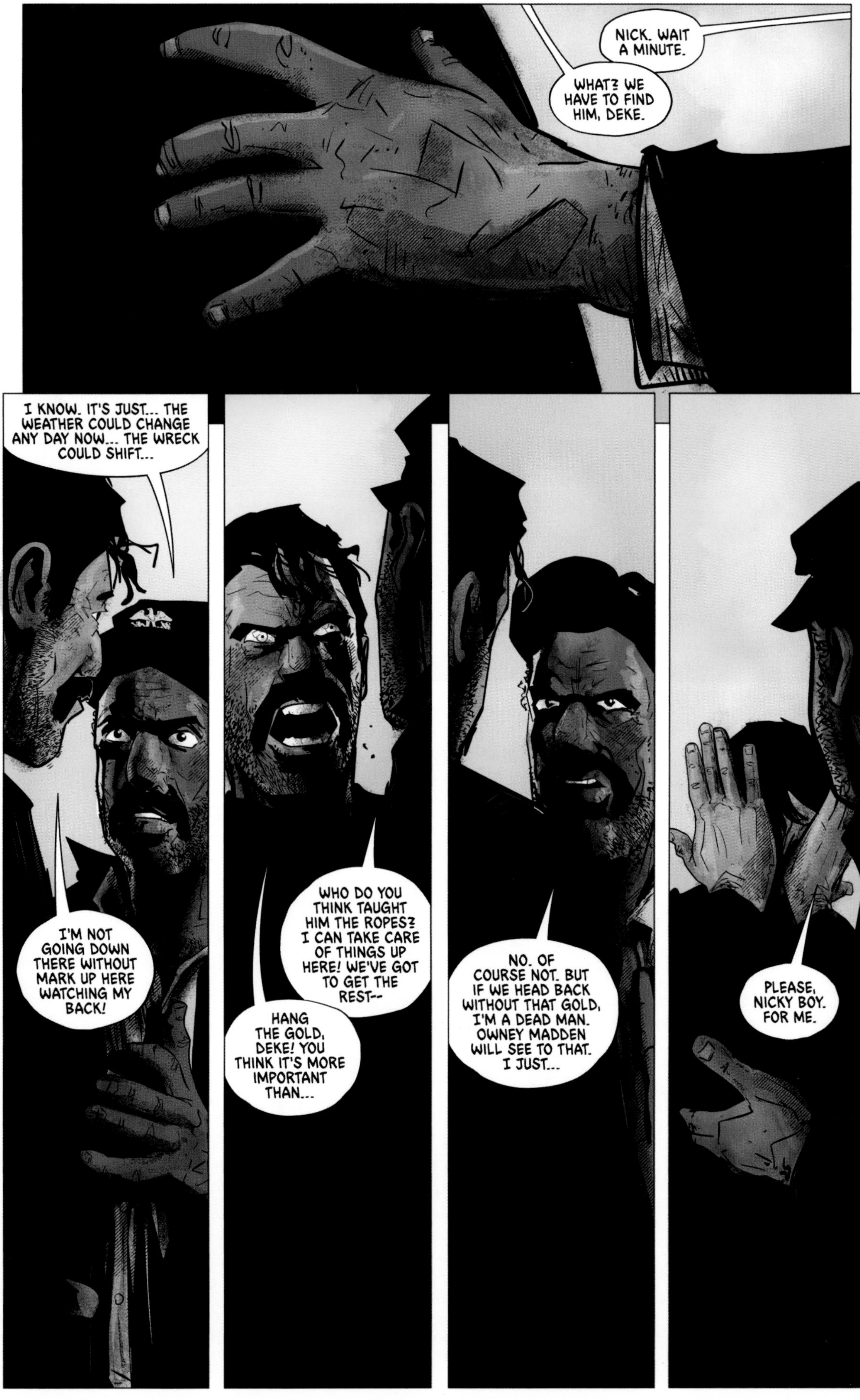
NICK. WAIT A MINUTE.
WHAT? WE HAVE TO FIND HIM, DEKE.
I KNOW. IT'S JUST... THE WEATHER COULD CHANGE ANY DAY NOW... THE WRECK COULD SHIFT...
I'M NOT GOING DOWN THERE WITHOUT MARK UP HERE WATCHING MY BACK!
WHO DO YOU THINK TAUGHT HIM THE ROPES? I CAN TAKE CARE OF THINGS UP HERE! WE'VE GOT TO GET THE REST--
HANG THE GOLD, DEKE! YOU THINK IT'S MORE IMPORTANT THAN...
NO. OF COURSE NOT. BUT IF WE HEAD BACK WITHOUT THAT GOLD, I'M A DEAD MAN. OWNEY MADDEN WILL SEE TO THAT. I JUST...
PLEASE, NICKY BOY. FOR ME.

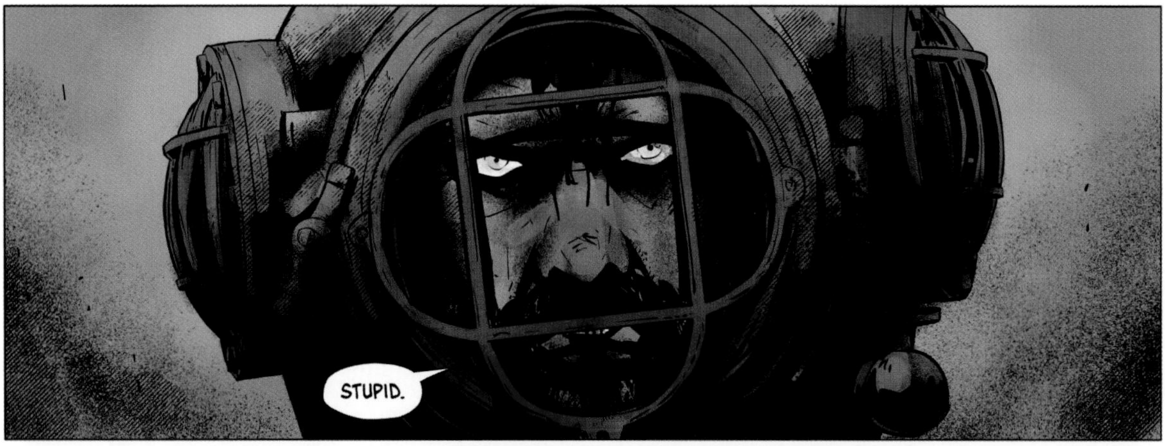
STUPID.

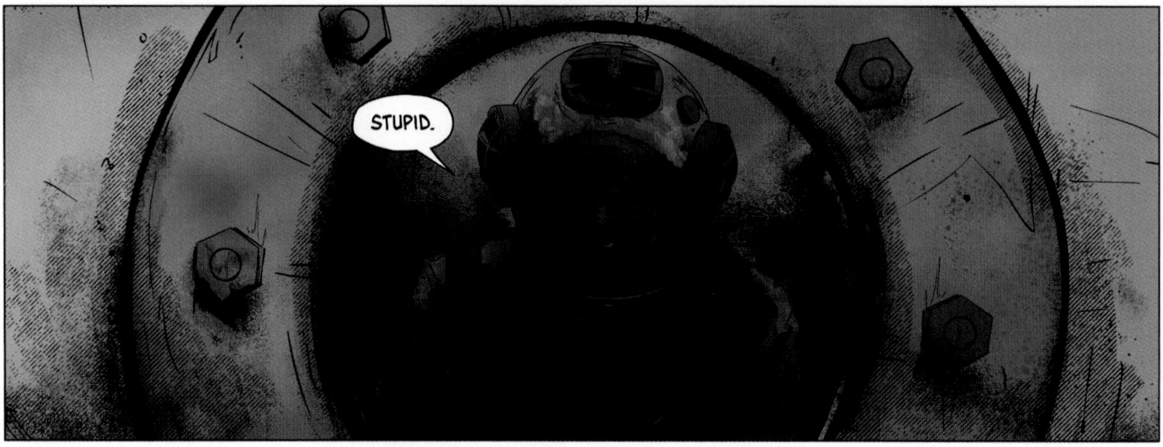
STUPID.

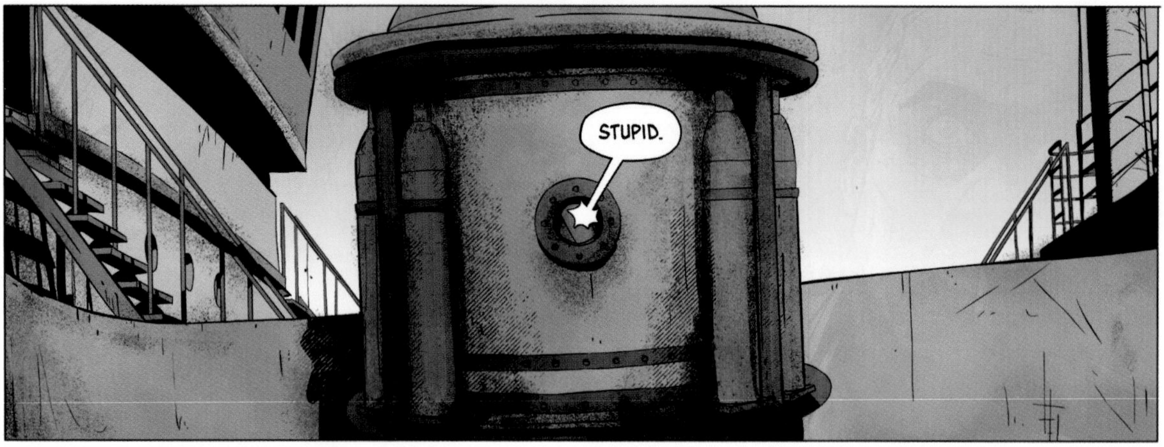
STUPID.

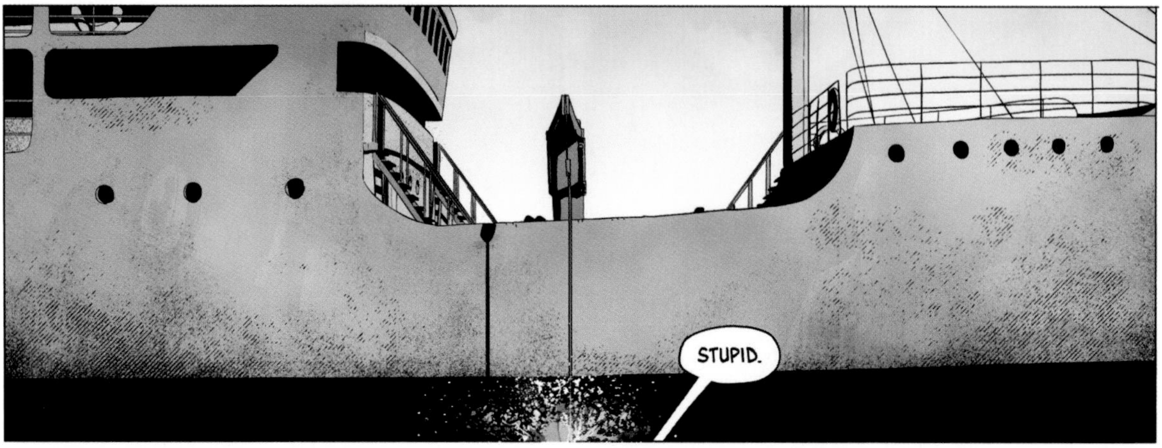
STUPID.

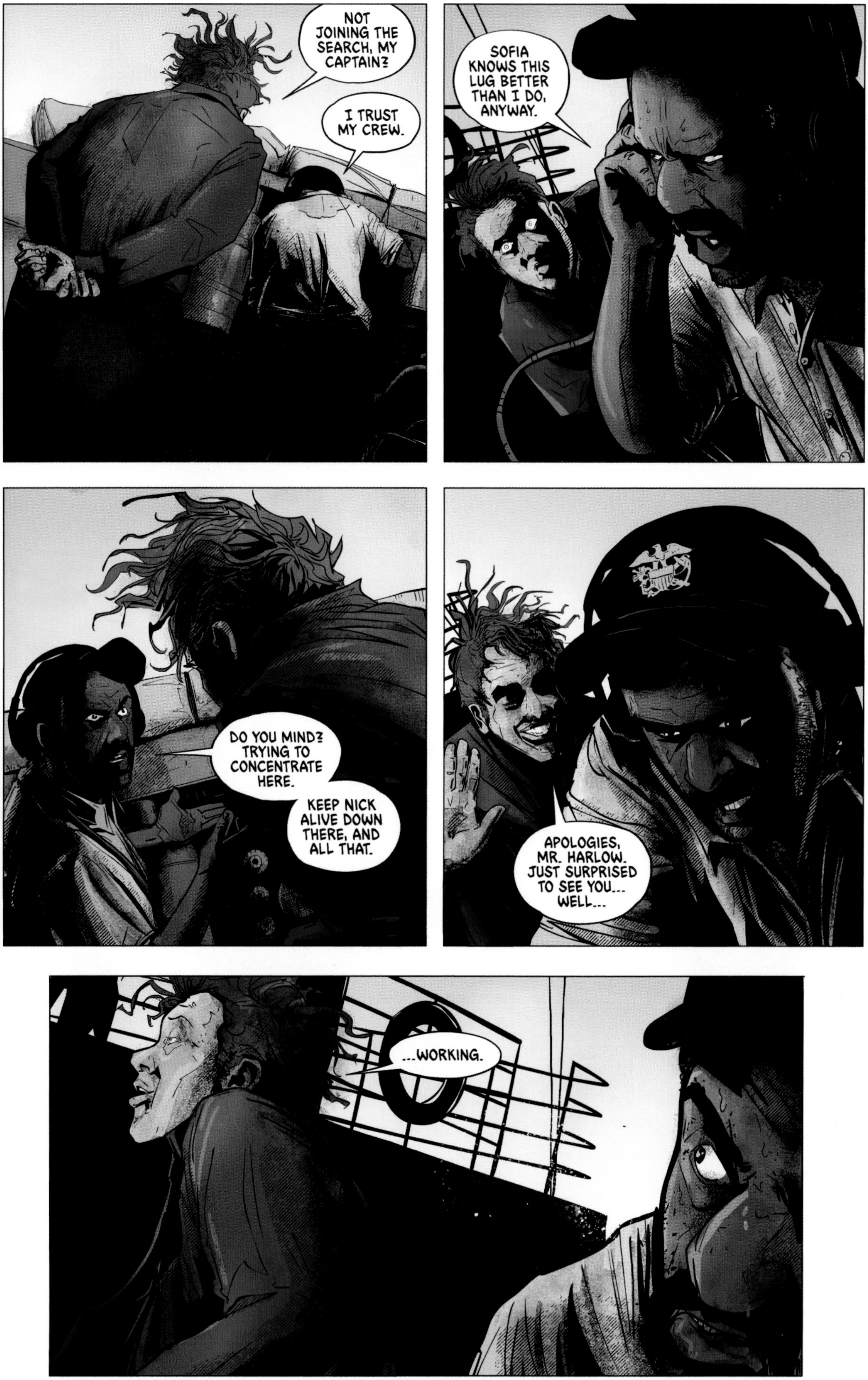
NOT JOINING THE SEARCH, MY CAPTAIN?
I TRUST MY CREW.
SOFIA KNOWS THIS LUG BETTER THAN I DO, ANYWAY.
DO YOU MIND? TRYING TO CONCENTRATE HERE.
KEEP NICK ALIVE DOWN THERE, AND ALL THAT.
APOLOGIES, MR. HARLOW. JUST SURPRISED TO SEE YOU... WELL...
...WORKING.

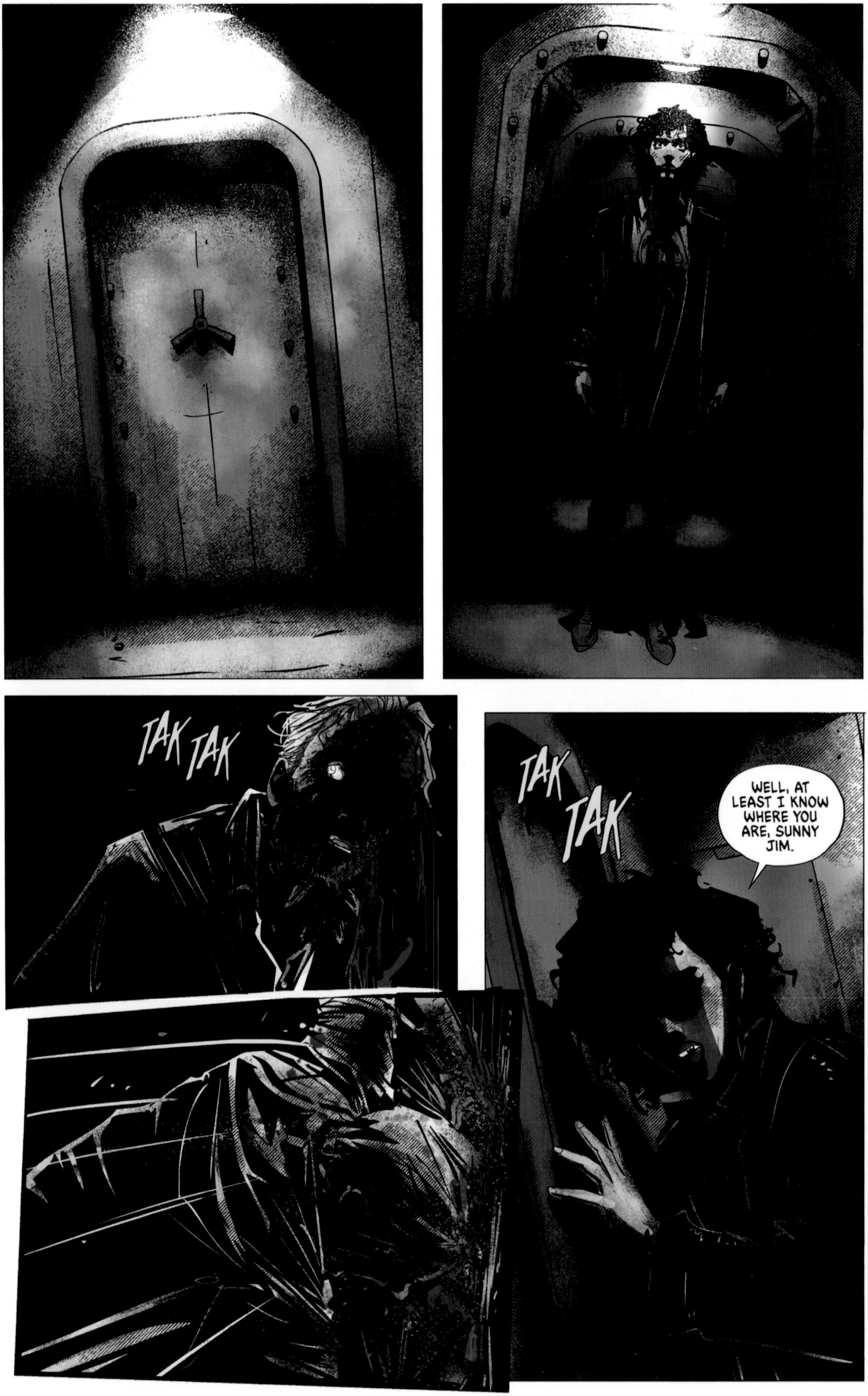
TAK TAK
TAK TAK
WELL, AT LEAST I KNOW WHERE YOU ARE, SUNNY JIM.

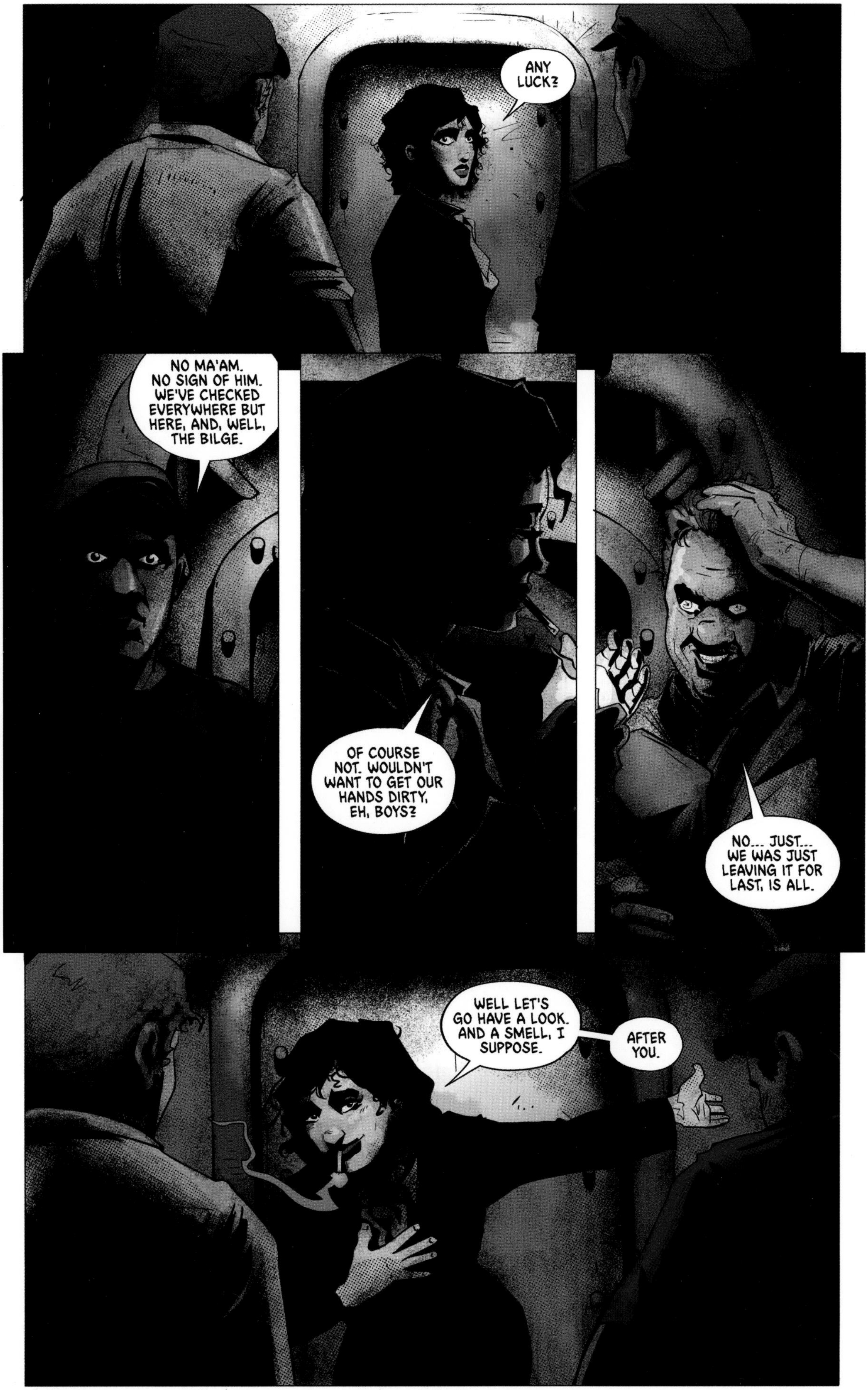
ANY LUCK?
NO MA'AM. NO SIGN OF HIM. WE'VE CHECKED EVERYWHERE BUT HERE, AND, WELL, THE BILGE.
OF COURSE NOT. WOULDN'T WANT TO GET OUR HANDS DIRTY, EH, BOYS?
NO... JUST... WE WAS JUST LEAVING IT FOR LAST, IS ALL.
WELL LET'S GO HAVE A LOOK. AND A SMELL, I SUPPOSE.
AFTER YOU.

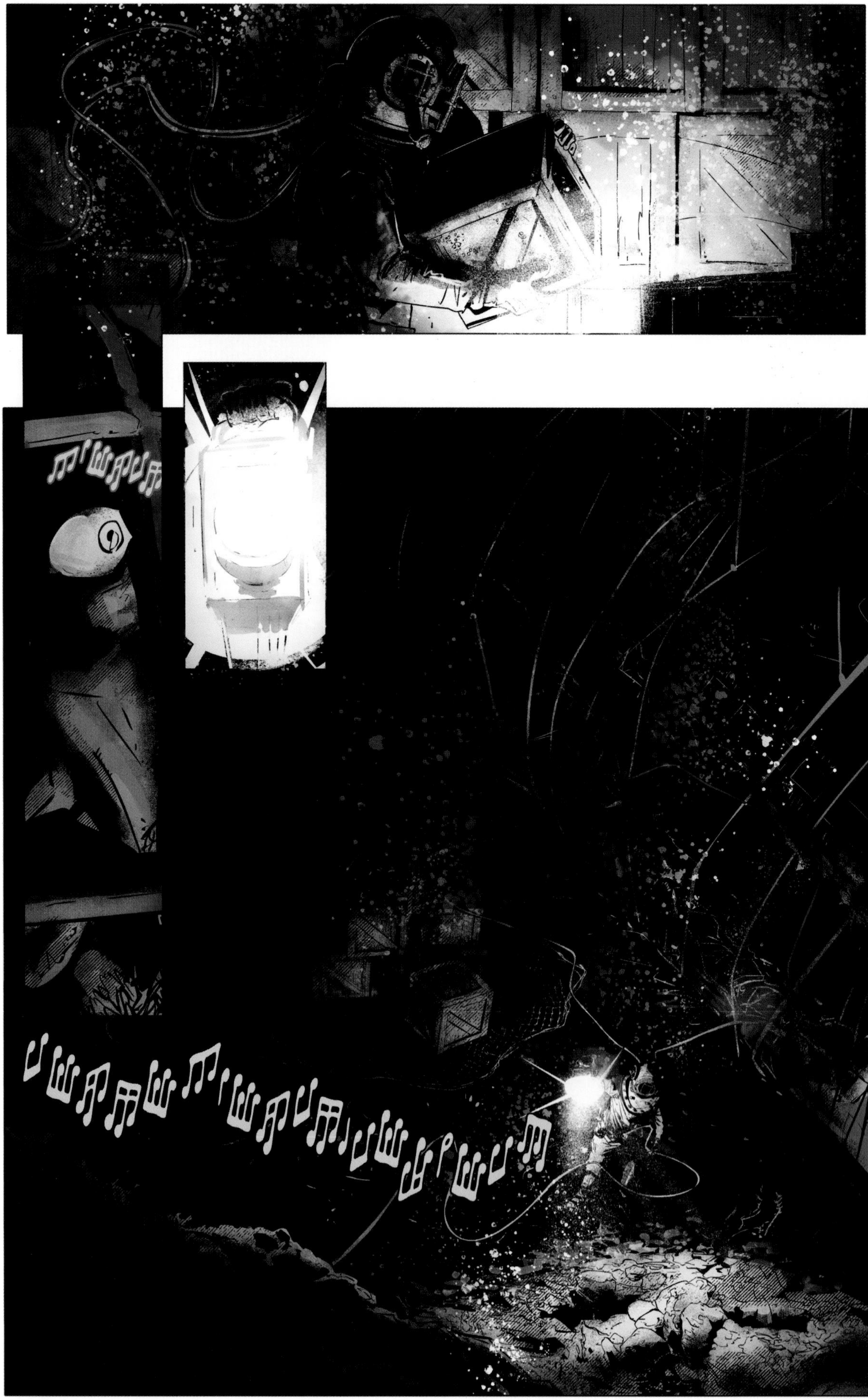

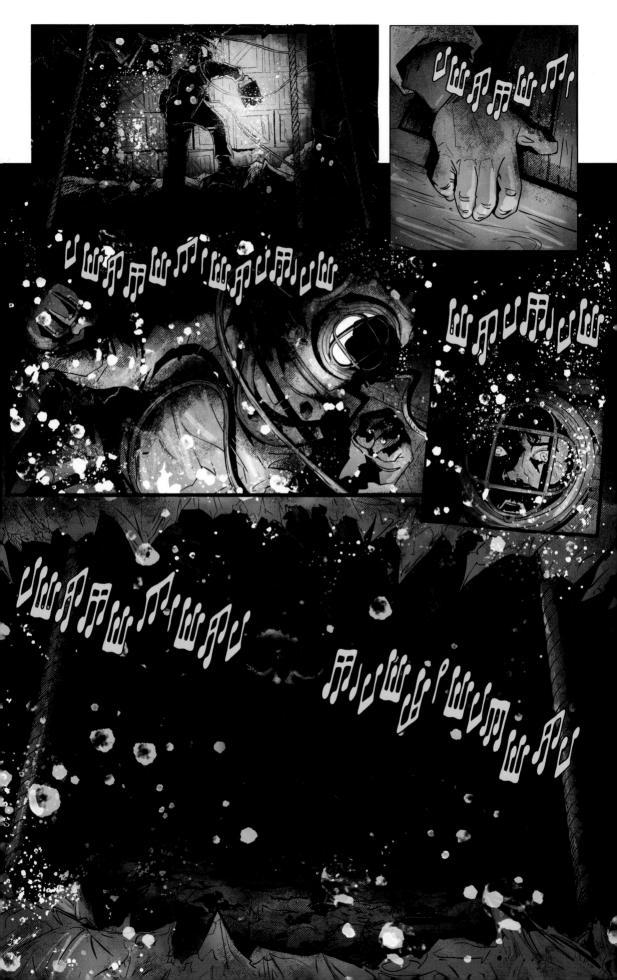

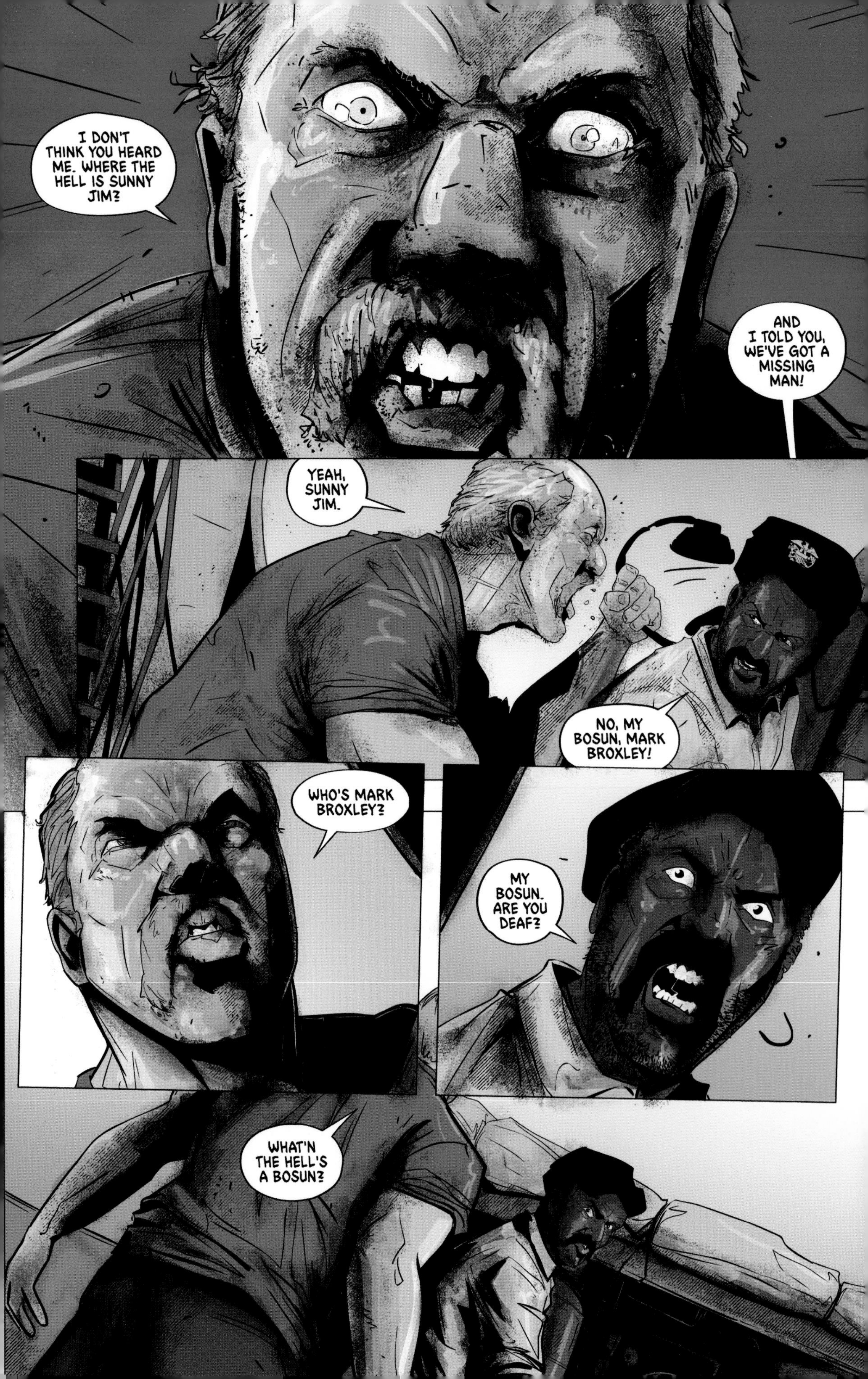
I DON'T THINK YOU HEARD ME. WHERE THE HELL IS SUNNY JIM?
AND I TOLD YOU, WE'VE GOT A MISSING MAN!
YEAH, SUNNY JIM.
NO, MY BOSUN, MARK BROXLEY!
WHO'S MARK BROXLEY?
MY BOSUN. ARE YOU DEAF?
WHAT'N THE HELL'S A BOSUN?

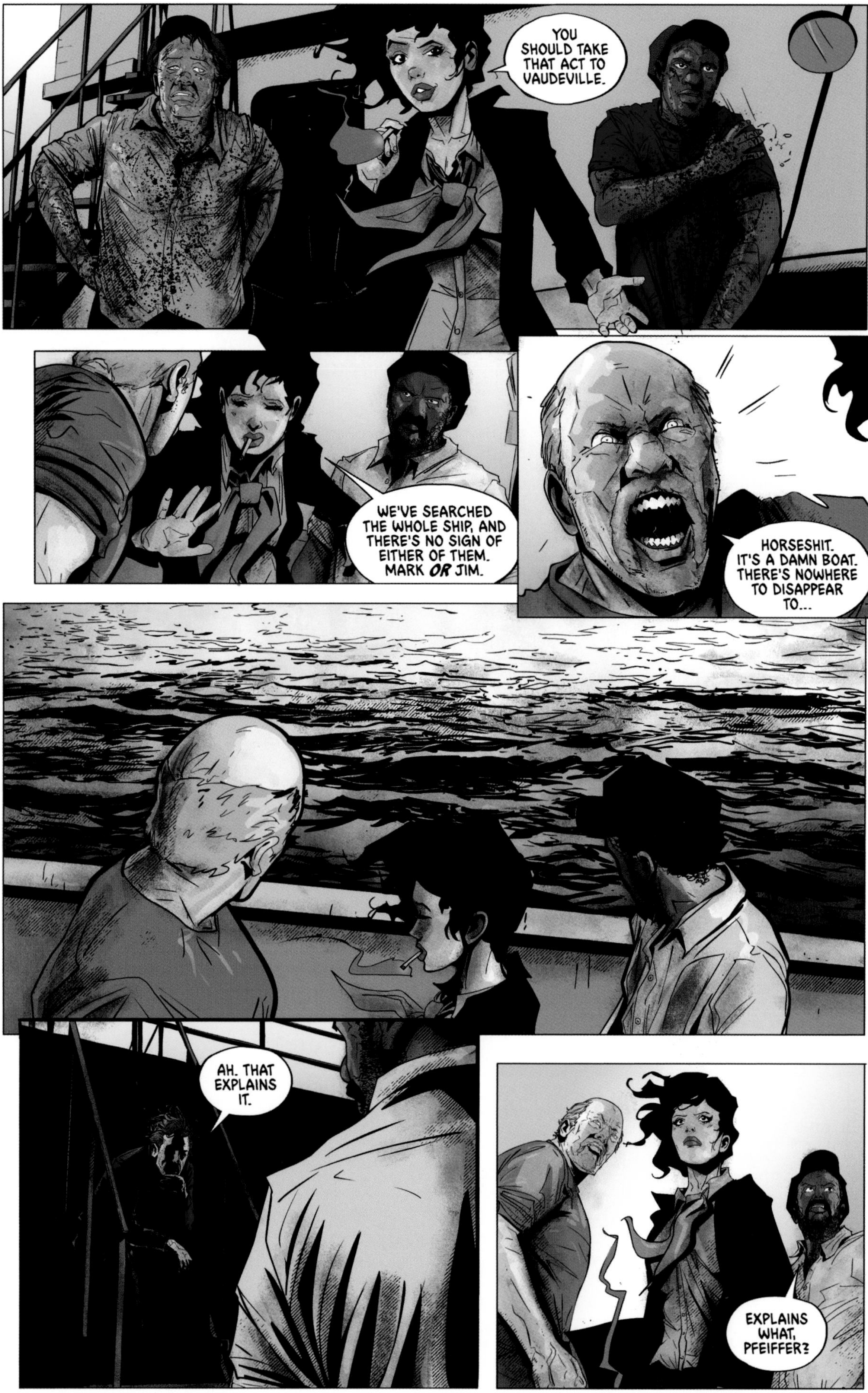

YOU SHOULD TAKE THAT ACT TO VAUDEVILLE.
WE'VE SEARCHED THE WHOLE SHIP, AND THERE'S NO SIGN OF EITHER OF THEM. MARK *OR* JIM.
HORSESHIT. IT'S A DAMN BOAT. THERE'S NOWHERE TO DISAPPEAR TO...
AH. THAT EXPLAINS IT.
EXPLAINS WHAT, PFEIFFER?

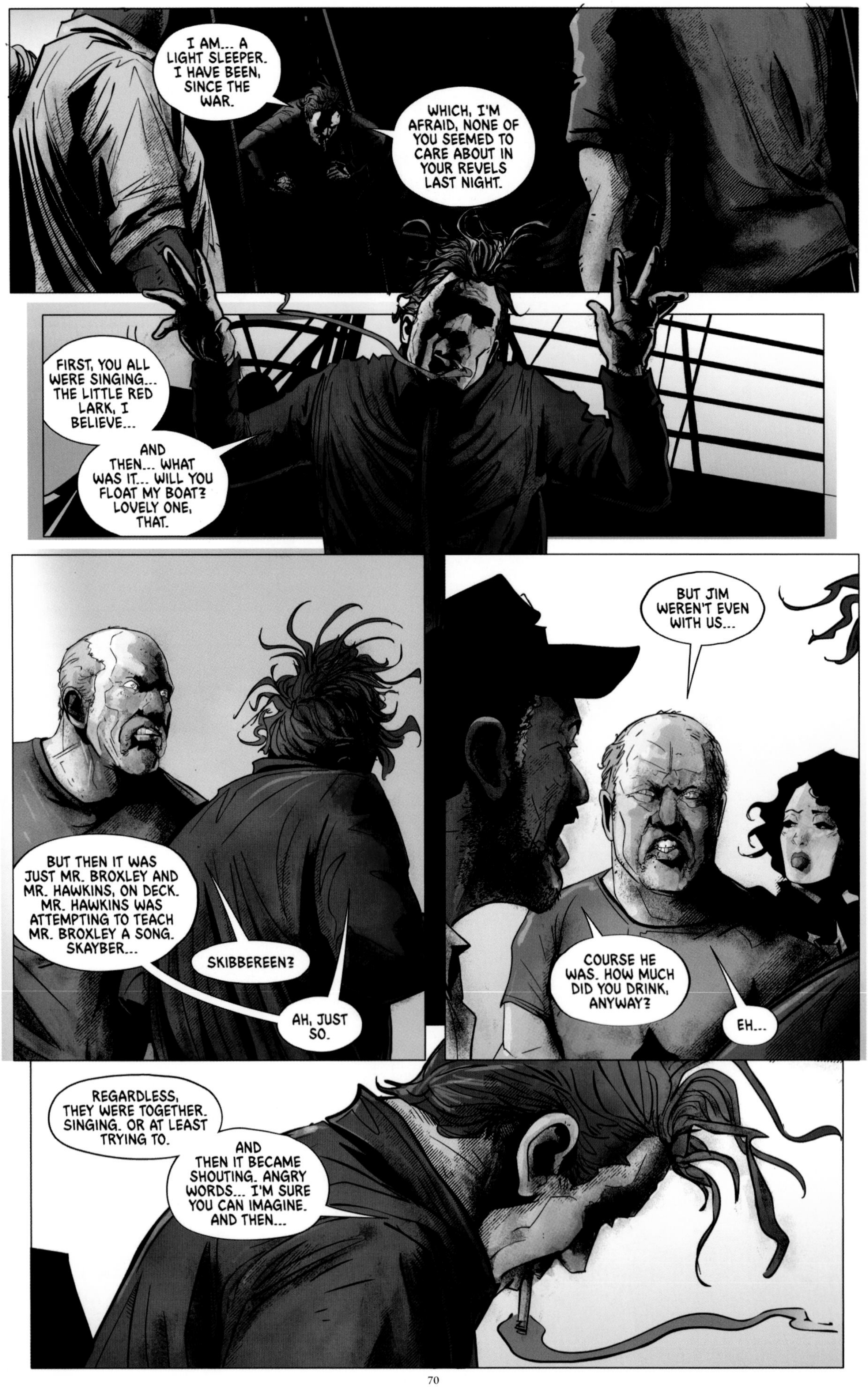
I AM... A LIGHT SLEEPER. I HAVE BEEN, SINCE THE WAR.
WHICH, I'M AFRAID, NONE OF YOU SEEMED TO CARE ABOUT IN YOUR REVELS LAST NIGHT.
FIRST, YOU ALL WERE SINGING... THE LITTLE RED LARK, I BELIEVE...
AND THEN... WHAT WAS IT... WILL YOU FLOAT MY BOAT? LOVELY ONE, THAT.
BUT THEN IT WAS JUST MR. BROXLEY AND MR. HAWKINS, ON DECK. MR. HAWKINS WAS ATTEMPTING TO TEACH MR. BROXLEY A SONG. SKAYBER...
SKIBBEREEN?
AH, JUST SO.
BUT JIM WEREN'T EVEN WITH US...
COURSE HE WAS. HOW MUCH DID YOU DRINK, ANYWAY?
EH...
REGARDLESS, THEY WERE TOGETHER. SINGING. OR AT LEAST TRYING TO.
AND THEN IT BECAME SHOUTING. ANGRY WORDS... I'M SURE YOU CAN IMAGINE. AND THEN...

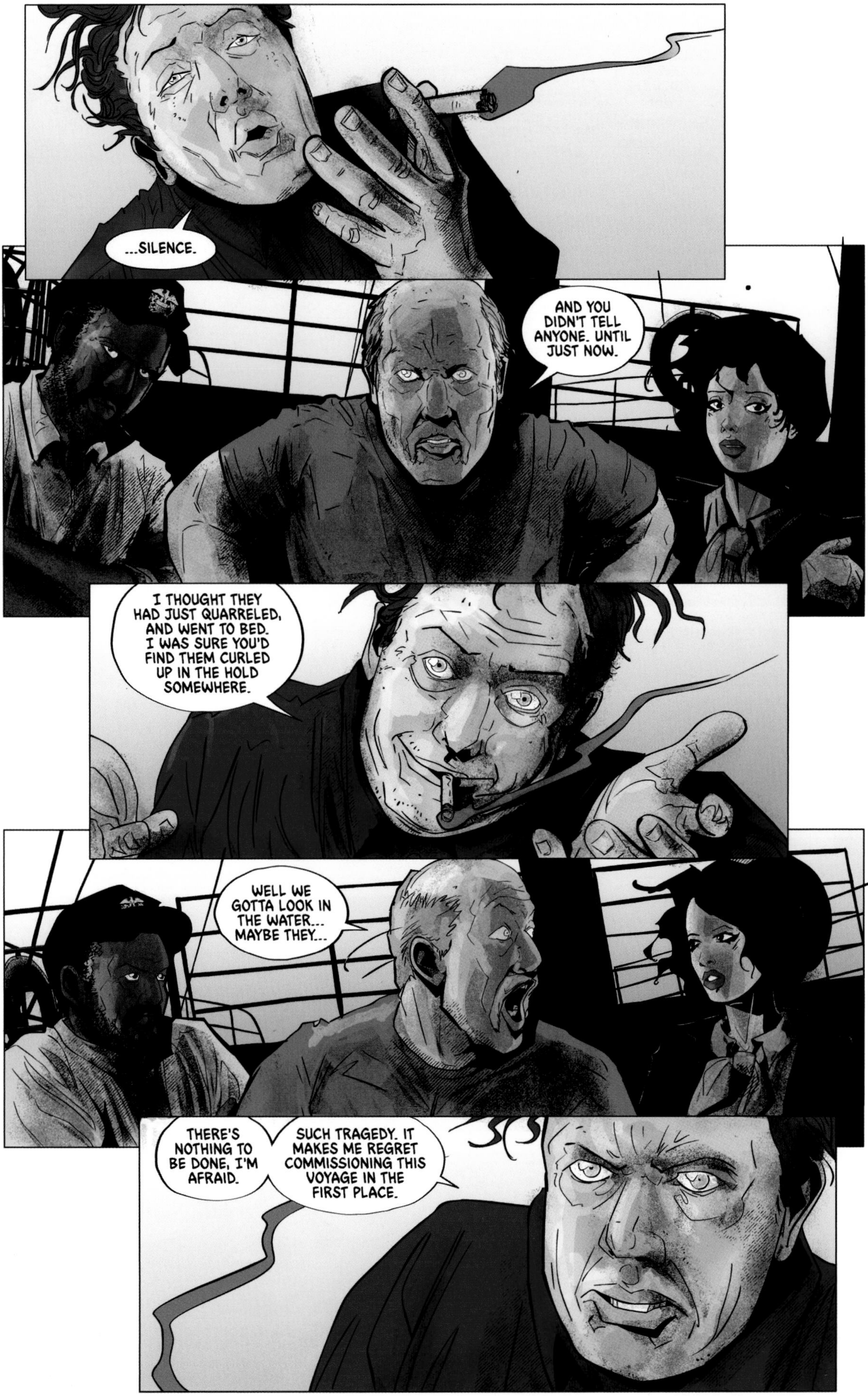
...SILENCE.
AND YOU DIDN'T TELL ANYONE. UNTIL JUST NOW.
I THOUGHT THEY HAD JUST QUARRELED, AND WENT TO BED. I WAS SURE YOU'D FIND THEM CURLED UP IN THE HOLD SOMEWHERE.
WELL WE GOTTA LOOK IN THE WATER... MAYBE THEY...
THERE'S NOTHING TO BE DONE, I'M AFRAID.
SUCH TRAGEDY. IT MAKES ME REGRET COMMISSIONING THIS VOYAGE IN THE FIRST PLACE.

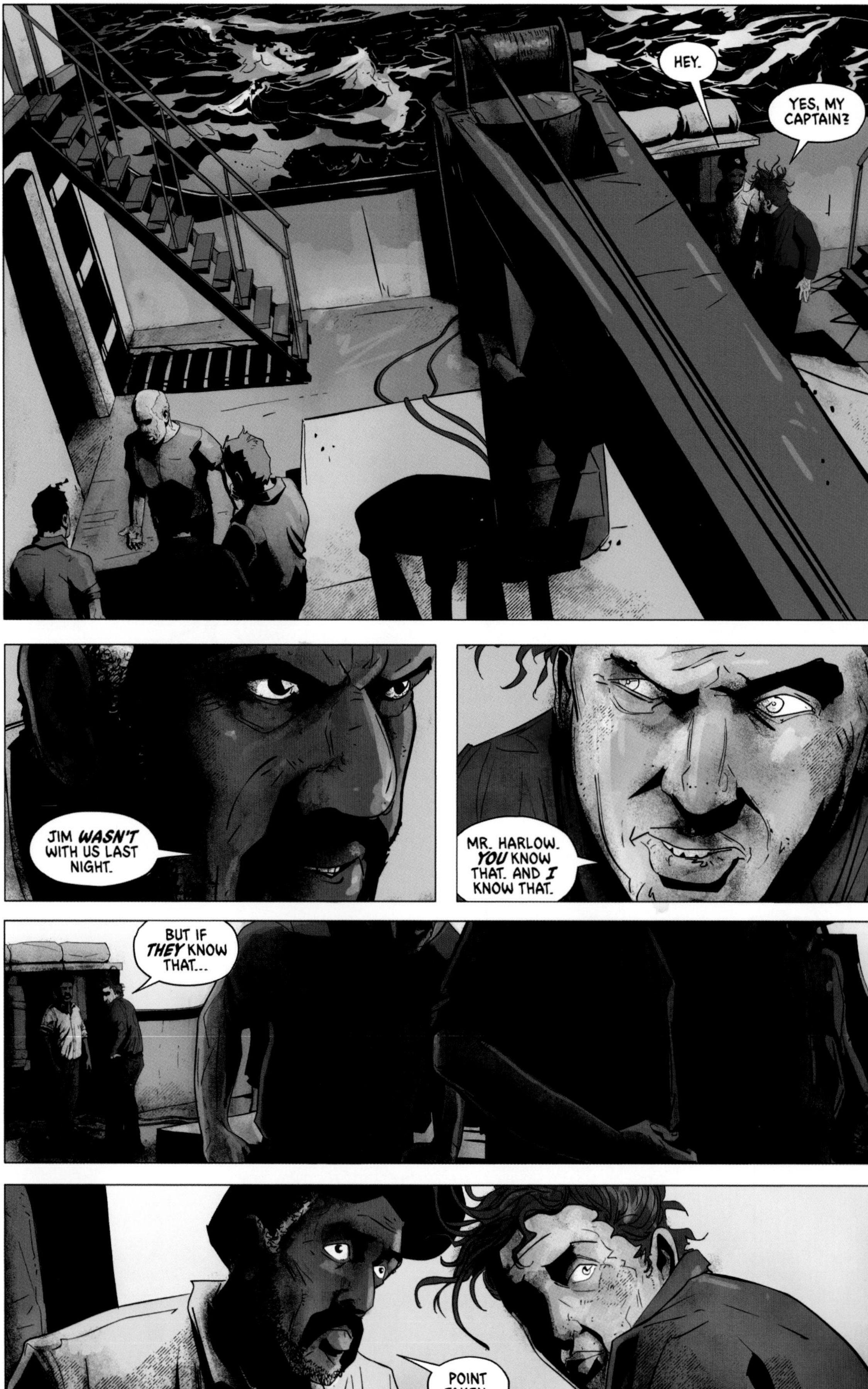
HEY.
YES, MY CAPTAIN?
JIM WASN'T WITH US LAST NIGHT.
MR. HARLOW. YOU KNOW THAT. AND I KNOW THAT.
BUT IF THEY KNOW THAT...
POINT TAKEN.

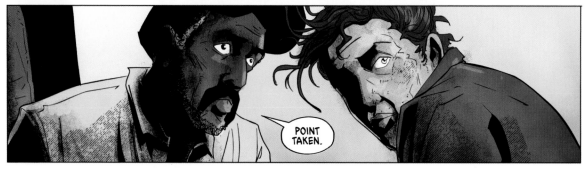

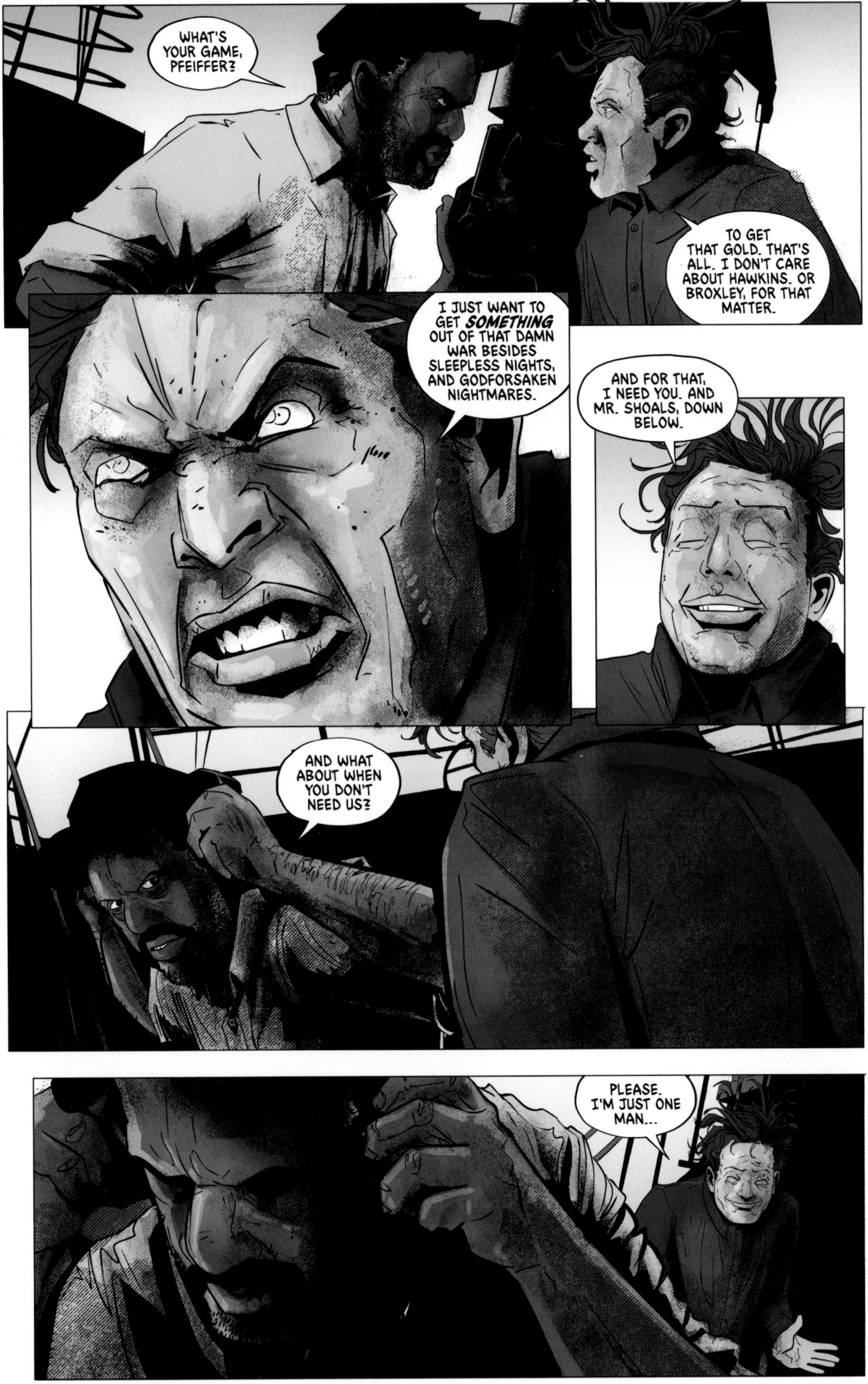
WHAT'S YOUR GAME, PFEIFFER?
TO GET THAT GOLD. THAT'S ALL. I DON'T CARE ABOUT HAWKINS. OR BROXLEY, FOR THAT MATTER.
I JUST WANT TO GET SOMETHING OUT OF THAT DAMN WAR BESIDES SLEEPLESS NIGHTS, AND GODFORSAKEN NIGHTMARES.
AND FOR THAT, I NEED YOU. AND MR. SHOALS, DOWN BELOW.
AND WHAT ABOUT WHEN YOU DON'T NEED US?
PLEASE. I'M JUST ONE MAN...

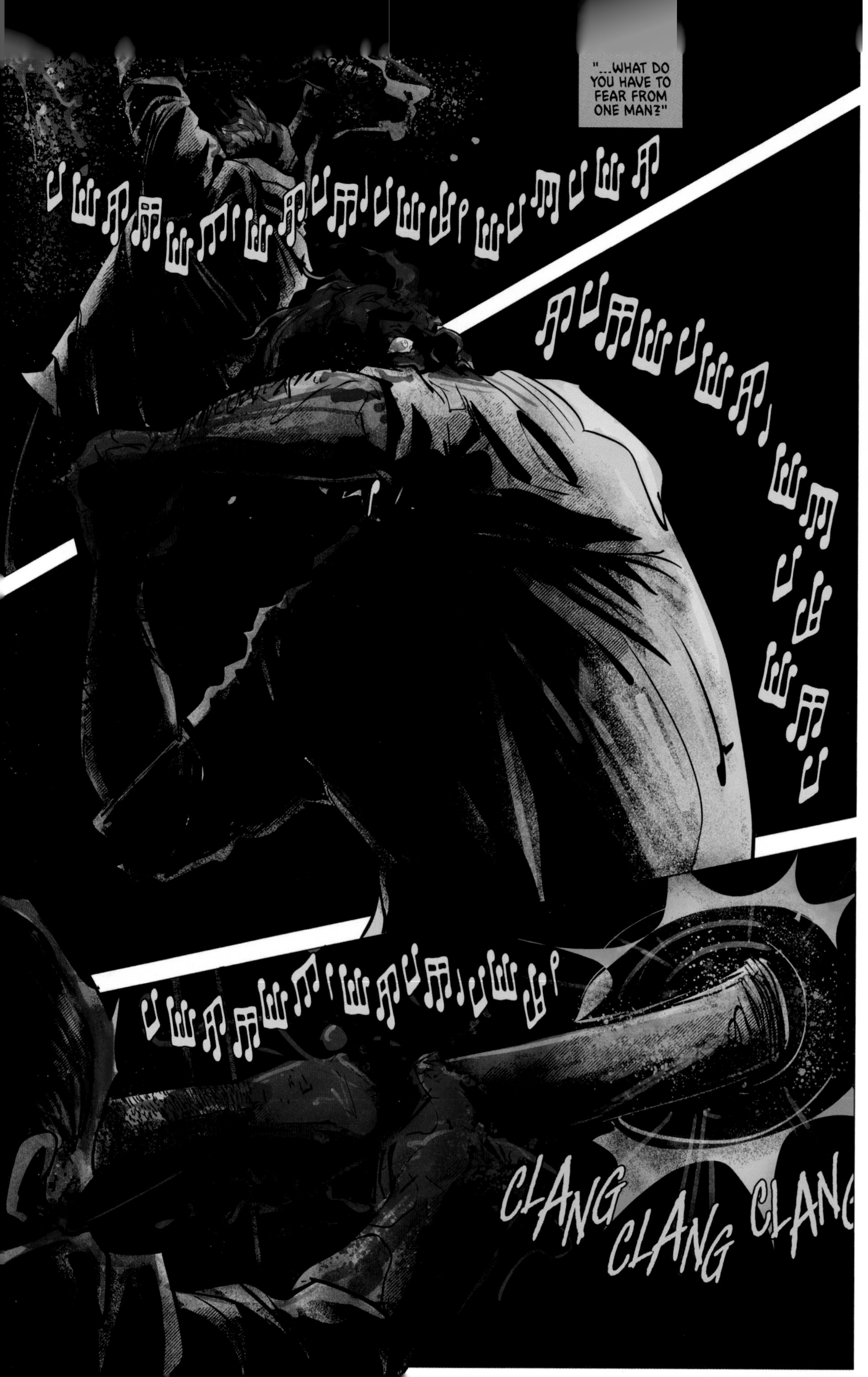
"...WHAT DO YOU HAVE TO FEAR FROM ONE MAN?"
CLANG
CLANG
CLANG

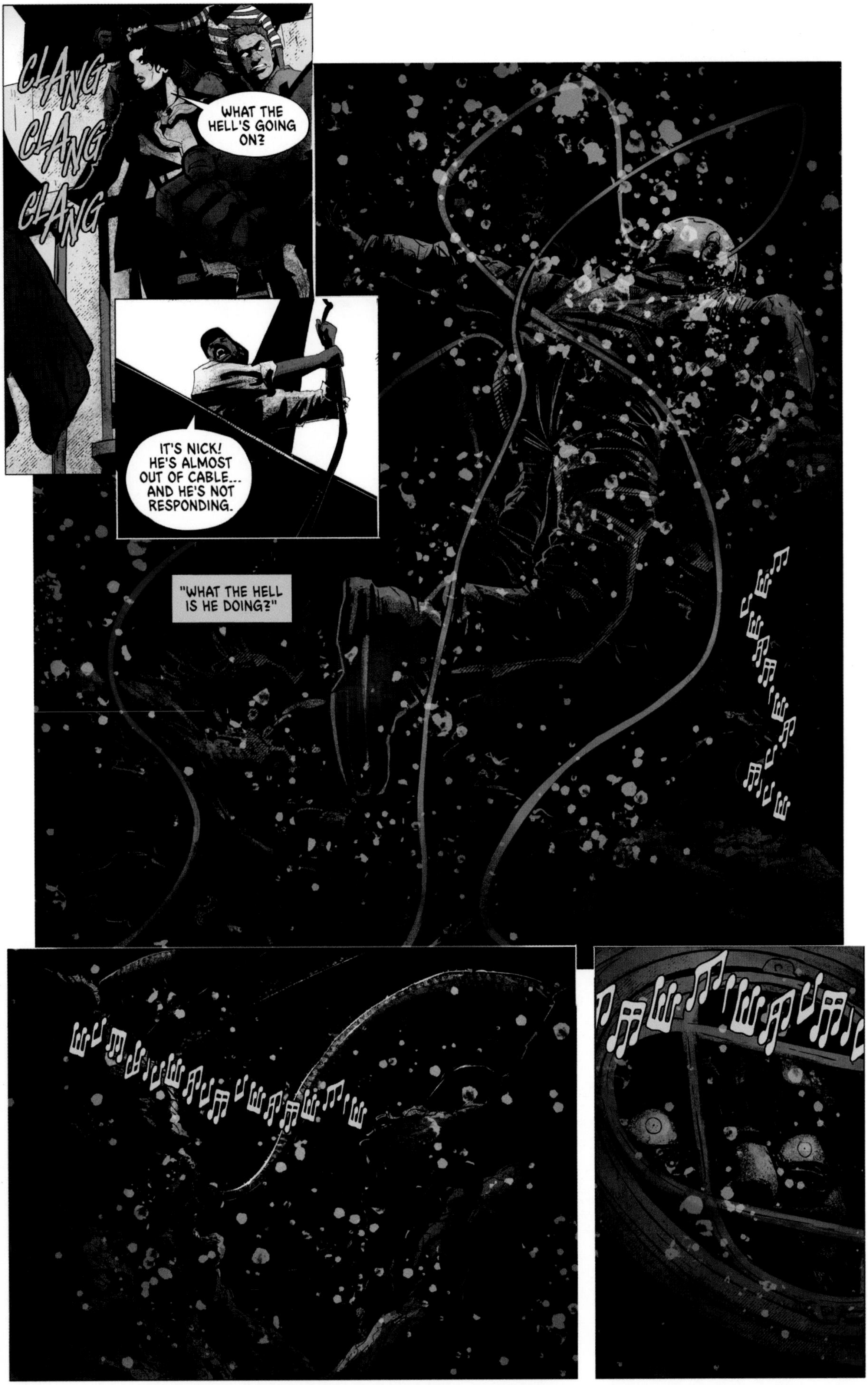
CLANG
CLANG
CLANG
WHAT THE HELL'S GOING ON?
IT'S NICK! HE'S ALMOST OUT OF CABLE... AND HE'S NOT RESPONDING.
"WHAT THE HELL IS HE DOING?"

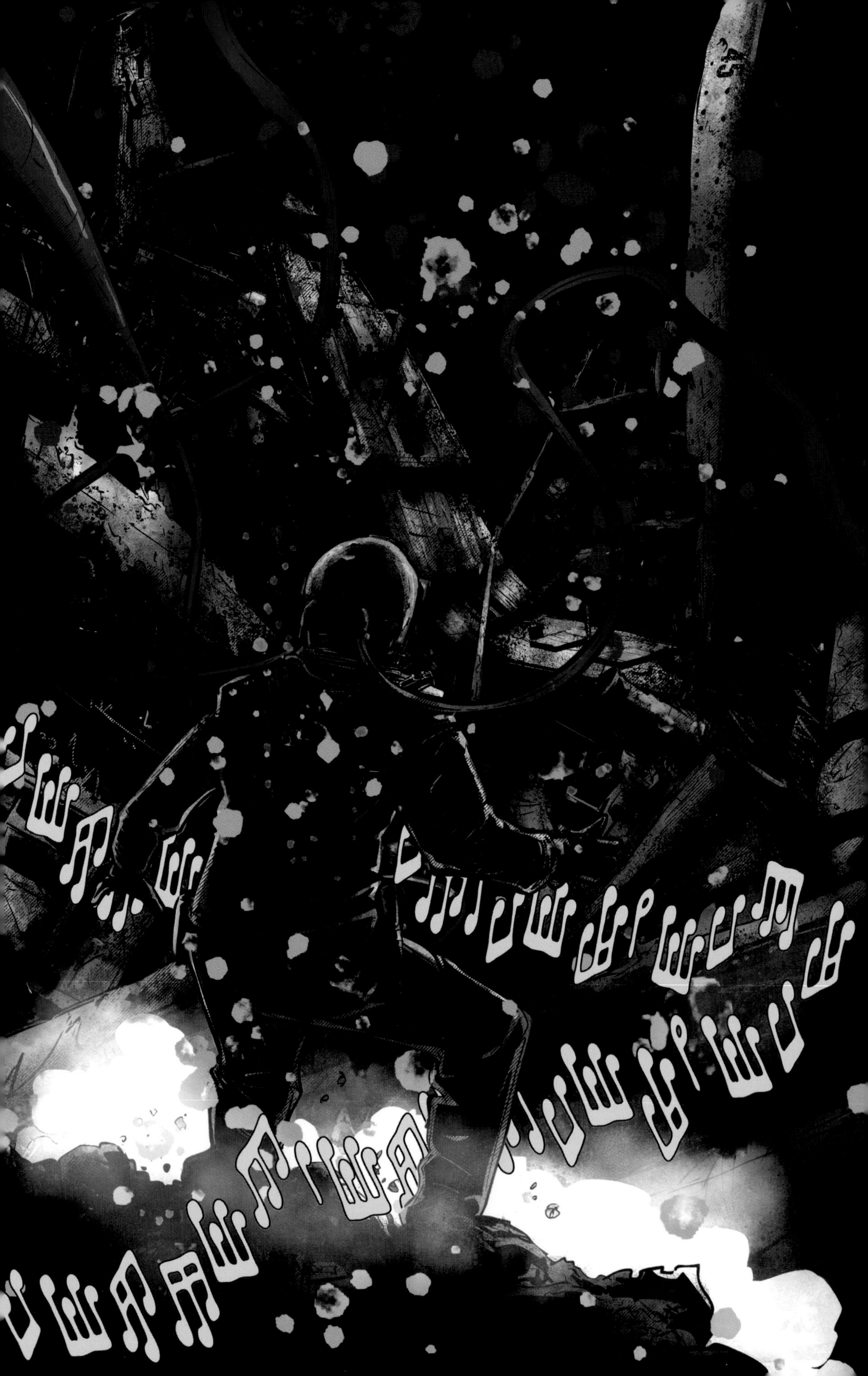

JOE MULVEY

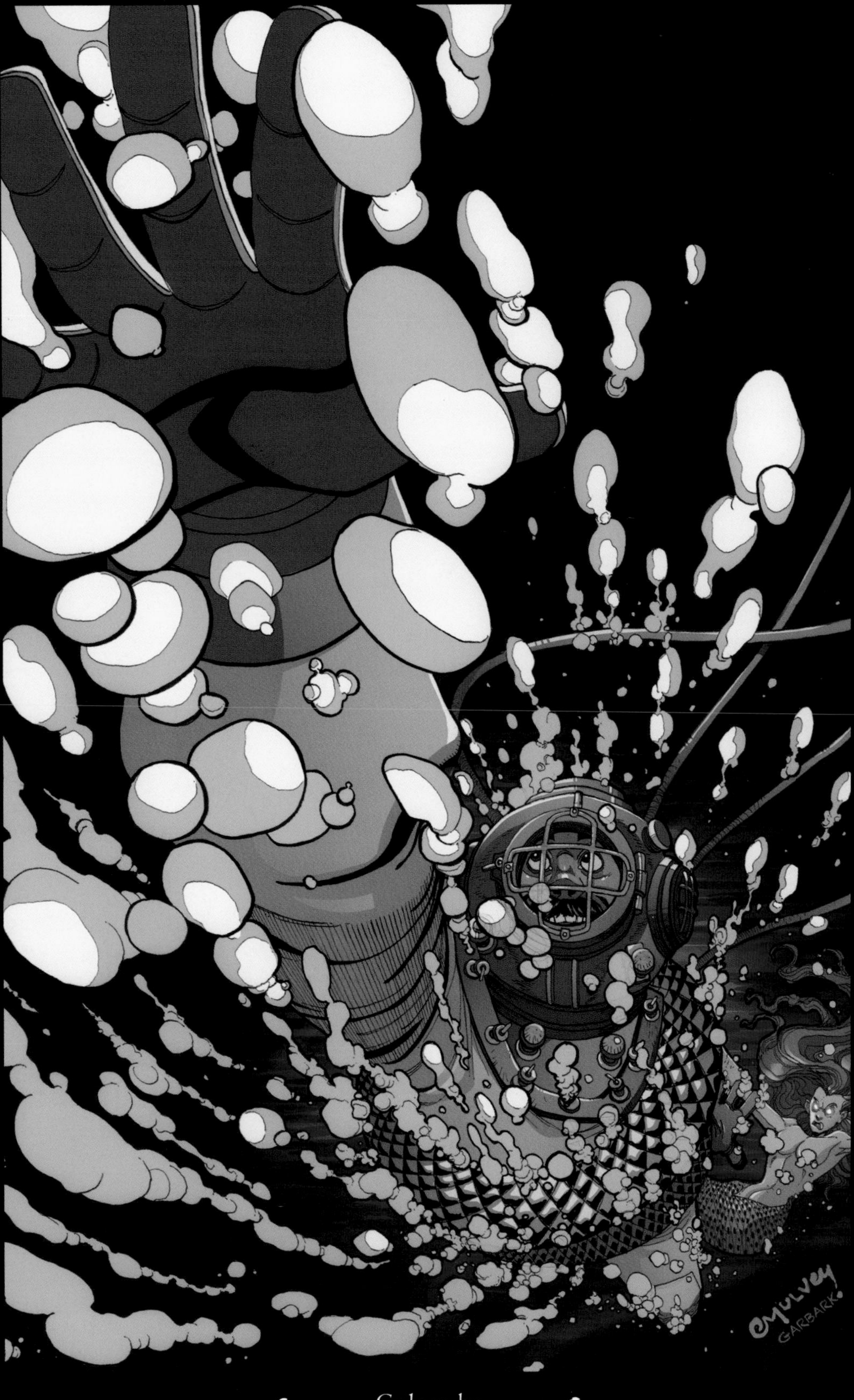
©MULVEY
GARBARK

Colors by

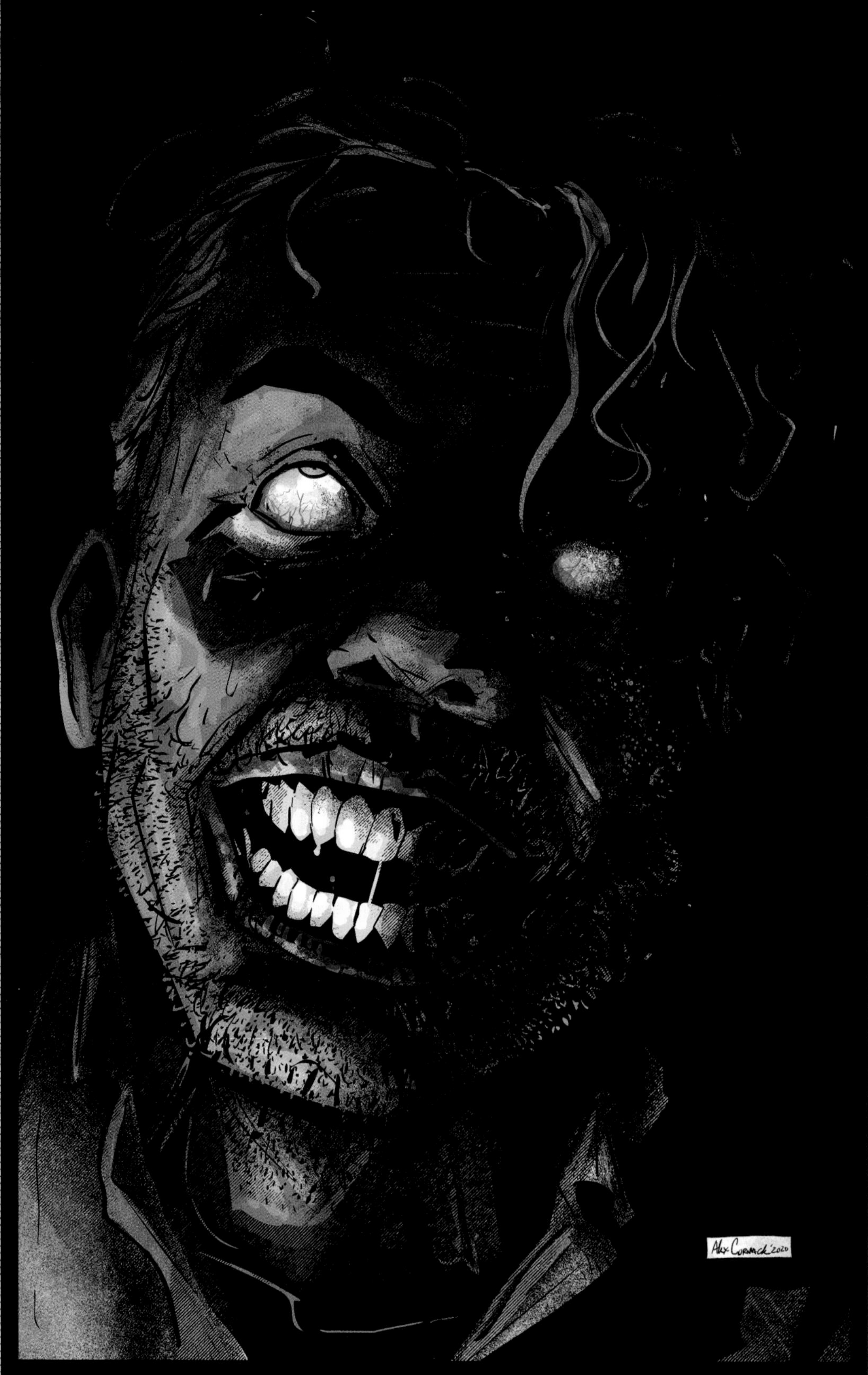
Alex Cormack '2020

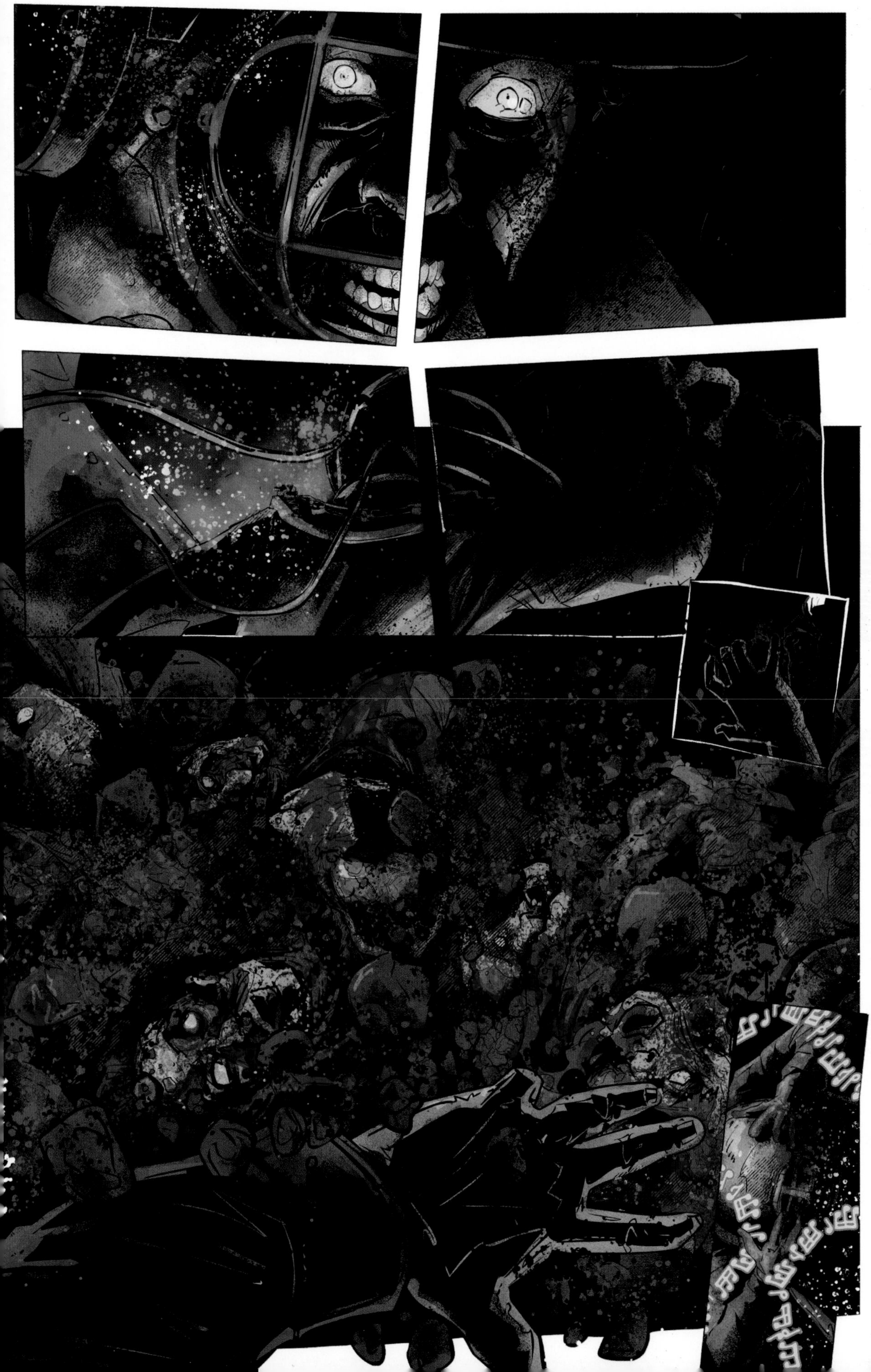

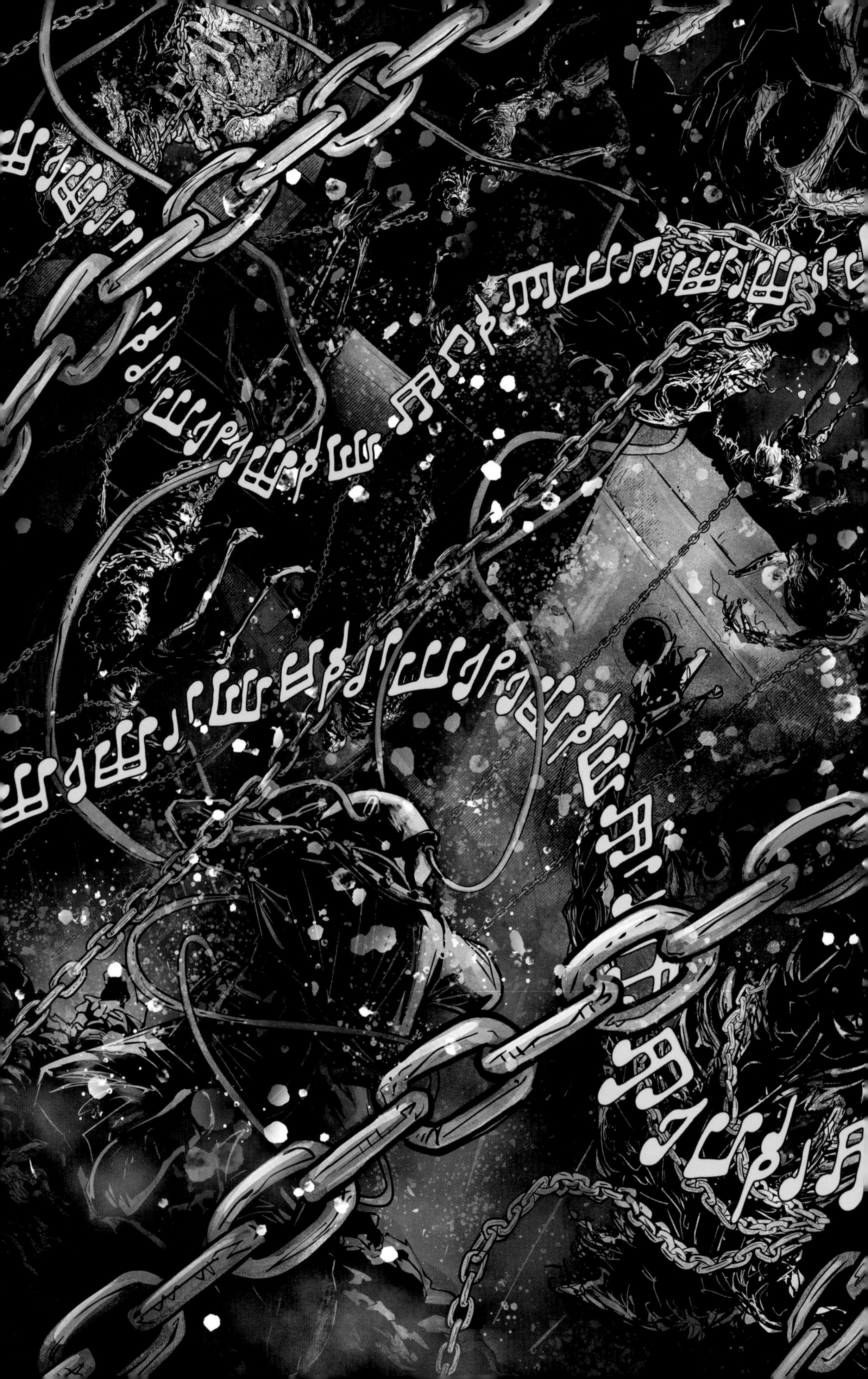

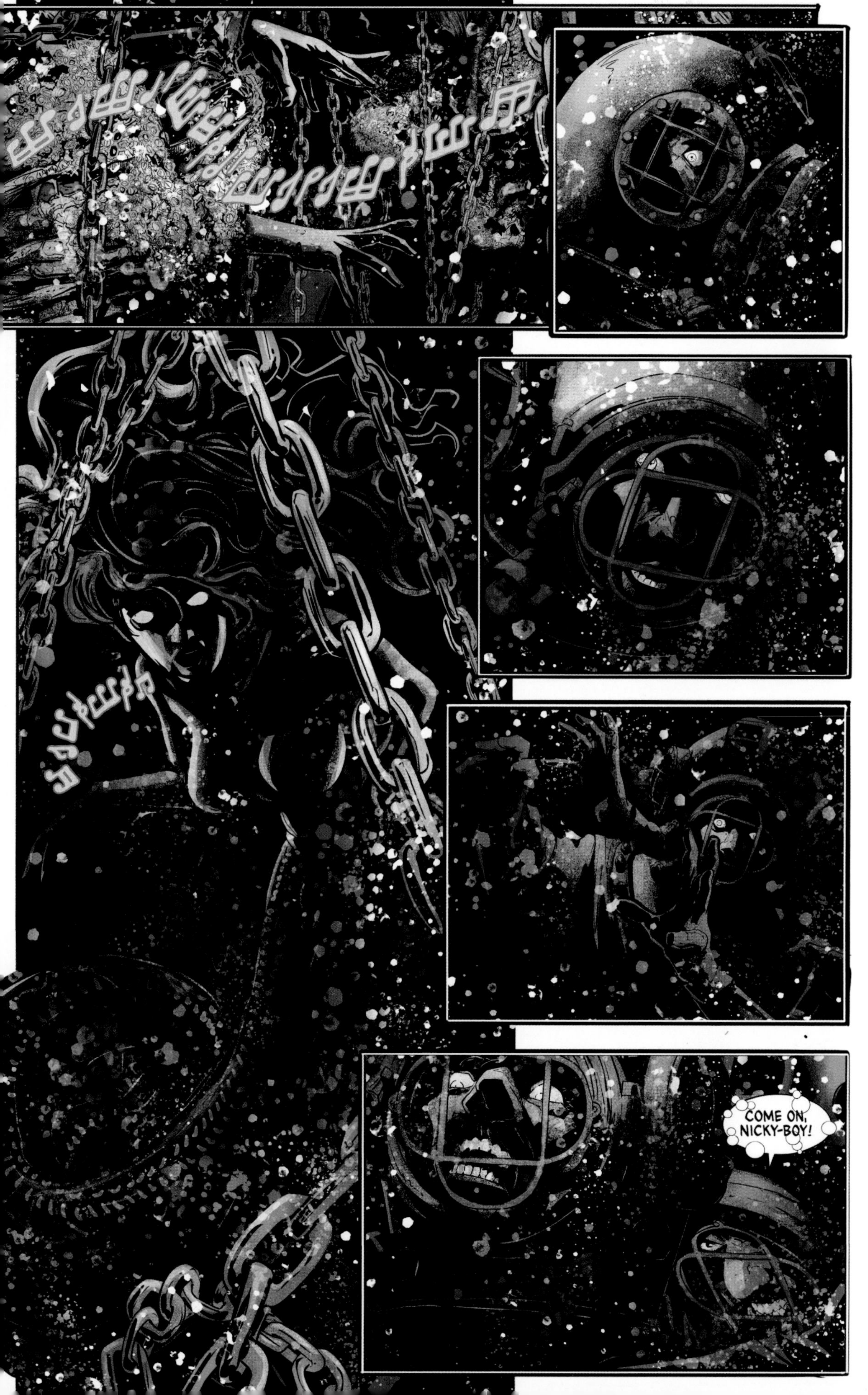
COME ON, NICKY-BOY!

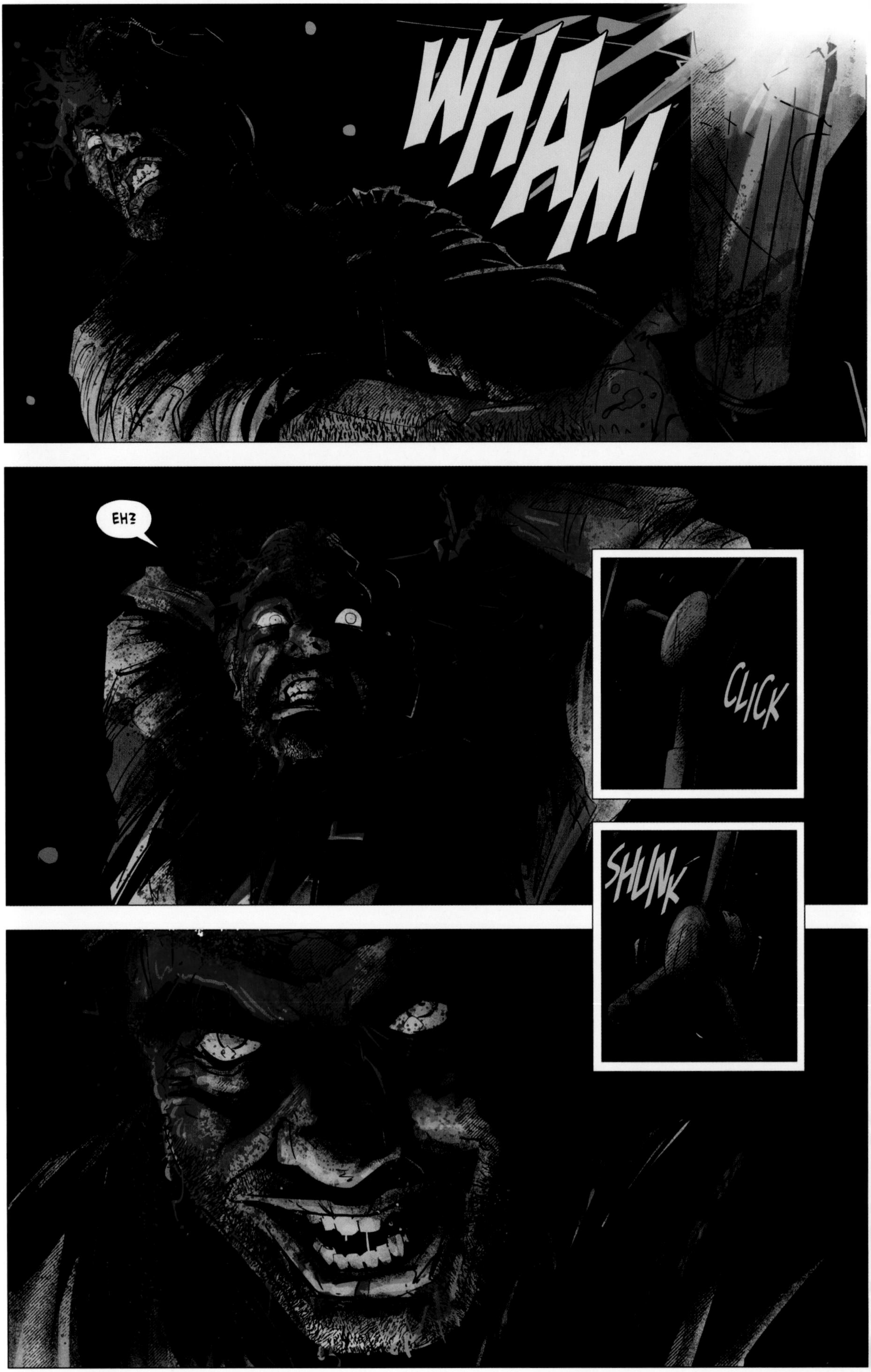
WHAM
EH?
CLICK
SHUNK

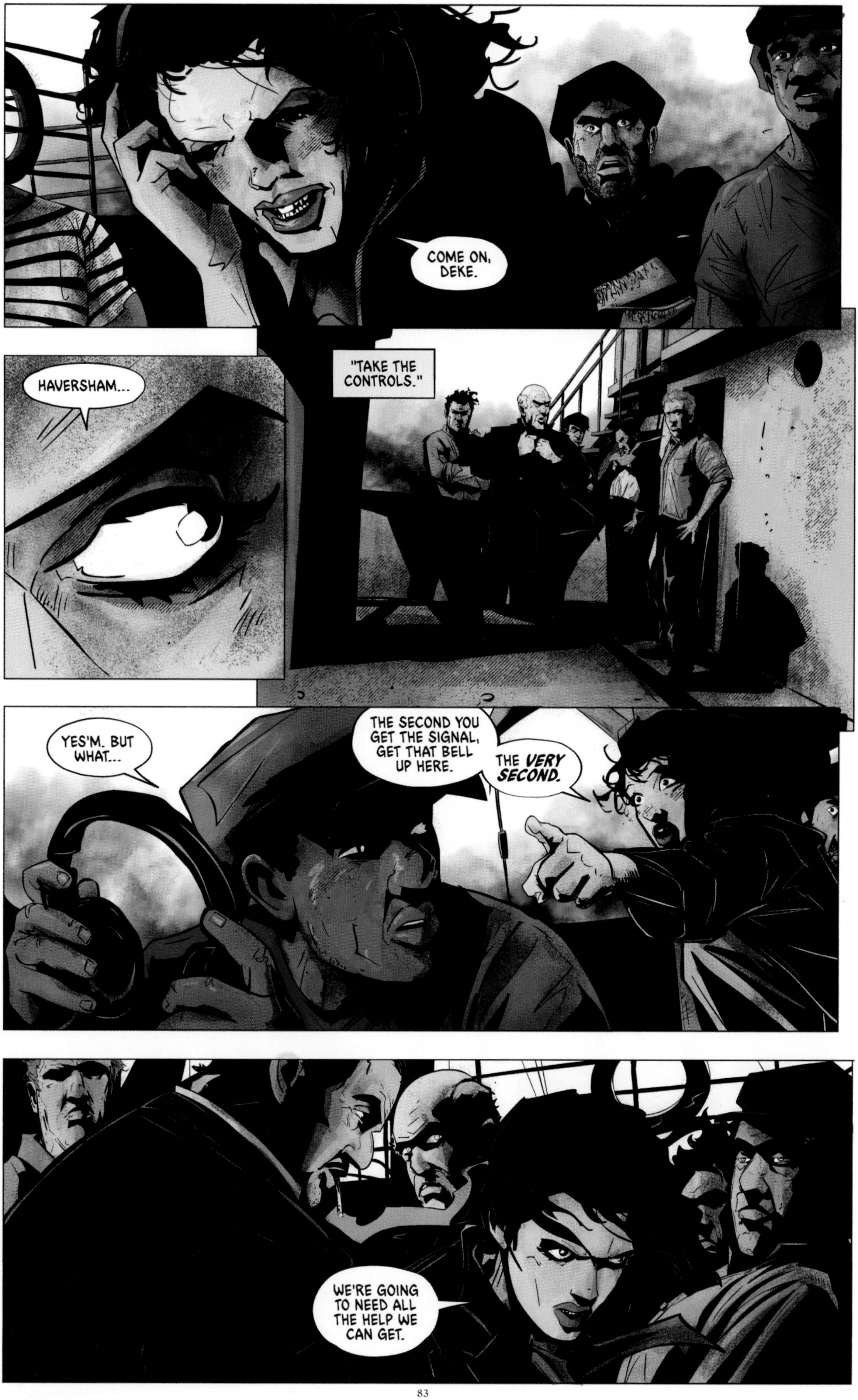
COME ON, DEKE.
HAVERSHAM...
"TAKE THE CONTROLS."
YES'M. BUT WHAT...
THE SECOND YOU GET THE SIGNAL, GET THAT BELL UP HERE.
THE *VERY SECOND.*
WE'RE GOING TO NEED ALL THE HELP WE CAN GET.

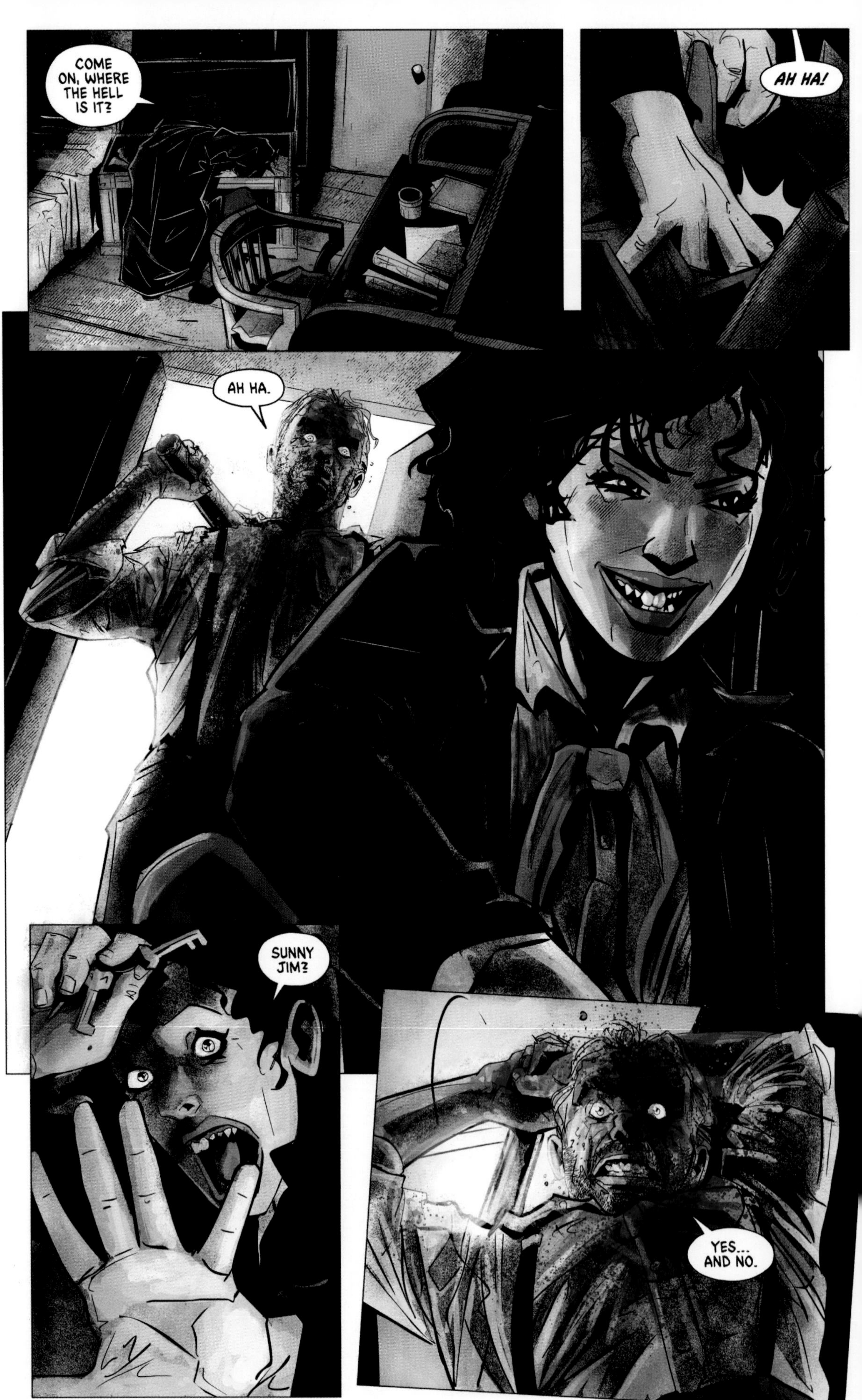
COME ON, WHERE THE HELL IS IT?
AH HA!
AH HA.
SUNNY JIM?
YES... AND NO.

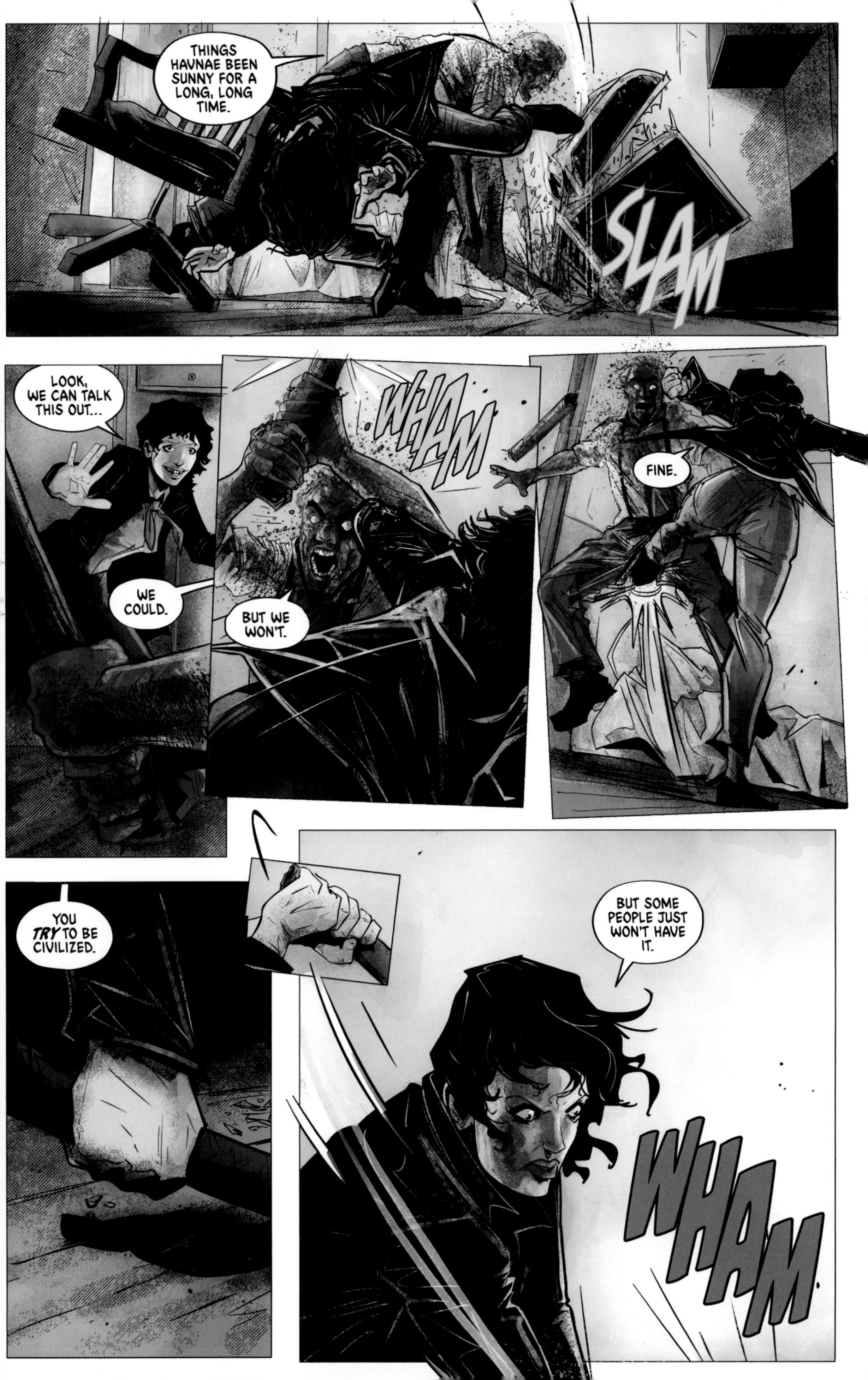

THINGS HAVNAE BEEN SUNNY FOR A LONG, LONG TIME.
SLAM
LOOK, WE CAN TALK THIS OUT...
WE COULD.
BUT WE WON'T.
WHAM
FINE.
YOU TRY TO BE CIVILIZED.
BUT SOME PEOPLE JUST WON'T HAVE IT.
WHAM

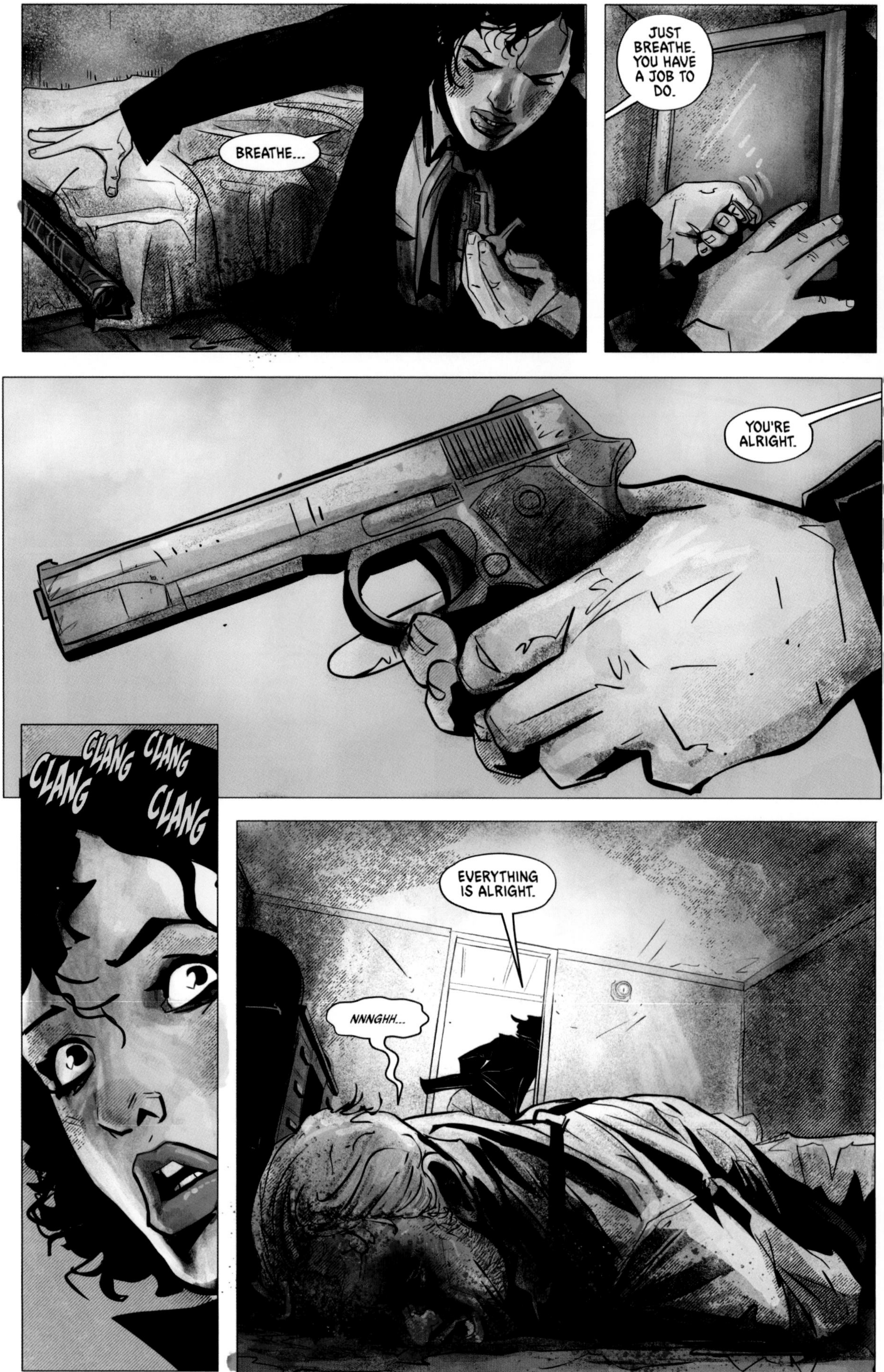
BREATHE...
JUST BREATHE. YOU HAVE A JOB TO DO.
YOU'RE ALRIGHT.
CLANG CLANG CLANG CLANG CLANG
EVERYTHING IS ALRIGHT.
NNNGHH...

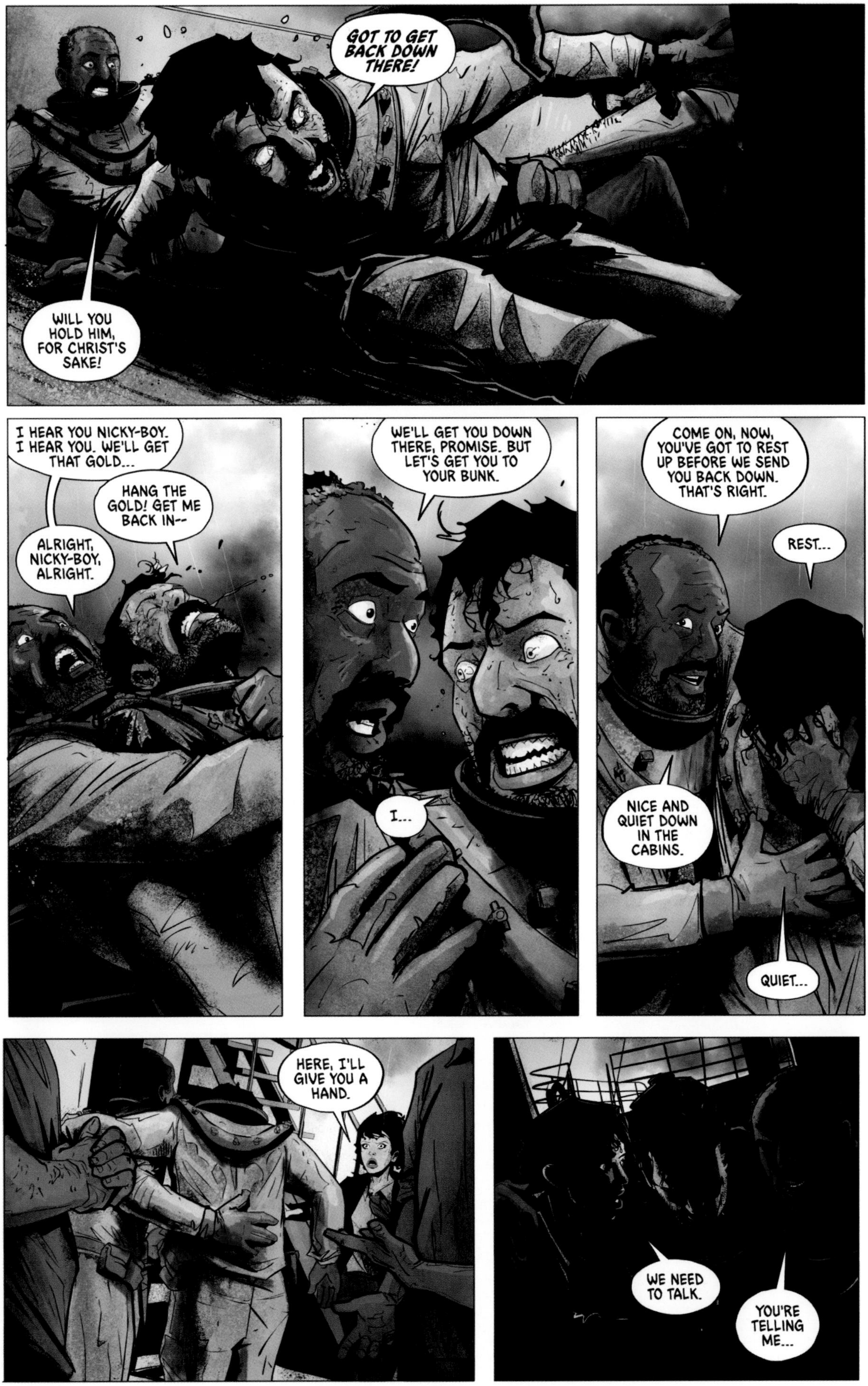
GOT TO GET BACK DOWN THERE!
WILL YOU HOLD HIM, FOR CHRIST'S SAKE!
I HEAR YOU NICKY-BOY. I HEAR YOU. WE'LL GET THAT GOLD...
HANG THE GOLD! GET ME BACK IN--
ALRIGHT, NICKY-BOY, ALRIGHT.
WE'LL GET YOU DOWN THERE, PROMISE. BUT LET'S GET YOU TO YOUR BUNK.
I...
COME ON, NOW, YOU'VE GOT TO REST UP BEFORE WE SEND YOU BACK DOWN. THAT'S RIGHT.
REST...
NICE AND QUIET DOWN IN THE CABINS.
QUIET...
HERE, I'LL GIVE YOU A HAND.
WE NEED TO TALK.
YOU'RE TELLING ME...

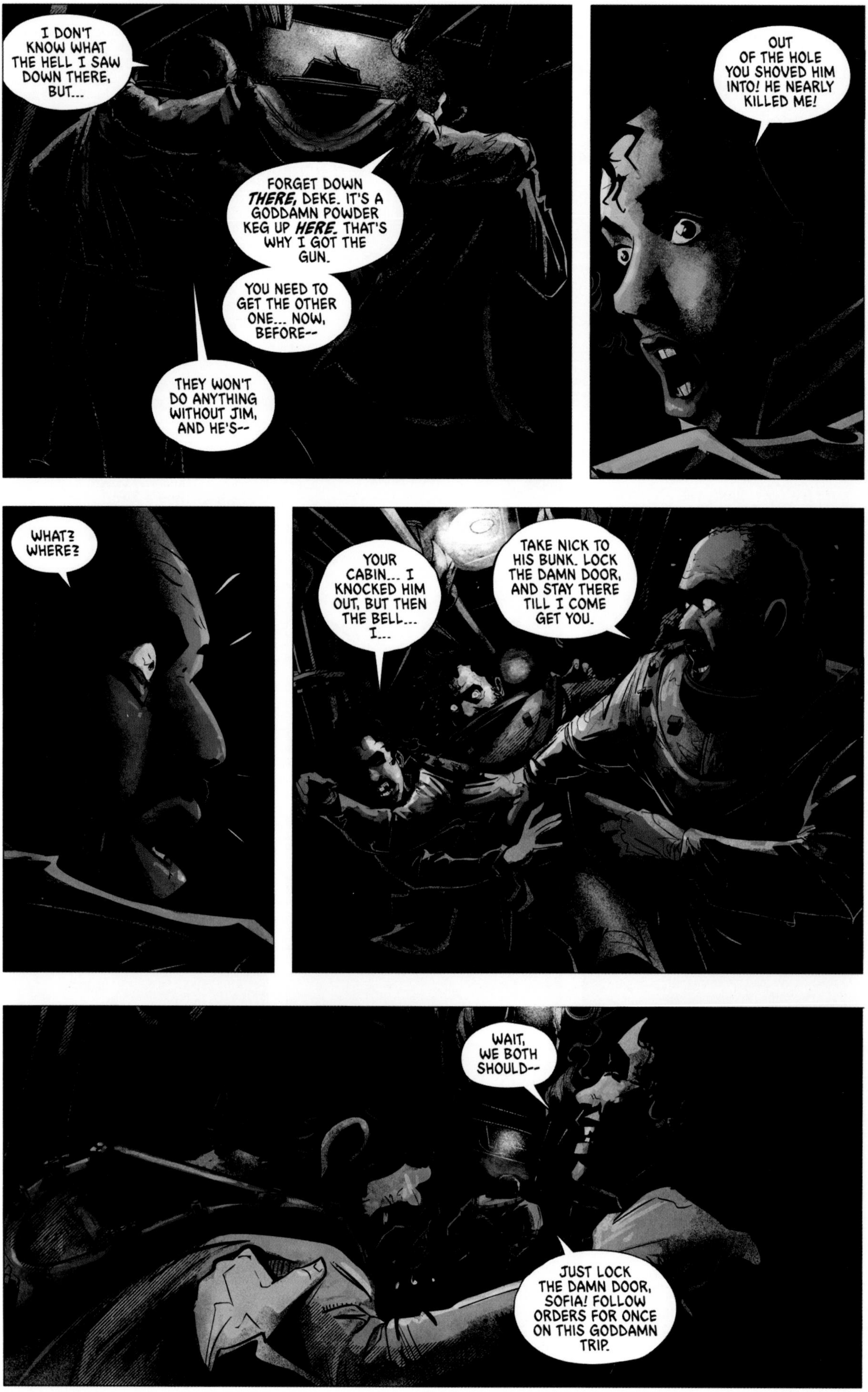
I DON'T KNOW WHAT THE HELL I SAW DOWN THERE, BUT...
FORGET DOWN ***THERE,*** DEKE. IT'S A GODDAMN POWDER KEG UP ***HERE.*** THAT'S WHY I GOT THE GUN.
YOU NEED TO GET THE OTHER ONE... NOW, BEFORE--
THEY WON'T DO ANYTHING WITHOUT JIM, AND HE'S--
OUT OF THE HOLE YOU SHOVED HIM INTO! HE NEARLY KILLED ME!
WHAT? WHERE?
YOUR CABIN... I KNOCKED HIM OUT, BUT THEN THE BELL... I...
TAKE NICK TO HIS BUNK. LOCK THE DAMN DOOR, AND STAY THERE TILL I COME GET YOU.
WAIT, WE BOTH SHOULD--
JUST LOCK THE DAMN DOOR, SOFIA! FOLLOW ORDERS FOR ONCE ON THIS GODDAMN TRIP.

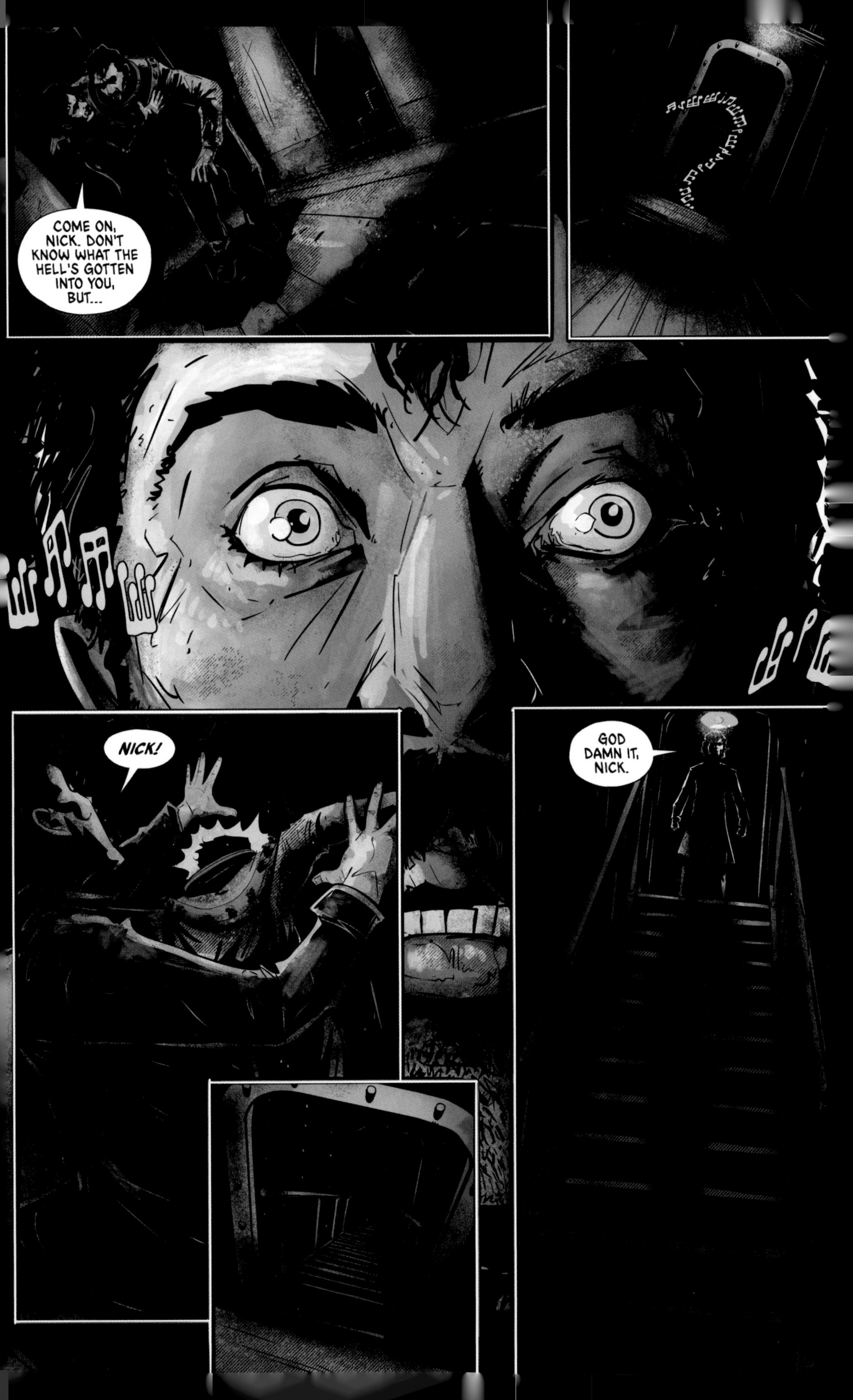
COME ON, NICK. DON'T KNOW WHAT THE HELL'S GOTTEN INTO YOU, BUT...
NICK!
GOD DAMN IT, NICK.

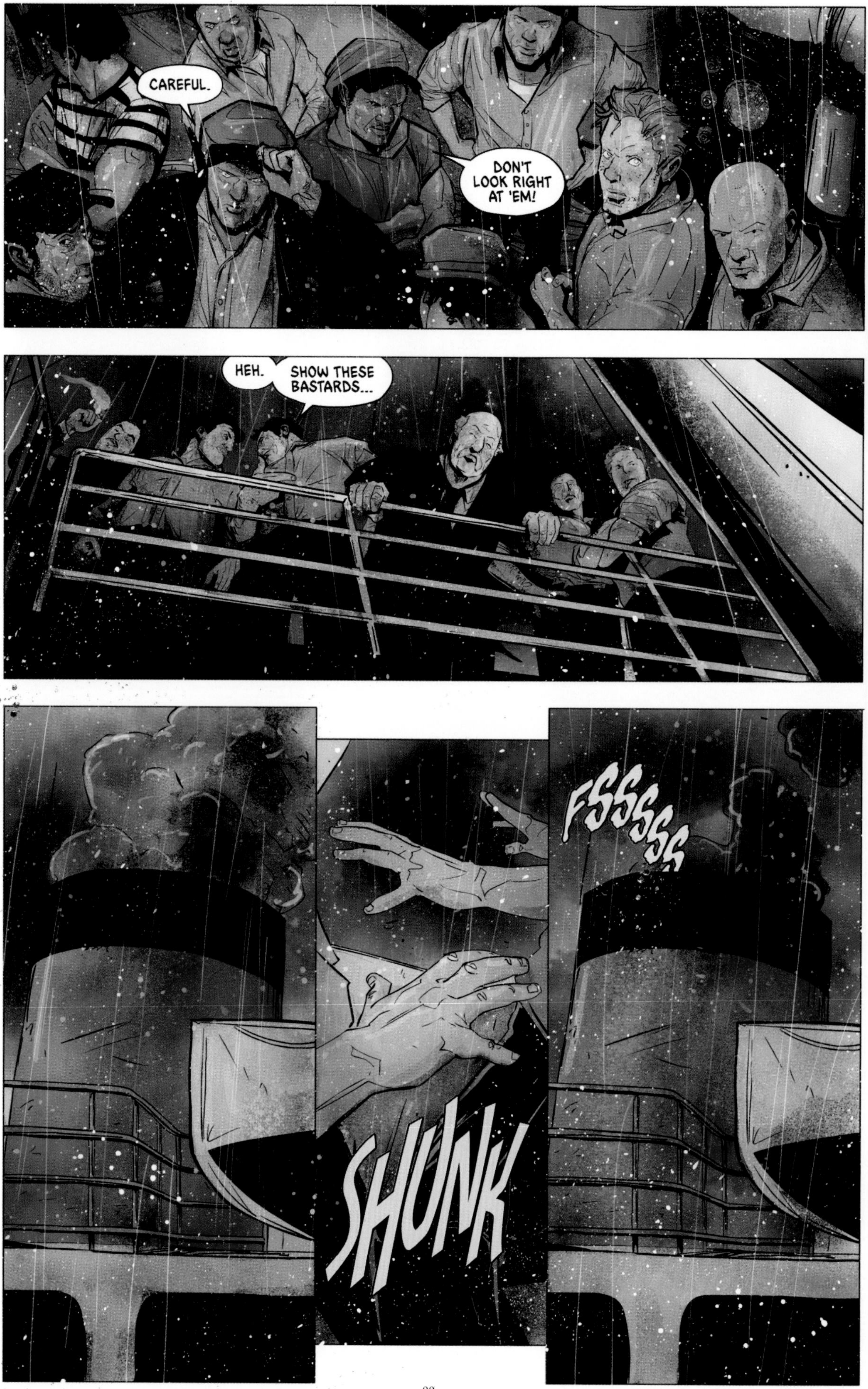
CAREFUL.
DON'T LOOK RIGHT AT 'EM!
HEH.
SHOW THESE BASTARDS...
SHUNK
FSSSSS

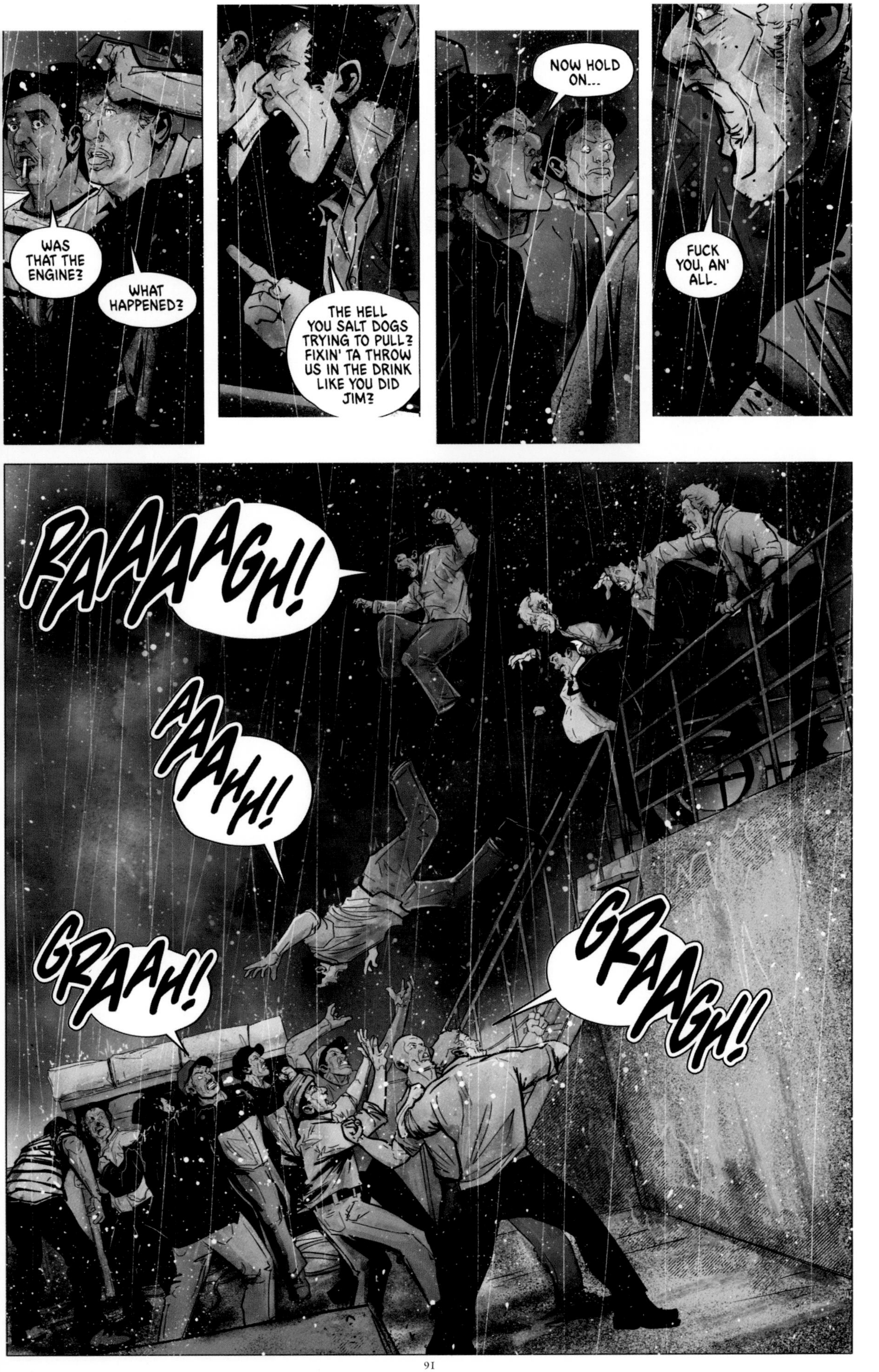
WAS THAT THE ENGINE?
WHAT HAPPENED?
THE HELL YOU SALT DOGS TRYING TO PULL? FIXIN' TA THROW US IN THE DRINK LIKE YOU DID JIM?
NOW HOLD ON...
FUCK YOU, AN' ALL.
RAAAAAGH!
AAAAHH!
GRAAH!
GRAAGH!

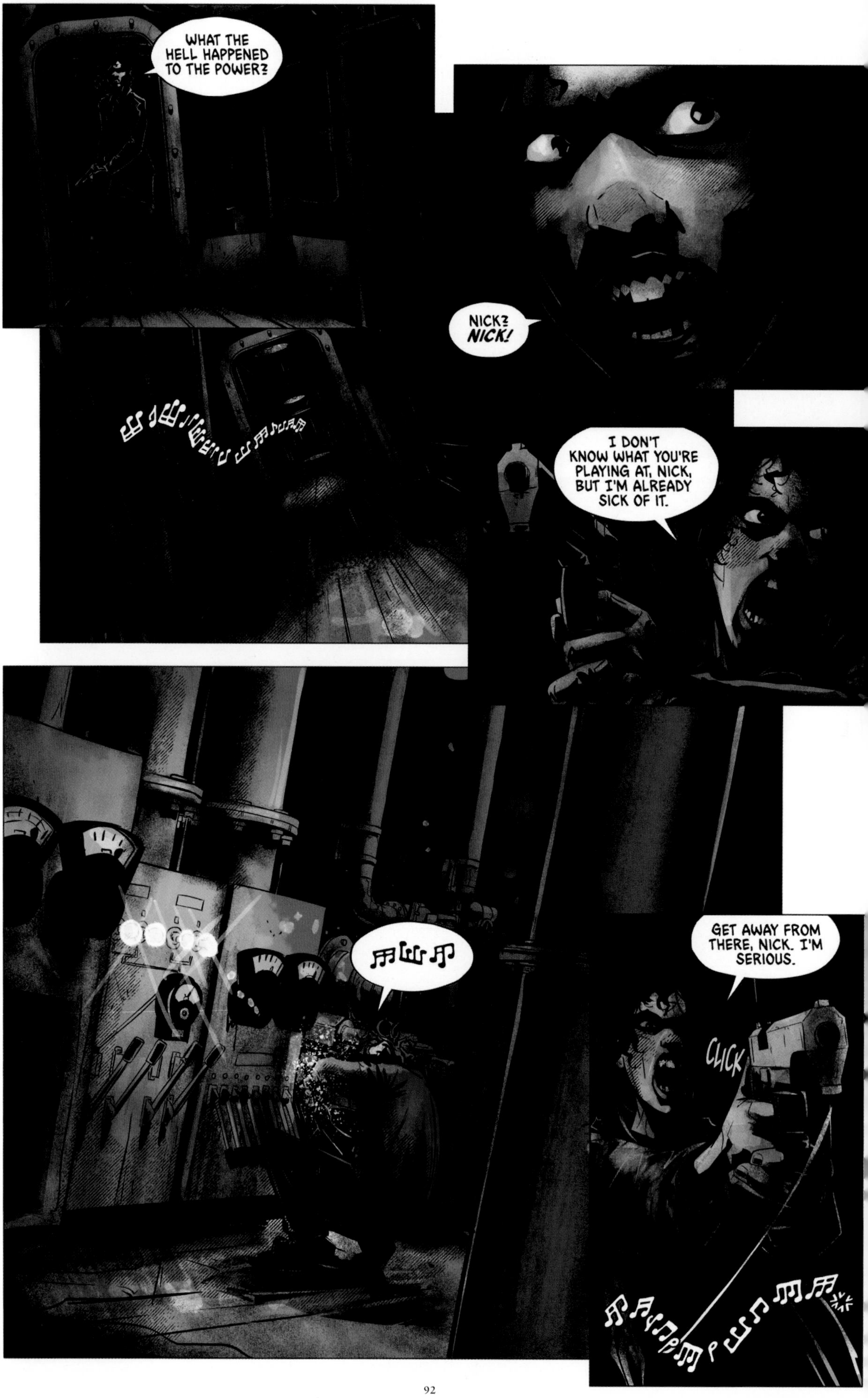
WHAT THE HELL HAPPENED TO THE POWER?
NICK? NICK!
I DON'T KNOW WHAT YOU'RE PLAYING AT, NICK, BUT I'M ALREADY SICK OF IT.
GET AWAY FROM THERE, NICK. I'M SERIOUS.
CLICK

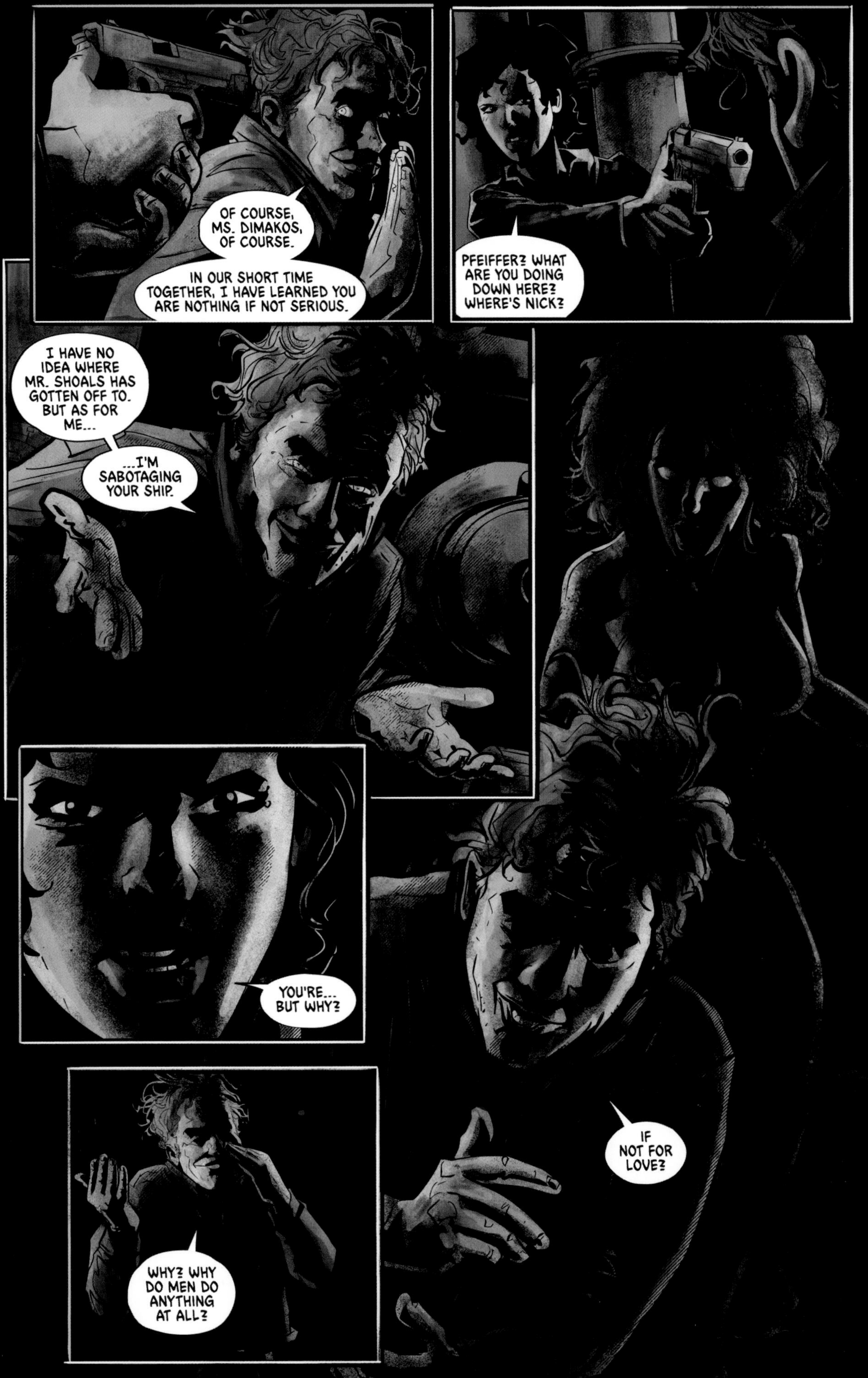

OF COURSE, MS. DIMAKOS, OF COURSE.
IN OUR SHORT TIME TOGETHER, I HAVE LEARNED YOU ARE NOTHING IF NOT SERIOUS.
PFEIFFER? WHAT ARE YOU DOING DOWN HERE? WHERE'S NICK?
I HAVE NO IDEA WHERE MR. SHOALS HAS GOTTEN OFF TO. BUT AS FOR ME...
...I'M SABOTAGING YOUR SHIP.
YOU'RE... BUT WHY?
WHY? WHY DO MEN DO ANYTHING AT ALL?
IF NOT FOR LOVE?

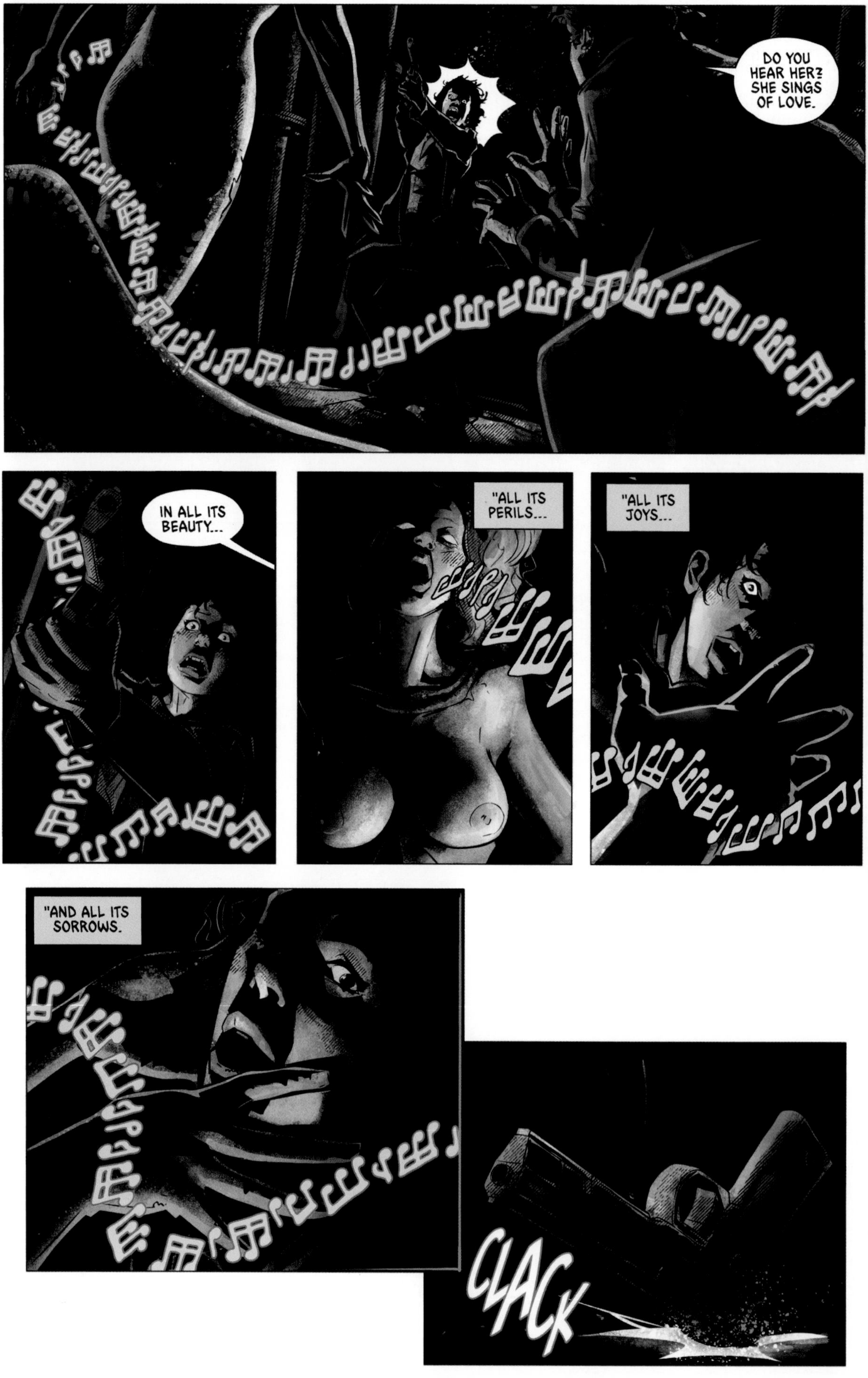
DO YOU HEAR HER? SHE SINGS OF LOVE.
IN ALL ITS BEAUTY...
"ALL ITS PERILS...
"ALL ITS JOYS...
"AND ALL ITS SORROWS.
CLACK

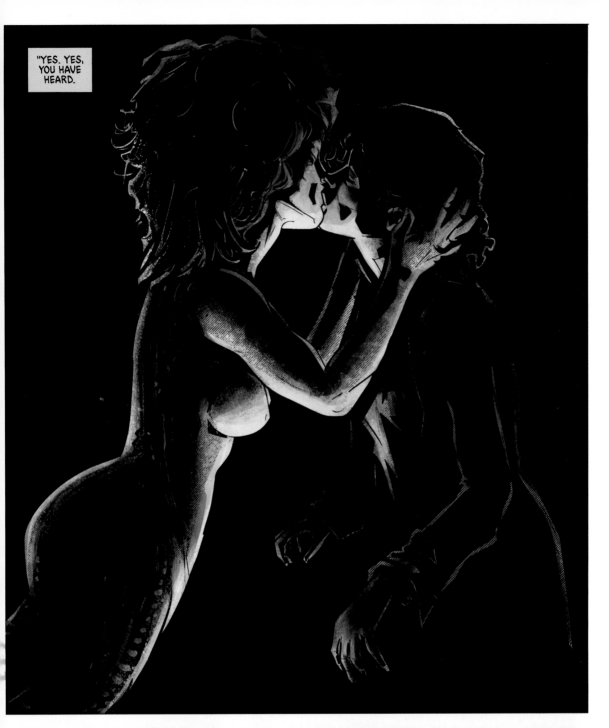

"YES. YES, YOU HAVE HEARD.

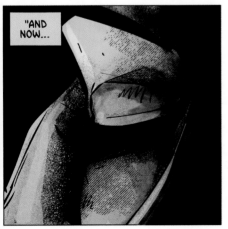

"AND NOW...

"NOW YOU WILL SEE."

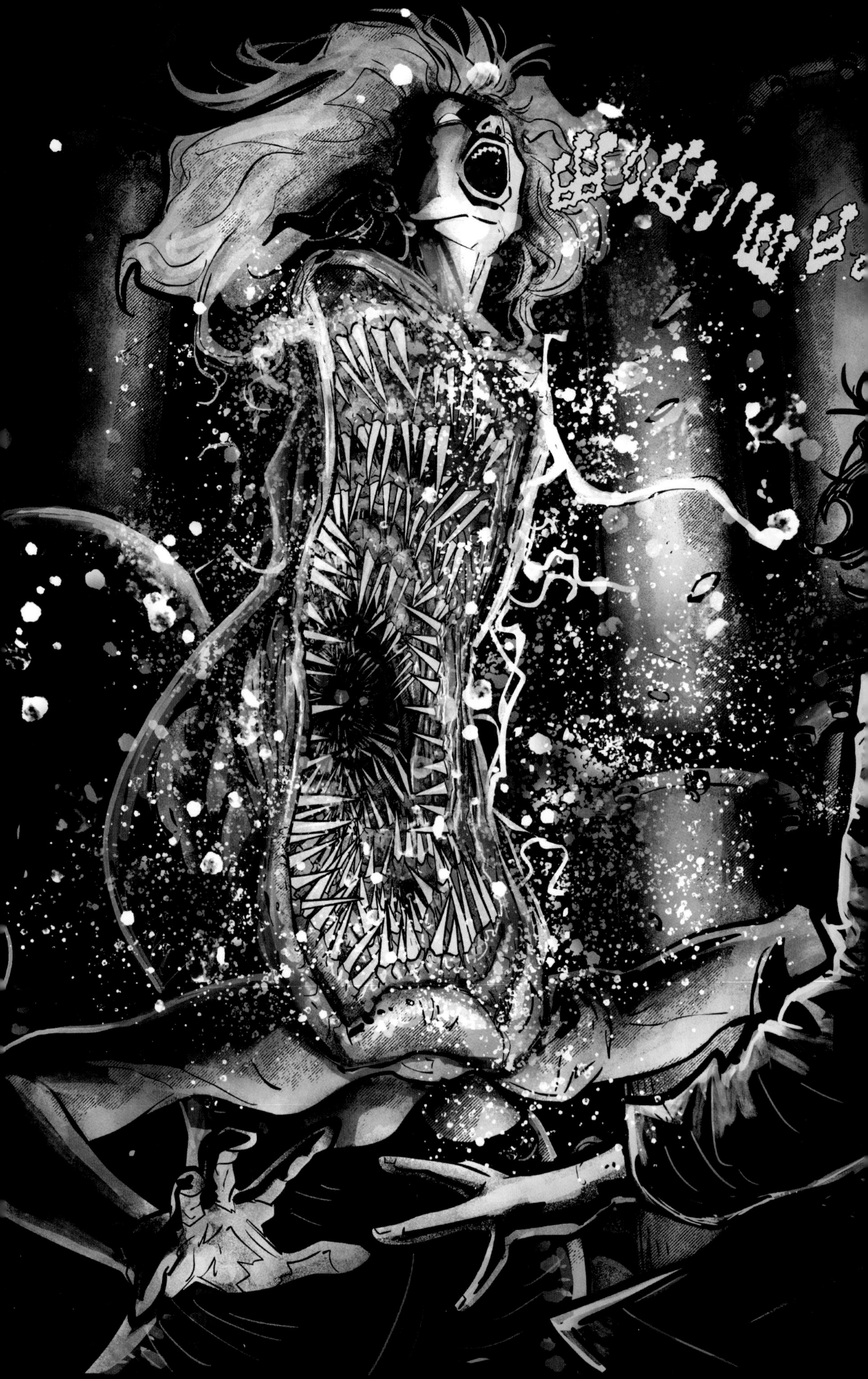

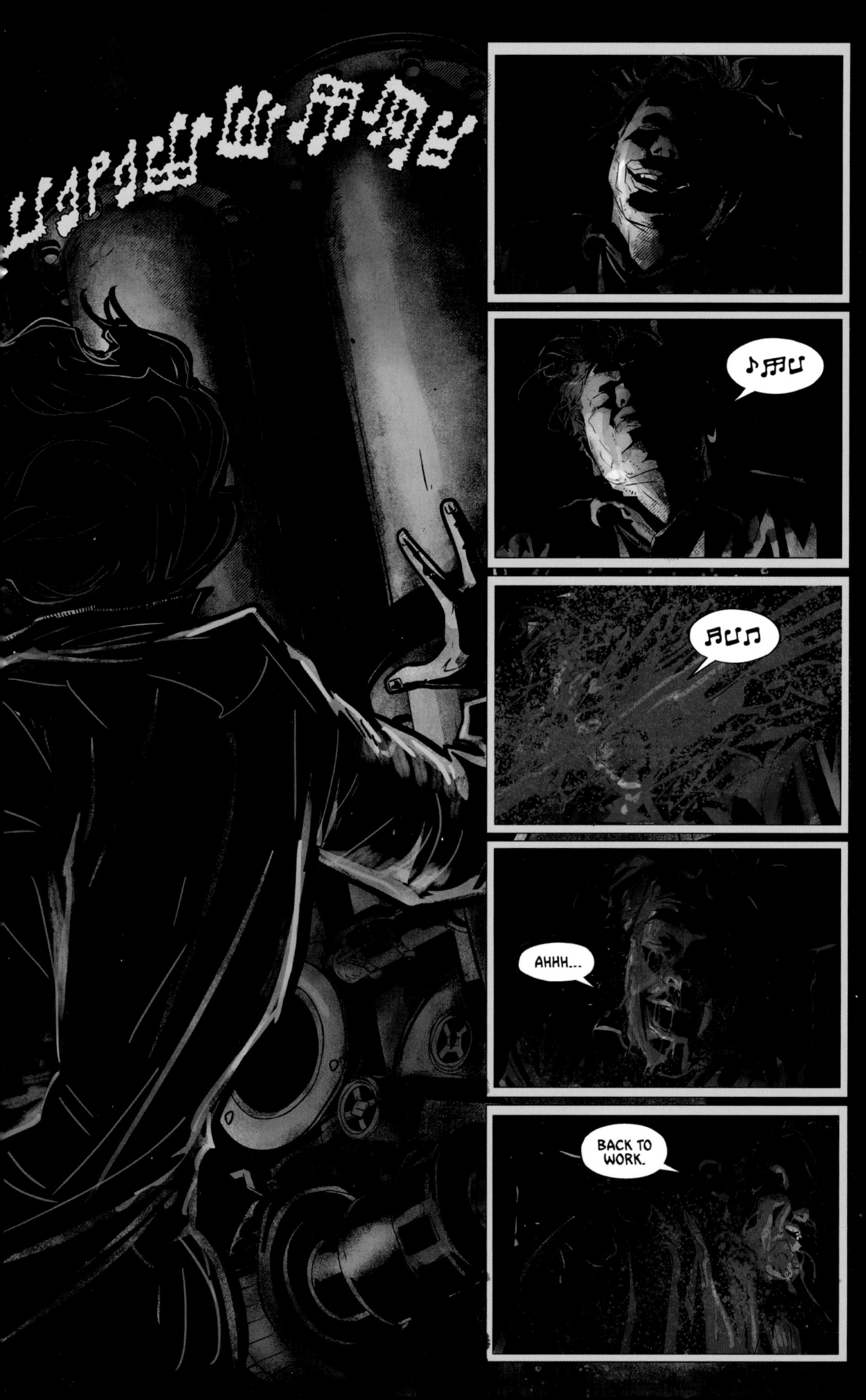
AHHH...
BACK TO WORK.

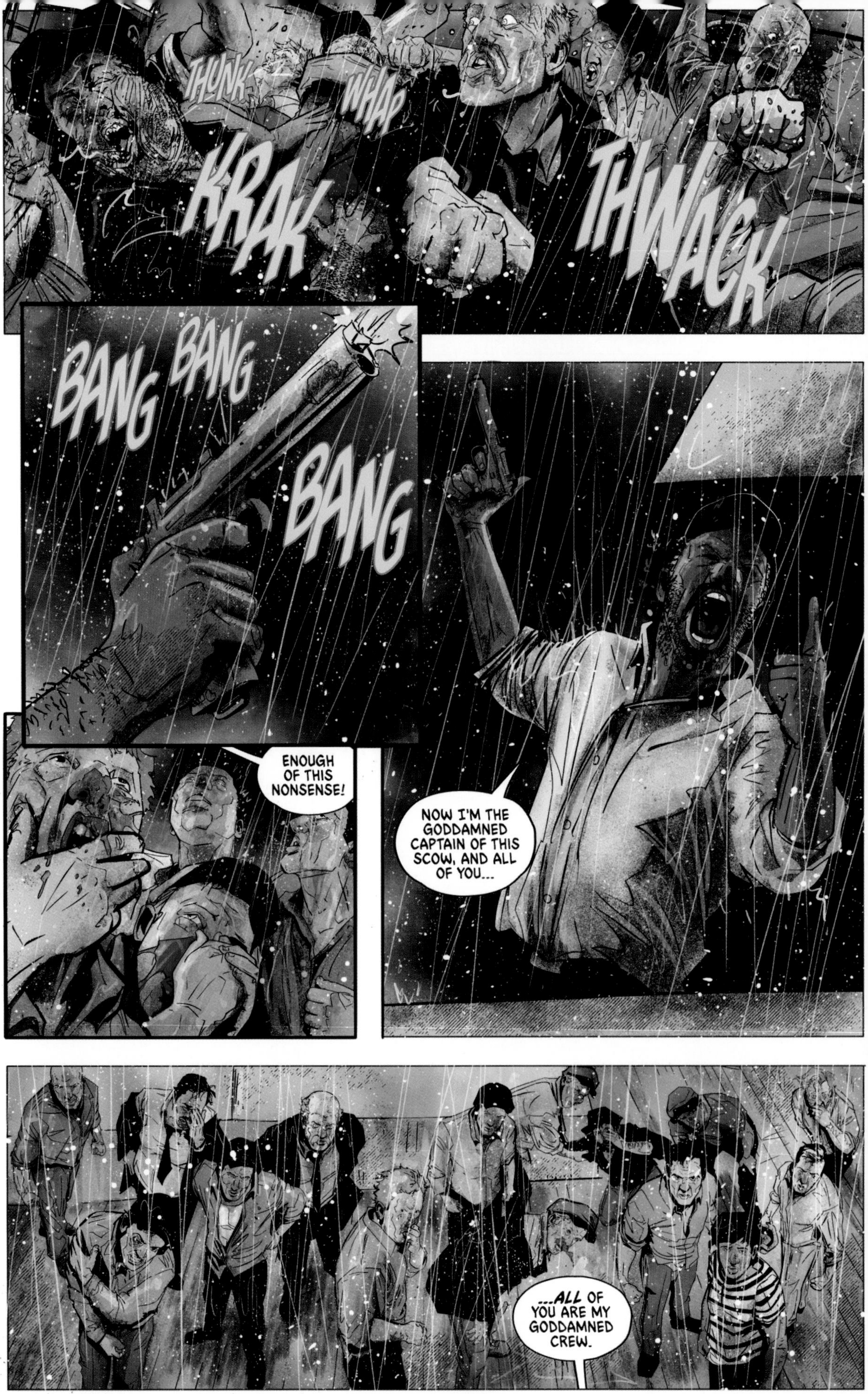
THUNK
WHAP
KRAK
THWACK
BANG BANG
BANG
ENOUGH OF THIS NONSENSE!
NOW I'M THE GODDAMNED CAPTAIN OF THIS SCOW, AND ALL OF YOU...
...ALL OF YOU ARE MY GODDAMNED CREW.

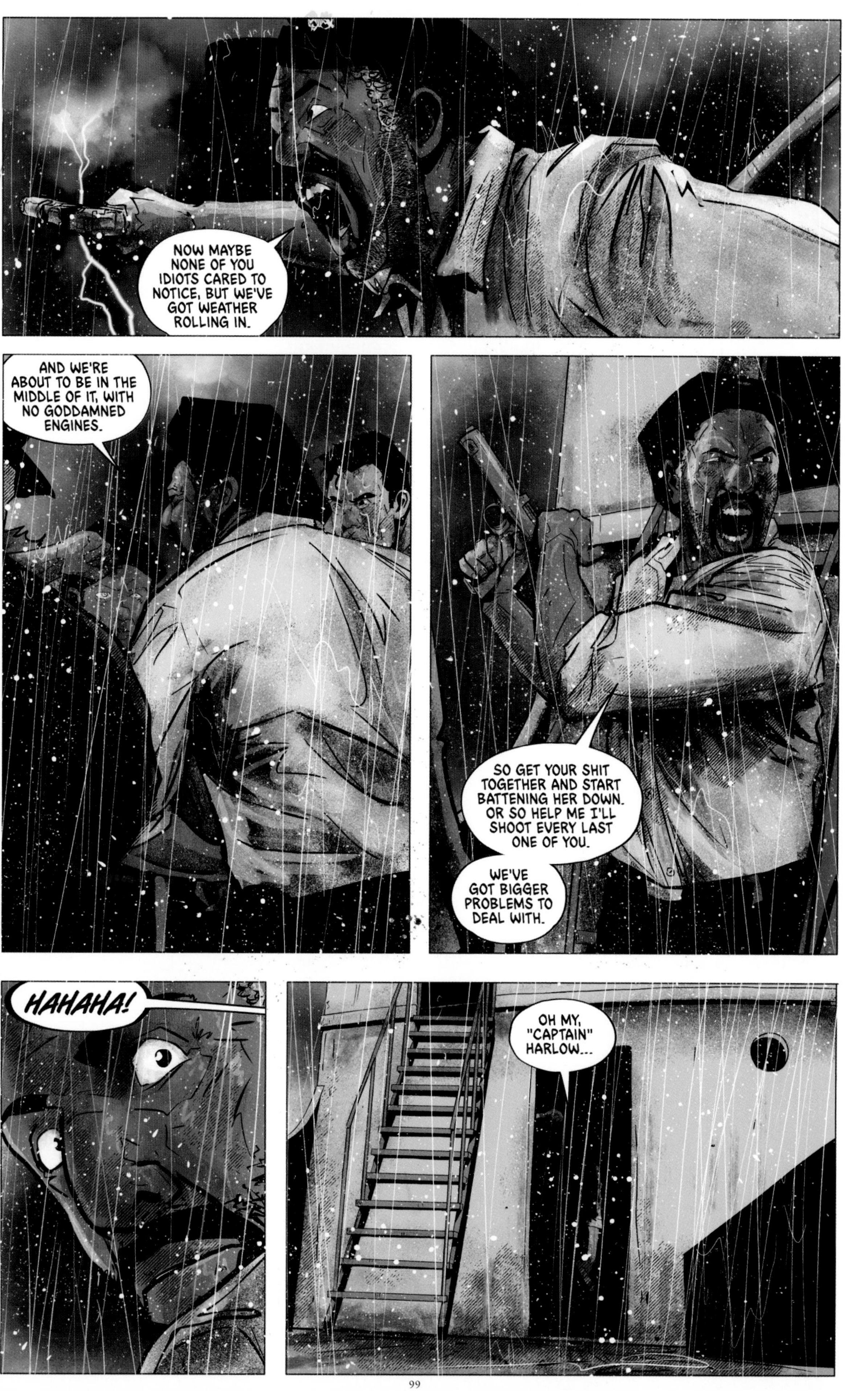
NOW MAYBE NONE OF YOU IDIOTS CARED TO NOTICE, BUT WE'VE GOT WEATHER ROLLING IN.
AND WE'RE ABOUT TO BE IN THE MIDDLE OF IT, WITH NO GODDAMNED ENGINES.
SO GET YOUR SHIT TOGETHER AND START BATTENING HER DOWN. OR SO HELP ME I'LL SHOOT EVERY LAST ONE OF YOU.
WE'VE GOT BIGGER PROBLEMS TO DEAL WITH.
HAHAHA!
OH MY, "CAPTAIN" HARLOW...

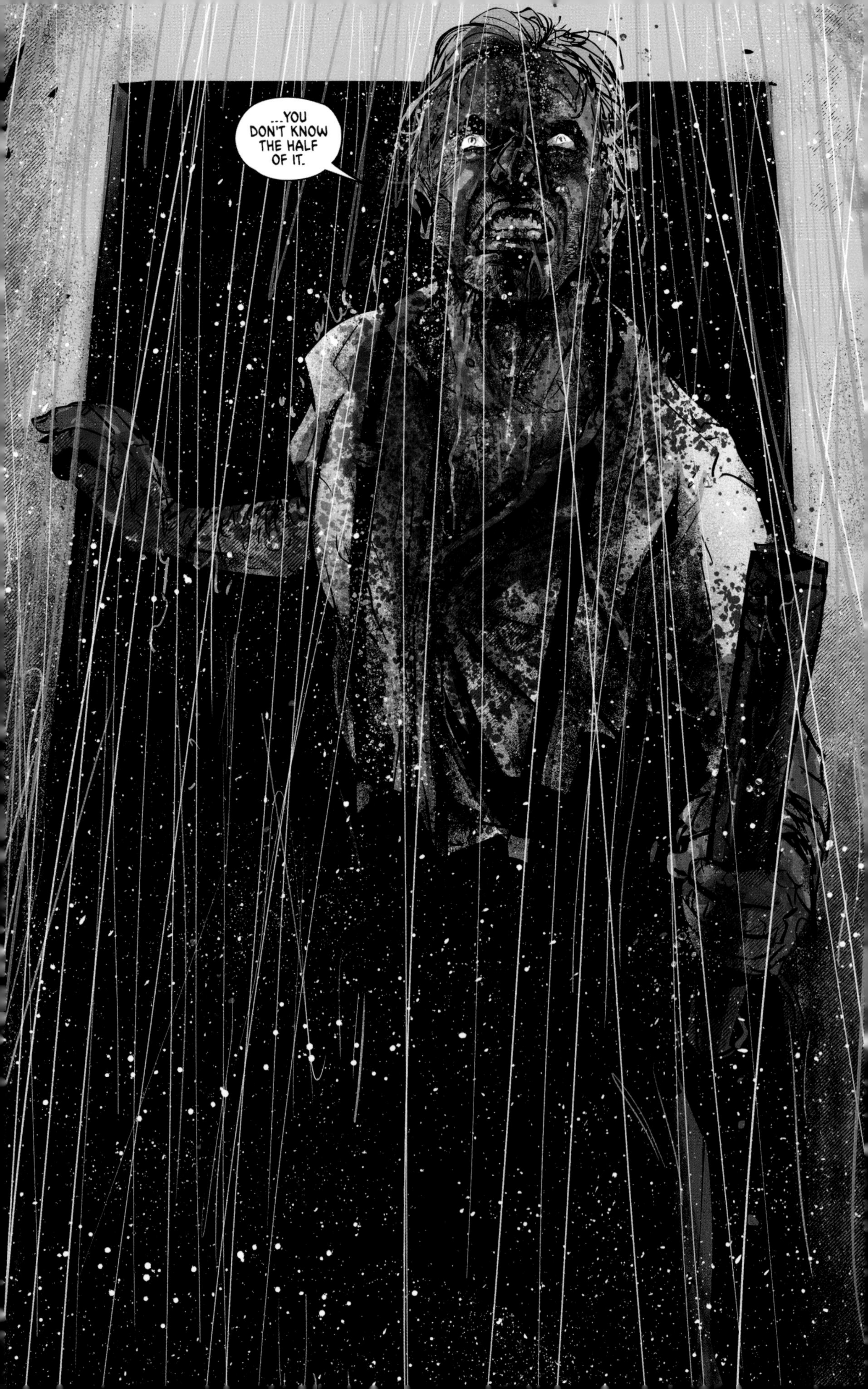
...YOU DON'T KNOW THE HALF OF IT.

Art by
BRIAN LEVEL

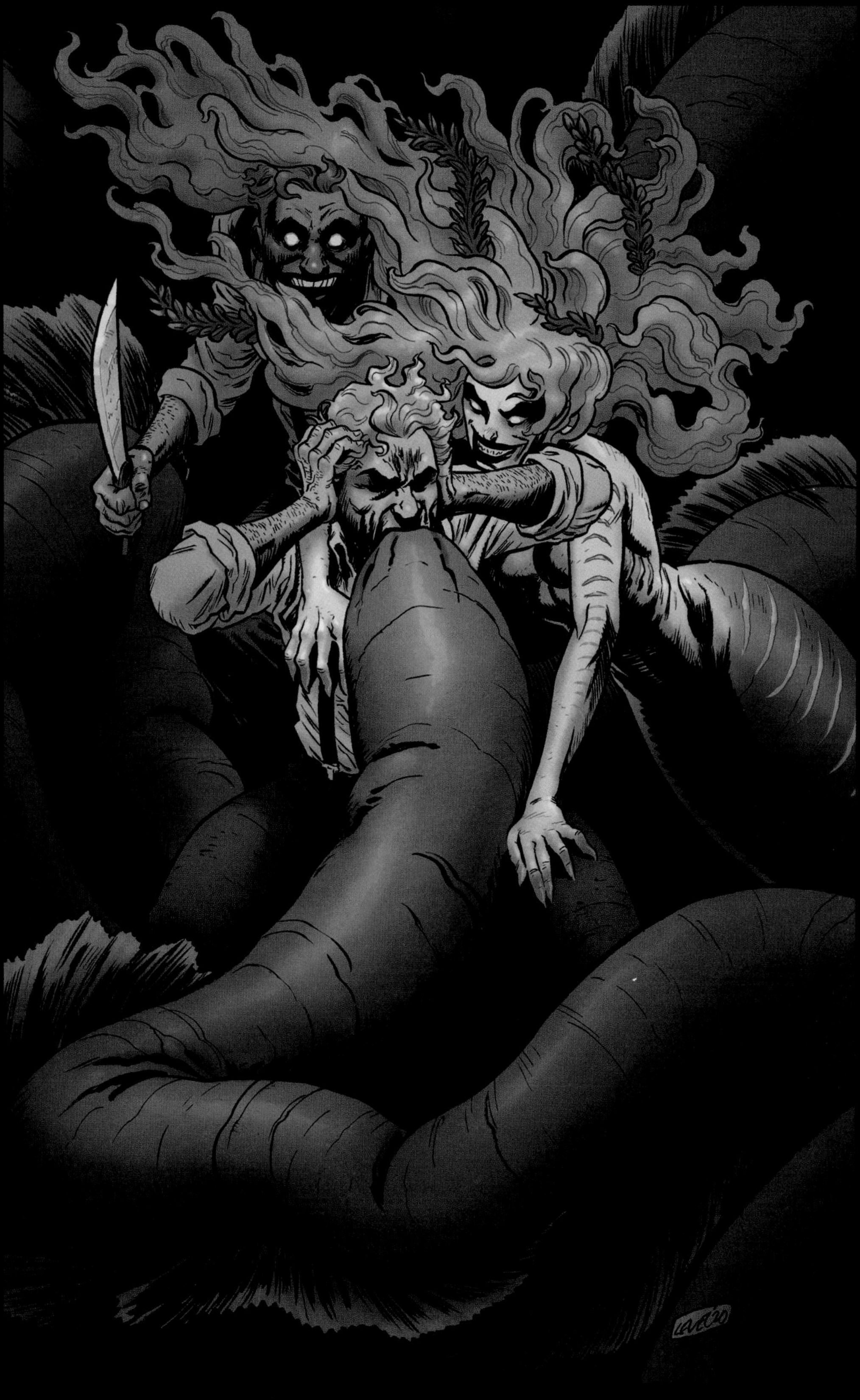

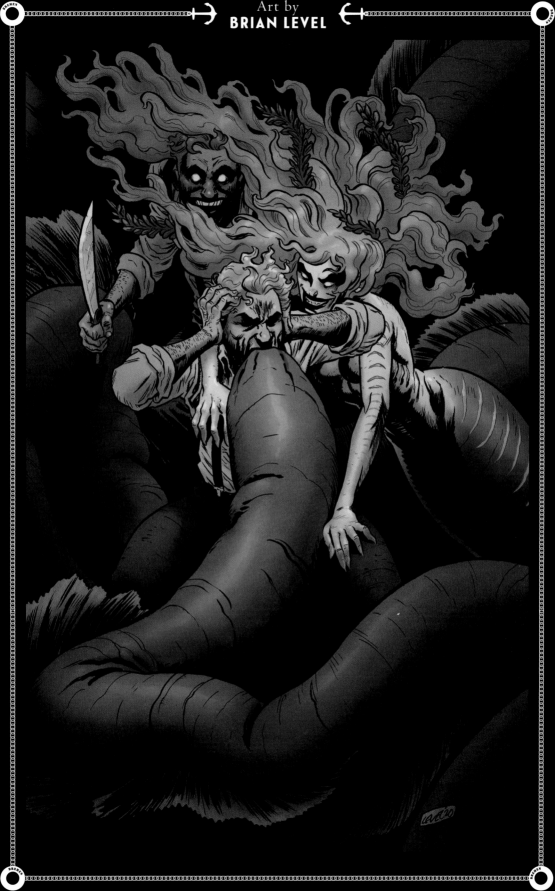

Art by
ALEX CORMACK

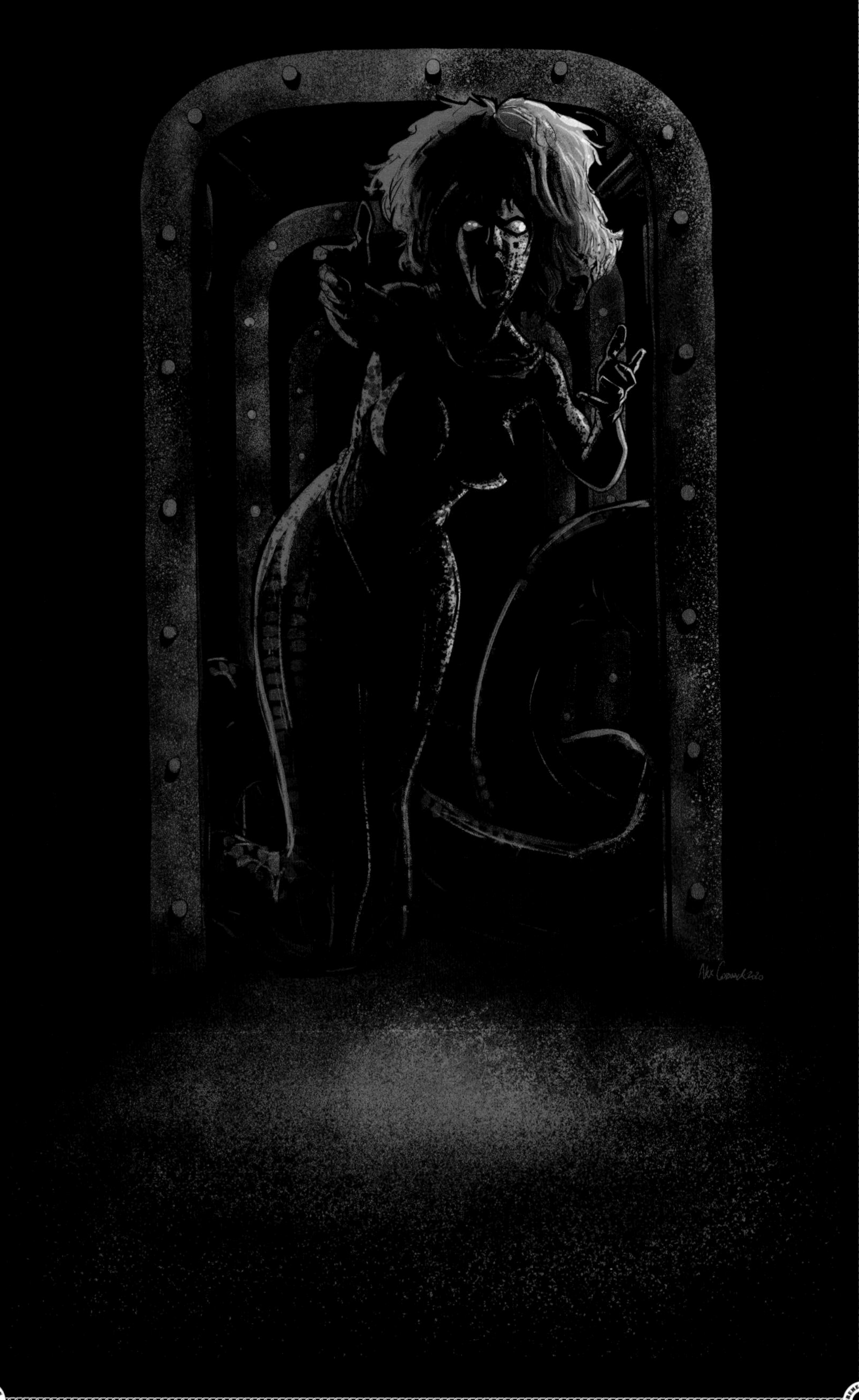

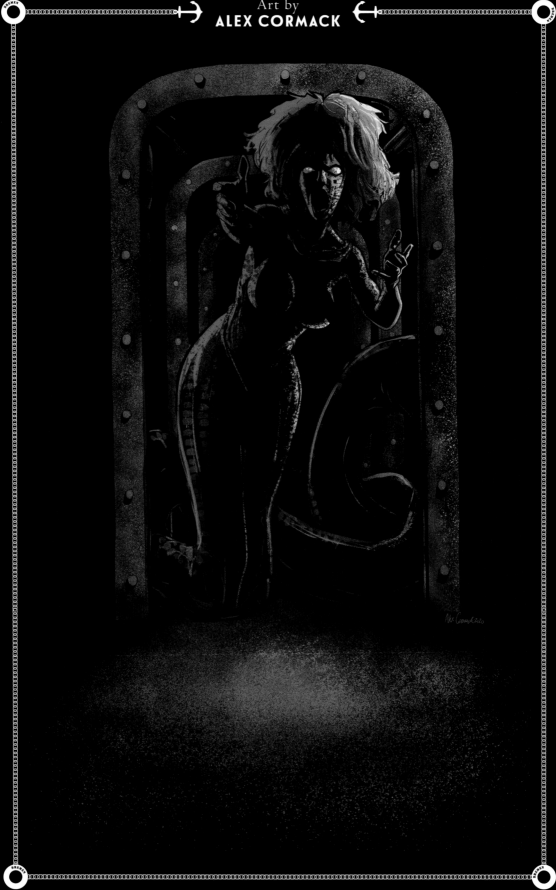

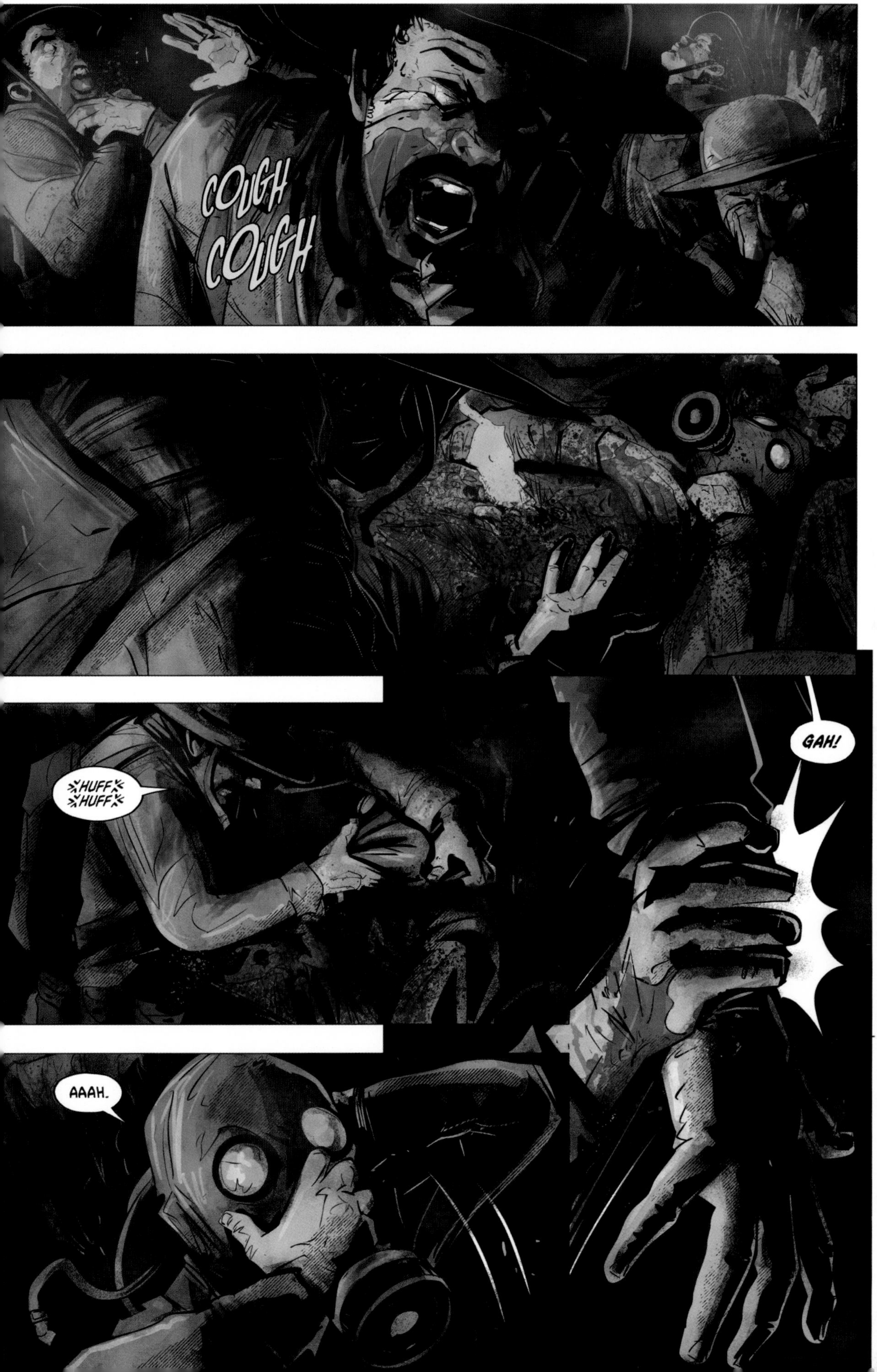
COUGH
COUGH
HUFF HUFF
GAH!
AAAH.

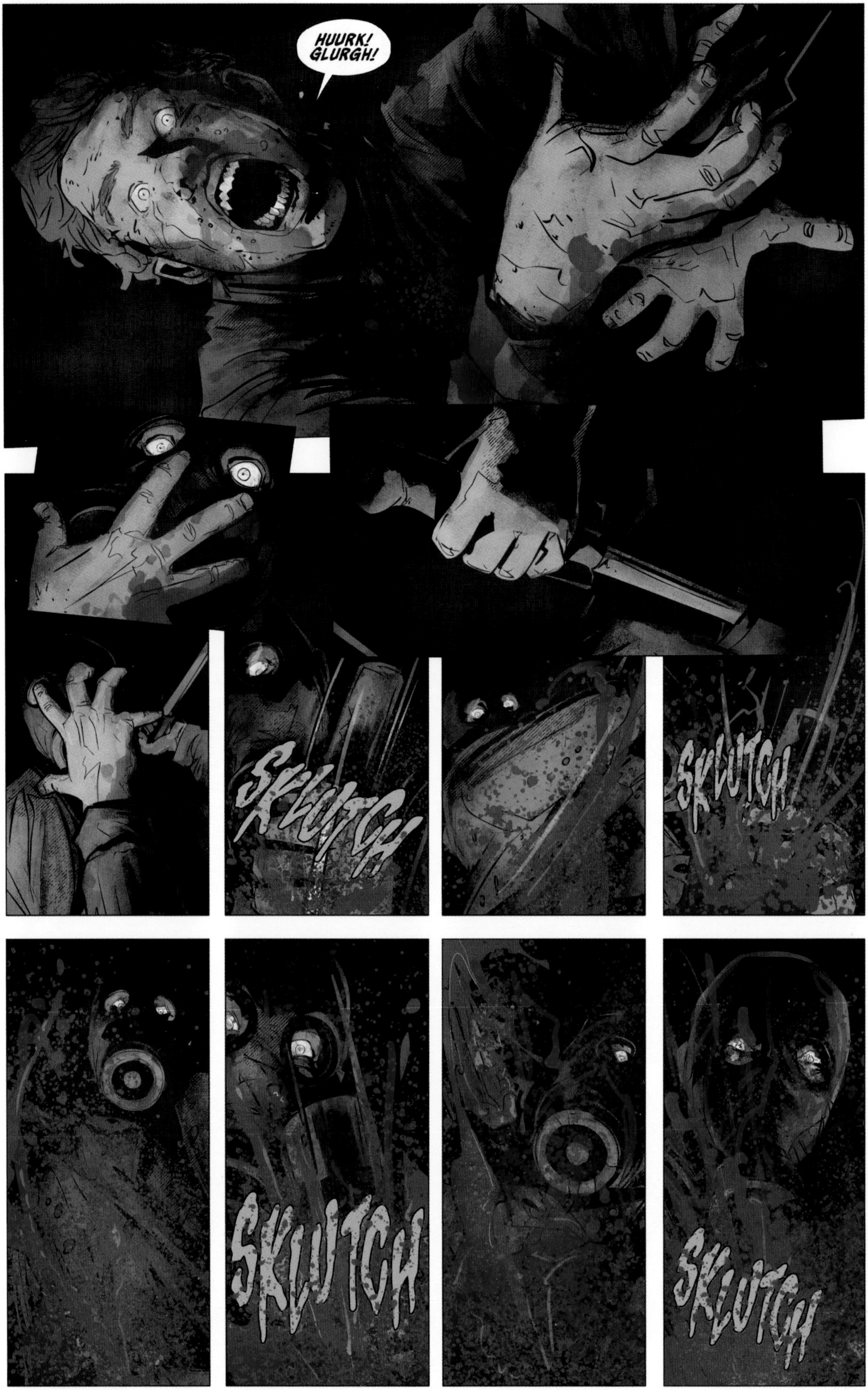
HUURK! GLURGH!
SKLUTCH
SKLUTCH
SKLUTCH
SKLUTCH

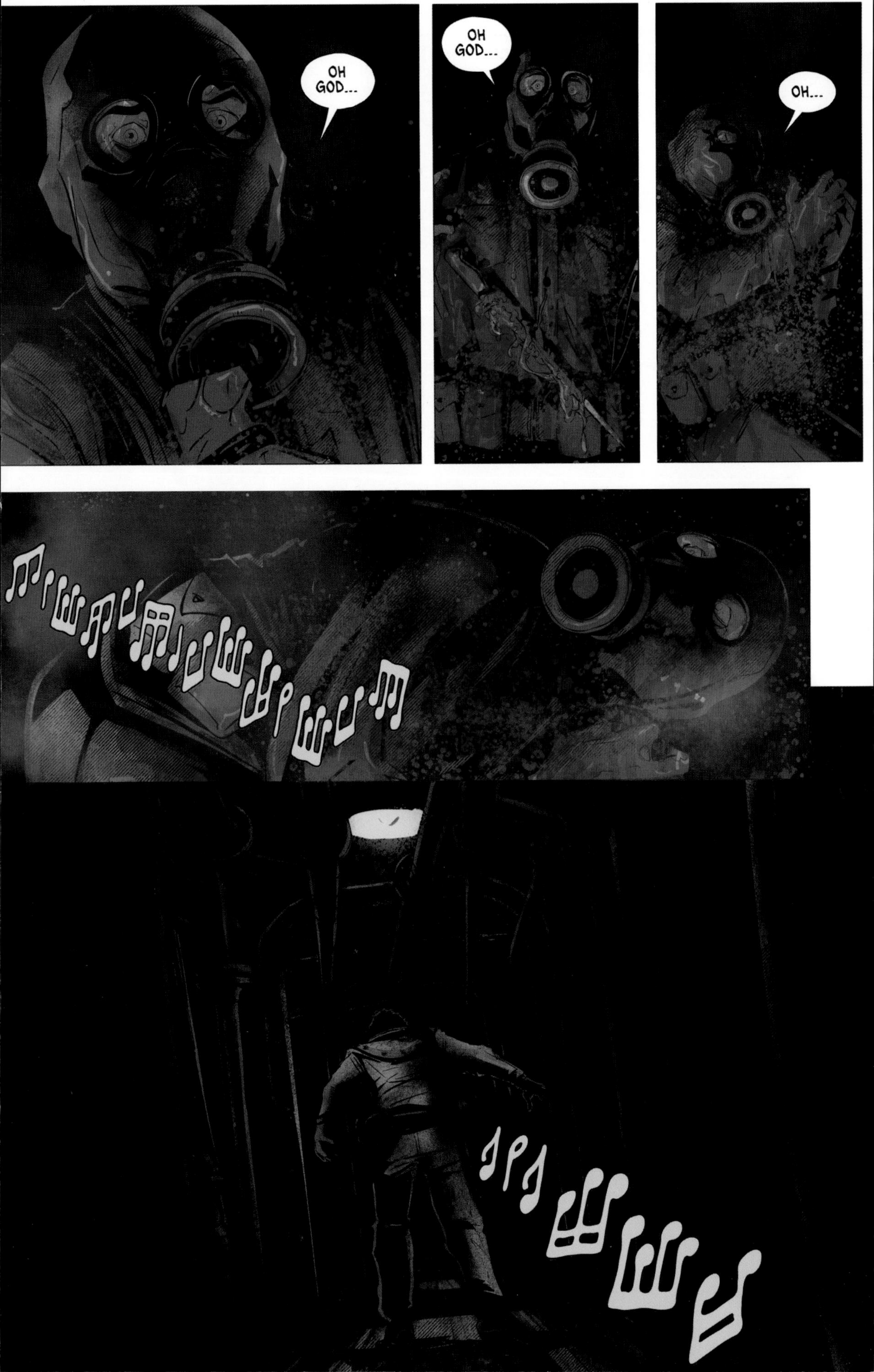
OH GOD...
OH GOD...
OH...

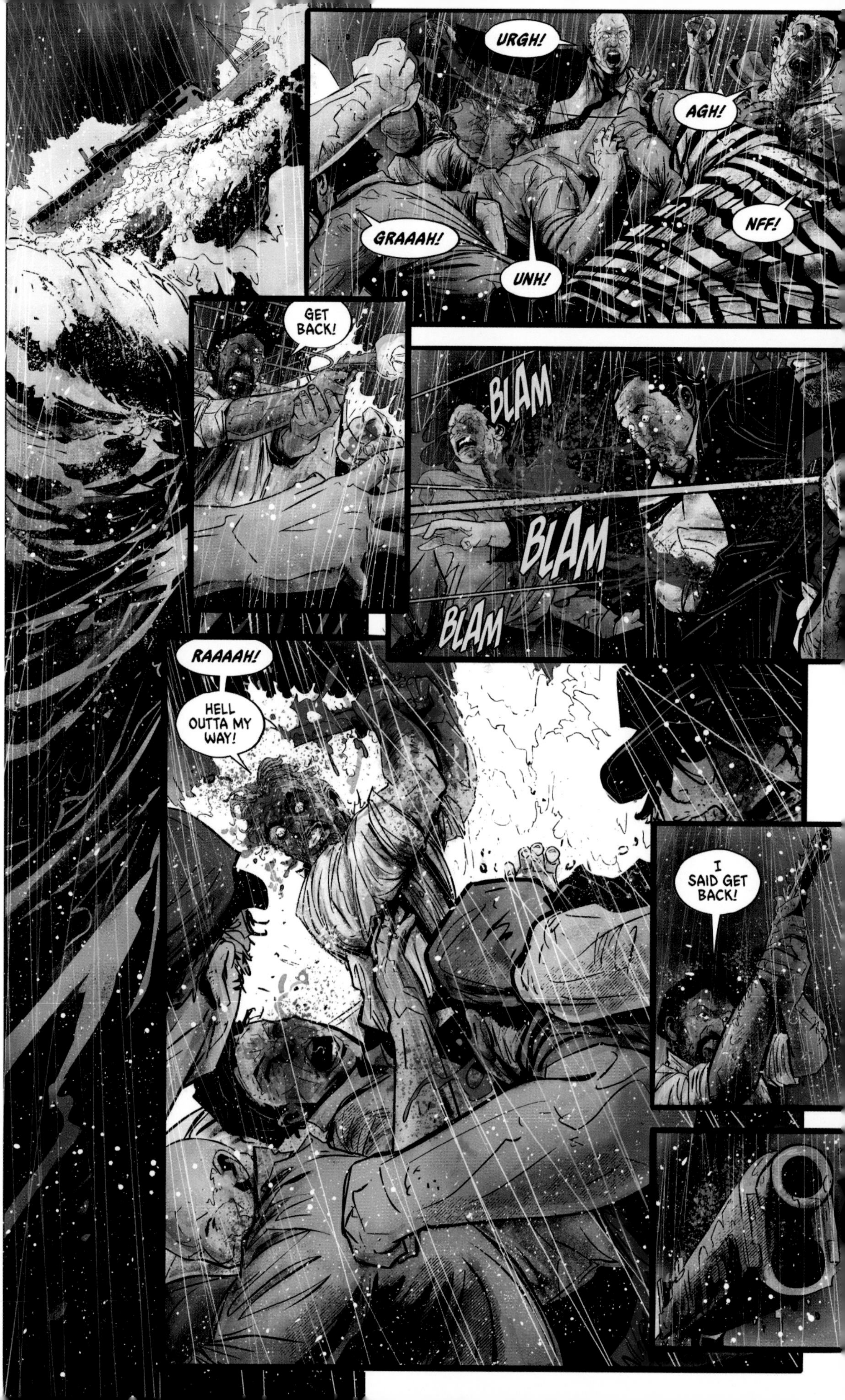
URGH!
AGH!
GRAAAH!
UNH!
NFF!
GET BACK!
BLAM
BLAM
BLAM
RAAAAH!
HELL OUTTA MY WAY!
I SAID GET BACK!

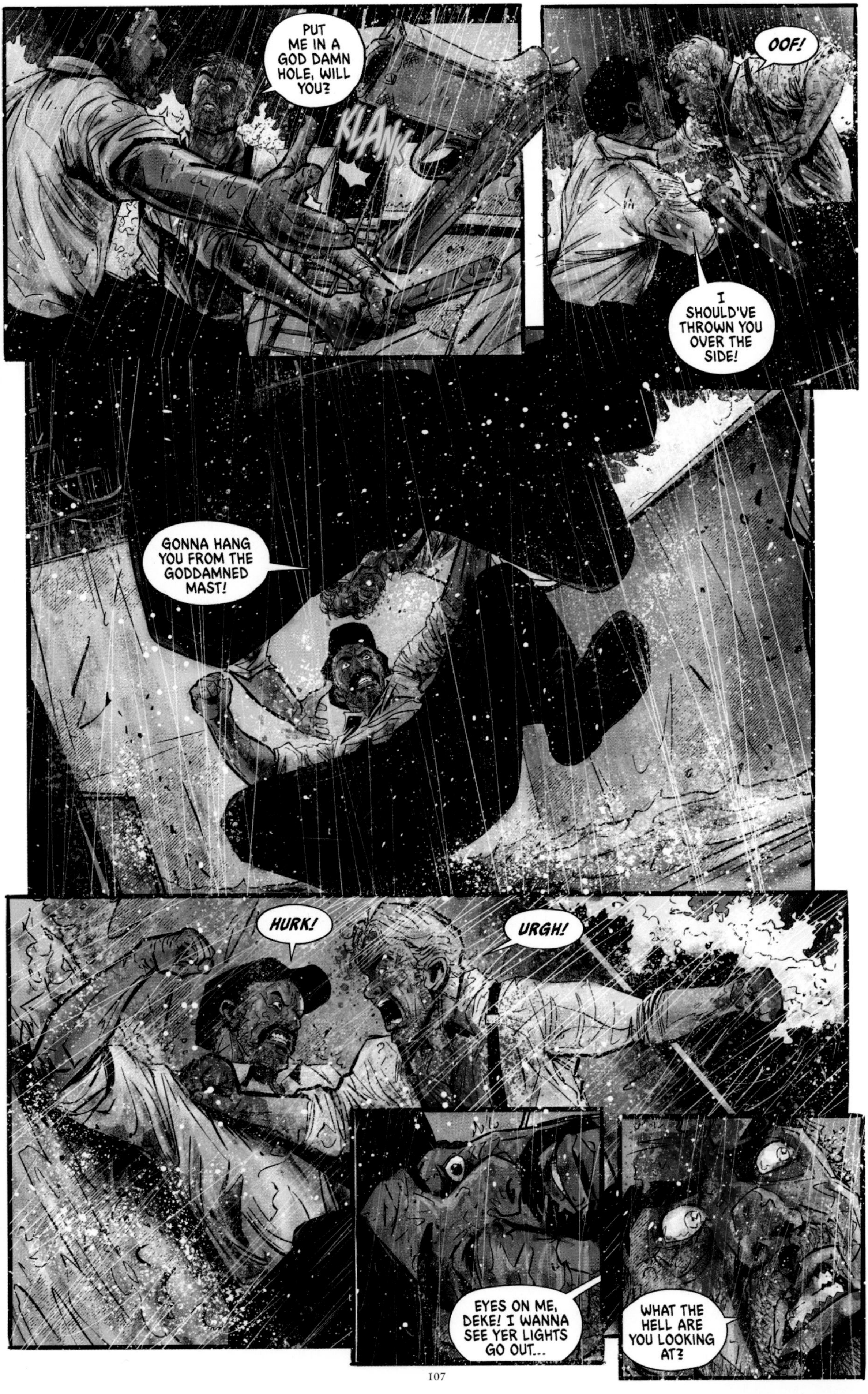
PUT ME IN A GOD DAMN HOLE, WILL YOU?
KLANK
OOF!
I SHOULD'VE THROWN YOU OVER THE SIDE!
GONNA HANG YOU FROM THE GODDAMNED MAST!
HURK!
URGH!
EYES ON ME, DEKE! I WANNA SEE YER LIGHTS GO OUT...
WHAT THE HELL ARE YOU LOOKING AT?

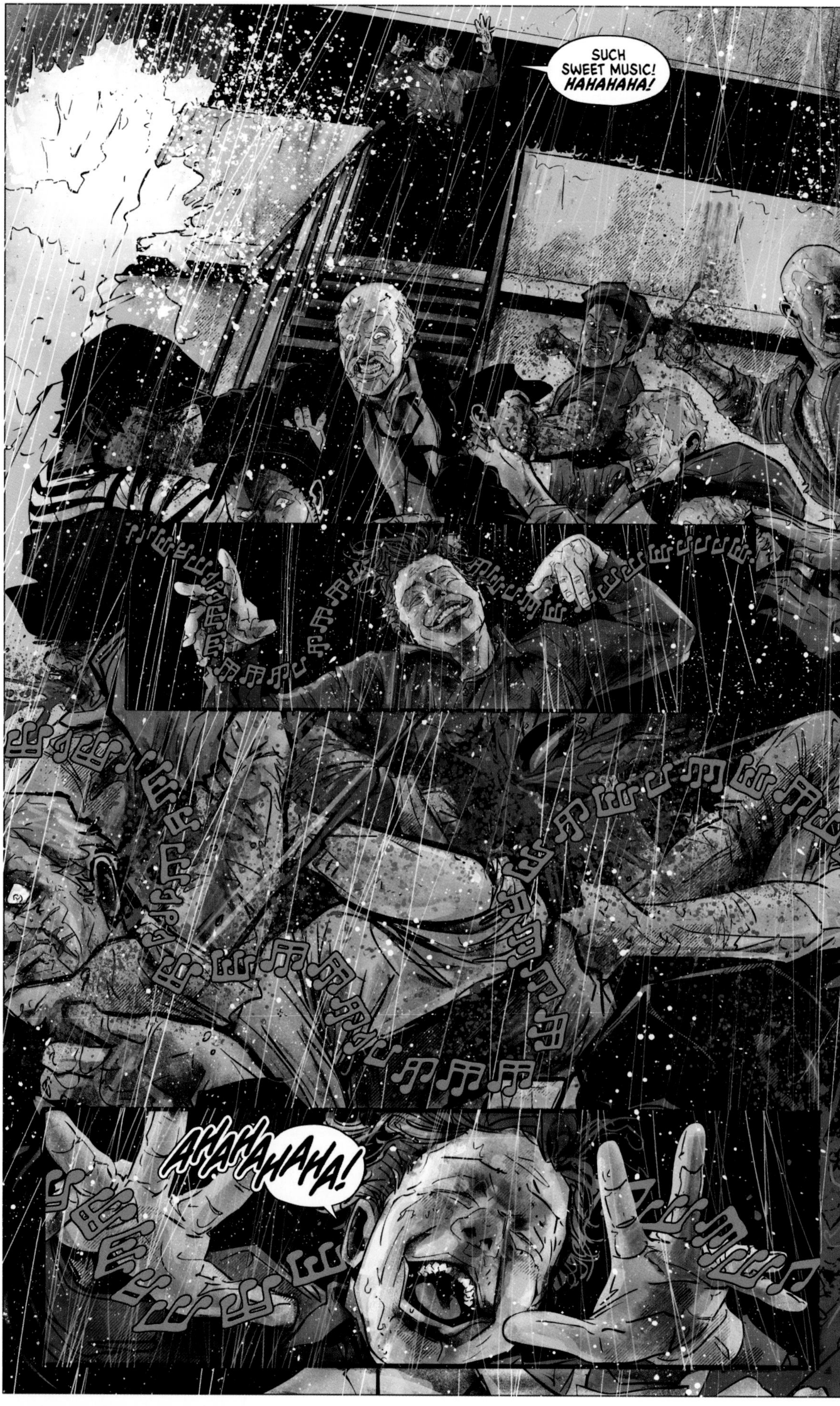
SUCH SWEET MUSIC! HAHAHAHA!
AHAHAHAHAHA!

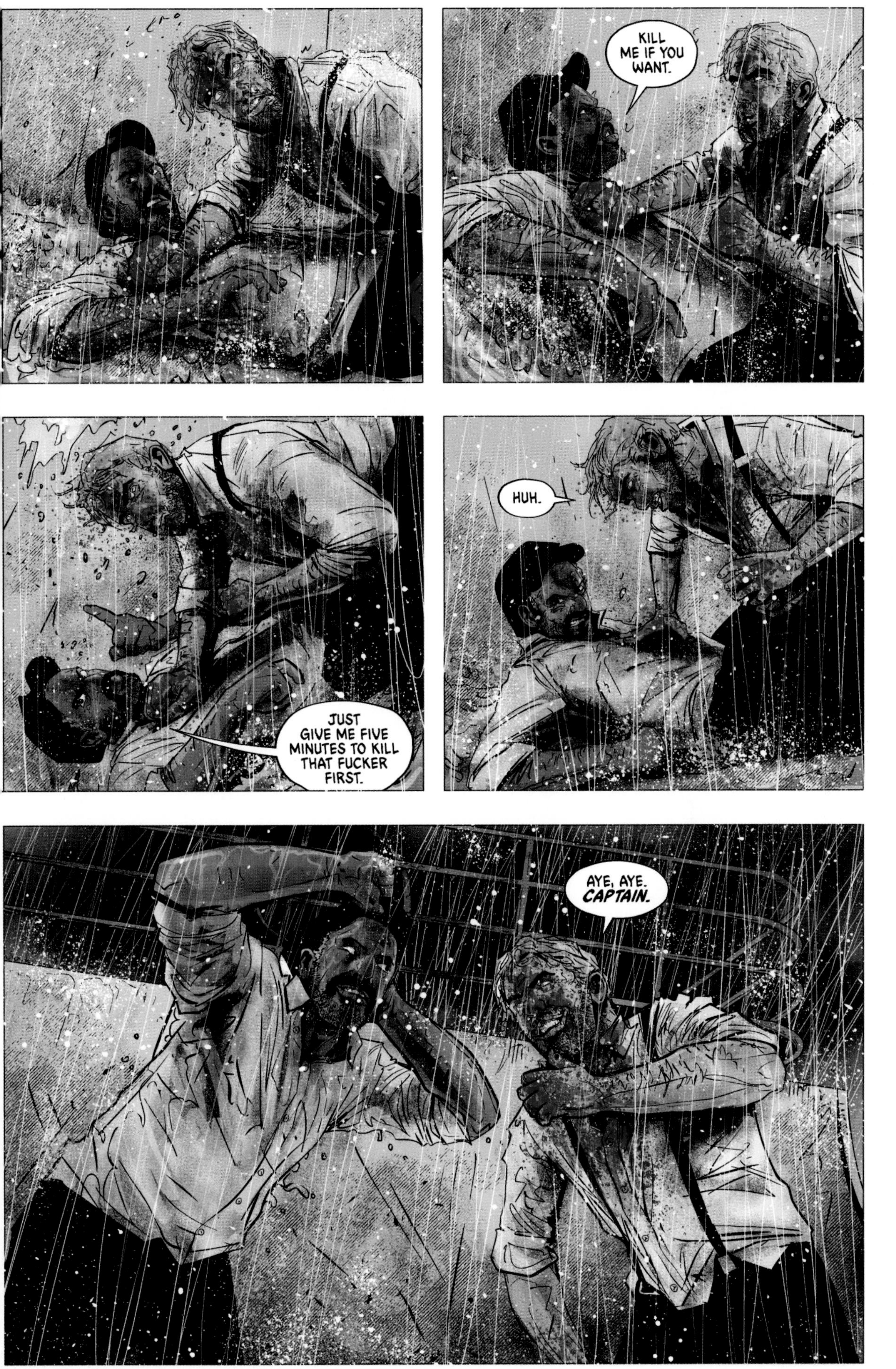
KILL ME IF YOU WANT.
JUST GIVE ME FIVE MINUTES TO KILL THAT FUCKER FIRST.
HUH.
AYE, AYE. CAPTAIN.

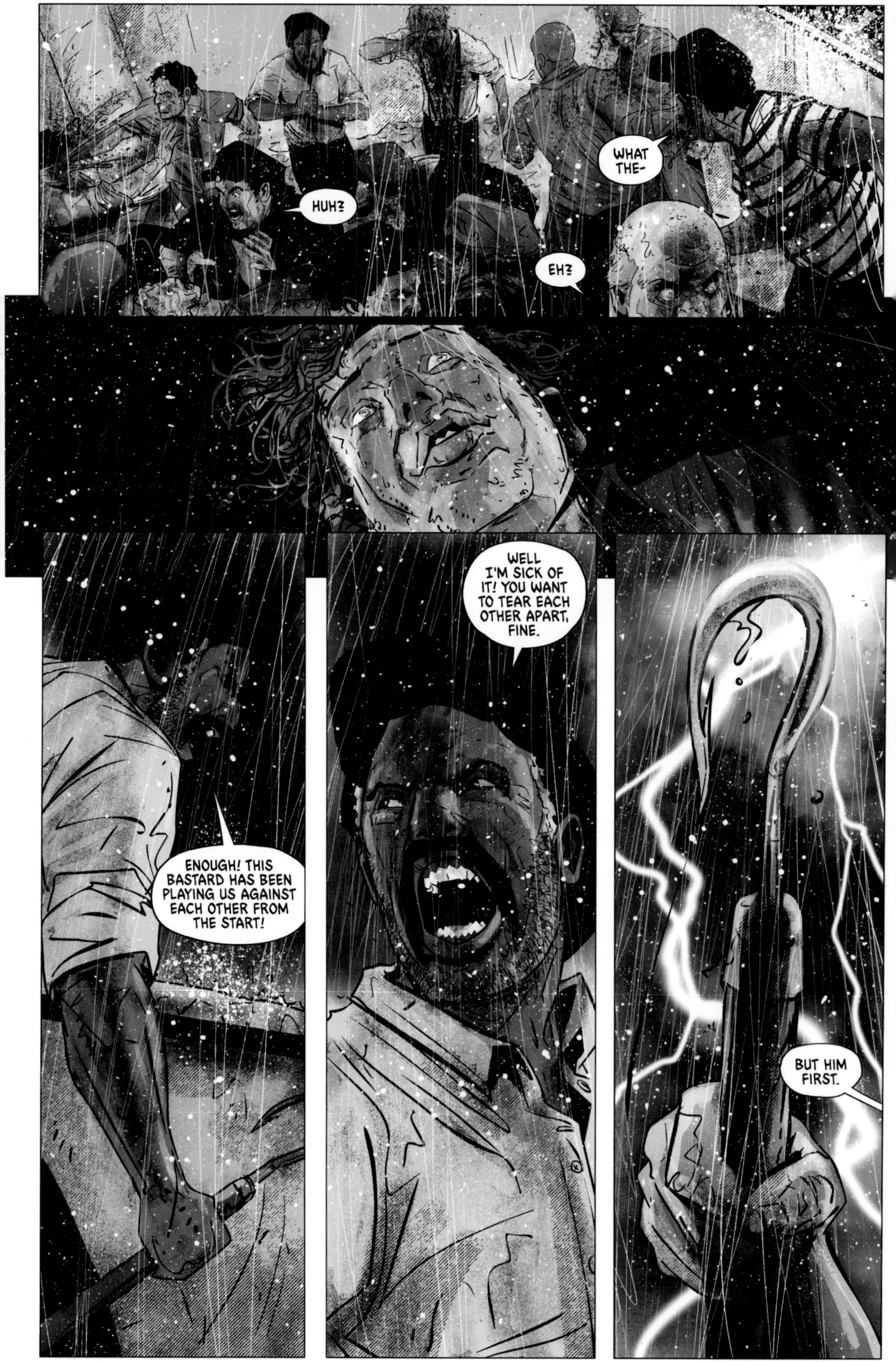
HUH?
WHAT THE-
EH?
ENOUGH! THIS BASTARD HAS BEEN PLAYING US AGAINST EACH OTHER FROM THE START!
WELL I'M SICK OF IT! YOU WANT TO TEAR EACH OTHER APART, FINE.
BUT HIM FIRST.

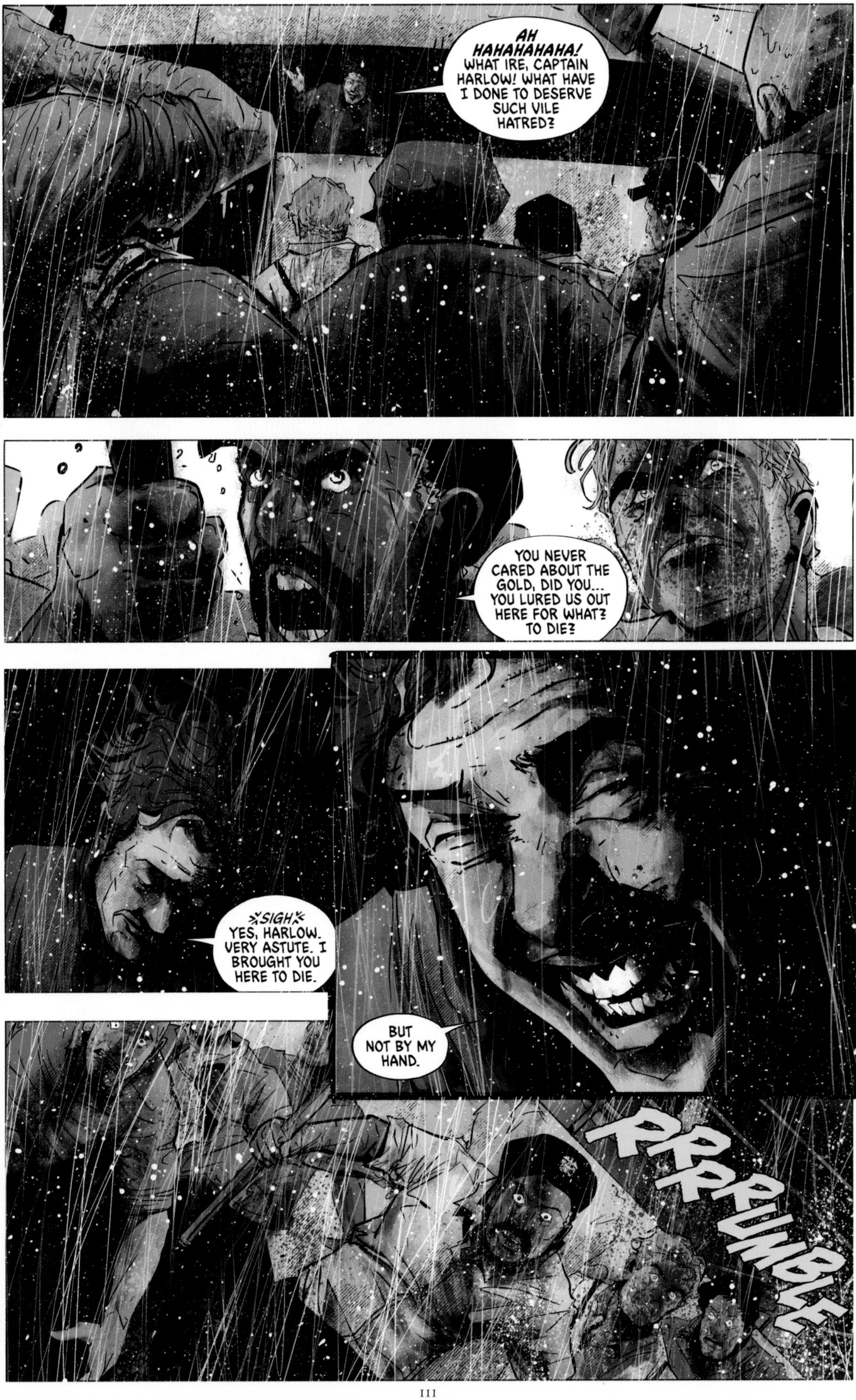
AH HAHAHAHAHA! WHAT IRE, CAPTAIN HARLOW! WHAT HAVE I DONE TO DESERVE SUCH VILE HATRED?
YOU NEVER CARED ABOUT THE GOLD, DID YOU... YOU LURED US OUT HERE FOR WHAT? TO DIE?
SIGH YES, HARLOW. VERY ASTUTE. I BROUGHT YOU HERE TO DIE.
BUT NOT BY MY HAND.
RRRUMBLE

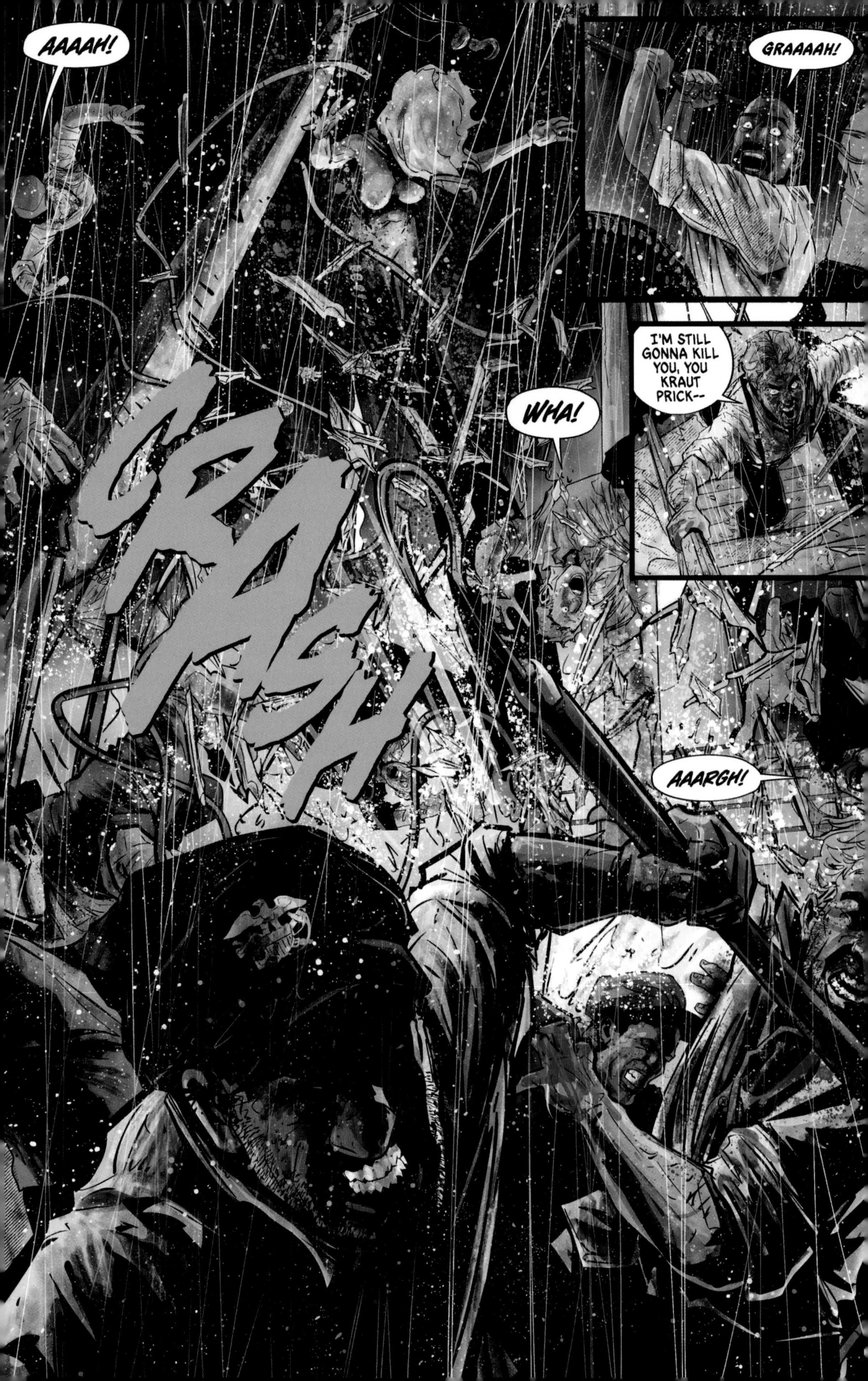
AAAAH!
GRAAAAH!
I'M STILL GONNA KILL YOU, YOU KRAUT PRICK--
WHA!
CRASH
AAARGH!

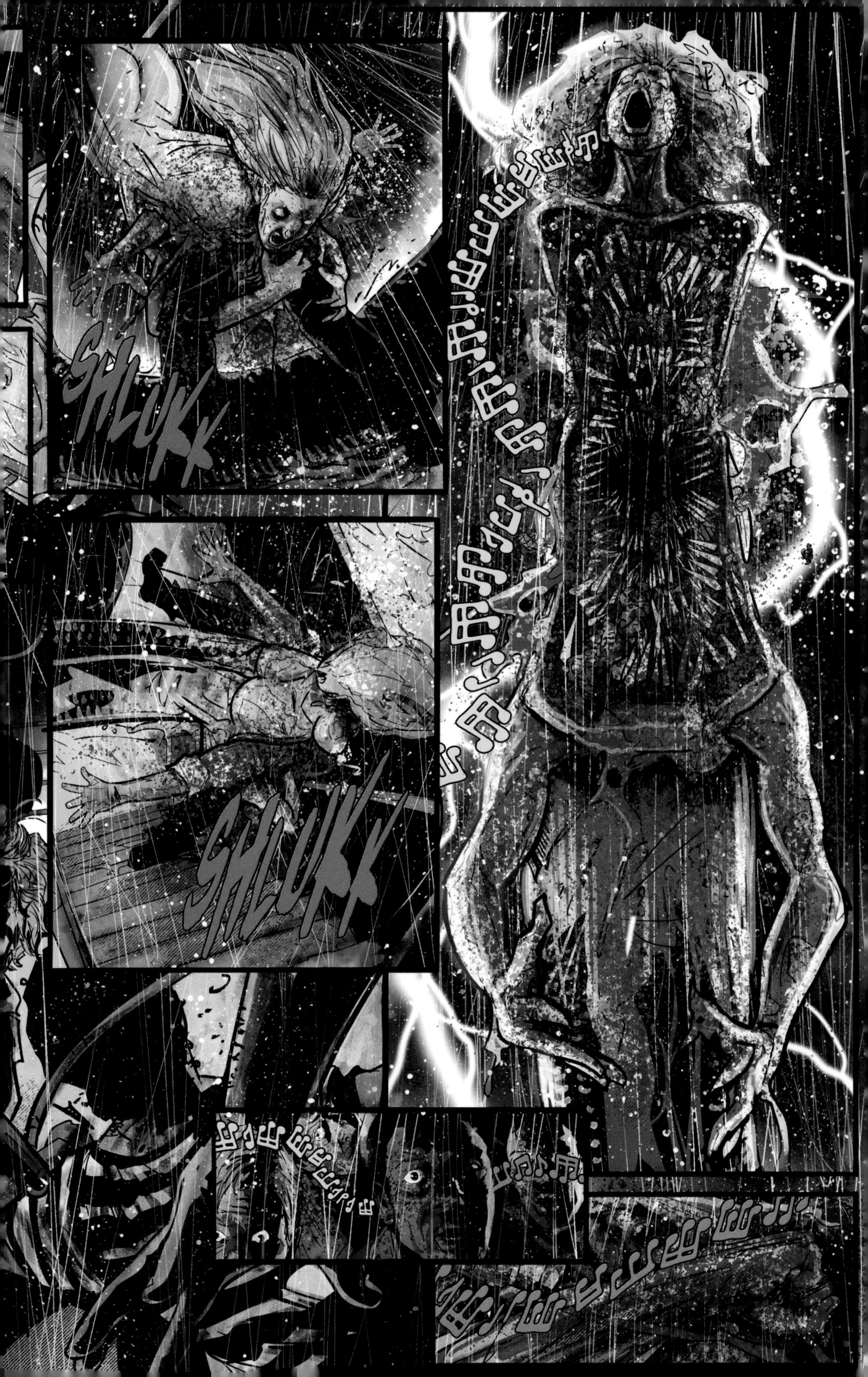
SHLUKK
SHLUKK

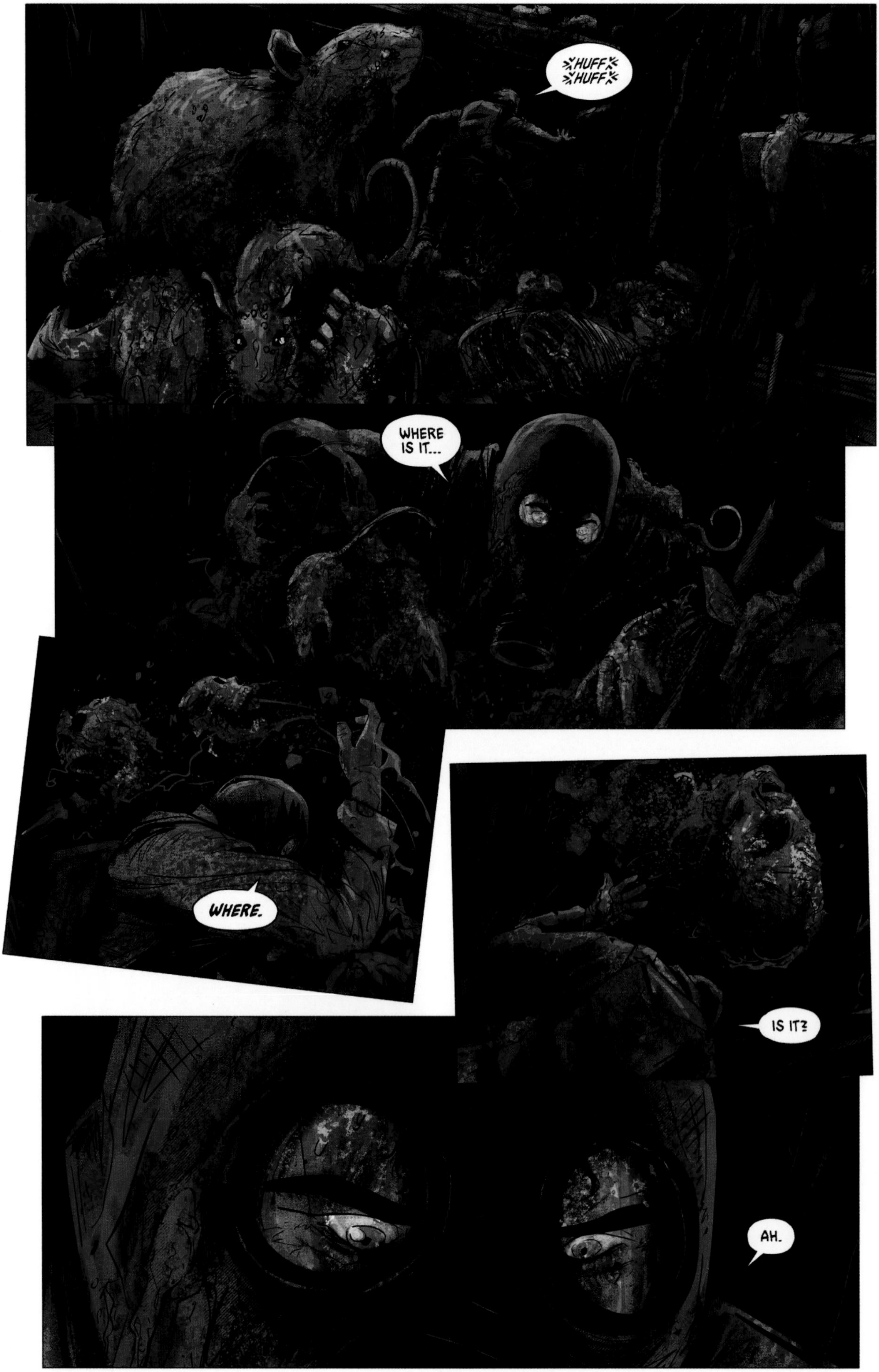

HUFF *HUFF*
WHERE IS IT...
WHERE.
IS IT?
AH.

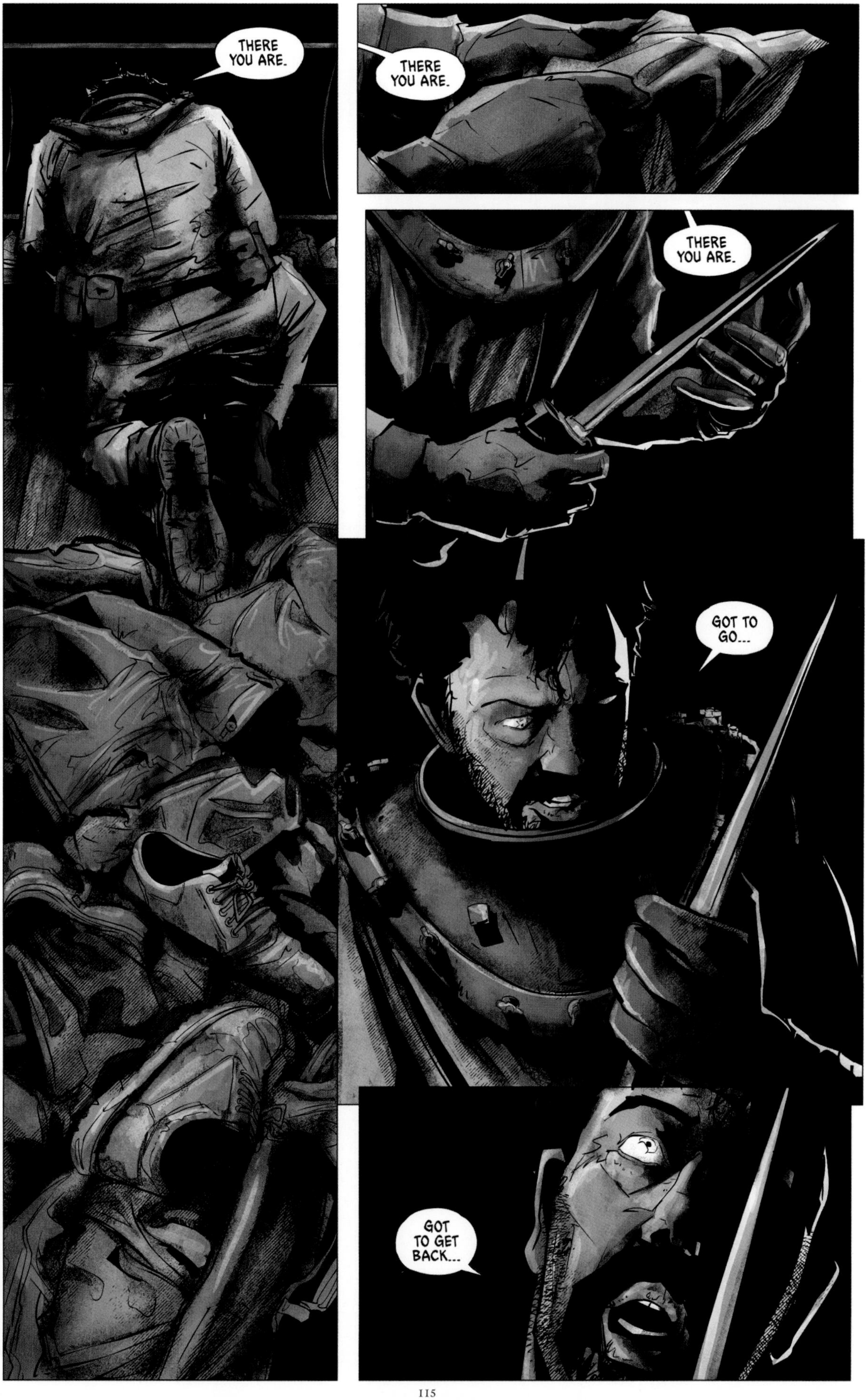
THERE YOU ARE.
THERE YOU ARE.
THERE YOU ARE.
GOT TO GO...
GOT TO GET BACK...

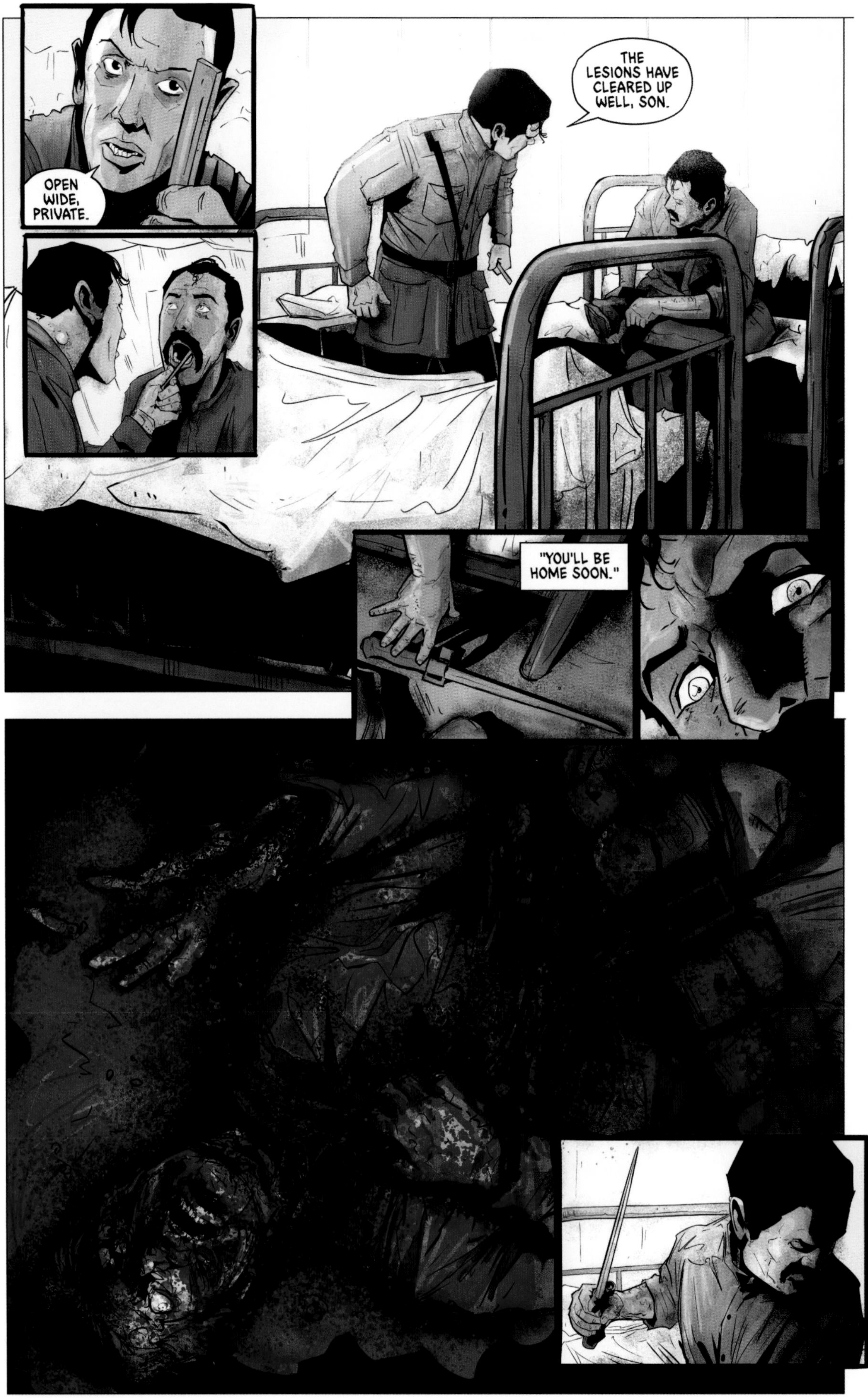
OPEN WIDE, PRIVATE.
THE LESIONS HAVE CLEARED UP WELL, SON.
"YOU'LL BE HOME SOON."

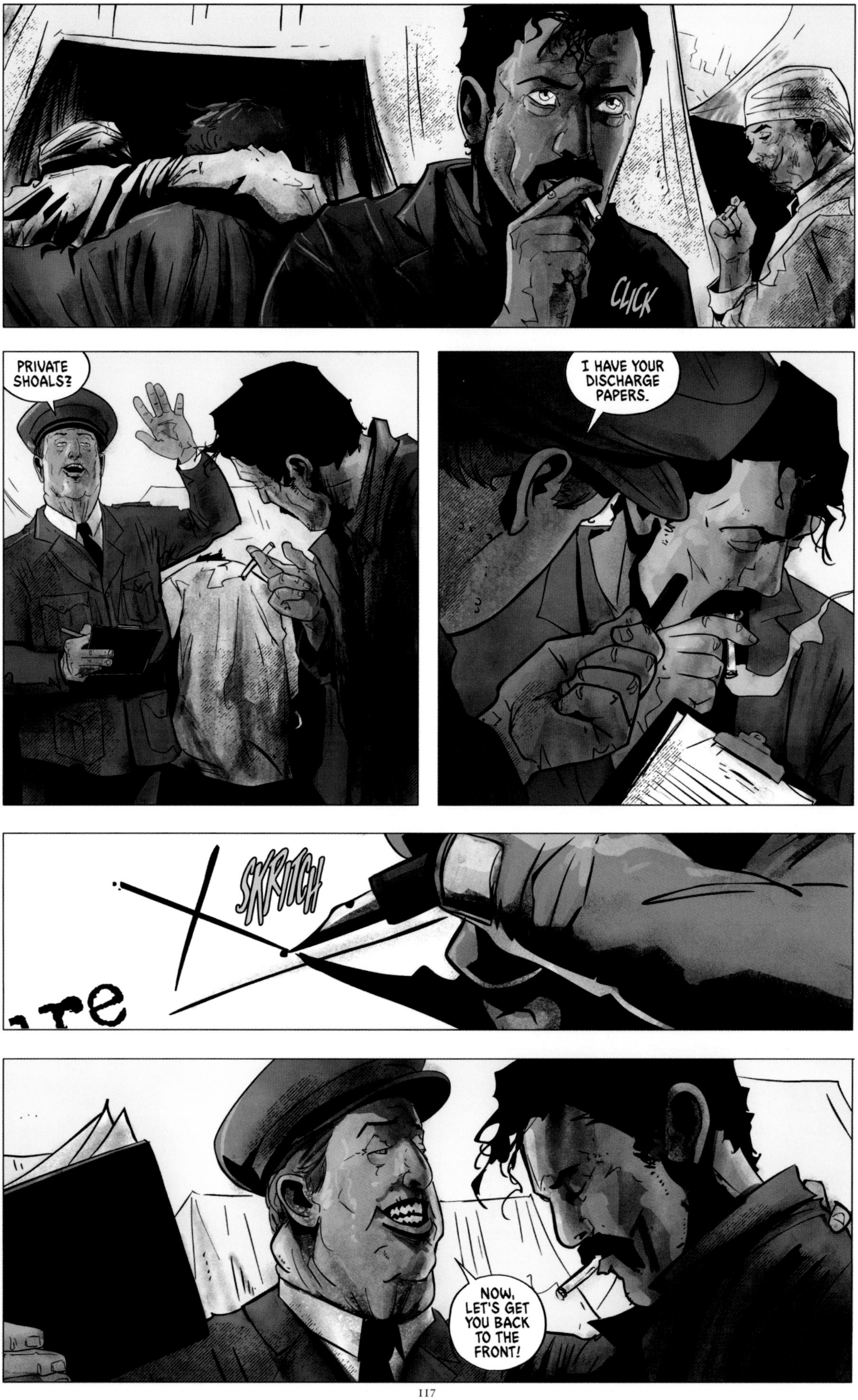
CLICK
PRIVATE SHOALS?
I HAVE YOUR DISCHARGE PAPERS.
SKRITCH
...
NOW, LET'S GET YOU BACK TO THE FRONT!

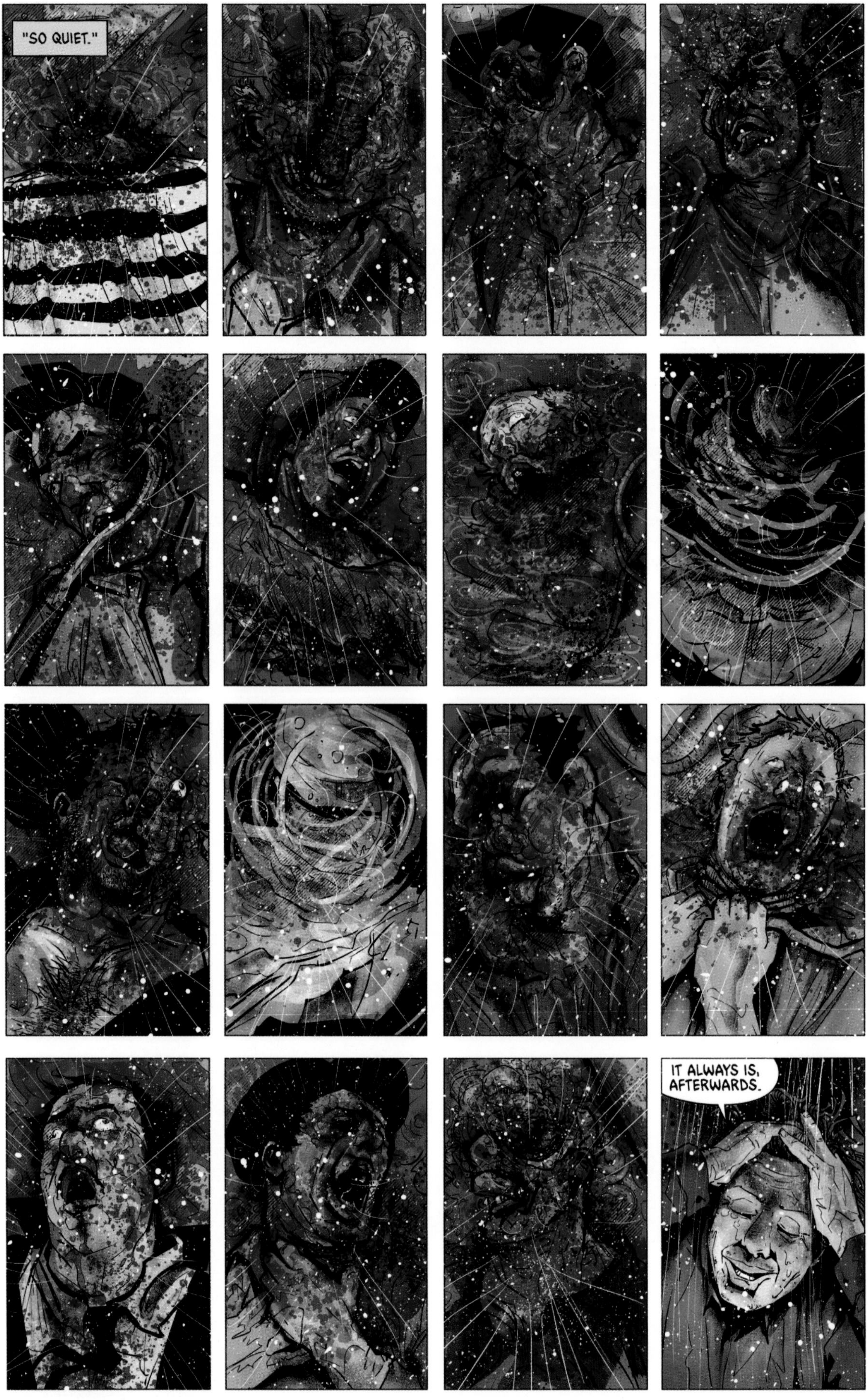
"SO QUIET."
IT ALWAYS IS, AFTERWARDS.

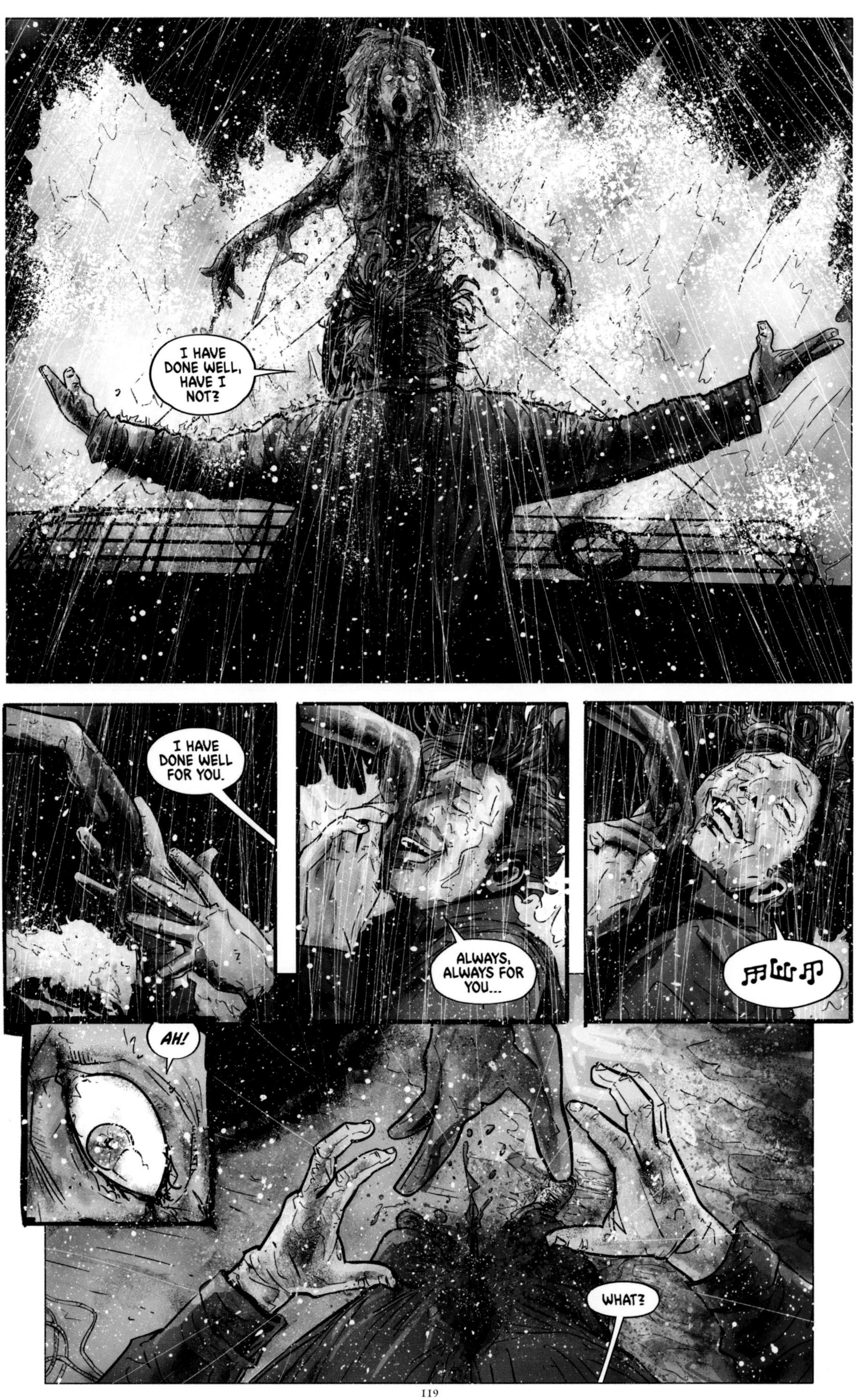
I HAVE DONE WELL, HAVE I NOT?
I HAVE DONE WELL FOR YOU.
ALWAYS, ALWAYS FOR YOU...
AH!
WHAT?

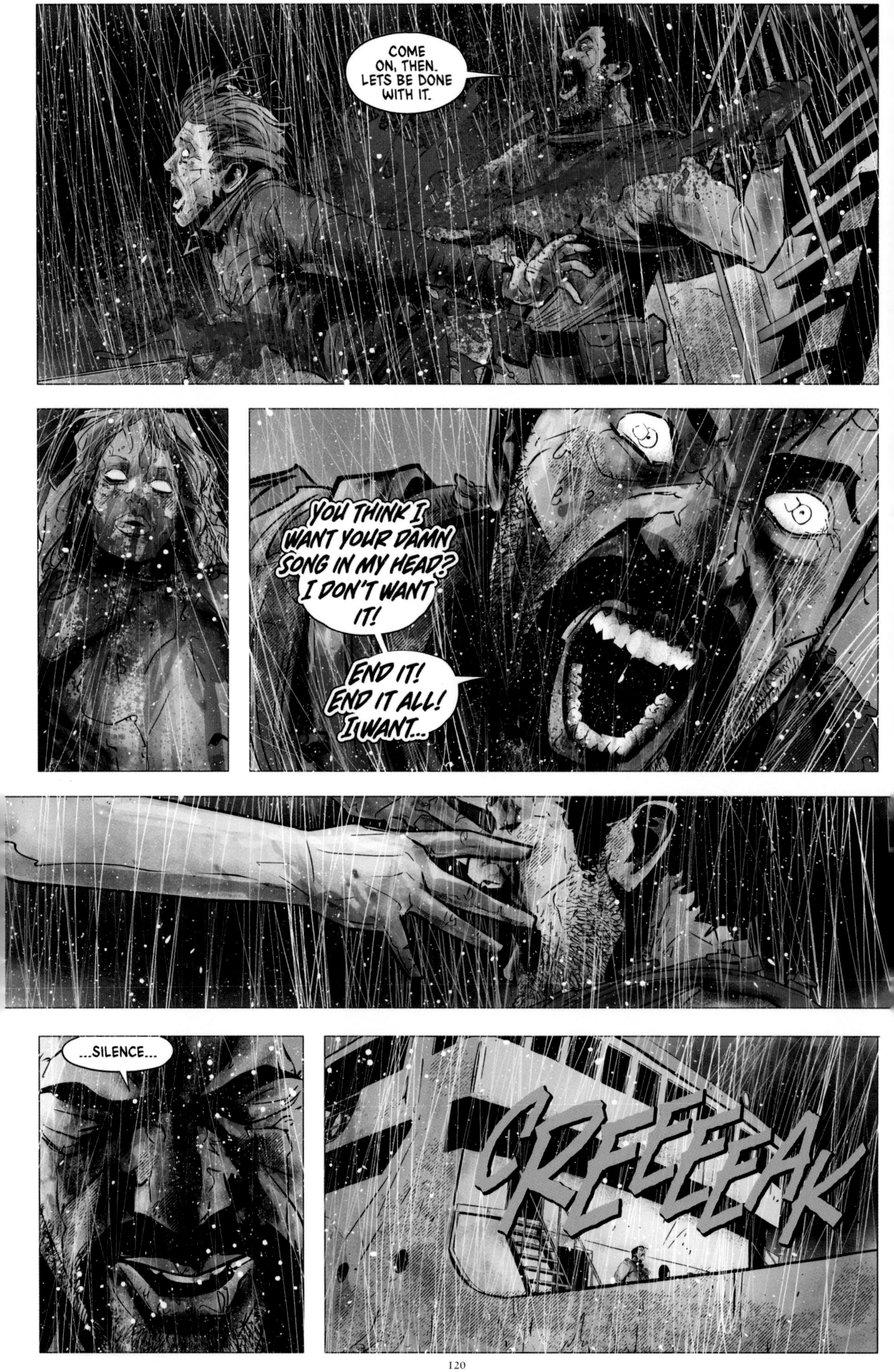
COME ON, THEN. LETS BE DONE WITH IT.
YOU THINK I WANT YOUR DAMN SONG IN MY HEAD? I DON'T WANT IT!
END IT! END IT ALL! I WANT...
...SILENCE...
CREEEAK

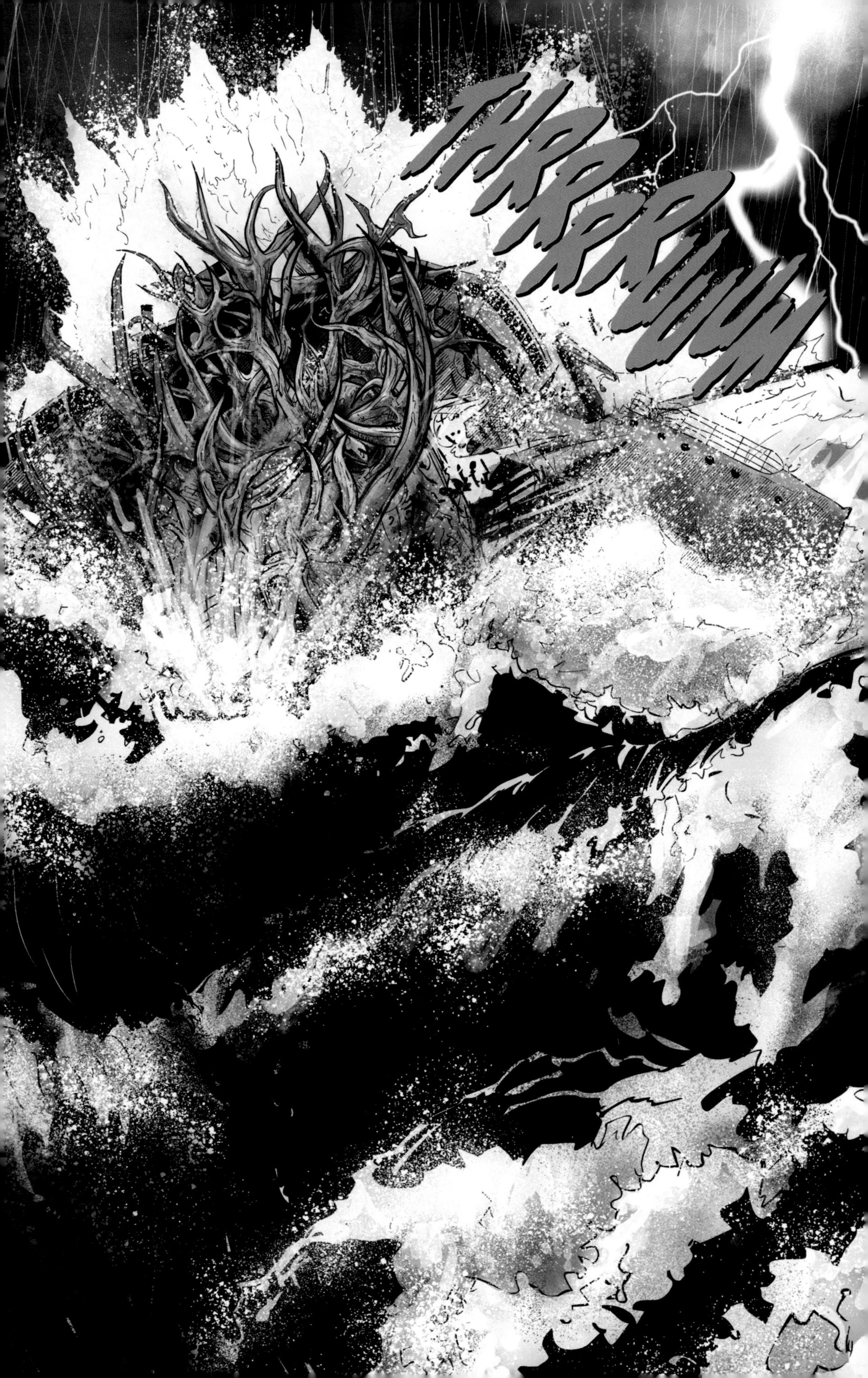
THRRRUUM

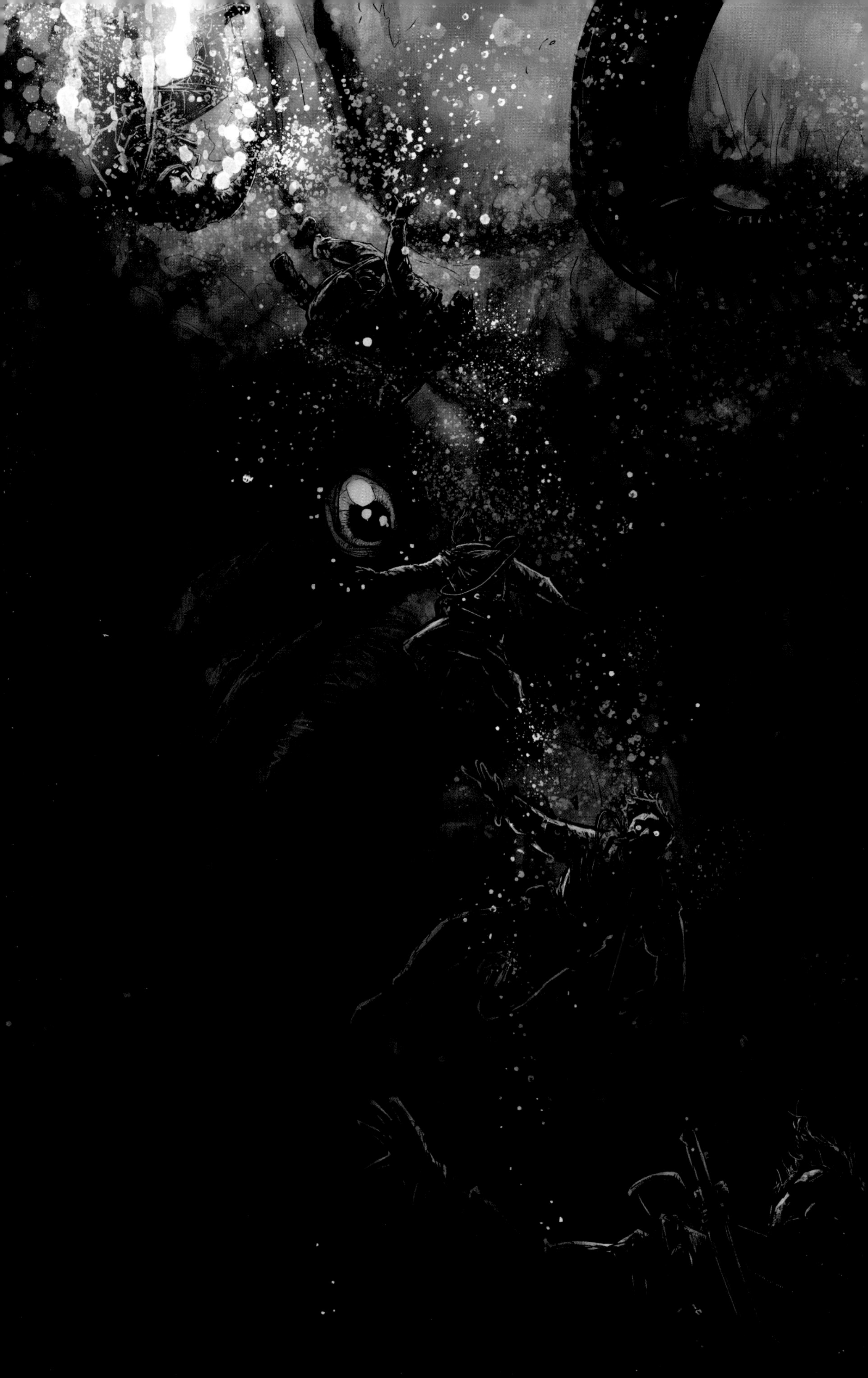

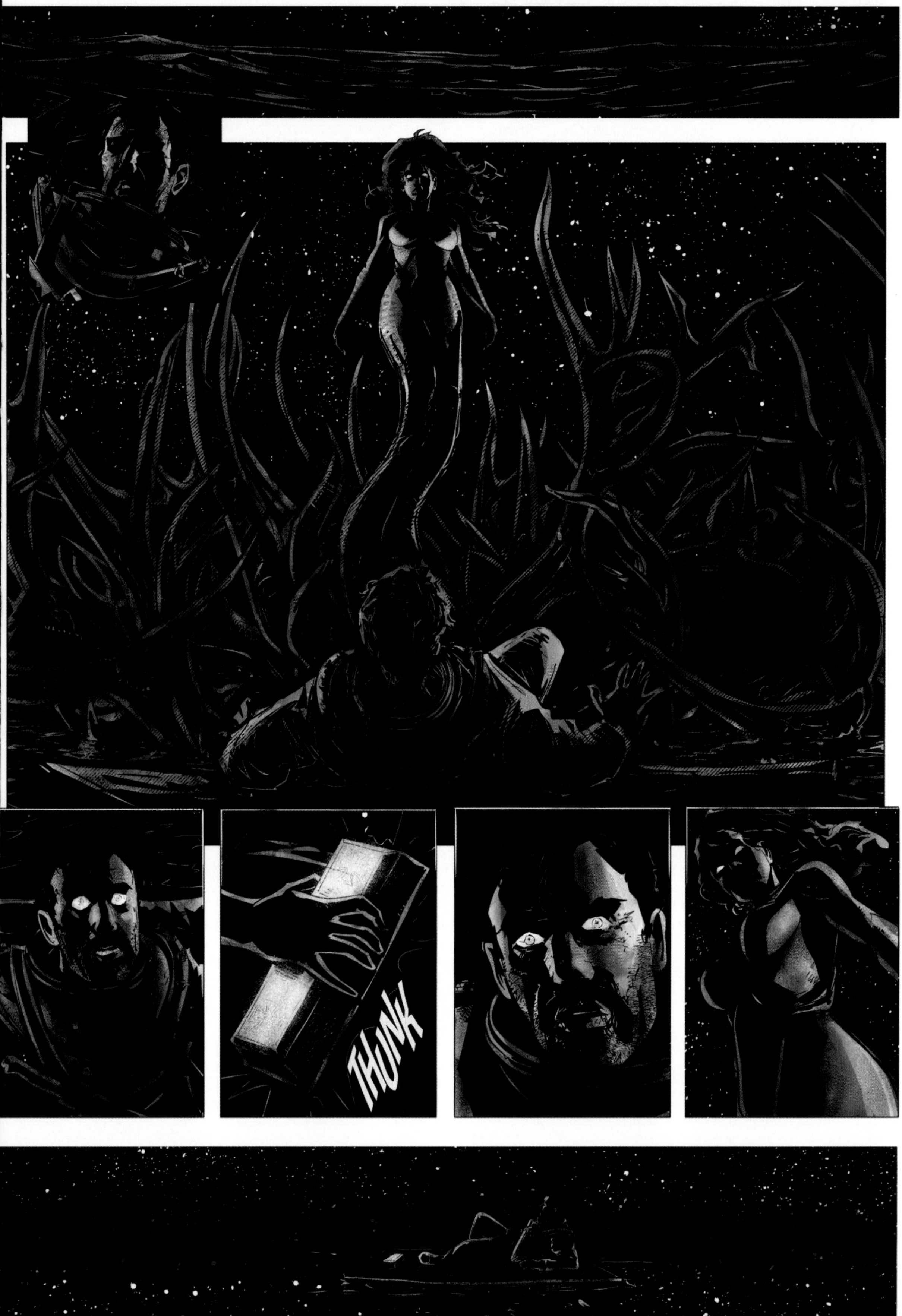
THUNK

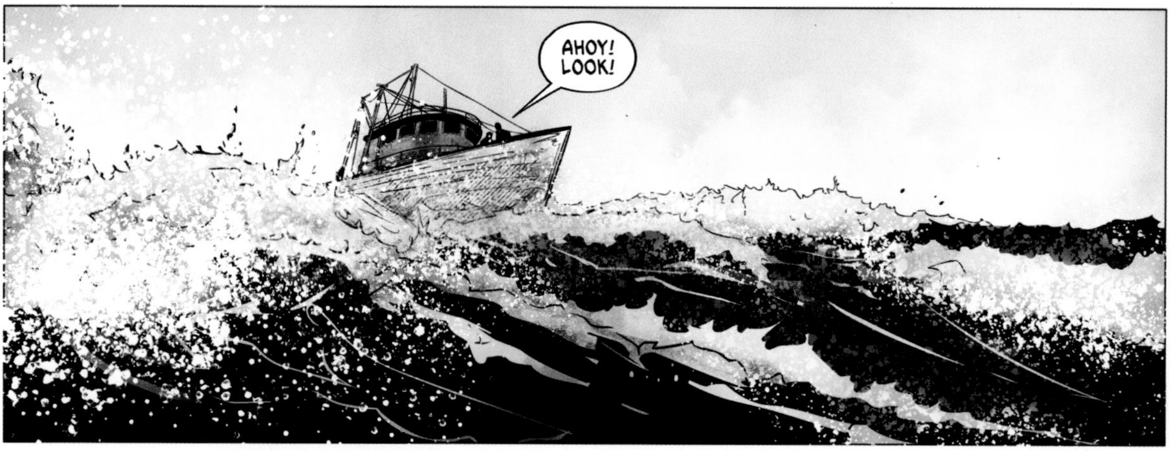
AHOY! LOOK!

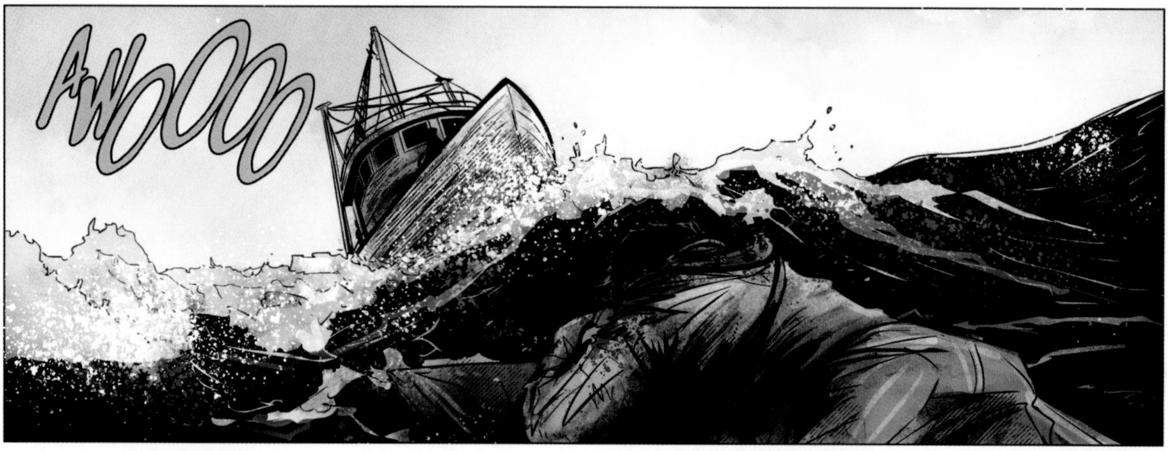
AWOOOO

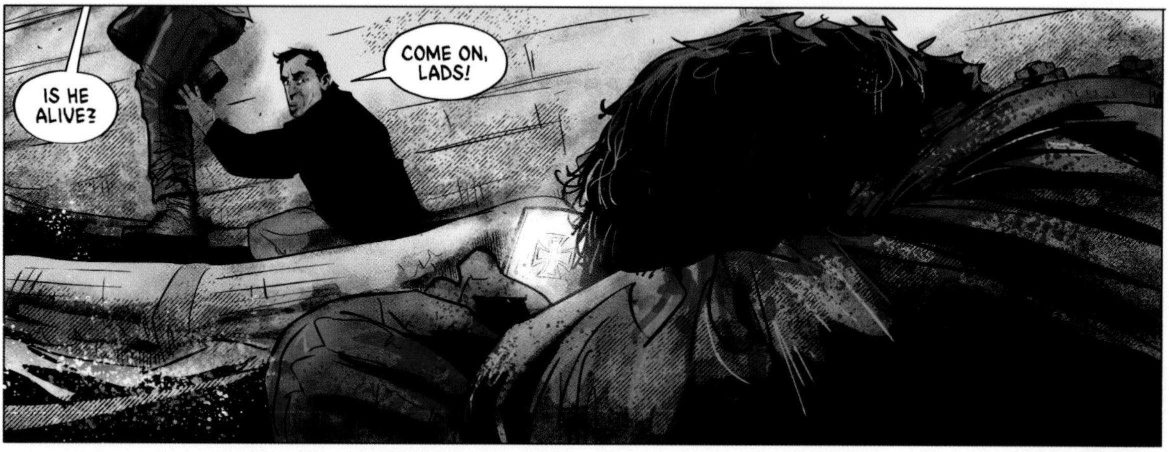
IS HE ALIVE?
COME ON, LADS!

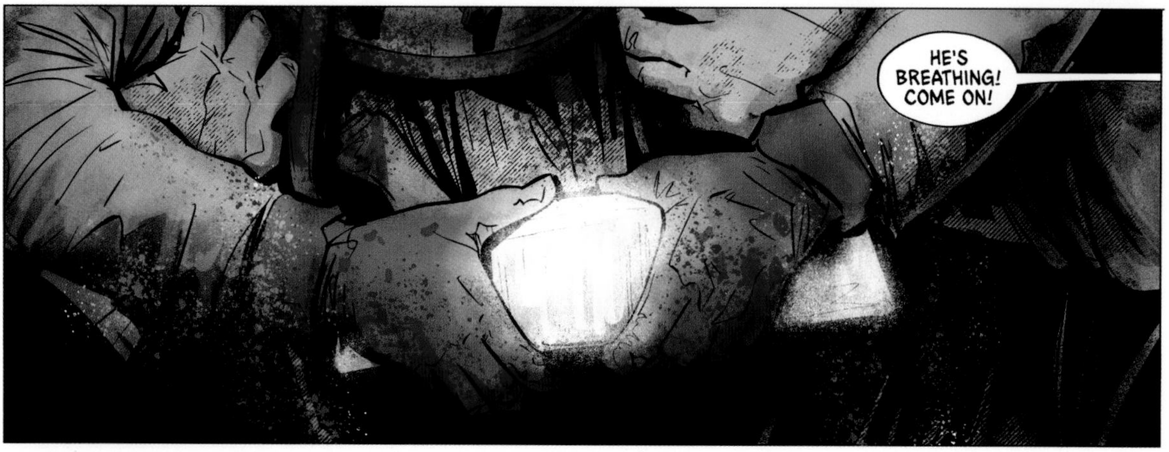
HE'S BREATHING! COME ON!

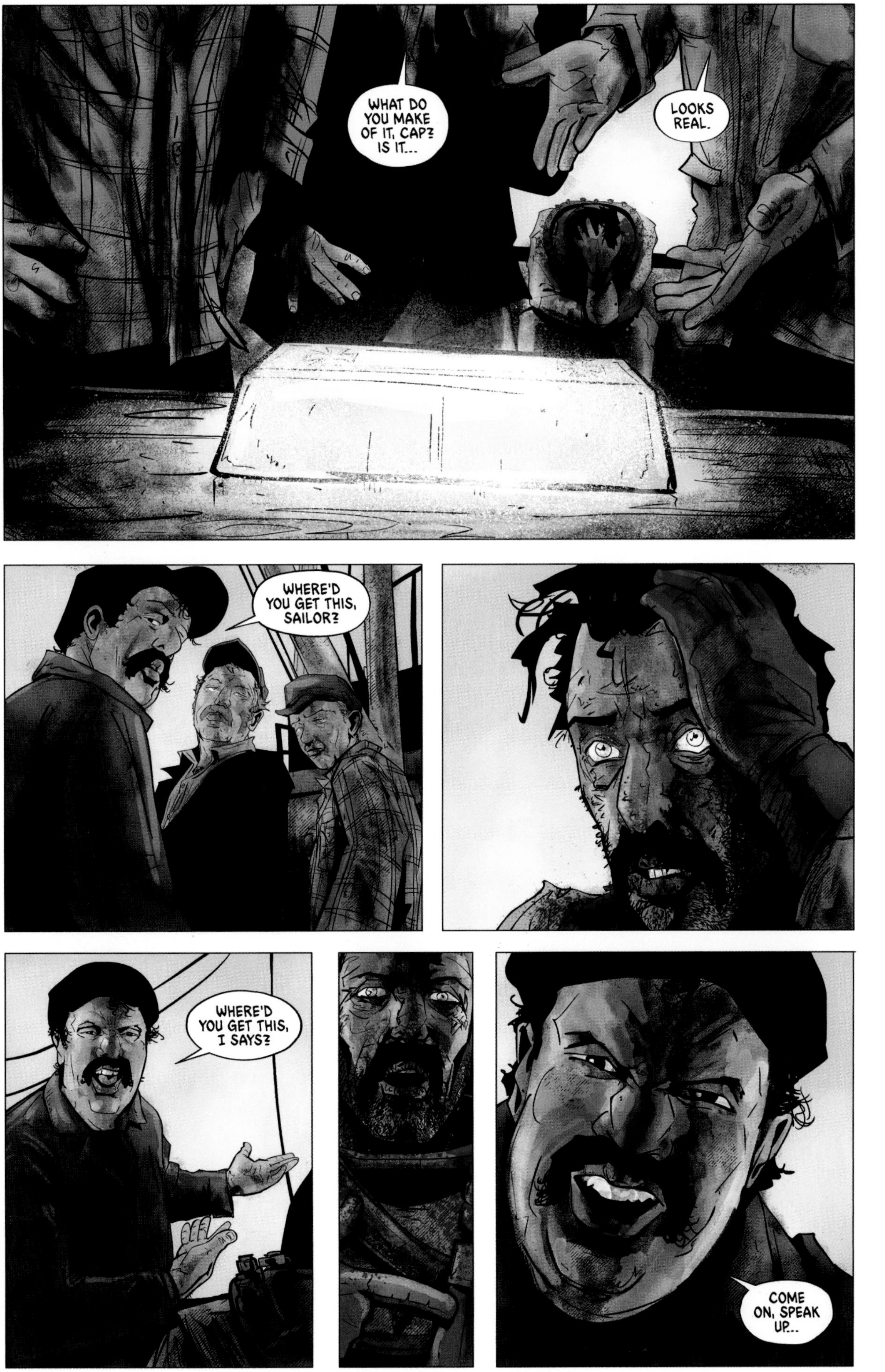
WHAT DO YOU MAKE OF IT, CAP? IS IT...
LOOKS REAL.
WHERE'D YOU GET THIS, SAILOR?
WHERE'D YOU GET THIS, I SAYS?
COME ON, SPEAK UP...

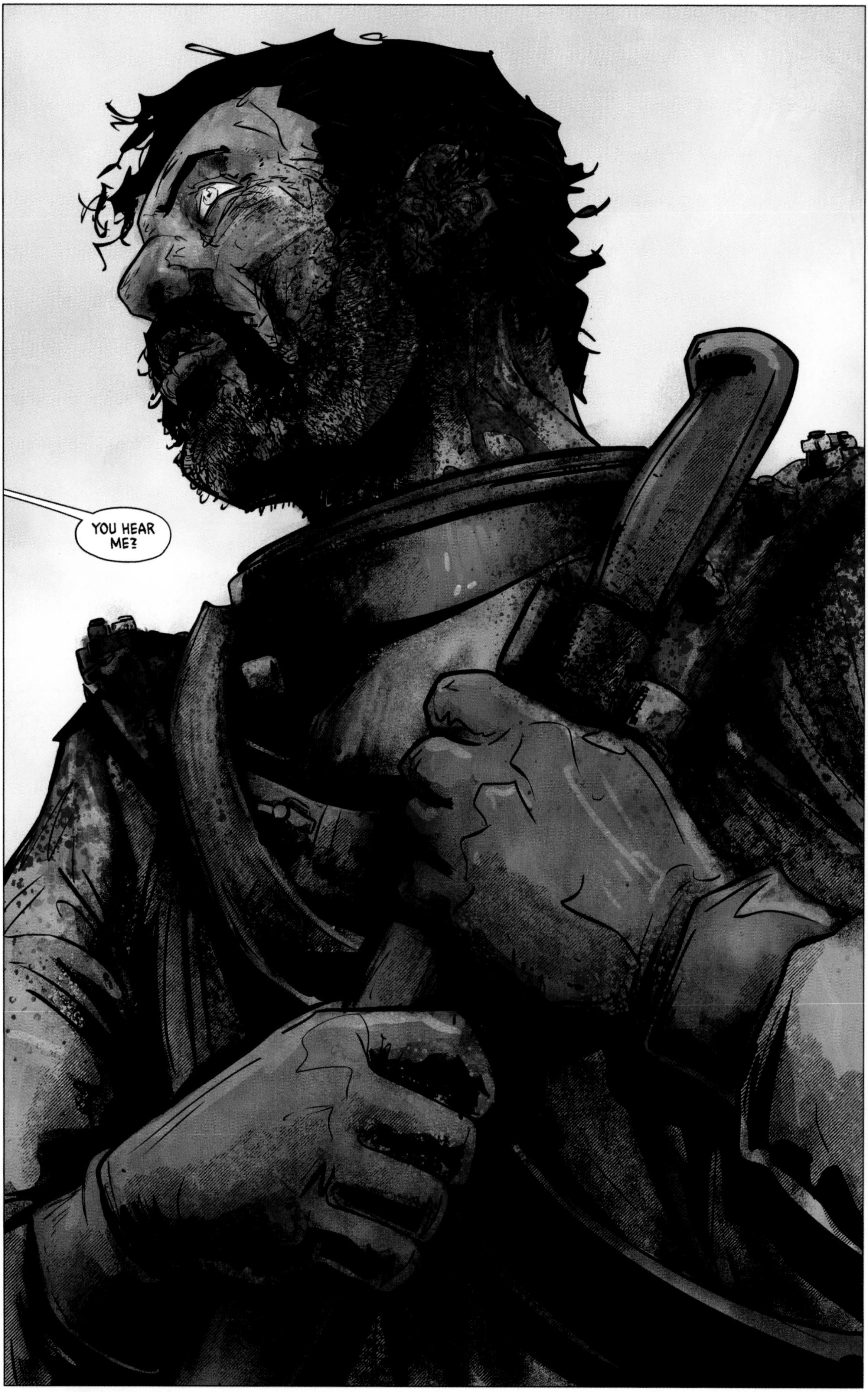
YOU HEAR ME?

Art by
ANDREW JERZ

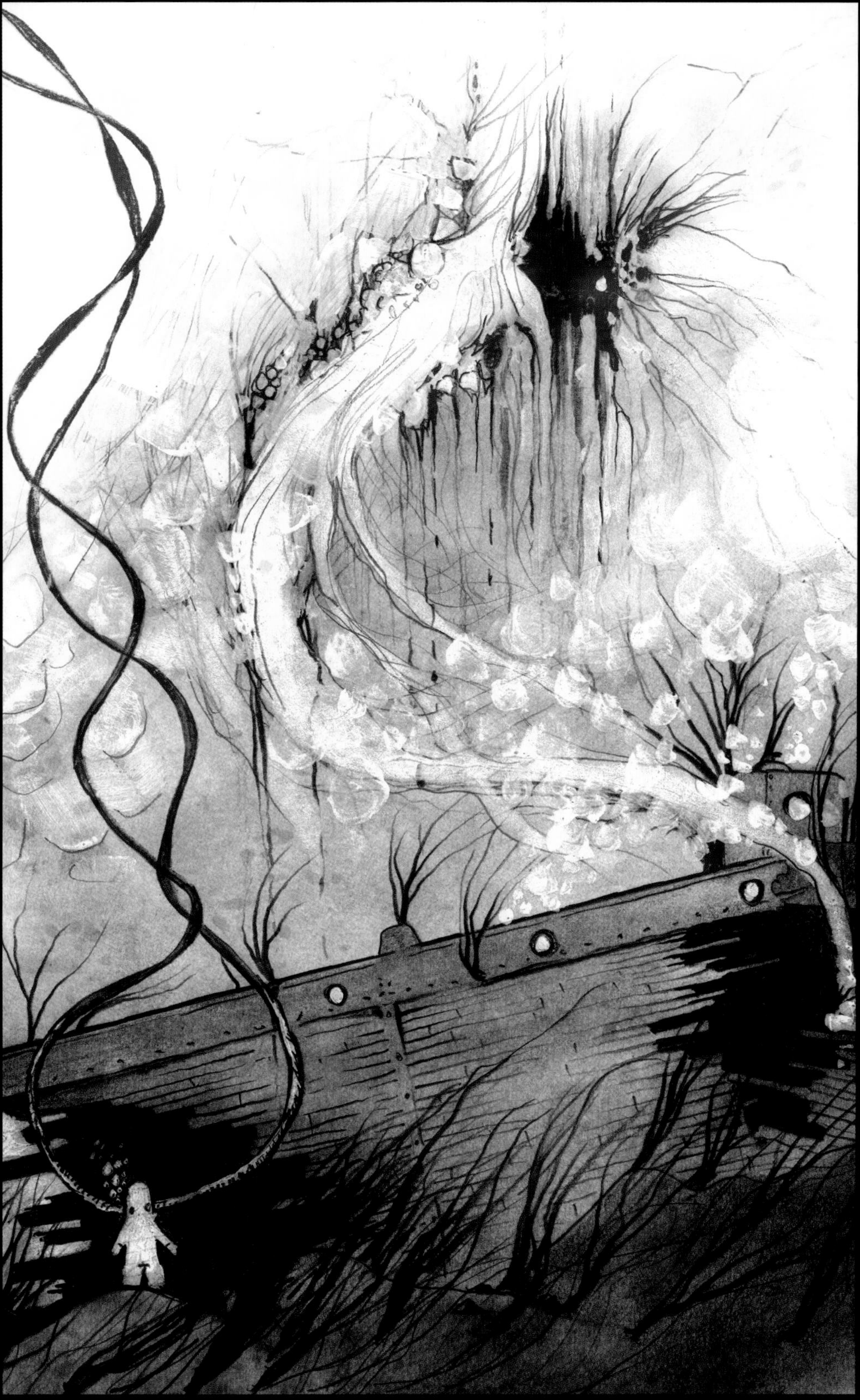

AFTERWORD

The most common question we get about *Sea of Sorrows* is, why didn't we do *Road of Bones 2*—and it's a good question, because a lot of people loved *Road of Bones*, so a direct sequel or prequel might have been a great project.

But, as much as we loved working on *Road of Bones*, we didn't want to tread the same ground over again. We also didn't want to get trapped into a cycle of diminishing returns that happens to a lot of horror sequels, or series, but the most important thing was we didn't want to destroy the mystery of just what happened out there on the icy tundra by overexplaining it, or expanding on how it ended. We loved the ending and the questions it raised, and it felt like answering it completely would take some of that magic out of it. So we needed something new.

And we found it with *Sea of Sorrows*. How we got here was really thinking about what we loved about making *Road of Bones*—the interplay of a horrific time and place in history, a supernatural creature, and the horror of what people can be driven to in desperate situations. We wanted to take all of that and use it to create a new story that would serve as a companion to *Road of Bones*—one where we'd be looking at the same evils, but through a different window.

The two books have a lot of differences—where *Road of Bones* was dominated by the color white, *Sea of Sorrows* is full of black. Where one story follows three men driven to survive, the other follows a larger group driven by greed—but both stories share the same dark heart—a stark look at the most horrifying parts of our souls.

We'd like to thank all the readers that followed us from the icy expanses of Siberia to the depths of the North Atlantic and welcome all the new readers who came on board with this series first. The human race has a long, long history of horror, and we hope to be able to explore more of it in the future.

We'll see you there.

Rich, **Alex**, and **Justin**

Art by
ERICA ROSE LEVINE

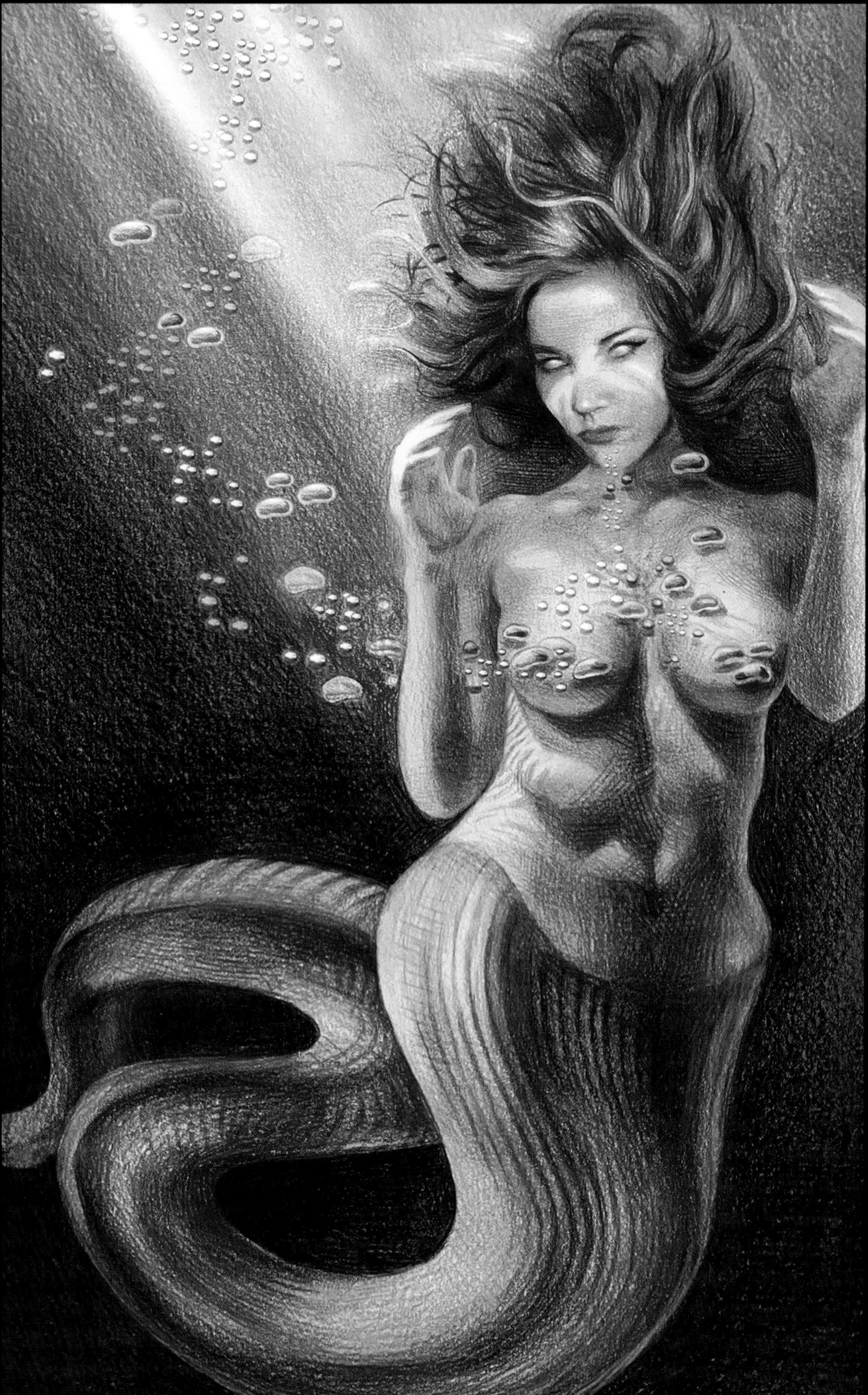

Art by
FRANCK UZAN

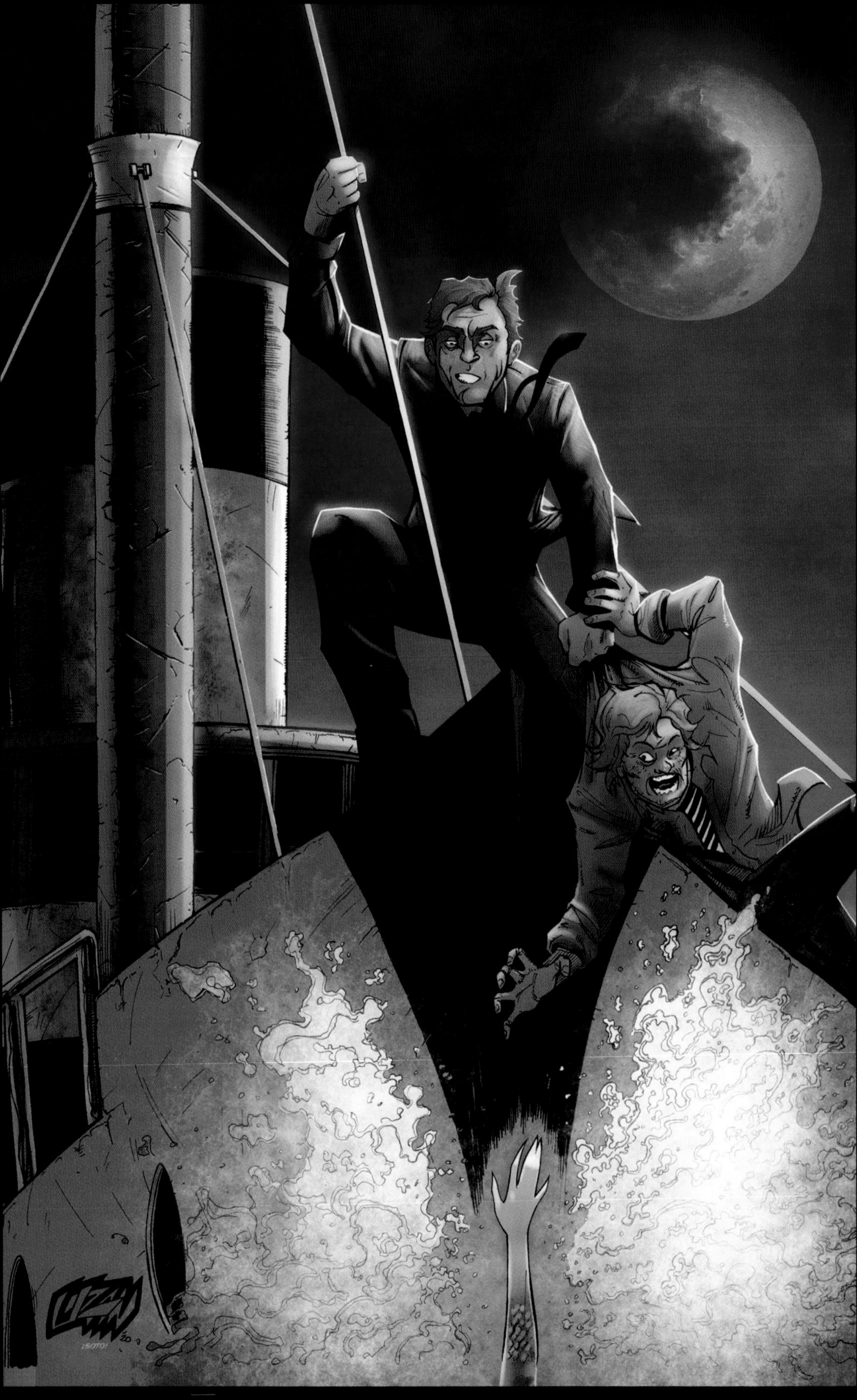

Art by
J. PAUL SCHIEK

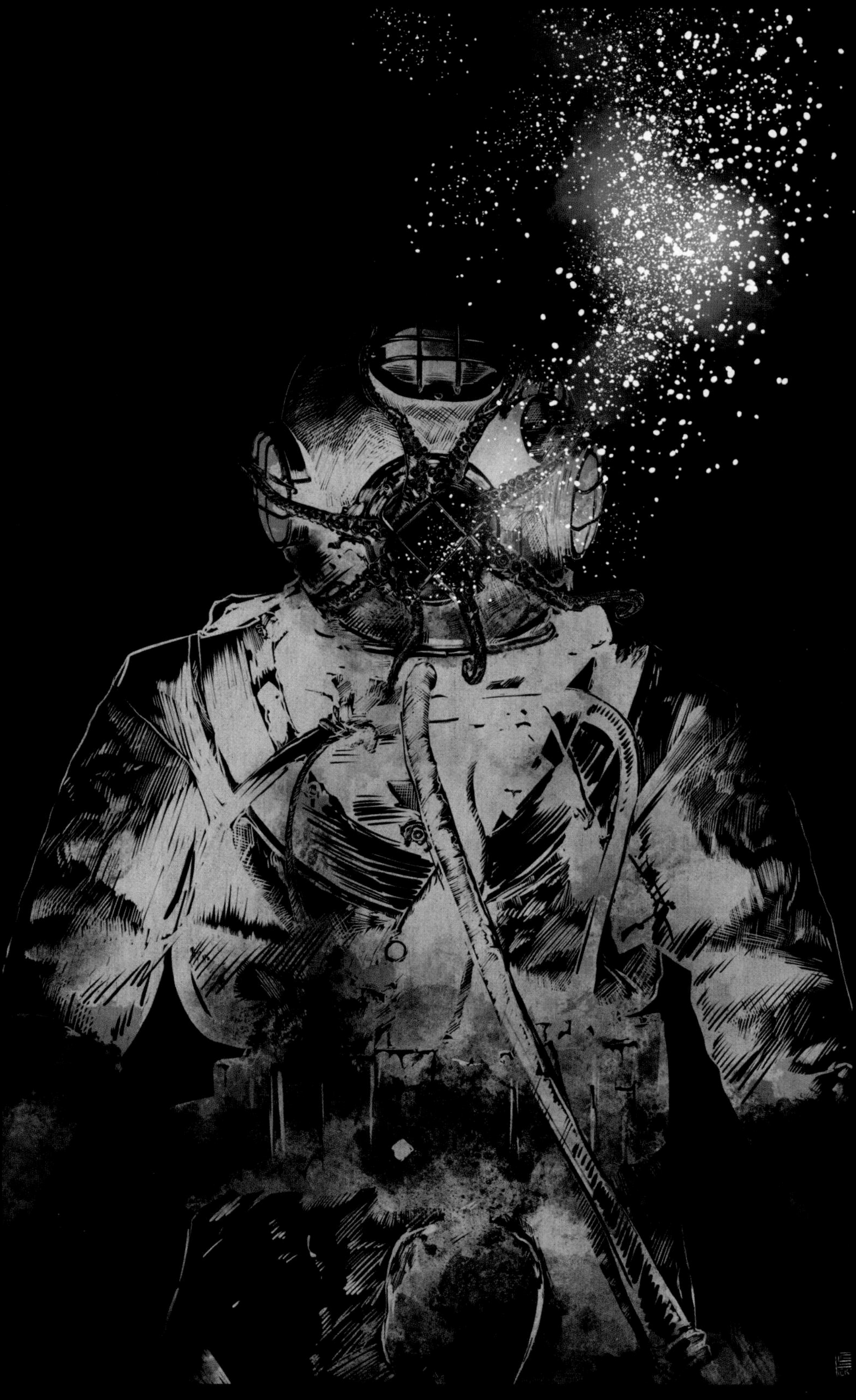

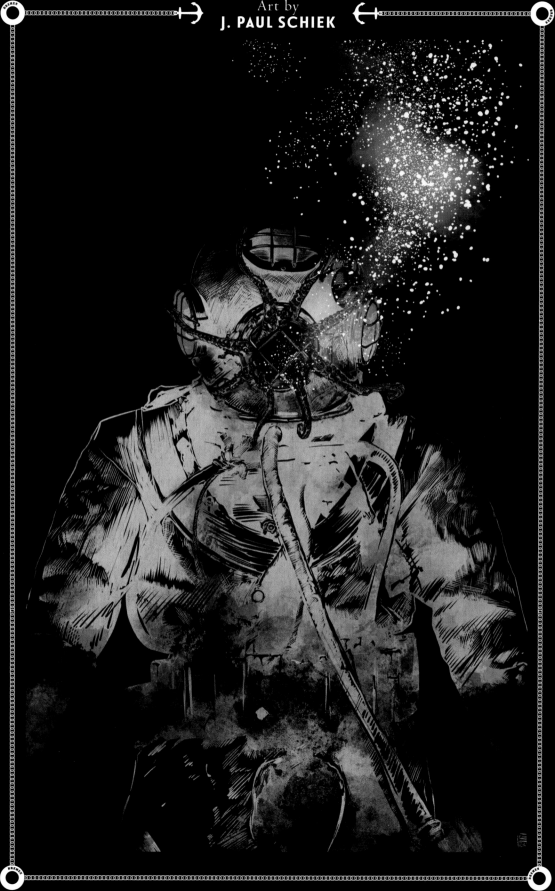

Art by
J. PAUL SCHIEK

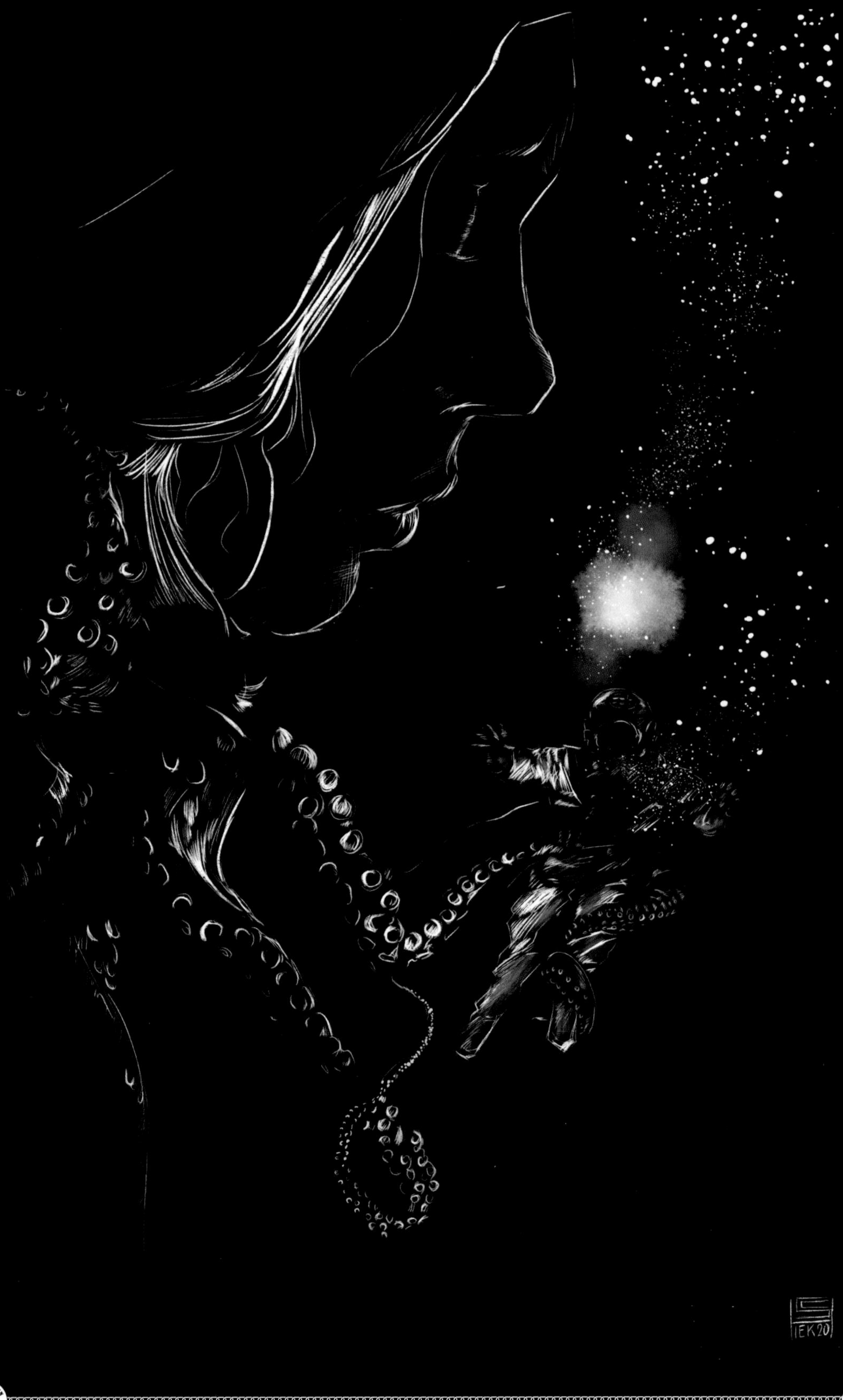

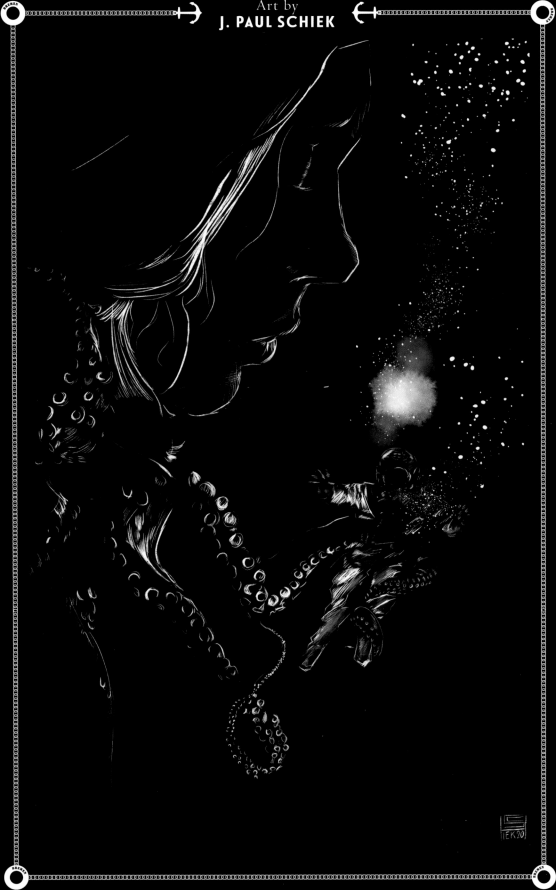

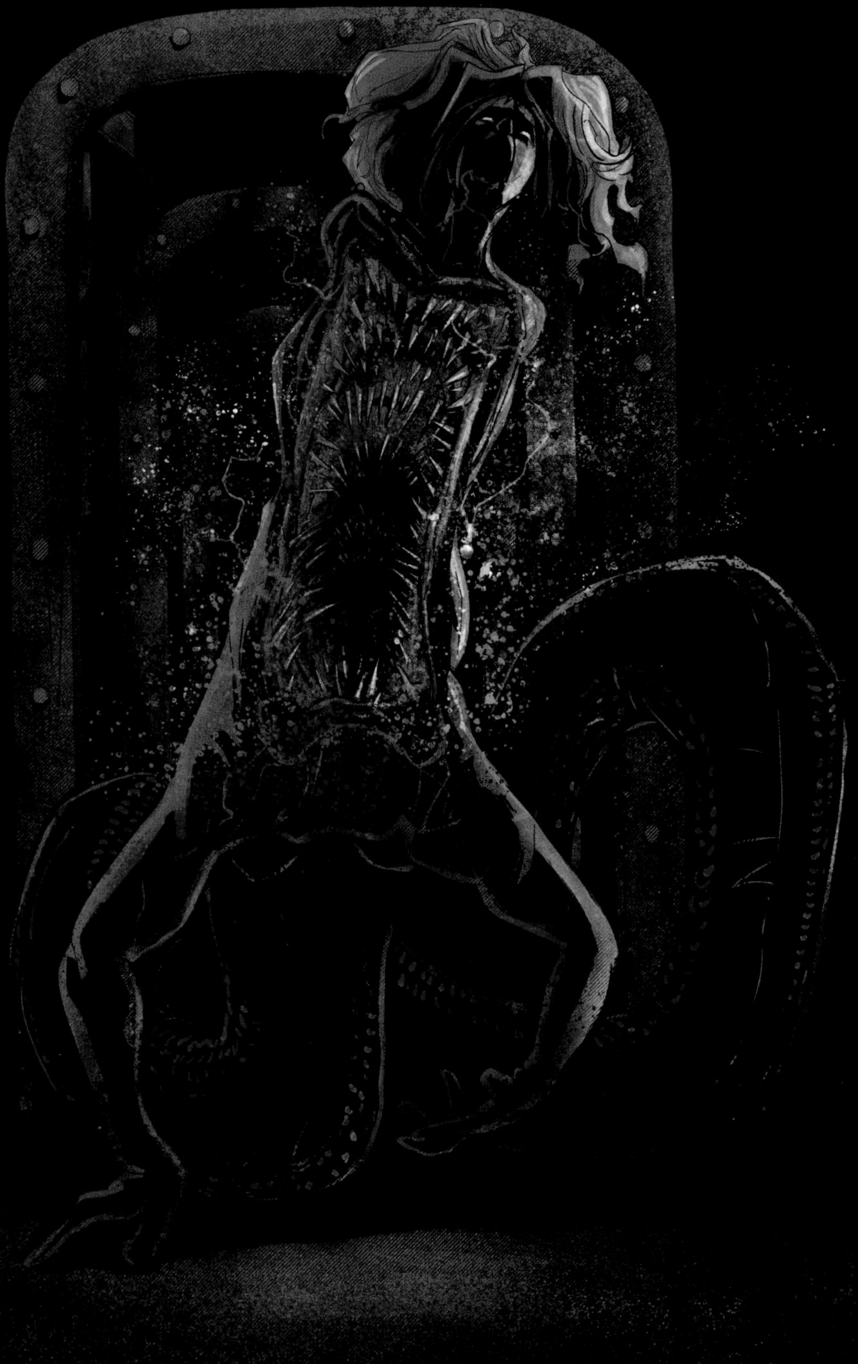

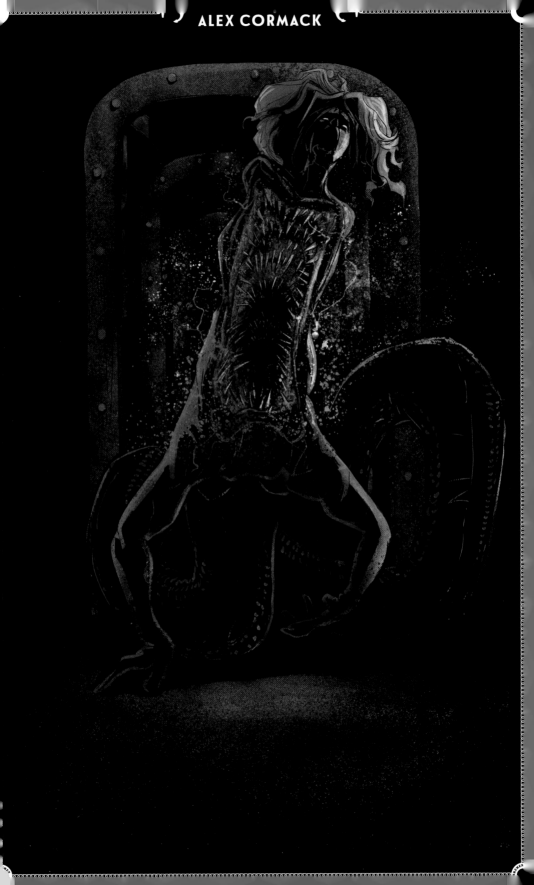

Concept Art by
ALEX CORMACK

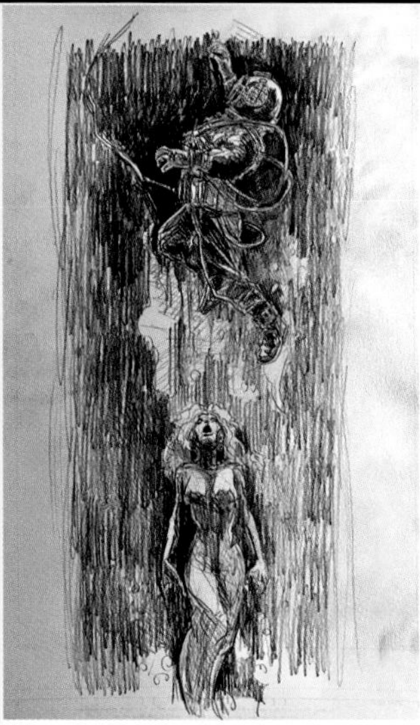

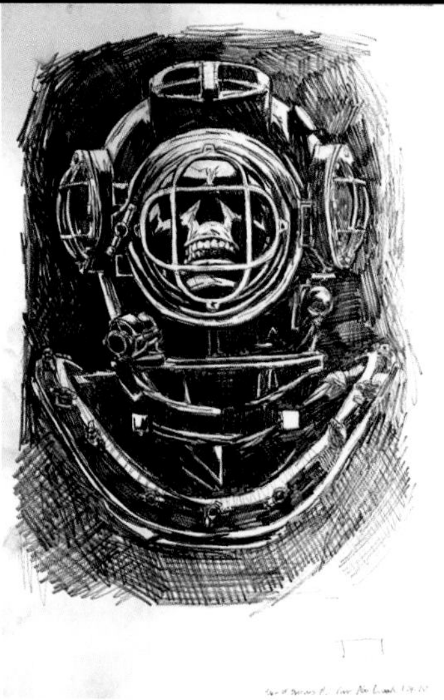

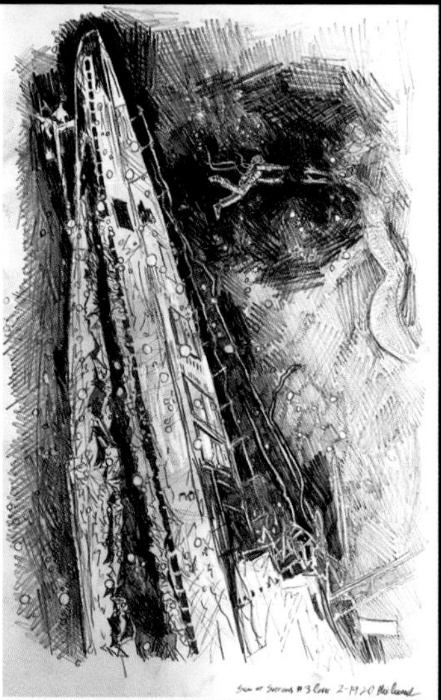

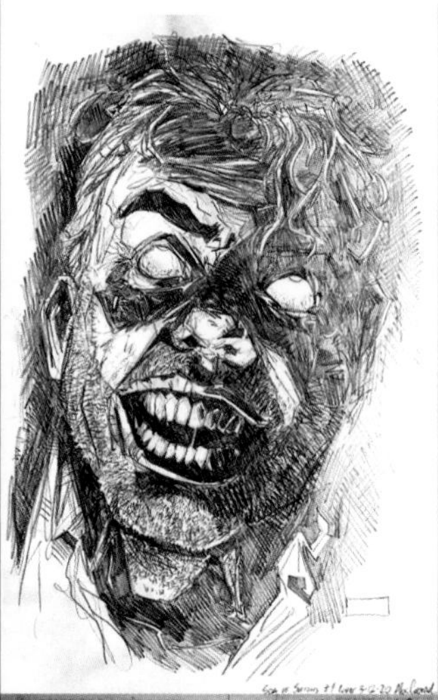

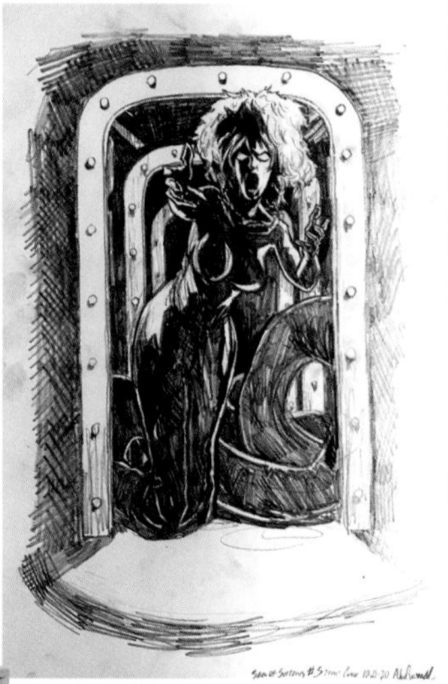

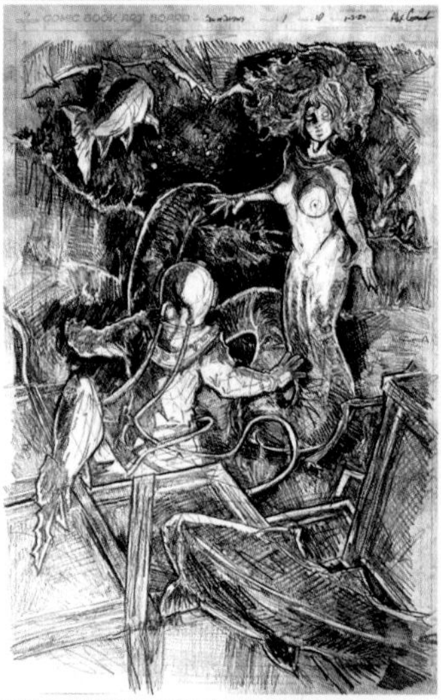

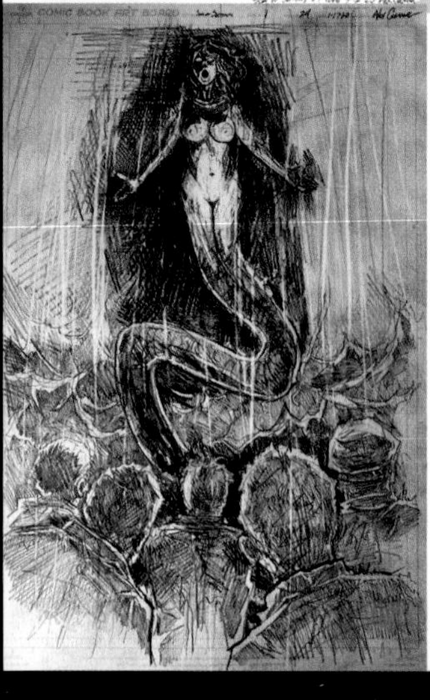

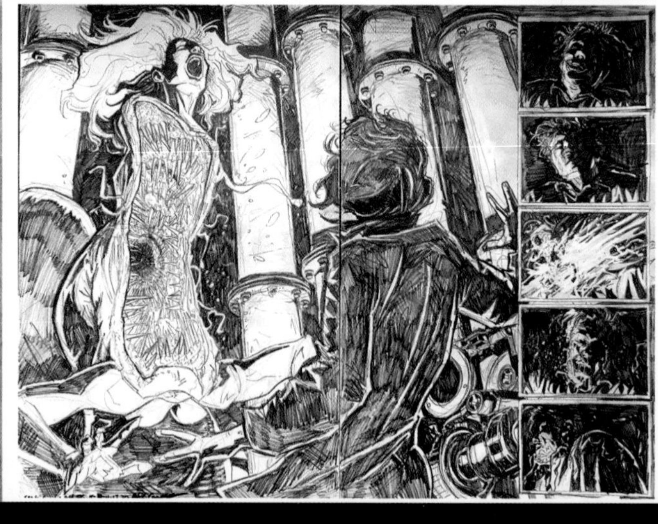

Concept Art by
ALEX CORMACK

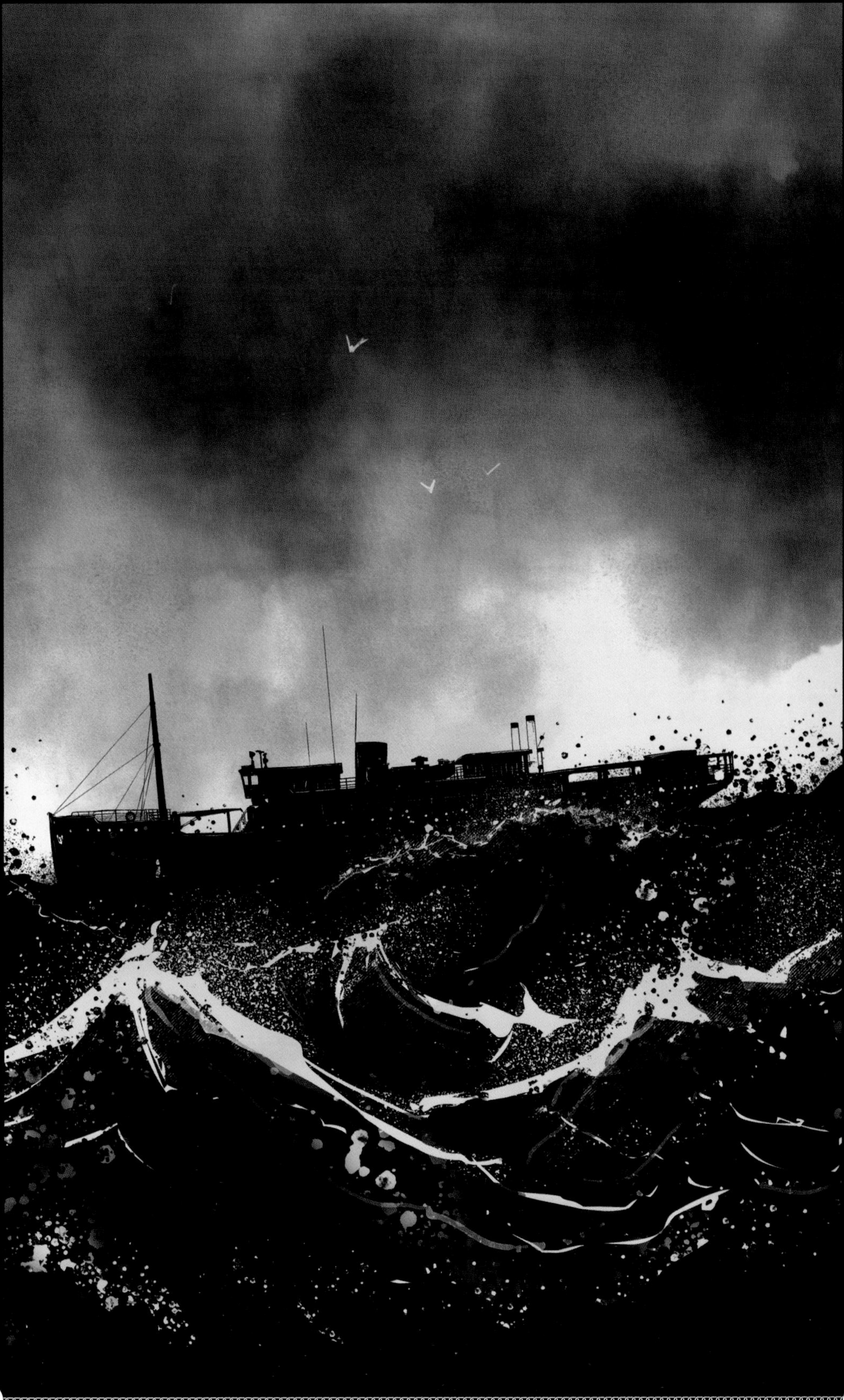

RICH DOUEK is a Bram Stoker Award-nominated writer, and creator of several independent comic series, such as *Sea of Sorrows*, *Road of Bones*, *Wailing Blade*, and *Gutter Magic*. He has written short stories in several anthologies, including *Superman: Red and Blue*, *Teenage Mutant Ninja Turtles Universe*, and the *New York Times*-featured *All We Ever Wanted*. He was born and grew up in Queens, NY, and currently lives with his family in New Jersey.

ALEX CORMACK is the Bram Stoker Award-nominated illustrator whose work includes *Sea of Sorrows*, *Road of Bones*, *Sink*, *Weed Magic*, *Crossing*, *Hardcore Akan* (the prequel to the film *Hardcore Henry*), and a bunch more. He lives in Vermont with his wife, son, and his cat, Destruction.